El Filibusterismo

by JOSE RIZAL

TRANSLATED BY LEON MA GUERRERO

GUERRERO PUBLISHING

First published 1961 by Longmans Group Ltd.
(formerly Longmans, Green & Co. Ltd), London.

World wide rights assigned to The Estate of
Leon Ma. Guerrero, 1994.

First published in the Philippines 1996 by
Guerrero Publishing, Manila

Exclusively distributed in the Philippines by Anvil Publishing Inc., 3/F,
Rudgen II Building, 17 Shaw Boulevard, Pasig, Metro Manila,
Philippines. Tel: (632) 633 6121 /6129 /6136. Fax: (632) 631 3766.

ISBN 971-27-0440-8 Book Paper edition
ISBN 971-27-0441-6 Newsprint edition

Set in Garamond 3, 11/13pt.
Printed in Manila by Insular Printing Corporation.
Typesetting by Frederick D. Ramos

Table of Contents

To the memory of the priests, Don Mariano Gómez, eighty-five, Don José Burgos, thirty, and Don Jacinto Zamora, thirty-five, who were executed on the scaffold at Bagumbayan on 28 February 1 872.

The Church, by refusing to unfrock you, has put in doubt the crime charged against you; the Government by enshrouding your trial in mystery and pardoning your co-accused has implied that some mistake was committed when your fate was decided; and the whole of the Philippines in paying homage to your memory and calling you martyrs totally rejects your guilt.

As long therefore as it is not clearly shown that you took part in the uprising in Cavite, I have the right, whether or not you were patriots and whether or not you were seeking justice and liberty, to dedicate my work to you as victims of the evil I am trying to fight. And while we wait for Spain to clear your names some day, refusing to be a party to your death, let these pages serve as a belated wreath of withered leaves on your forgotten graves. Whoever attacks your memory without sufficient proof has your blood upon his hands.

J. RIZAL

* Gómez was actually eighty-four, Burgos thirty-five, and Zamora thirty-seven, when they were executed on 17 February 1872. –L.Ma.G.

INTRODUCTION

A novel of Omens and Prophecies

IN the Introduction to my translation of *Noli Me Tangere,* of which *El Filibusterismo (Subversion)* is the sequel, I suggested that their author, Jose Rizal, had a good claim to being the first Asian nationalist. An extremely talented Malay born a hundred years ago in a small town near Manila, educated partly in the Philippines and partly in Europe, Rizal inspired the Filipinos by his writings and example to make the first nationalist revolution in Asia in 1896, to establish its first democratic republic, which survived until 1901, and in 1946, exactly half a century after his execution by the Spanish colonial regime, to become the first Asians to win independence from Western colonialism.

This impression grew all the stronger while I was actually engaged in translating the *Fili,* as it is known to Filipinos, off and on during 1960-61 when nationalism was capturing nearly the whole of Africa and a quite startling number of new states were achieving independence or were on the verge of it. Day after day I found Rizal's novel (published in Spanish as far back as 1891 and, ominously enough, in Ghent, Belgium) anticipating the apprehensions, prejudices, self-justification, anger and sense of betrayal of the white settlers in Africa and their spokesmen in European parliaments, that were being reported in the London newspapers seventy years later, as well, of course, as the counter-balancing idealism, liberalism and legislation to the inevitable both in the colonies and in the metropolises. In fact, as events rushed headlong across the front pages, some shockingly savage, others reassuring, I had the feeling that in the Fili there were, if they had only been read, portents and prophecies for the Asians, Africans and Europeans of our generation as much as for Rizal's own generation in the Philippines.

The theme of the *Fili* is what would now be called colonialism. It asks the questions that are still being asked today. Does a 'civilizing mission' justify the permanent subjection of one race to another? Should the colony aim at 'assimilation' with the metropolis or independence? If independence, should it be achieved through a process of peaceful evolution or by force of arms?

The *Fili* is equally contemporary in its treatment of the obsession with the 'prestige' of the ruling race and the conflict of nationalisms. 'I have a great liking for the natives,' says an old hand in the colony, a civil servant with pretensions to liberalism, 'but one must not praise them for anything, that only spoils them... Some are born to command, others to serve; of course, one cannot say this sort of thing out loud, although it is true enough, but it can be put into practice without talking too much about it.'

Another old hand, a friar who will have no truck with such innovations as schools and technical experts, protests: 'But the natives should not be allowed to learn Spanish, don't you realize that? When they do, they start arguing with us and they have no business arguing, all they should do is pay and obey.'

He is answered by another friar who is more foreseeing: 'Why should we always be at odds with the people when, after all, we are the few and they are the many?... For the time being they are short on knowledge and power, I agree, but they will not be the same tomorrow or the day after. Then they will be the stronger, they will know what is good for them and we shall not be able to stop them from getting it any more than children can be prevented, when they have reached a certain age from knowing a number of things...'

And a high colonial official, driven to frankness by the obstinacy of the Governor-General, declares: 'Let us put ourselves in the place of the Filipinos and ask ourselves what we would do... If things do not change for the better, some day they will rebel and, in truth, justice will be on their side as well as the sympathies of all honest men.' Then, having submitted his resignation, he tells his native lackey: 'When you declare yourselves independent some day, remember that there were not lacking hearts in Spain that beat for you and some who fought for your rights.'

But divisions also exist among the natives. The superstitious still believe that their ancient King, chained within a mountain, will soon shake himself free and solve all their problems; others, the great majority, are held in thrall by a Church that is Spanish rather than Catholic. The intellectuals, the elite who have managed to wrest an education from systematized obscurantism, are split between a natural desire for a conformist, unobtrusive existence that will allow them to enjoy their advantages, and a hazy idealism which at first seeks progress through assimilation with the metropolis and is driven to the assertion of a separate national identity only by the frustration of their dreams of equal rights with the white man.

The case for nationalism is put by Simoun, the central character, who upbraids one of the idealists in a memorable passage: 'You ask parity of rights, the Spanish way of life, and you do not realize that what you are asking is death, the destruction of your national identity, the disappearance of your homeland, the ratification of tyranny. What is to become of you? A people without a soul, a nation without freedom; everything in you will be borrowed, even your very defects. You ask for Hispanization and do not blush for shame when it is denied you... What you should do is take advantage of the prejudices of our rulers. So they refuse to integrate you into the Spanish nation. So much the better! Take the lead in forming your own individuality, try to lay the foundations of a Filipino nation. They give you no hopes. All the better! Hope only in yourselves and in your own efforts... Instead of aspiring to be a mere province, aspire to be a nation; develop an independent, not a colonial, mentality... Resignation is not always a virtue; it is a crime when it encourages oppression. There are no tyrants where there are no slaves.'

Simoun's plans for a revolution are frustrated and on his deathbed, a suicide, a native priest tells him that he has failed and deserved to fail because the Filipinos are not yet ready for independence and must first cultivate the civic virtues. Until they have done so, 'why give them independence? With or without Spain they would be the same, perhaps worse. What is the use of independence if the slaves of today will be the tyrants of tomorrow? And no doubt they will, because whoever submits to tyranny, loves it!'

This is rhetoric, no doubt, but it is superb rhetoric. The vitality of this debate, carried on simultaneously in the two camps, is shown, by its timelessness or, more precisely, its timeliness in another world and another age. But the *Fili*, like the *Noli*, is more than a political novel. It is a romantic, witty, sometimes satirical portrait of a colonial society at the end of the nineteenth century.

SUMMARY OF THE NOLI

The bare plot of the *Noli* may be summarized here for those who have not read it.

Crisóstomo Ibarra, the son of a wealthy Creole landlord, is betrothed from early youth to María Clara, the only daughter of Santiago (Capitán Tiago) de los Santos. Ibarra is sent abroad to study; in his absence his father, who has Spanish blood himself, runs afoul of the authorities by accidentally killing a Spanish tax-collector. He dies in gaol and, as a free thinker who had stopped going to Confession, is denied Christian burial by Father Dámaso, the parish priest of their lakeside home town of San Diego. When Ibarra returns and learns of his father's fate he is at first overcome with rage but, dedicated to the uplift of his people through education, he puts aside his plans for revenge in order to secure official approval for the establishment of a town school. But Father Salví, who has replaced Father Dámaso as parish priest, is himself in love with María Clara. At the laying of the school's cornerstone Ibarra is almost killed in an obviously contrived accident and is saved only by the intervention of Elias, a mysterious boatman whom he had rescued from death during an outing on the lake. Father Dámaso too is vehemently and openly opposed to the marriage between Ibarra and María Clara. At a public dinner after the school opening ceremony he insults the memory of Ibarra's father; Ibarra loses his head and is about to kill him when María Clara stops his hand. Ibarra, automatically excommunicated for laying violent hands on a priest, is forbidden to see María Clara again. Father Dámaso arranges for her marriage instead to a Spanish relative of his Linares. Worse is still to happen; Father Salví's head sacristan recruits the desperate and the oppressed in San Diego for a rising in the name and allegedly with the money of Ibarra; the rising is denounced by the parish priest to the Constabulary and is suppressed; the young liberals of the town, with Ibarra at their head, are seized and charged with rebellion. There is no proof against Ibarra until María Clara is persuaded to surrender to Father Salví and the authorities some letters of dubious loyalty which Ibarra had written to her from abroad. Ibarra is found guilty but he is liberated from gaol by Elias. He confronts María Clara with her treachery and she confesses that she was forced to exchange his letters for some of Father Dámaso, which Father Salví had found in the parish house. The letters would have proved that her real father was the friar. Ibarra, having forgiven María Clara, flees with Elias up river to the lake but they are sighted by a Constabulary patrol; one of them is killed; who survives remains a mystery but a dying man buries Ibarra's treasure at the foot of his grandfather's grave. María Clara, believing Ibarra dead, refuses to go on with her marriage to Linares; she had planned to run away afterwards to join her lover. Father Dámaso pleads with her; he had not realized how much she loved Ibarra, he had only opposed their marriage and persecuted Ibarra's family because, as her real father, he could not bear the thought of her becoming the wife of a native, without privileges, without rights. When she threatens to kill herself he consents at last to her entering a nunnery of Poor Clares; here the chaplain is Father Salví, who is waiting for the promotion which is due him for frustrating the rising in San Diego. The story ends with a glimpse of a young nun on the roof of the convent bewailing her wrongs amid the thunder and lightning of a storm.

All this may sound very Victorian in the pejorative sense of the word, and indeed it is. In fact the *Fili,* which continues the *Noli,* was partly written in Victorian London. The modern reader may find it difficult to suspend his disbelief in the unlikely coincidences of the plot and the extravagant emotions of the main characters but who are we to say that another generation were extravagant in their emotions or that their reactions are unlikely?

It may be of interest to note that many of the incidents and characters in the *Fili* are taken from the Philippine society of Rizal's time. The young intellectuals' project for a secular academy of the Spanish language, which causes such a stir in official circles, is based on an identical proposal made in Rizal's lifetime by a group of progressive young women in the provincial town of Malolos in Bulakan; Rizal wrote them an open letter of encouragement that has a part in Philippine history. The quarrel for precedence among the guilds of natives and halfbreeds actually took place. Simoun's first attempt at rebellion, which partly depends for its success on the suburbs of Manila rising in protest against a decree for the demolition of nipa huts, has a clear parallel in history with the destruction of the houses of dispossessed tenants, among them Rizal's own family, of an estate belonging to the Dominican Order near Manila; this high-handed act may have changed Rizal's whole life. The oblique references to the personages of the colonial regime are only thinly disguised: the Governor-General is almost certainly Valeriano Weyler, Marquess of Tenerife, who had well-known disagreements with the liberal counsellor of his predecessors, a 'high official' in the colony by name of Quiroga, who was forced to resign. Sometimes Rizal does not even bother to mask the factual basis of his story, as in the case of Cabesang Tales whose experiences are obviously meant to reflect those of Rizal's own family in the Dominican estate of Kalamba.

Finally, a word may be said about the meaning of *Filibusterismo.* Rizal himself explained it in a letter to his dearest friend, the Austrian anthropologist Blumentritt: 'The word *Filibusterismo* is very little known in the Philippines. The masses do not know it yet. I heard it for the first time in 1872 when the tragic executions took place. I still remember the panic that this word evoked. Our father forbade us to say it... The Manila newspapers and the Spaniards use this word to describe those whom they want to render suspect of revolutionary activities. The educated Filipinos fear its scope. It does not have the meaning of *pirate;* it means rather a *dangerous patriot who will soon be on the gallows,* or else *a conceited fellow.*' In the context of the novel the word *Filibusterismo,* it seems to me, can only be translated for the present generation as 'subversion' if it is to be correctly understood as a non-conformist attitude of mind, as an overt attempt to overthrow an established order of society.

It is Rizal's main claim to glory, although many in the Philippines would now much rather forget or minimize it, that in his time he defied what the British call The Establishment and subverted it with his writings and his death.

L.Ma.G.

Embassy of the Philippines in London
May Day of the Centenary of Rizal's Birth, 1961.

ACKNOWLEDGMENT

I would be ungrateful and less than loving were I to neglect to make public acknowledgment of my debt to my dear wife Anita, who amid the chores and cares of an Ambassador's wife at the Court of St James's found time to question my lapses into Hispanisms and to type with her own hands the whole of this Anglicizing of the *Fili*.

L.Ma.G

DEDICATION

This edition of *El Filibusterismo* is dedicated to the memory of its translator.

David Guerrero

Manila
Rizal Day, 1996.

1 • On the Upper Deck

This way to the stars

ONE December morning the steamship *Tabo* struggled upstream along the winding Pasig, carrying a great number of passengers to the province of La Laguna. It was a ponderously shaped vessel almost as round as the native water-dipper, usually made of half a coconut shell, after which it had been named. It was rather dirty in spite of its pretensions to whiteness and managed to appear stately by dint of going slowly. For all that, it was looked upon with a certain affection in the region, perhaps because of its Tagalog name, or because it was typical of the country, something like a triumph over progress, a steamship that was not quite a steamship, changeless, defective but an indisputable fact, which, when it wanted to look modern, was perfectly happy with a new coat of paint.

No doubt the ship was genuinely Filipino! With a little good will it could even be taken for the Ship of State itself built under the supervision of Most Reverend and Illustrious personages.

Bathed by the morning sun, which quivered on the river and danced on the pliant bamboo along the banks, the ship's white figure moved on, waving a black plume of smoke—the Ship of State too expels a lot of hot air! Its steam-whistle hooted continuously, hoarse and demanding, like a tyrant who wants to rule by shouting, so that no one aboard could make himself understood. It threatened everything in its way, now seeming about to crush rickety fishing traps that had the look of giant skeletons saluting a prehistoric turtle, now to all appearances rushing straight into a bamboo thicket or upon the riverside restaurants that, set among hibiscus and other flowers, seemed like timid bathers with their toes in the water but still holding back from the plunge. At other times, following a course outlined in the river with bamboo poles, the steamship went along with an air of being sure of itself, but then a sudden shock threw the passengers off balance: it had struck an unsuspected mudbank.

Nor did its similarity to the Ship of State stop there; it was even carried to the distribution of the passengers. Below decks could be seen brown faces and black hair: natives, Chinese, half-breeds, jammed in among baggage and cargo, while above them on the upper deck, under an awning that protected them from the sun, a handful of passengers dressed in European style, friars and officials, were seated in comfortable armchairs, smoking huge cigars and admiring the view, without taking the slightest notice of the efforts of the skipper and the crew to negotiate the difficulties of the passage.

The skipper was a man with a kindly face, rather on in years, an old sailor who had sailed much wider seas in faster ships in his youth and now in his old age found he had to exert greater diligence, care and vigilance to save pettier perils. They were, moreover, such hackneyed perils: the same mudbanks, the same problem of maneuvering the bulk of the ship, like a fat woman stuck in a crowd, past the same twists and bends. So the good skipper had, by the minute, to stop, go astern, or half-speed ahead, sending to port and starboard five sailors, equipped with punting-poles, to emphasize the turns of the tiller. He was like an old soldier who, having led battalions in hazardous campaigns, had turned in his old age tutor to a wilful, disobedient and lazy child.

Doña Victorina, the only lady in the European group, could have described exactly how wilful, disobedient and lazy the *Tabo* was. Her nerves were as bad as ever and she hurled invective against the barges, boats and coconut rafts of the natives, and even against the laundresses and bathers on the river banks whose noisy gaiety put her in a bad humour. Oh, the *Tabo* would go very well indeed if there were not so many natives about in the river, in fact in the whole country, the whole world, Doña Victorina would have said, forgetting that the steersmen were natives, natives the crew above and below decks, natives ninety-nine per cent of the passengers, and she herself a native if the make-up were scraped off her and if she were stripped of her pretentious gown. That morning Doña Victorina was even more unendurable than ever because the passengers in her group paid her little attention, and the character of the company certainly gave her reason for resentment. For among them were three friars convinced that out of pure perversity the world would go backward the day they went forward; the tireless Don Custodio, most renowned of official counsellors, quietly snoozing with satisfaction over his plans and programmes; the prolific writer Ben Zayb (a pen-name which was the anagram of Ybáñez) who believed that, if there was any intellectual life in Manila to speak of, it was only because he was an intellectual; Father Irene, the canon, who gave lustre to the clergy with his well-shaved rosy face and beautiful Jewish nose, and an elegantly cut and delicately buttoned silk soutane; and the fabulous jeweller Simoun, who had the reputation of being the adviser and true author of all the acts of His Excellency the Governor-General. To find these indispensable pillars of the country gathered together in pleasant conversation but not at all attracted to a renegade Filipina who had even dyed her hair blonde, was enough to try the patience of a Job—or rather of a Jobess, for that was how Doña Victorina invariably described herself, in her atrocious version of Spanish, whenever she had a grievance.

Her bad temper rose every time the sailors, at the skipper's command of 'port' or 'starboard', ran back and forth with their long punting poles, and pushed now against this bank, now against the other, preventing the ship's hull from hitting it with the strength of their legs and shoulders. In these circumstances the Ship of State seemed to change from turtle to crab every time danger came near.

'But, Captain, why also these stupid peoples are now going over there?'

'Because, ma'am, we are not drawing enough water on that side,' replied the skipper very deliberately and with a slow wink.

He had acquired this little idiosyncrasy as if to warn his words to come slowly, very very slowly.

'And why also only half-speed, half-speed all the time?' protested Doña Victorina contemptuously. 'Why not full speed?'

'Because then we would find ourselves sailing down those rice-fields, ma'am,' answered the skipper imperturbably, pointing with his lips toward the nearby fields and giving two slow winks.

Doña Victorina was well known in the country for her extravagance and whims. She was very active socially and was tolerated because of her niece Palette Gómez, a ravishing girl of vast wealth, orphaned of both father and mother, to whom Doña Victorina was a kind of guardian. Rather late in life Doña Victorina had married a Spaniard who was down on his luck, Don Tiburcio de Espadaña by name, and at the time of these events had had fifteen years of marriage, wigs, and semi-European dress. Her whole ambition had been to Europeanize herself and from the ill-omened day of her wedding she had gradually succeeded, thanks to measures that were nothing short of criminal, in changing her appearance to such an extent that the most eminent anthropologists would have been hard put to classify her among the known races of man. Her husband, for his part, after enduring many years of marriage with a resignation worthy of an Indian holy man, submitting to all his wife's impositions, finally arrived at the moment of truth one unhappy day and gave her a magnificent whaling with his cripple's crutch. Madam Jobess was so amazed by this change in her husband's character that she did not immediately feel the physical effects and it was only when she had recovered from the shock and when her husband had got safely away that she began to feel aches and pains and took to her bed for a number of days to the great amusement of Paulita, who loved to make fun of her aunt. The husband, awed by his own wickedness, which seemed to him to amount almost to dreadful parricide, had fled the house with all the speed that his limp allowed him, pursued by the household furies—two lapdogs and a parrot. He took the first hackney-coach he found, transferred to the first boat he caught sight of in the river, and, a Philippine Ulysses, went from town to town, from one province to another, from this island to that, followed and pursued by his Calypso in pince-nez. Doña Victorina, who bored everyone who travelled with her with this tale, had now heard a report that her husband was hiding out in a town in the province of La Laguna and she was on her way to seduce him with her dyed locks.

Her travelling companions, in self-defence, kept up a lively conversation among themselves on any subject that came to mind. At that point the turns and twists of the river course had led them to talk about straightening it out and then by a natural sequence to the subject of port works.

Ben Zayb, the writer who looked like a friar, was arguing with a young religious, who in turn looked like a gunner. They were shouting at each other, gesturing, waving their arms, throwing up their hands, stamping their feet, as they talked of water levels, fish corrals, the river at San Mateo, barges, natives and other kindred subjects, to the delight of their hearers and the open annoyance of an aged Franciscan, extraordinarily thin and haggard, and a handsome Dominican who allowed a mocking smile to play about his mouth.

The gaunt Franciscan understood the meaning of the Dominican's smile and cut the discussion short by intervening. They must have had the greatest respect for him; with a gesture he silenced both just as the friar-gunner was talking of experience and the writer-friar of technical experts.

'Have you any idea what technical experts are like, Ben Zayb?' asked the Franciscan in a hollow voice, scarcely moving in his chair and with the barest gesture of his withered hands. 'Look at the Bridge of Whims, built in the provinces by one of our brethren. It was never finished because your so-called technical experts, on the basis of their theories, criticized it as being flimsy and unsafe. Well, the bridge is still standing in spite of floods and earthquakes!'

'That's it, by golly, that's exactly what I was going to say,' cried the friar-gunner, who was called Father Camorra, hitting the arms of his wicker chair with his fists. 'Bridge of Whims, technical experts, that's what I was going to say, Father Salví!'

Ben Zayb, half-smiling, did not reply, either out of deference to Father Salví or because he really had nothing to say. Yet he was the only intellectual in the Philippines!

Father Irene nodded approvingly, rubbing his long nose.

Seemingly satisfied with the general acquiescence Father Salví continued amid the respectful silence:

'But that does not mean that you don't have just as much reason on your side as Father Camorra. The trouble lies in the lake itself.'

'The difference is that the lakes in this country are no good also,' interrupted Doña Victorina, who appeared to be truly indignant about this deficiency and who now prepared to make another attempt to join the conversation.

Her travelling companions exchanged apprehensive looks and, with the air of a commanding officer, Simoun went promptly to their rescue.

'The remedy is very simple,' he said with a strange accent, half English and half Latin-American. 'Really, I can't see why nobody has ever thought of it before.'

All turned to him with the greatest attention, even the Dominican. The jeweller was a lean, tall, sinewy man, very deeply tanned, who dressed in the English fashion and wore a pith helmet. His most striking feature was his long hair, completely white, which set off a black goatee so sparse that it suggested he was a half-breed. To protect himself from the sun he always wore a pair of huge dark glasses that covered his eyes and part of his cheeks completely, giving him the appearance of a man who was either blind or suffered from some defect in his eyesight. He stood with his legs apart, as if to keep his balance, hands thrust in the pockets of his jacket.

'The remedy is very simple,' he repeated, 'and it would not cost a penny.'

The interest of his hearers rose. After all it was said in informed circles in Manila that this man exercised a decisive influence on the Governor-General, and all could already see the solution adopted and in force. Don Custodio himself turned in his chair.

'It is to dig a canal straight through from the lake to Manila, that is to say, to make a new river channel and close up the old Pasig. Land will be saved, distances shortened, and mudbanks avoided.'

The plan left everyone dazed; they were not used to such drastic proposals.

'How typically Yankee,' commented Ben Zayb, who wanted to please

Simoun. The jeweller had spent some time in North America.

Everyone found the plan impressive and nodded approval. Only Don Custodio, in his capacity as a liberal with independent views and high office, thought it his duty to attack a programme that owed nothing to him. This was usurpation of powers, pure and simple!

He cleared his throat, stroked his mustaches, and said in the significant tones he usually reserved for sessions of the Municipal Council:

'Pardon me, Mr Simoun, esteemed friend, if I say that I disagree with you. It would cost a very great deal, and besides some villages might have to be destroyed.'

'Destroy them,' replied Simoun coldly.

'And the money for the workers?'

'They do not have to be paid. Use prison labour...'

'There are not enough prisoners, Mr Simoun.'

'Then let all the towns furnish labour. Make the old, the young, even the children contribute to the State, not the usual fifteen days of conscript labour, but three, four, five months, with the additional obligation of furnishing their own food and tools.'

Don Custodio, shocked, looked over his shoulder to see if they could be overheard by some native. Fortunately those near them seemed to be peasants, and the two helmsmen were engrossed in following the twisting course of the river.

'But Mr Simoun...'

'Let's face it, Don Custodio,' continued Simoun drily 'It's the only way to accomplish great works with little means. That is how the Pyramids, the Lake of Moeris, and the Colosseum in Rome were built. The populations of whole provinces came from the desert, carrying a few onions for their food. Old and young, even children, worked, hauling stone, cutting it, carrying it on their shoulders, under the whip of some official. Those who survived returned to their homes, if they did not perish in the sands of the desert. Then it was the turn of other provinces, and others still, relieving one another in the work for years. The work was finished, and now we admire it; we go abroad, to Egypt and Rome; we praise the Pharaohs, the Antonines... Face it: the dead are dead; posterity gives its verdict only to the strong.'

'But, Mr Simoun, such measures may provoke disturbances,' protested Don Custodio, made uneasy by the trend of the argument.

'Disturbances!' Simoun laughed. 'Did the Egyptian people rebel? Did the Jewish prisoners of war rise against the upright Tito? My dear fellow, I thought you knew a little more history.'

Obviously Simoun was either very conceited or had no manners. To tell Don Custodio to his face that he did not know history was enough to make anybody lose his temper. And indeed Don Custodio forgot himself and retorted;

'But you are not dealing with Egyptians or Jews!'

'And these people,' added the Dominican with a certain reluctance, 'have risen more than once. In the days when they were made to haul timber to build the galleons, if it had not been for the friars...'

'Those days are far away,' replied Simoun, even more curtly than usual. 'These islands will not rise again, no matter what conscription or taxation is imposed on them. Tell me, Father Salví,' he added, turning to the thin Franciscan, 'were you not singing the praises just now of the house and hospital in the town of Los Baños where His Excellency is now spending a few days?'

Father Salví nodded and looked askance.

'Well, then, did you not tell us that both buildings were constructed by compelling the townspeople to do it under the whip of a lay brother? Probably the Bridge of Whims was built in the same way. Now tell me, were there disturbances in those towns?'

'The point is, they rose once,' replied the Dominican. '*Ab actu ad posse valet illatio,* that is to say, what happened before can happen again.'

'Nonsense, nonsense, nonsense,' said Simoun, making ready to go down the hatchway to the saloon. 'I will not change a word I have said. And you, Father Sibyla, don't give me your silly Latin. What are you friars for if the people can make trouble after all?'

Paying no heed to expostulations and rebuttals, Simoun went down the hatchway to the lower deck, muttering scornfully: 'Come, come!'

Father Sibyla had lost colour; never before had he, the Vice Rector of the University, been called silly. Don Custodio was in a rage; he had never met such an opponent in any council session he had ever attended. It was too much.

'American mulatto!' he growled.

'British Indian!' Ben Zayb muttered.

'American, I tell you. I know what I am talking about,' insisted Don Custodio in a temper. 'His Excellency told me so himself. Simoun is a jeweller whom he met in Havana, and who, I suspect, lent the General the money he needed to get this assignment to the Philippines. That is why, to repay him,

Simoun has been allowed to come and do what he likes, to make even more money, selling diamonds... fake diamonds, maybe, who knows? And he is so ungrateful that after taking the natives' money, he even wants to... bah!'

And he ended his sentence with a very significant gesture of the hand.

Nobody wanted to join in these diatribes; Don Custodio could put himself in the wrong with His Excellency if he felt like it, but neither Ben Zayb nor Father Irene nor Father Salví nor the outraged Father Sibyla had any confidence in the discretion of the rest.

'The trouble is that the fellow is an American and no doubt he thinks we are dealing with Red Indians... To talk of these things aboard a steamer! Compelling, forcing people! He was the one responsible for the expedition to the Carolines and the Mindanao campaign that is going to be our dishonour and our ruin! It was he who offered to take a hand in the construction of the new cruiser. What does a jeweller, I ask you, no matter how rich or well-read, know about naval engineering?'

Don Custodio was addressing all this to his neighbour Ben Zayb, his voice rumbling in his throat, gesturing, shrugging, and looking for support from the rest who in turn replied with non-committal nods and shakes of the head. Father Irene permitted himself an ambiguous smile which he half-concealed with his hand as he caressed his nose.

'I tell you, Ben Zayb,' Don Custodio continued, shaking the writer by the arm, 'the whole trouble is that the people who have lived here for years and years are never consulted. A high-sounding project, a project above all involving a great deal of expenditure, expenditure in nice round figures, fascinates and is immediately accepted—because of this!' Don Custodio rubbed the tips of his fingers together.

'There is something to that, something,' Ben Zayb felt it his duty to comment; after all, as a newspaper man he was supposed to be well-informed.

'Look here, before the port works were started I had submitted a plan to clear the mudbanks from the lake, a plan that was original, simple, useful, economical and feasible, but which was not adopted because it would not have given—this!' And he repeated the gesture with his fingertips, shrugged his shoulders, and looked round as if to ask whether anyone had ever heard of anything so outrageous.

'Can you tell us what the plan was? Come now!' His hearers drew up closer and cocked their ears; Don Custodio's projects had just as great a reputation as a quack doctor's prescriptions.

Don Custodio was tempted not to tell them, he was so resentful at not having found support for his diatribes against Simoun. They wanted him to speak up when it was safe, did they, but when it was not, they kept their mouths shut! Still, it was too good an opportunity to lose; if his plan could not be carried out, at least it could be made known and admired.

After two or three puffs at his cigar and some coughing and spitting out of the side of his mouth he slapped Ben Zayb on the thigh and asked: 'Have you ever seen duck?'

'Well, I think so,' replied Ben Zayb, taken aback; 'we have gone shooting for them on the lake.'

'No, I don't mean wild duck, I mean domesticated duck like the ones raised in Pateros and Pasig. You know what they feed on?'

Ben Zayb the intellectual did not know; he was not a duckbreeder, after all.

'Snails, man, snails!' Father Camorra supplied the answer. 'You don't have to be a nigger to know that, all you need is a pair of eyes!'

'Exactly. Snails,' Don Custodio repeated, shaking a finger. 'And do you know where you get them?'

The intellectual did not know that either.

'Well, if you had lived in this country as long as I have, you would know that they are gathered in mudbanks.'

'And your plan?'

'I was coming to that. I would have compelled all the towns in the vicinity of the mudbanks to breed duck, and then you would have seen how on their own initiative they would have eliminated the mudbanks gathering snails. Nothing more or less than that, nothing less and nothing more.'

Don Custodio flung his arms wide and happily contemplated the amazement of his audience; nobody had ever had such a marvellous idea.

'Would you allow me to do a short article on that?' asked Ben Zayb. 'There is so little thinking done in this country...'

'But, Don Custodio,' Doña Victorina protested with pouts and grimaces, 'if also everybody is breeding ducks, therefore there will be too much eggs like the ones the niggers eat when the little ducks is not yet born. How nasty also! Better only the mudbanks!'

2 • On the Lower Deck

OTHER scenes were taking place below decks, where the great majority of the passengers were seated on benches or wooden stools among suitcases,

boxes, baskets and straw holdalls, two feet away from the engine, and washed
by the heat of the boilers, the odour of human bodies and the stench of oil.
Some of the passengers gazed silently upon the varied scenery of the river
bank; others played cards or tried to carry on a conversation amid the clatter
of the paddle-wheels, the noise of the engine, the hiss of escaping steam, the
roar of moving waters and the hooting of the steamwhistle. In a corner, piled
up like corpses, some Chinese pedlars slept or tried to sleep. Seasick, they
were pale and dribbling at the mouth and bathed in a thick sweat. Only a
few young men, for the most part easily recognizable as students by their
spotless white suits and their well-groomed appearance, had the spirit to
move about from stern to bow, scrambling over baskets and boxes, gay with
the expectation of the Christmas holidays. Now they discussed the movements
of the engine, trying; to recall forgotten lessons in Physics; now they were
paying court to a convent school girl or to the rosy-lipped pedlar of betel-
nut with the garland of flowers round her neck, whispering in their ears
words that made them smile or cover their faces with a painted fan.

Two of the students, however, instead of engaging in these passing
flirtations, were deep in conversation at the bow with an elderly gentleman
who for all his age held himself proudly erect. Both the young men, to judge
from a certain deference displayed towards them by their fellows, appeared
to be well known and respected. The elder one, dressed all in black, was
Basilio, now a student of medicine and already known for his successful
cures and surprisingly good prescriptions. The other, bigger and stronger
although much younger, was Isagani, one of the poets, or at least versifiers,
produced that year by the Ateneo, an original character. usually reserved
and rather taciturn. The gentleman who was conversing with them was the
rich Capitán Basilio, who had been shopping in Manila.

'No, sir, Capitán Tiago shows no improvement,' said the medical student
shaking his head. 'He will not submit to any treatment. Somebody has advised
him to send me to San Diego on the pretext of keeping an eye on his house
there but it is only so he will be left completely free to smoke opium.'

Basilio, in referring to 'somebody', meant Father Irene, a great friend and
trusted adviser of Capitán Tiago in his last days.

'Opium is one of the modern plagues,' observed Capitán Basilio with the
contempt and indignation of a Roman senator. 'The ancients knew it but
never abused it. Now mark you, young fellows, opium was only a medicine
as long as the study of the classics was popular. If you don't believe me, tell
me who smoke the most opium. Why, the Chinese, who, of course, don't

know a word of Latin. Ah, if Capitán Tiago had only taken up Cicero!'

His well shaven Epicurean face displayed the most classic loathing. Isagani seemed fascinated by this gentleman who suffered from a nostalgia for antiquity.

'But to go back to that academy for the teaching of Spanish,' continued Capitán Basilio, 'I can assure you that you will never get it established.'

'On the contrary, sir,' replied Isagani, 'we are expecting the permit any day now. Father Irene, whom you may have seen on the upper deck, has promised it to us. We gave him a pair of chestnut horses and he is going to see the Governor-General himself.'

'He can do nothing. Father Sibyla is opposed.'

'Let him oppose it. Father Irene is going to Los Baños precisely so that in front of the Governor-General...'

And Basilio showed what he meant by striking one of his fists against the other.

'I understand,' said Capitán Basilio with a laugh. 'But even if you get the permit, where will you raise funds?'

'We have them, sir. Each and every student is contributing fifteen centavos.'

'And the professors?'

'We have them too, half of them Filipinos, the other half Spaniards from Spain.'

'And the building?'

'The wealthy Makaraig is letting us have one of his houses.'

Capitán Basilio had to concede defeat. These young men had everything ready.

'Well, as far as it goes,' he said, shrugging his shoulders, 'the idea is not wholly bad. If our young people cannot learn Latin, let them at least learn Spanish. There you have, my dear namesake, a proof that we are deteriorating. In our time we learned Latin because our textbooks were in Latin; now you learn it a little but you no longer have books in Latin; instead your books are in Spanish but you are not taught Spanish. *Aetas parentum pejor avis tulit nos nequiores,* as Horace used to say. The age of our fathers, worse than that of their fathers, has bred us even worse than them.'

Having declaimed this he moved away with the majesty of a Roman emperor. The two young men smiled.

'These old-timers find obstacles to everything,' complained Isagani. 'If anything is proposed to them, they notice the disadvantages without seeing the advantages. They want everything as smooth and round as a billiard ball.'

'Well, he is happy enough with your uncle, Father Florentino. They talk of old times,' said Basilio. 'Listen, that reminds me, what does your uncle think of Paulita?'

Isagani flushed.

'He gave me a sermon on the proper choice of a wife. I answered that there was nobody in Manila like her, beautiful, well brought up, an orphan...'

'With a great fortune, excellent taste, and wit, and with no defects other than a ridiculous aunt,' added Basilio with a laugh in which Isagani joined.

'That reminds me. Do you know she has asked me to look for her husband?'

'Doña Victorina? And naturally you promised to do so in order to keep her on your side.'

'Of course! The trouble is that the husband is hiding out precisely in my uncle's house!'

Both burst out laughing again.

'That is why,' continued Isagani, 'my uncle, who is very conscientious, has not gone to the upper deck. He is afraid Doña Victorina will ask him about Don Tiburcio. Imagine! And Doña Victorina was looking down her nose at me because she thought I was a deck passenger.'

Going down the hatchway Simoun saw the two students, and called out in a protective tone:

'Hello there, Basilio! Are you off on your holidays? Ah, and this young man is, I suppose, a townmate of yours?'

Basilio introduced Isagani to Simoun and explained that although they were not townmates they did not live far apart. Isagani's home was by the Pacific, across the island from the lake.

Simoun was scrutinizing Isagani so intently that the latter took umbrage and looked him in the face somewhat provocatively.

'And how are things in your province?' asked Simoun, turning to Basilio.

'You mean you don't know?'

'How the devil should I know when I have never set foot in it? They tell me it is very poor and does not buy much jewellery.'

'We do not buy jewellery because we don't need it,' answered Isagani curtly, hurt in his regional pride.

Simoun smiled.

'Do not take offence, young man,' he replied. 'I meant none. But they assured me that almost all the parishes there were in the hands of native priests and I told myself: the friars would give their lives for a parish, and the Franciscans, especially, would be satisfied with even the poorest, so that when they all let the secular priests have the parishes of this province it must be because it has never seen a peso. Come, gentlemen, let us have a drink of beer and toast the prosperity of your province!'

The young men thanked him and excused themselves, saying they did not drink beer.

'That's wrong,' answered Simoun visibly annoyed. 'Beer is a good thing. I have heard Father Camorra say that the lack of energy in this country is due to the fact that its inhabitants drink so much water.'

Isagani, who was almost as tall as the jeweller, drew himself up. Nudging him under cover Basilio hastened to intervene:

'Well, you can tell Father Camorra that, if he drank water instead of beer or wine, perhaps we would all be the better for it and there would not be ground for so much gossip.'

'And you can also tell him,' added Isagani, ignoring his friend's elbow, 'that water is sweet to drink but it can drown out wine and beer and put out fire; that water when heated becomes steam, and when angry becomes such a flood as once destroyed the human race and shook the world to its foundations!'

Simoun raised his head and, although his dark glasses hid his eyes, it was plain that he had been taken by surprise.

'Well answered,' he said, 'but I am afraid Father Camorra will take it as a joke and ask me when the water will turn to steam, or into another Deluge. He is rather sceptical and very much of a wag.'

'The water will turn to steam when the fires are lighted under it, and it will become a Deluge when all the little streams that are now scattered in their hidden channels come together, driven by fate, in the abyss that human society is digging,' countered Isagani.

'I think, Mr Simoun,' said Basilio taking a jesting tone, 'you had better recite to Father Camorra instead my friend Isagani's verses:

'We are water, you the fire,
Or so you say, let it be so!
Let us live in peace together,
Never think the other foe,
As fireman when the flames do blow.
United, rather, fire, water,
The way that men of science know,

In the boilers of an age of progress
Soon combining by their glow
In a new creation, vapour, show
How life and light can forward go!'

'Utopian!' Simoun said drily. 'Your engine is about to collide with… well, in the meantime, I'll have my beer.'

Without saying good-bye he left the two friends.

'But what's the matter with you today? You were bent on picking a fight,' said Basilio.

'I don't know. That man antagonizes me, almost terrifies me.'

'I kept nudging you. Don't you know they call him the Brown Cardinal?'

'The Brown Cardinal?'

'Or, if you like, His Black Eminence.'

'I don't understand you.'

'Cardinal Richelieu, who was once the all-powerful Prime Minister of France, had a Capuchin adviser who was known as His Grey Eminence because, although clad in the humble grey habit of a friar, he was as powerful as His Eminence the Cardinal himself. Well, Simoun is said to play exactly the same role with the Governor-General.'

'Really?'

'I have heard it from Father Irene who always talks against him behind his back and flatters him to his face.'

'Does he call on Capitán Tiago too?'

'From the very day he arrived. Actually Father you-know-who looks on him as a rival for Capitán Tiago's inheritance. I think he is now going to see the Governor-General about the teaching of Spanish.'

They were interrupted by a servant who told Isagani that he was wanted by his uncle.

Father Florentino was seated on one of the benches astern together with other passengers and was gazing at the view unrolled before him. His neighbours made room for him, those who passed by raised their hats, and the gamblers dared not put up their tables near him. The priest said little and did not smoke. He was not haughty and was not above mixing with other men, returning their greetings with courtesy and grace as if he felt truly honoured by their esteem. He was quite old, his hair was almost wholly white, but he seemed to be in good health and, even seated, he kept his body erect but without pride or conceit. A certain air of self-possession and gravity, of one who was conscious of the dignity of his person and the holiness of his office, distinguished him from the ordinary run of native priests. These, few in number in any case, served at that time merely to assist the friars as coadjutors in their parishes or administered others provisionally. A brief study of the old priest's appearance, if not his white hair alone, revealed immediately that he belonged to another era, another generation, when the best young men were not afraid to expose their human dignity to outrage by taking Holy Orders, when the native secular priests could look upon any friar as an equal, and when their calling, not yet defamed and degraded, attracted free men, not slaves, superior minds not subservient wills. The tranquillity of a soul strengthened by study and meditation, and perhaps tested by intimate moral sufferings, was evident in his grave and severe countenance. His story can be told briefly.

Born to a wealthy and well-connected Manila family, he had never felt a vocation for the priesthood. Moreover, he had charm and all the best opportunities to make a name for himself in the world. But his mother, in fulfilment of certain promises or vows, compelled him to enter a seminary after a long struggle and many violent quarrels. She was a great friend of the Archbishop; also, she was inexorable, like any pious woman who thinks to interpret the will of God. The young Florentino protested and pleaded in vain; in vain he provoked scandals with his affairs; a priest he had to be, and a priest he became at the age of twenty-five. The Archbishop himself ordained him; his first Mass was celebrated with great pomp and three days of festivities; and his mother died happy and satisfied leaving him all her fortune.

But in the struggle Florentino had received a wound which was never healed. Weeks before he said his first Mass the woman whom he had loved best of all married a nobody in despair. The blow was the heaviest he had ever suffered; he lost his spiritual energies, and life weighed on him and was unbearable. But his unhappy love, if not his virtue and respect for his holy office, saved him from the depths to which the parish priests of the Philippines, friars and seculars, so often fell. He dedicated himself to his parishioners out of a sense of duty, and cultivated his liking for the natural sciences.

When the events commonly known as the Cavite Mutiny occurred in 1872, and three Filipino priests, identified with the movement to turn the parishes over to the native clergy, were charged with complicity in the rebellion and executed, Father Florentino feared that the rich revenues of his own parish would attract attention towards him and, above all a lover of peace, he applied for retirement. He had lived since then as a private person in his family lands on the shores of the Pacific. There he had adopted his nephew Isagani, according to malicious gossip his own son by his old love after she had been widowed, or, according to the more serious and well-informed, the natural son of a cousin of his in Manila.

The skipper of the vessel had recognized the priest and urged him to go to the lounge on the upper deck.

'If you don't,' he had added to persuade him, 'the friars will think you don't want to mix with them.'

Father Florentino was bound to agree and had sent for his nephew to let him know what was afoot and to warn him not to be found near the lounge.

'If the Captain sees you he will ask you in too and we would be abusing his hospitality.'

How my uncle does carry on, thought Isagani, all that just so I won't have a chance of talking to Doña Victorina!

3 • Legends

I want to cry,
I don't know why!

WHEN Father Florentino paid his compliments to the little group the bad temper aroused by the previous discussions had been dissipated, perhaps by the sight of the charming houses of the town of Pasig, or by the glasses of sherry they had been taking to sharpen their appetites for luncheon, or by the prospects of a good meal; whatever the reason; they were all laughter and banter, including even the gaunt Franciscan. But his good humour was noiseless; his laughs had the appearance of the grimaces of the dying.

'Bad times, bad times,' Father Sibyla was saying merrily.

'Come now, don't say that, Vice-Rector,' Father Irene replied, giving the Dominican's chair a push. 'You are making money hand over fist in Hong Kong and putting up such buildings that... well!'

'Now, wait a while, you have no idea what our expenses are like, and the tenants on our estates are starting to talk back...'

'That's enough, by golly,' Father Camorra interrupted gaily, 'no more complaints or you'll make me cry. Franciscans don't complain and we have neither estates nor banks. And I must tell you that the natives in my parish have also got it into their heads to jew down my sacramental fees and to insist on the official rates! Imagine telling me about the official rates, and no less than the rates fixed by Archbishop Sancho last century, by golly, as if prices hadn't gone up since then! Why should a baptism be different from a chicken? But I turn a deaf ear, charge what I can get away with, and never complain. We're not greedy, are we, Father Salví?'

At this point Simoun's head appeared at the hatchway.

'But where have you been keeping yourself?' Don Custodio greeted him, all his annoyance forgotten. 'You have missed the best part of the trip!'

'Oh well,' Simoun replied, going up, 'I have seen so many rivers and so many landscapes that now I am interested only in those that have some legend connected with them.'

'The Pasig has a number of legends,' said the skipper who did not relish criticism of the river where he sailed and made a living. 'You have the legend of *Malapad-na-bato,* the "broad rock", sacred home of spirits before the coming of the Spaniards. Afterwards, when the myth had been destroyed and the rock profaned, it became a nest of bandits who made easy prey of the boats that had to struggle against both the current and these pirates. Later still, in our own times, one story or another is told of a boat mysteriously overturned, and if I did not have all my six senses with me when I go past it I would dash myself against it. Then there is another legend for you, that of Doña Gerónima's cave, which Father Florentino can tell you...'

'Everybody knows that one,' Father Sibyla observed scornfully But neither Simoun nor Ben Zayb nor Father Irene nor Father Camorra did know it, and they asked for the story, some in jest and others with real curiosity. The secular priest, putting on the light manner of some of those who had asked him to tell the story, said with the air of a nanny giving children a fairy tale:

'Once upon a time there was a student who promised to marry a country maid. He never again gave her another thought but she was faithful and waited for years and years. Her youth passed away and she became an old maid. Then one day she heard that her old sweetheart was now the Archbishop of Manila. So she disguised herself as a man, came here round the Cape, and asked His Grace to keep his promise. But what she asked was impossible and the Archbishop had a cave built for her by the river's edge; you may have seen it, walled and decorated at its mouth with tangled vines. There she lived and died and there she was buried. We are told that Doña Gerónima was so fat that she had to enter the cave sideways. She had the reputation of being a magician because, after the lavish banquets she would serve to her gentlemen guests, she had the habit of throwing all the silver into the river; in fact there was a net stretched underneath the surface, and thus the silver was washed and cleaned. Scarcely twenty years ago the river passed by the mouth of the cave but how it has slowly receded, just like her memory among the natives.'

'A pretty tale,' said Ben Zayb, 'I am going to write it up. So sentimental!'

Doña Victorina promptly decided to go and live in a cave of her own and was about to announce her plan when Simoun got ahead of her.

'What do you think of it, Father Salví?' he asked the Franciscan, who seemed sunk in meditation. 'Don't you think that His Grace, instead of giving her a cave, should have put her in a nunnery, say, the Poor Clares?'

Father Sibyla was startled to see Father Salví shudder and stare.

'Because,' Simoun continued coolly, 'it is not at all gentlemanly to give someone whose hopes we have defrauded a rock for a home; it was not pious at all to expose her thus to all sorts of temptations, living in a cave, on a river bank; it has a pagan air of nymphs and dryads. It would have been more gentlemanly, more pious, more romantic, more in keeping with the customs of this country, to shut her up in the nunnery of St Clare like a new Heloise and to visit and comfort her from time to time. What do you say?'

'I neither can nor should sit in judgment on the conduct of archbishops,' answered the Franciscan reluctantly.

'But you are the ecclesiastical governor of the archdiocese and you stand in the place of our archbishop. What would you have done if it had happened to you?'

Father Salví shrugged and answered coldly:

'It is a waste of time to think about what cannot happen. But since we are talking about legends, you should not forget the one that is the most beautiful because it is the truest, the one that tells of the miracle wrought by St Nicholas, the ruins of whose church you may have seen. I must tell it to Mr Simoun who cannot have heard about it. It seems that once upon a time the river, like the lake, was infested with crocodiles so huge and voracious that they attacked the boats, overturning them with a blow of the tail. Our chronicles record that one day a heathen Chinese, who had up to then refused to be converted, was going down the river past St Nicholas's church when suddenly the Devil appeared before him in the shape of a crocodile and overturned his boat to devour him and take him to Hell. Inspired by God at this crucial moment the Chinese called for help to St Nicholas and immediately the crocodile was turned to stone. The old timers say that in their day it was possible to recognize the monster in the fragments of stone that still remained of it I myself can say that I was able to make out the head of the reptile and judging from it the monster must have been enormous!'

'Marvellous, what a marvellous tale!' exclaimed Ben Zayb. 'Very suitable for an article! Description of the monster, the Chinaman's terror, the waters of the river, the canefields... And then again, it lends itself to a comparative study of religions. You will observe that the heathen Chinaman in the moment of his great danger invoked, of all people, a saint whom he knew of only by hearsay and in whom he did not believe. The saying that the devil we know is better than the saint we don't, obviously did not apply in this case. For myself, if I were to find myself in such a danger in China, I fear I would call upon the least known saint in the calendar before calling upon Confucius or Buddha. Whether this argues toward the manifest superiority of Catholicism or toward the logical inconsistency of the yellow race can be elucidated only after profound anthropological investigation.'

Ben Zayb had adopted the manner of a professor and traced circles in the air with his index finger, amazed by his own ingenuity which had derived so many allusions and consequences from the most insignificant premises. Seeing Simoun thoughtful and believing that the jeweller was cogitating on what he had just said, he asked Simoun what he was thinking about.

'About two rather important things,' said Simoun, 'two questions you should raise in your article. First: what the devil can have happened to the Devil when he suddenly found himself encased in stone? Did he escape? Did he stay there? Was he crushed? And second: can the fossils I have seen in the museums in Europe possibly be the victims of some antediluvian saint?'

The jeweller spoke so seriously, leaning his brow on the point of his index finger, that Father Camorra said gravely:

'Who knows?'

'Well,' Father Sibyla interrupted, 'since we are talking about legends, and we are just entering the lake, the Captain, I am sure could tell us a number...'

The steamer was just then entering the lake and the view was really magnificent. Everyone was impressed. The beautiful lake, ringed by green banks and blue mountains, stretched out before them like an immense mirror in a frame of emeralds and sapphires here Heaven might look at itself. To the right a series of bays mate graceful curves in the low shore, with farther on, half-blurred the hook of Sugay; ahead, as a background, was Mount Makiling, majestic, imposing, crowned with light clouds; to. the left, the island of Talim and the *Susong Dalaga,* the 'Maiden's Breasts', with the soft undulations which had given it its name.

A spanking breeze delicately curled the great expanse.

'Come to think of it, Captain,' said Ben Zayb, turning in his deck chair, 'do you know where in the lake a certain Guevara—Navarra—or Ibarra—was killed?'

All turned towards the skipper except for Simoun who had turned sideways as if to search for something on the shore.

'Ah really, where, Captain?' asked Doña Victorina. 'Maybe we can see some signals in the water?'

The skipper gave a series of winks, showing he was most annoyed, but aware of the curiosity in all eyes he went forward to the prow and stared out to shore.

'Look there,' he said in a hushed voice, after looking round to make sure he was not being overheard by strangers. 'According to the corporal who was in charge of the chase, Ibarra, seeing himself cut off, dived from his boat there, near the *Kinabutasan,* and swam under water for more than two miles, fired upon every time he showed his head above water to take a breath. Farther on they lost track of him, and a little farther on near the shore they found what seemed like traces of blood... It is just thirteen years to the day, exactly, that this happened.'

'And so his body...' inquired Ben Zayb.

'Joined his father's,' Father Sibyla put in. 'Wasn't he an agitator too Father Salví?'

'Now that's what I would call a cheap burial, eh, Father Camorra?' asked Ben Zayb.

'I have always said,' countered Father Camorra with a jolly laugh, 'that you can't expect these subversives to pay the bills for a first-class funeral.'

'And what's the matter with you, Mr Simoun?' asked Ben Zayb seeing the jeweler withdrawn in his own thoughts. 'Don't tell me you're sick! You, an experienced traveller, sick on a drop of water like this?'

'Well, let me tell you,' said the skipper, who had grown quite fond of those parts, 'don't call this a drop of water. It is bigger than any lake in Switzerland or all the lakes in Spain put together. I have seen old sailors get sick here.'

4 • *Cabesang Tales*

THE woodcutter who had sheltered Basilio in the mountains as a boy was still alive and healthy, although his hair had turned completely white. He no longer went hunting or wood-gathering; his fortunes had improved and now he made brooms as a pastime.

His son Telesforo, Tales for short, had first worked as a share-tenant; later, having acquired two carabaos and saved some hundreds of pesos, he had struck out on his own with the help of his father, wife and three children.

They had cleared a thickly forested tract on the edge of the town which they thought belonged to no one. The entire family, one after the other, had gone down with fever when they were breaking up and draining the ground; the wife of Tales and his elder daughter Lucía, in the prime of youth, wasted away and died. It was only to be expected from the nature of their task but the family blamed it on the vengeful guardian spirit of the forest, resigned themselves, and went on with their work confident that the spirit had been appeased. Then, on the eve of their first harvest, a religious Order which owned lands in the neighbouring town had claimed ownership of the newly cleared fields, alleging that they were within the limits of its property, and to establish its claim immediately attempted to put up boundary markers. The administrator of the religious Order's estate, however, let it be understood that out of pity he would allow Tales the enjoyment of the land for an annual rental, a mere trifle, a matter of twenty or thirty pesos.

Tales, as peace-loving as the next man, as averse to litigation as many more, and compliant to the friars like few, was weak enough to give in under such pressure, arguing to himself that he knew no Spanish and had no money for lawyers. Besides, he said, he did not want to match his clay pot against the iron pan of the friars. In any case Old Selo, his father, counselled:

'Patience! You will spend more in one year in court than if you pay for ten years what the white Fathers want. Oh well, maybe they'll pay you back in Masses. Make believe you lost the thirty pesos gambling, or that you dropped them in the river and a crocodile swallowed them.'

The harvest was good and sold for such a good price that Tales planned to build a wooden house in the hamlet of Sagpang in the, town of Tiani, near San Diego.

Another year went by; the harvest was just as good; and giving one reason or another the friars raised the rental to fifty pesos. Tales paid to avoid a quarrel, and also because he hoped to sell his sugar crop well.

'Patience,' said Old Selo to console him. 'Make believe the crocodile has grown.'

That year they were able to make their dreams come true: to live in a wooden house in town, in the hamlet of Sagpang. Father and grandfather now dreamed of sending the three children to school, especially the girl,

Juliana, Julí; as they called her, who gave promise of being talented and pretty. After all, Basilio was already a student in Manila and his origins were just as humble as theirs.

But it was a dream which it seemed would never come true.

As the family slowly prospered human society took notice and named its most hard-working member, Tales, chief tax-collector of his hamlet. After all, his elder son, Tano, was only fourteen years old. Tales, then, became Cabesang Tales, that is to say, Tales the headman. He had a European jacket made, bought himself a felt hat, and braced himself for further expenses. Soon, in order to avoid disputes with the parish priest and the local authorities, he found; himself making up out of his own pocket the losses in the revenues from identity cards; he paid for those who had died or who had simply not reported. He wasted much time trying to collect the required fees, and travelling to the provincial capital to make his report.

'Patience,' said Old Selo with a placid smile. 'Make believe the crocodile's family has joined the party.'

Cabesang Tales, whenever he heard his daughter speak about how Basilio was getting along in Manila, said: 'Next year I will send you to Manila to study, all dressed up, like the young ladies in town!'

But next year never came; instead there was another increase in the land rent, and Cabesang Tales frowned and scratched his head. The clay pot was giving up its rice to the iron pan.

When the annual rent reached two hundred pesos Cabesang Tales was not satisfied with sighing and scratching his head; he grumbled and protested, to which the friar-administrator replied that if Tales could not pay, then another could have the use of the lands; there were many eager applicants.

Cabesang Tales thought the friar was joking but the friar was speaking in earnest; he even singled out one of his servants to take over. The unfortunate Tales blanched, there was a buzzing in his ears, and he saw red. The images of his wife and daughter rose before him, pale, gaunt, the death rattle of the fever in their throats. He saw the thick forest turned to open field, the furrows watered with the sweat of his body; he saw himself, poor Tales, ploughing in the noonday sun, tearing his feet on rocks and roots, while this friar rode in his coach, followed like a slave by his chosen successor. But he would never consent to that: rather let the earth swallow his fields and all of them! Who was this foreigner that he should have any rights to the land of Tales? Had he brought from his own country the merest handful of that land? Had he bent a single finger to pull out a single root in it?

Exasperated by the threats of the friar, who wanted to assert his authority at all costs because the other tenants of the estate were present, Cabesang Tales rebelled, refused to pay a single penny, and still seeing red declared that he would only yield his fields to the first man that watered them with his own blood.

Old Selo, when he saw his son's face, did not dare to talk of the crocodile but tried to calm him down by speaking instead of earthen pots and reminding his son that in lawsuits even the winner ended up by losing his shirt.

'We shall all end up in the earth, father,' Tales replied, 'and were born without a shirt.'

He resolutely refused to pay the rent or to yield a single square inch of his fields unless the friars first proved with some document bat their claims were legitimate. But the friars had no such document and went to court instead. Tales defended the suit believing, if not all, at least some of the judges loved justice and Would enforce the law.

'I serve and I have served the King with my money and my work,' he told those who tried to discourage him. 'I ask him now do me justice and he must give it to me.'

Obeying some fatal compulsion to stake his future and that of his children on the outcome of the case, he spent his savings gradually on lawyers, notaries and solicitors, not to mention the court officials and clerks who exploited his ignorance and predicament. He went back and forth to the provincial capital, too busy to eat and too worried to sleep. He could speak only of pleadings, evidence, appeals, and all the apparatus of the law. This was a fight as had never before been seen in the Philippines: a poor native, unlettered, without friends, confident in his rights and the justice of his cause, doing battle against a most powerful religious Order before which justice lowered her head and judges dropped their scales and surrendered their swords. Tales fought stubbornly like the ant that bites although it knows it will be crushed, like the fly that hurls itself upon the window-pane when it sees the open space beyond. There was something impressive about this earthen pot defiantly dashing itself to pieces against the iron vat; it had the sublimity of despair. When he was not in court Tales spent his time patrolling his fields, armed with a shotgun. There were outlaws around, he explained, and he had to have means of self-defence so as not to fall into their hands and thus lose his case. As if to perfect his aim he shot down birds and fruits, even butterflies, with such skill that the friar-administrator no longer dared to go to Sagpang without a Constabulary escort, and his protégé-servant, who had caught a glimpse from afar of the imposing figure of Cabesang Tales making the rounds of his fields with the air of a sentry in a beleaguered fort, gave up all his ambitions in a panic.

But the justices of the peace and later the judges in the provincial capital did not dare adjudicate in favour of Tales, fearing they would lose their jobs, and with good reason, for one of their number who had shown signs of impartiality had been immediately dismissed. For sure, the judges were not wicked men; they were conscientious and upright, good citizens, excellent fathers, dutiful sons, and they knew the plight of poor Tales better than Tales himself. Many of them were acquainted with the scientific and historical principles of property; they knew that the friars under the Rule of their Order could not own property; but they also considered that, having left their distant homes and crossed the seas to discharge with the best of intentions the duties of a post which it had cost them so much to obtain, it was too much to expect them to lose it all just because some native fancied that justice should be done on earth as it is in Heaven! They had their families whose needs were surely greater than the family of that native. One judge had to send money home to his mother, and what duty could be more sacred than the duty of honouring one's mother? Another one had marriageable sisters who would need dowries; a third had many children, fledglings in the nest who must be fed and who would surely starve to death if he lost his job; a fourth was worried about his wife back home, a long way away, who might be tempted if she did not receive her monthly allowance... And so all those justices and judges, most of them with vigilant consciences and the most upright moral principles, believed they were doing the best they could in the circumstances by advising a compromise under which Cabesang Tales would pay the required rentals. But Tales, with the simplicity of a clean conscience, would not swerve from his path once he had seen justice to be his goal. He demanded proofs, documents, written evidence, titles, and the friars had none, resting their case on the implied admission of their ownership which he had made by paying rentals in the past.

But Cabesang Tales countered:

'If I give alms to a beggar every day to be rid of him, can I be compelled to go on doing it if he afterwards takes advantage of my generosity?'

Nothing could shake him from that position and no threats could intimidate him. The Provincial Governor made a trip especially to see him and perhaps make him come to his senses, but Tales turned away all arguments by saying:

'You can do what you like, Mr Governor. I am an uneducated man without resources. But I have worked those fields; my wife and my daughter died helping me to clear them; and I will yield them only to someone who can do more for them than I did. Let him water the land first with his own blood and bury his wife and daughter there!'

Because of his intransigence the honourable judges found in favour of the friars and all laughed at him, saying that lawsuits were not won with argument. But Tales filed an appeal, shouldered his shotgun, and calmly patrolled his boundaries. He lived as in a fever. His son Tano, a youth as tall as his father and as good-hearted as his brother, was conscripted but Tales would not buy the services of a substitute and allowed his son to be marched off.

'I have to pay the lawyers,' he told his weeping daughter. 'If I win the case, I will know how to get him out of the army. If I lose, I will need no sons.'

The son went off and nothing more was heard of him except that they had shaved off his hair and that he slept under a cart. Six months later it was rumoured that he had been seen shipped off to the Carolines; others thought they had seen him in a Constabulary uniform.

'Tano in the Constabulary! Jesus, Mary, Joseph! they cried, wringing their hands. 'Tano, so good, so honest! God rest his soul!'

Tano's grandfather would not speak to Tales for a long time. Julí fell ill, but Cabesang Tales did not shed a single tear. For two days he stayed home, as if he feared the reproachful eyes of the neighbourhood. He was afraid they would call him his son's executioner. But on the third day he was out again with his shotgun.

He was suspected of planning murder. Some well-meaning soul whispered that he had heard Tales threaten to bury the friar-administrator in one of the furrows in his fields. The friar was overtaken by real panic. As a result the Governor-General issued a decree against the carrying of firearms, ordering their immediate surrender. Cabesang Tales turned in his shotgun but kept on his rounds armed with a long *bolo*.

'I must guard my crops,' he answered. 'Each sugar cane is like a bone from my wife's body.'

His *bolo* was taken away by the authorities, who found it of an illegal length. Tales brought out his father's old woodsman's hatchet and shouldered it on his brooding rounds.

Whenever he left home Old Selo and Julí trembled for his life. The latter left her loom, ran to the window, fell on her knees to pray, made promises to the saints, and started novenas. The old man, fumbling with the hoop of one of his brooms, sometimes talked of going back to the woods. In that house life was becoming impossible.

In the end what they feared came true. The fields were far from town and Cabesang Tales, in spite of his hatchet, fell in the hands of the outlaws, who had guns and revolvers. They told him that, since he had money for lawyers and judges, he should have it too for the forsaken and oppressed. Through a peasant they let it be known that his ransom was fixed at five hundred pesos, to be paid in two days, and that if anything happened to their intermediary Cabesang Tales would pay with his life.

The news plunged the distraught family into despair which became even greater when it was learned that the Constabulary were going out after the outlaws. Everybody knew that if an encounter took place the prisoner would be the first casualty. Old Selo could not raise a finger and Julí, despondent and panic-stricken, could not utter a word. Then an even more terrible possibility, an even more cruel thought, shook them out of their stupor. The peasant sent by the outlaws said that the gang would probably have to move fast and if they delayed payment of the ransom much longer the two days would be over before he could catch up with them and they would cut Cabesang Tales's throat.

This drove the two out of their heads; they were both weak, both without resources. Old Selo sprang to his feet no sooner he had sat down, went up and down stairs, wondering where to go, to whom to appeal. Julí turned to her holy images; she counted her money over and over again but her two hundred pesos did not increase, were not multiplied like the loaves and the fishes. On an impulse she would dress up, gather all her jewels together, and ask her grandfather for advice; she would go and see the Mayor, the Municipal Judge, the municipal clerk, the Constabulary lieutenant. The old man said yes to everything and agreed equally when she changed her mind. A number of neighbours came round, some of them relatives, others friends of the family, some poorer than others, but all ingenuous and full of noisy sympathy. The cleverest of them all was Sister Balí, a great gambler, who had just come back from Manila where she had undergone spiritual exercises in the Jesuit retreat-house for women.

It was decided that Julí should sell all her jewels except for a diamond-and-emerald reliquary which Basilio had given her. This jewel had a story behind it; a nun, Capitán Tiago's daughter, had given it to a leper; the leper in turn had given it to Basilio, who had treated his disease. She would not sell it without letting Basilio know first.

Julí's combs, earrings and rosary were quickly disposed of to the richest of the neighbours and there were fifty pesos more, but she was still short two hundred and fifty. Would she pawn the reliquary? Julí shook her head. Another neighbour proposed that the house be sold and Old Selo agreed, happy enough to return to the forest and gather firewood as in the old days. But Sister Balí observed that it could not be done in the absence of the owner of the house.

'The Judge's wife once sold me an overskirt for a peso, but her husband said the sale was not valid because it had been made without his consent. Well, can you imagine, he took back the overskirt, but she has not given me back my peso to this day! Well, I don't pay her when she wins at cards, and that way I have recovered twelve centavos; that's the only reason I play cards, really; I can't bear it when people don't pay their debts!'

A neighbour was going to remind Sister Balí about a trifling debt of her own, but she was not given a chance because the card-player smartly went on:

'Do you know what can be done, Julí? Borrow two hundred and fifty pesos with the house for security, payable when the lawsuit is won.'

This seemed to be the best advice and they decided to follow it that very same day. Sister Balí offered to accompany Julí and the two went the rounds of the rich families of Tiani, but nobody would agree to the condition: the lawsuit, they said, was as good as lost, and to help an enemy of the friars would be to expose oneself to their reprisals. In the end a pious old woman took pity and lent Julí the money on condition that the girl should stay with her as a servant until the debt was paid. In any case Julí would not have to do very much except sew, pray, accompany her to Mass, and fast for her once in a while. The girl accepted with tears in her eyes and took the money, promising to enter the old woman's service the next day, Christmas Day.

When her grandfather learned of what amounted to the sale of his granddaughter, he burst into tears like a child. What, a servant to be scolded and punished, with hands roughened, sent to sleep in any corner and awakened at any hour; all this for his granddaughter whom he had never allowed to go out in the sun to save her complexion, Julí of the delicate fingers and rosy heels, the prettiest girl in the neighbourhood, and perhaps in the whole town, beneath whose window so many had spent the night serenading, his only granddaughter, his only child, the only joy of his tired eyes, whom he had dreamed of seeing in a long-skirted gown, speaking Spanish, and toying with a painted fan like the daughters of the rich, Julí, a servant-maid!

He wept, and talked of hanging himself or going on hunger strike.

'If you go,' he kept on saying, 'I am going back to the woods and never set my foot again in town.'

Julí tried to calm him down; it had to be done if her father was to return, and in any case they would soon win the lawsuit and redeem her from servitude.

It was a sad night for both of them. Neither could eat a mouthful and the old man refused to go to bed, spending the night in a corner, without saying a word or moving a muscle. Julí, for her part, tried to sleep but for a long time was unable to close her eyes. Reassured about her father's fate, she thought now of herself and wept, choking down her sobs to keep her grandfather from hearing them. Tomorrow she would be a servant, and it was just the day when Basilio usually came from Manila bringing her gifts. From now on she would have to give up her love; Basilio, who would soon be a physician, should not marry a kitchen slavey. She imagined him going to church with the prettiest and richest girl in town, both dressed in their best, happy and smiling, while she, Julí, walked behind her mistress, carrying prayer-books, betel-nut chew and a spittoon. At this point the girl felt an immense knot in her throat, a heavy weight on her heart, and she asked the Virgin to let her die first.

Still, said an inner voice, he will at least know that I preferred to put myself in pledge rather than pawn the reliquary he gave me.

This thought somewhat soothed her and she yielded to vain fancies. Who could tell? A miracle could happen: she might find the two hundred and fifty pesos under the image of Our Lady—she had read about so many miracles of that kind! The sun might not rise, morning might not come, and in the meantime the lawsuit might be won. Her father might suddenly come back, or Basilio come to the rescue; she might find a bag of gold in the orchard, or the outlaws might send her one, or the parish priest Father Camorra, who was always at her with his jokes, might turn out to be the chief of the outlaws... her thoughts grew ever more confused and disordered until at last, exhausted by sorrow, she went to sleep to dream of her childhood in the depths of the forest. She was bathing in the stream together with her two brothers; little fishes of all colours swam about and let themselves be caught, and she was exasperated because it was no fun catching such stupid fishes; Basilio was under water but, she did not know why, he had the face of her brother Tano. Her new mistress watched them from the bank.

5 • A Rig-Driver's Christmas Eve

BASILIO arrived in San Diego when the Christmas Eve procession was going round the town. He had been delayed many hours because the driver of his hired rig had forgotten to carry his identity card and had been arrested by the Constabulary, hit with a rifle-butt, and taken to the barracks.

Now they were being held up once again by the procession. The unfortunate rig-driver reverently uncovered himself and said an Our Father before the first of the images on wheels, the image, it seemed, of a great saint, an old man with the longest of beards, seated on the edge of a pit, under a tree whose branches were loaded with stuffed birds of all kinds. All he had by him were a native earthen stove, a pot, a mortar, and the utensils to make betel-nut chew, as if to suggest that the old man lived and had his meals on the very brink of the grave. In the Philippines this religious image represented Methuselah; his European counterpart and perhaps contemporary was called Noel, and was jollier and more cheerful.

'In the time of the saints,' the driver mused, 'there cannot have been many Constabulary soldiers. Being hit with a rifle-butt certainly does not help one to live to be as old as that.'

After the bearded old man came the Three Magi on horseback. Their steeds kept rearing, particularly that of the black King Melchior which seemed about to hit the horses of the two white kings Gaspar and Balthassar.

'Can't have been, can't have been many constables,' the driver concluded from this exhibition, sighing inwardly for such happy times. 'Otherwise that Negro who allows himself all these liberties beside those two Spaniards would be in gaol by now.'

Then, seeing that the Negro wore a crown and was just as much a king as the two Spaniards, he naturally remembered the King of the Natives and sighed.

'Do you know, sir,' he asked Basilio respectfully, 'whether or not his right foot is free by now?'

'Whose right foot?'

'The king's,' the driver replied in a conspiratorial whisper. 'Which king?'

'Our king, the King of the Natives...'

Basilio smiled and shrugged his shoulders.

The driver heaved another sigh. The peasants of that day kept alive a legend that their king, imprisoned in chains in the cave of San Mateo, would one day return to free them from oppression. Every hundred years he had broken one of his chains, and now he already had freed his arms and his left leg. Only his right leg was still held fast. It was he who caused earthquakes as he flailed about and struggled against his chains: he was so strong that one could shake hands with him only by stretching out a bone, which crumbled in his grasp. For no apparent reason the natives called him King Bernardo, confusing him perhaps with Bernardo del Carpio, the semi-mythical Spanish hero of the ninth century who was said to have defeated the French Roland at Roncesvalles.

'When he gets his right foot free,' muttered the driver with a suppressed sigh, 'I shall give him my horses, put myself under his orders, and die for him. He will free us from the Constabulary.'

He followed the Three Kings with mournful eyes as they rode away.

The boys of the town came next in two files, sad-faced, sullen, as if they had been compelled to attend. Some carried torches, others tapers, and still others lanterns made of paper and bamboo. They were reciting the Rosary aloud, so loudly in fact that they seemed to be carrying on a quarrel. St Joseph followed on a modest float, his face resigned and melancholy, carrying a staff that flowered into lilies, and between two Constabulary soldiers who looked as if they had arrested him. The driver understood at last why the saint looked like that and, either because the sight of the soldiers had unnerved him, or because he had no great respect for a saint that kept such company, he did not even say the prayers for the dead. After St Joseph came the girls in the procession, their heads covered with kerchiefs knotted under the chin, likewise reciting the Rosary although less angrily than the boys. In their midst a number of children could be seen, pulling paper rabbits with raised tails that were lighted with little red candles; the children joined the procession with these toys to amuse the new-born Babe. The rabbits, plump and round like eggs, seemed so cheerful that likely as not they gave a little leap, lost their balance, fell, and went up in flames; their owners ran up to quench their ardour, blew and blew or beat out the fire, but seeing their pets destroyed burst into tears. The driver here perceived with a certain melancholy that every year the paper rabbits were decimated as if they had been attacked by the rinderpest like live animals. It was enough to recall to him two magnificent horses of his which, to preserve them from the disease, he had had blessed for ten pesos, upon the advice of the parish priest; neither the government nor the priests, he had been told, had found a more efficacious cure for the epidemic. All in vain; they had died on him all the same; although he had not been wholly disconsolate because, after having been sprinkled with holy water and had Latin read over them by the priest, the beasts had put on such airs, had given themselves such importance, that they had refused to be hitched, and he, like a good Christian, had not dared to whip them because a member of a religious confraternity had warned him that they were 'sanctified'.

The procession was closed by the Virgin, dressed for her trip to Bethlehem as the Divine Shepherdess in an elaborate wide-brimmed feathered hat. To suggest the impending Birth the parish priest had ordered the image's waist to be thickened and its skirts padded with rags and cotton-wool so that no one might have any doubts about its condition. It was a very beautiful image, pathetic in visage like all images carved by the Filipinos, and now with also a rather embarrassed air, perhaps because of the position in which the parish priest had placed it. The Virgin was preceded by a number of carollers, and followed by musicians and the inevitable Constabulary escort. The parish priest, as might have been expected after what he had perpetrated, had not come along; that year he was much put out because he had had to use all his diplomacy and talent for intrigue to persuade the townspeople to pay thirty pesos for the Masses in the Christmas season instead of twenty as in the past.

'You are turning subversive,' he had muttered.

The things he had seen in the procession must have been so much on the driver's mind that, when the procession had passed and Basilio ordered him to go on, he did not notice that his vehicle's lights had gone out. Basilio did not notice it either because he was too engrossed in looking at the houses along the street, lighted inside and out with little paper lanterns fashioned in fanciful shapes and various colours, stars within hoops with long tails that shivered deliciously in the breeze, or fishes with movable heads and tails and oil lamps in their bellies, hanging from the eaves to give a charming holiday air, both inviting and intimate. Yet Basilio thought these illuminations on the decline, the stars in eclipse, and this year with less ornaments and pendants than the year before, just as last year's had had less than the year before that. There was scarcely any music to be heard in the streets; not all the houses were abustle with preparations in the kitchen. He blamed it on the bad times: sugar prices were low, the rice harvest had been lost, half the work animals had died, rentals and taxes were rising no one knew why or what for, while more and more abuses by the Constabulary discouraged merrymaking in the towns.

He was thinking on just these abuses when a brisk order to halt cut through the night. They were passing in front of the Constabulary barracks and one of the sentries had noticed that the vehicle's lights were out. It just would not do; a rain of insults fell upon the driver who explained in vain that processions lasted too long. It was bound to lead to an arrest for violation of regulations, and perhaps a piece in the newspapers; Basilio, peace-loving and prudent, left the vehicle and went on his way on foot, carrying his luggage.

This was San Diego, the town which he called home but where he did not have a single relative.

The only house which seemed to him to have a holiday air was that of Capitán Basilio, his namesake, where hens and chickens were saying noisy farewells amid the rapid clatter of knives on chopping blocks and the sputtering of lard in frying pans. There was a promise of good eating in the succulent smells of stews and sweetmeats that reached out to the street.

Basilio caught a glimpse of Sinang in the ground floor, as short as ever, although rather plumper and rounder now that she was married. Farther in he saw to his great surprise, chatting with Capitán Basilio, the parish priest, and the Constabulary lieutenant, no other than Simoun the jeweller, in his familiar dark glasses as nonchalant as ever.

'Agreed, Mr Simoun,' Capitán Basilio was saying. 'We shall go to Tiani to see your jewels.'

'I would go too,' said the lieutenant, 'because I need a watch-chain, but I have so many things to do. If you could get me one, Capitán Basilio...'

Capitán Basilio would do so with the greatest of pleasure and, since he wanted to be in the good graces of the officer so that the latter would leave his field hands alone, he refused to accept the money which the lieutenant was trying to fish out of his pocket.

'Let it be a Christmas gift from me!'

'I cannot allow it, Capitán, I cannot permit it!'

'Well, all right, we can settle accounts later,' said Capitán Basilio with an elegant gesture.

The parish priest wanted a pair of lady's earrings and likewise asked Capitán Basilio to get them for him.

'I want them to be of the best quality, and we can settle it later too.'

'Not to worry, Father,' said the good man who also wanted to be at peace with the Church.

An unfavourable report by the parish priest might cause him great harm and make him spend twice the money; these earrings were compulsory gifts.

In the meantime Simoun was praising his stock.

'This man is unbearable,' the student thought. 'He does business everywhere. If we are to believe some stories, he buys back at half-price from certain people the jewels that he himself has sold to be given to them as presents. Everybody does business in this country except we Filipinos!'

He went on to his house, or rather that of Capitán Tiago, which was in the care of a trusted employee. The latter, who had held the medical student in awe ever since the day he had seen Basilio perform surgical operations with the same nonchalance as if chickens had been concerned, was waiting to give him the news. Two of the field hands had been arrested, one was going to be deported, a number of work animals had died...

'The old story, it's always the same,' interrupted Basilio ill-humouredly. 'You always meet me with the same complaints.'

The young man was not a martinet but, since he was often scolded by Capitán Tiago, he liked in turn to scold those under him. The old man searched his mind for some fresh news.

'One of our tenants, the gamekeeper, died and the parish priest refused to give him a pauper's funeral because, according to him, the dead man's landlord was rich enough.'

'What did he die of?'

'Old age.'

'Good grief, old age! If at least he had died of some disease.'

Basilio was eager for autopsies.

'Is there nothing new you can tell me? You make me lose my appetite telling me the same things over and over again. Have you any news of Sagpang?'

The old man then told him the story of the kidnapping of Cabesang Tales. Basilio grew thoughtful and said nothing. He had lost his appetite for good and all.

6 • *Basilio*

WHEN the church bells of San Diego started pealing for the midnight Mass on Christmas Eve, and those who preferred a good night's sleep to rites and festivities were turning over in their beds, grumbling about the noisy merry-making, Basilio cautiously went downstairs and, after doubling back two or three times along various streets to make sure that nobody was watching or following him, went along unfrequented paths towards the old forest of the Ibarras, which Capitán Tiago had acquired when the Ibarra properties had been confiscated and sold.

That year the moon was on the wane at Christmas and it was pitch dark in the wood. The bells had stopped ringing and now only the last slow separate peals could be heard in the night's silence over the murmur of the windswept branches and the regular beat of the waves in the nearby lake, the heavy breathing of Nature sunk in her immense sleep.

Impressed by the place and the time the young man walked with head downcast as if trying to peer at the ground through the dark. From time to time he raised his head to seek the stars in the clearings between the treetops; then went ahead again pushing aside the bushes and tearing down the vines in his way. Sometimes he retraced his steps, or his foot became entangled in a shrub, or he stumbled on an exposed root or a fallen tree-trunk. After half an hour he reached a small stream on whose opposite bank rose something like a hillock, a black and shapeless mass that in the dark took on the proportions of a mountain. Basilio crossed the creek, jumping from one stone to another among those that gleamed darkly in the bright waters. He climbed the hillock and went towards a small enclosure with old and crumbling walls. A *balete* tree rose in its centre, huge, mysterious, awesome, with its tangle of intertwined branches and roots that rose and fell.

He stopped before a heap of stones, uncovered himself, and seemed to pray. His mother was buried there, and every time he went to San Diego his first visit was to this unknown and unremarked grave. He was fulfilling this duty tonight because the next day he would have to call certain superfluities and puerilities the method followed in the Ateneo filled him with admiration, and the zeal of the professors, with gratitude. His eyes filled with tears when he thought of the four previous years when he had been unable to study in that school for lack of means. He had to make extraordinary efforts to catch up with those who had had a good start, and in that one year he might be said to have really covered for the first time all the first five years of the six-year bachelor of arts course. He was awarded his degree to the great satisfaction of his professors. They made their pride in him obvious at the final oral examinations conducted by visiting Dominicans, who had been assigned to inspect the standards of the school. One of them, to dampen the enthusiasm of the Jesuits, asked Basilio where he had started his Latin studies.

'In San Juan de Letran, Father,' replied Basilio.

'Ah,' the Dominican commented with a slight smile. 'He's not too bad in Latin really.'

Out of a natural inclination he chose to take up Medicine. Capitán Tiago would have preferred him to take up Law so that he would have a lawyer for nothing, but in the Philippines a thorough knowledge and understanding of the laws is not enough to build up a practice; one must also have connections and influence in certain circles, and know one's way around. In the end Capitán Tiago gave way, when he remembered that medical students were always playing around with corpses. For some time now he had been looking for an effective poison to smear on his fighting cock's spurs and the most deadly that he knew of was the blood of a Chinese who had died of a venereal disease.

Basilio took up his medical studies with the same, if not greater, profit than he had so far shown, and even from his third year in the course he began to make some fortunate cures, which not only augured a brilliant future but also gave him enough money to enable him to dress with a certain elegance and even to put aside some savings.

This was the last year of his studies and in two months he would become a full-fledged physician, set up practice in his home town marry Julí, and live happily ever after. He not only thought his graduation sure; he expected it to be brilliant, the crowning success of his student life. He had been chosen to deliver the valedictory address at the graduation ceremonies and already he could see himself in the middle of the stage before the assembled faculties and student body of the university, the centre of attention. All the most eminent men of science in Manila, half buried in their doctors' capes, all the curious women who had looked on him a few years ago with indifference if not contempt, all those gentlemen whose coaches would have run over him when he was a boy as indifferently as if he had been a dog, would now listen to him attentively, and he for his part would tell them something far from trivial, never before heard in that auditorium. He would forget self and would speak for the needy students of the future. With that speech he would make his entrance into the world.

7 • *Simoun*

BASILIO was thinking of these things at his mother's grave. He was about to return to town when he thought he perceived a light among the trees, a clatter of branches, the sound of footsteps, a rustling of leaves. The light went out but the noise became gradually more distinct and soon he saw a shadow appear in the enclosure and proceed directly to where he stood.

Basilio was not superstitious by nature and was even less so after dissecting so many corpses and assisting at so many deaths, but the old legends about that melancholy place, the time, the dark, the dismal whistling of the wind, and the fairy stories he had heard as a child, had their effect on him and he felt his heart beating faster.

The shadow stopped at the other side of the *balete* tree and the young man, watching between two hanging roots which with time had grown as thick as tree-trunks, saw the newcomer take out a powerfully focused lamp and place it on the ground. The light shone on a pair of riding boots; otherwise the unknown remained in darkness. He seemed to be going through his pockets; then, as he leaned forward to adjust the blade of a spade to the end of a thick stick, Basilio thought he recognized, to his amazement, the features of the jeweller. It was indeed Simoun.

As the jeweller was digging, the lantern lighted his face from time to time. He was not wearing the dark glasses that so greatly altered his features. Basilio shuddered. This was the face of the unknown man who thirteen years ago had dug his mother's grave; only age had changed him, his hair had turned white and he now had a moustache and a goatee; but the bitter look in his eyes, the troubled brow, the powerful arms, perhaps a little leaner now, the angry energy, these had not changed. Past sensations revived in Basilio; he felt again the heat of the funeral pyre, his hunger and despair that night, the smell of freshly dug earth. His discovery unnerved him. So Simoun the jeweller, who had been taken for an Indian, a Portuguese, a South American, or a mulatto, the Brown Cardinal, His Black Eminence, the evil spirit of the Governor-General, as he was known to many, was no other than the unknown man of mystery who had appeared and vanished with the death of the heir to these lands. But of the two unknown men that night, the one who died and the one who survived, which had been Ibarra?

He had often asked himself this question whenever the death of Ibarra was spoken of, and now it returned to him as he watched the enigmatic jeweller. The man who had died had two wounds which, in the light of his later medical studies, he judged to have been caused by firearms, suffered probably during the chase on the lake. Therefore he must have been Ibarra, who had come to die on the grave of his ancestor. His desire to be cremated could thus be explained by Ibarra's stay in Europe, where this practice was common. If so, then who was the other, the one who had survived, and who now returned, immensely rich, the friend of the powerful? Here was a mystery which the student, with characteristic *sangfroid*, was determined to solve at the first opportunity.

Simoun had kept digging in the meantime, but Basilio could see that he was not so strong as he once was. He was panting, breathed with difficulty, and had to rest frequently.

Fearing that he would be discovered at any rate, Basilio made a sudden decision. He stood up and leaving his hiding place asked in a normal voice:

'Can I help you, sir?'

Simoun leapt up like a tiger attacked by surprise. He put his hand in the pocket of his jacket and stared at the student, pale and menacing.

'Thirteen years ago, sir, you did me a great service,' Basilio continued unmoved, 'by burying my mother's body in this very place. I would be happy if I could help you in return.'

Simoun drew a revolver, without taking his eyes from the young man, and cocked it.

'Who do you take me for?' he asked, stepping back.

'For someone sacred to me,' answered Basilio with some emotion, thinking he was on the point of death. 'For one whom all, except I, believe to be dead, and for whose misfortunes I have always grieved.'

An impressive silence followed these words, a silence which to the young man seemed endless. However, Simoun after much hesitation approached him and, putting a hand on his shoulder, said in a voice trembling with emotion:

'Basilio, you know a secret which can ruin me and now you have discovered another which puts me entirely in your hands. If you should reveal it all my plans would be ruined. For my own security and for the sake of my objective I should silence you for ever. What is the life of one man compared with the end which I pursue? I have every opportunity. Nobody knows I have come here. I am armed and you are defenceless. Your death would be blamed on outlaws or attributed to other causes, perhaps supernatural. And yet I shall spare you, and I hope I will not regret it. You have worked and struggled with energy and perseverance and, like myself, you have some accounts to settle with human society. Your brother was murdered, and your mother was driven mad, and human society has called neither the murderer nor the torturer to account. You and I are among those who thirst for justice and we should help, not destroy, each other.'

Simoun paused, stifling a sigh, and then continued slowly with a faraway look:

'Yes, it was I who came thirteen years ago, spent and heartsick, to pay a last tribute to a great and noble soul who wished to die for my sake. The victim of a vicious system, I wandered through the world, working night and day to amass a fortune which would enable me to carry out my plans. Now I have returned to destroy that system, to hasten its putrefaction, to give it the last push into the abyss to which it blindly runs, even if it should mean measureless blood and tears. It has condemned itself, it is doomed, but I would not die without seeing it with my own eyes dashed to pieces at the bottom of the abyss.'

Simoun stretched out his arms towards the ground as if to keep the broken remnants from ever rising. His voice had turned cold and sinister, and the student shuddered.

'I have returned to these islands summoned by the vices of their rulers. In the guise of a merchant I have gone from town to town, opening all doors with money, and everywhere I have seen greed in its most abominable forms, hypocritical one time, shameless the next, always cruel, battening on a dead social system like a vulture on a corpse. I asked myself why the corpse did not distill in its entrails some infection, some venom, some deadly virus that would kill the loathsome bird, but the corpse let itself be torn to pieces and the vulture had its fill. I could not bring back this corpse to life and turn it against its oppressor. On the other hand its decay and total disintegration were taking too long. So I incited even greater greed; I facilitated its satisfaction, and injustices and abuses have multiplied. I have encouraged crime and cruelty to accustom the people to the thought of death. I fostered insecurity to drive them to seek the most desperate solutions. I crippled business so that the country, impoverished and ruined, would no longer have anything to fear. I whetted appetites for the public funds. When this did not prove enough to make the people rise, I wounded them in their most sensitive spot. I made the vulture insult and pollute the very corpse on which it lived. But when I was about to achieve the spontaneous combustion of all this corruption, this loathsome accumulation of garbage, and when frenzied greed, taken unawares, was rushing about to seize whatever was at hand like an old woman surprised by fire, you showed up with your slogans of pro-Hispanism, with your calls for confidence in the Government and faith in what will never come! Suddenly the vulture finds fresh food offered to it: new flesh, warm with life, uncorrupted, young, healthy, pulsing with blood and enthusiasm. Ah, youth, fatuous and full of dreams, always running after butterflies and flowers! You pool your efforts thinking to unite your country with Spain with rosy garlands, and in reality you forge iron chains. You ask parity of rights, the Spanish way of life, and you do not realise that what you are asking is death, the destruction of your national identity, the disappearance of your homeland, the ratification of tyranny. What is to become of you? A people without a soul, a nation without freedom; everything in you will be borrowed, even your very defects. You ask for Hispanization, and do not blush for shame when it is denied you. And even if it were given you, what would you do with it? What do you have to gain? At best, to become a country of military revolts, a country racked by civil wars, a republic of the greedy and the needy like some republics of South America. Now you ask for the teaching of Spanish, an aspiration that would be ridiculous if it did not entail such deplorable consequences. For you would add one more language to the more than forty already spoken in these islands, no doubt so that you may understand one another less and less!'

'On the contrary,' objected Basilio, 'if the knowledge of Spanish may bring us closer to the Government, it can also unite all the islands.'

'A gross mistake,' interrupted Simoun. 'You let yourselves be fooled by big words and never get to the bottom of things to study the ultimate consequences. Spanish will never be the national language because the people will never speak it. That tongue cannot express their ideas and their emotions. Each people has its own way of speaking just as it has its own way of feeling. What will you do with Spanish, the few of you who will get to speak it? You will only kill your individual personality and subject your thoughts to other minds. Instead of making yourselves free, you will only make yourselves truly slaves. Nine out of ten among you who presume to be educated are renegades to your own country. Whoever among you speaks Spanish is so indifferent to his own language that he can neither write nor understand it. How many have I seen who pretend not to know a single word of their native tongue! Fortunately you have a stupid Government. While Russia compels the Poles to study Russian in order to enslave them, while Germany prohibits the use of French in the provinces she has conquered from France, your Government fights to keep alive your native languages, while you, on the other hand, an extraordinary people under an incredible government, struggle to get rid of your national identity. Both of you forget that as long as a people keeps its own language, it keeps a pledge of liberty, just as a man is free as long as he can think for himself. Language is a people's way of thinking. Fortunately your independence is secure. Human passions watch over it.'

Simoun stopped and drew his hand across his brow. The moon was rising and sent its feeble light through the branches. White-haired, his stern face lighted from below by the lantern, the jeweller seemed to be the ill-omened spirit of the forest brooding on some sinister scheme. Silenced by so many reproaches Basilio listened with head bent low. Simoun continued:

'I have spent many anxious nights since I saw the start of your pro-Spanish movement, because I knew that among you were young men of rare intelligence and good will sacrificing themselves for a cause which they believed to be good, although in reality they were working against their own country. How often I have wanted to address you, to unmask myself and try to destroy your illusions! But my reputation is such that anything I might have said would I have been misinterpreted and perhaps had the opposite effect. How often I have wanted to approach your Makaraig, your Isagani! Other times I considered killing them...'

Simoun paused.

'That is the reason why, Basilio, I spare you now and run the risk that some day you may betray me through some careless word. You know who I am and how much I must have suffered. You believe in me. You do not share the common opinion that Simoun the jeweller encourages the authorities to commit abuses so that the victims may buy his wares as bribes to save themselves. I am the Judge come to punish a social system through its own crimes, to make war upon it by indulging it. I need your help. I want you to use your influence among the youth to fight these stupid yearnings for Spain and the Spanish way of life, for equality of rights... That will only lead at best toward becoming a poor imitation and our people should aim higher. It is folly to try to influence the thinking of those who rule us; they have their own plans and their eyes are closed to anything else. You will not only lose your time but also fool the people with vain hopes and help to bend their neck to the tyrant yoke. What you should do is to take advantage of the prejudices of our rulers. So they refuse to integrate you into the Spanish nation. So much the better! Take the lead in forming your own individuality, try to lay the foundations of a Filipino nation. They give you no hopes. All the better! Hope only in yourselves and your own efforts. They deny you representation in the Spanish parliament. Good for you! Even if you were able to elect representatives of your own choosing, what could you do there but be drowned among so many voices, yet sanction by your presence the abuses and wrongs which may be afterwards committed? The less rights they recognize in you, the more right you will have later to shake off their

yoke and return evil for evil. If they refuse to teach you, their language, then
cultivate your own, make it more widely known, keep alive our native culture
for our people, and instead of aspiring to be a mere province, aspire to be
a nation, develop an independent, not a colonial, mentality, so that in
neither rights nor customs nor language the Spaniard may ever feel at
home here, or ever be looked upon by our people as a fellow citizen, but
rather, always, as an invader, a foreigner, and sooner or later you shall be
free. That is why I want you to live.'

Basilio sighed as if a great weight had been lifted from his shoulders, and
after a brief pause replied:

'Sir, the honour you do me by confiding your plans to me is so great that I
must be frank and say that what you want me to do is beyond my strength.
I do not play politics. If I signed the petition for the teaching of Spanish I
did so only because I thought it would be helpful to our studies, nothing
more. I have another end in life: my only ambition is to alleviate the physical
ills of my fellow citizens.'

The jeweller asked with a sneer:

'What are physical compared with moral ills? What is the death of one
man beside the death of a community? One day you may become a great
physician, if they leave you alone; but much greater will be the physician
who can give new life to this enfeebled people. What are you doing for the
country that made you what you are, that gives you life and knowledge?
Don't you realize that a life which is not dedicated to a great idea is useless?
It is a pebble lost in the field, when it should form part of some building.'

'But I do not stand by with arms crossed,' protested Basilio. 'I am working
as all are working to raise from the ruins of the past a country whose citizens
shall be united, each of them conscious in himself of the spirit and life of
the whole. But, enthusiastic as my generation may be, we realize that in
the great factory of society there must be a division of labour. I have chosen
my line of work and devote myself to science.'

'Science is not the end of man,' Simoun observed.

'It is the goal of the most cultured nations.'

'Yes, but only as a means to attain happiness.'

'Science will last longer than politics,' replied the young man in a burst of
enthusiasm, 'because it is more human, more universal. In a few centuries,
when humanity shall have been redeemed by knowledge, when racial
differences shall have disappeared, when all peoples shall be free, when there
are no longer tyrants and slaves, colonies and empires, when there is one rule

of justice, when man shall be a citizen of the world, only the pursuit of science will remain; the word patriotism will sound like mere fanaticism, and whoever shall. then take pride in patriotic virtues will surely be I locked up as a dangerous maniac, a disturber of the harmony of Society.'

Simoun smiled grimly and said, nodding his head:

'Of course, no doubt. But to reach that state it will be necessary to eliminate tyrants and slaves among the nations; it is necessary that man should learn, wherever he may go, to respect in others the rights of his own person; and for this it is necessary to shed much blood. A struggle cannot be avoided. Before the old fanaticism which oppressed consciences was vanquished many had to perish at the stake and thus horrify the conscience of society into liberating the conscience of the individual. It is just as necessary now for all to answer the question which the nation asks when it lifts up its shackled hands. Patriotism is a crime only in imperialist countries because then it is only a beautiful name for exploitation. However perfect humanity may become, patriotism will always be a virtue in oppressed peoples because it will always mean the love of justice, freedom and self-respect. Let us be done, therefore, with dreams and illusions and idylls fit for women. A man is great not because he goes ahead of his generation, which is in any case impossible, but because he guesses what it wants. The unlettered may think that geniuses are ahead of their time, but they only appear so to those who look at them from afar or who mistake the rearguard for a whole generation.'

Simoun stopped. Then, realizing that he had failed to awaken any enthusiasm in the student's frigid soul, he had resort to another argument and asked in a different tone:

'And what are you doing for your dead mother and brother? Is it enough to come here every year and weep over a grave like a girl?'

He laughed mockingly.

He had hit his mark. Basilio flushed and took a step forward.

'What do you want me to do?' he asked angrily. 'I am from the lower classes and without resources. Do you think I can bring their murderers to justice? I would be only one more victim and dash myself like a piece of glass thrown against a rock. You are wrong to remind me of them. You reopen a wound to no purpose.'

'And if I should offer to help you?'

Basilio shook his head and said thoughtfully:

'The vindication of the courts, pure revenge, all this put together would not bring back one hair on my mother's head or the smile on my brother's face. Let them sleep in peace. What would I get out of avenging them?'

'You would prevent others from suffering what you have suffered. You would save other sons from being murdered, other mothers from being driven mad. Resignation is not always a virtue; it is a crime when it encourages oppression. There are no tyrants where they are no slaves. Man is by nature so evil that he always abuses his powers when he is not resisted. I thought the way you do now, and you know what happened to me. Those who caused your misfortunes watch you night and day; they suspect you are only awaiting a favourable opportunity; they see in your thirst for knowledge, in your love of study, even in your very impertubability a burning desire for vengeance. The day they can get rid of you, they will do to you what they did to me. They will not let you attain your full growth because they fear and hate you.'

'Hate me? Hate me after all they have done to me?' asked Basilio aghast.

Simoun let out a laugh.

'It is natural for man to hate those whom he has injured, said Tacitus, confirming Seneca. When you want to measure the good or the evil that one country has done to another, you have only to see whether it loves or hates the other. That is why those who have enriched themselves here in high office slander and insult their victims once they have gone back to Spain. I repeat that it is natural for man to hate those whom he has injured.'

'But there is room for everyone! They are left free to enjoy power. I ask only to be allowed to work on, to live my own life...'

'And to raise peace-loving sons who will in their turn bow their necks to the yoke,' added Simoun in a cruel imitation of Basilio's voice. 'You are certainly preparing a beautiful future for them. They will have you to thank for a life of humiliation and suffering. Congratulations, young man! When somebody is dead it is useless to try to wake him up. Twenty years of uninterrupted slavery, of systematic humiliation, of constant prostration, can make a soul so hunch-backed that it will take more than a day to straighten it up. Children inherit from their fathers their ways of thought, good or bad. Long live then your ideas of a happy life, long live the dreams of the slave who only asks for a rag with which to wrap his chains so they won't make so much noise or bruise his skin. Your ambition is a cosy little home: a woman of your own and a handful of rice. Behold the model Filipino! Well, you will be lucky to get what you want.'

Basilio, who had grown used to obeying and enduring the caprices and bad temper of Capitán Tiago, and who was now dominated by Simoun, a terrible and sinister figure, it seemed to him, against his background of blood and tears, tried to explain himself. He did not think he was suited for politics; he had formed no definite opinions on these matters because he had never studied them; for all that, he was always ready to serve whenever he should be needed; but for the time being he saw only one thing needed, the education of the people—Simoun cut him short with a gesture. It was almost dawn.

'Young man, I will not suggest that you keep my secret. I know that discretion is one of your virtues. Even if you should want to betray me, the word of Simoun the jeweller, the friend of the authorities and of the religious Orders, will always carry more weight than that of Basilio, a mere student, already suspect of subversion by the very fact that, although a native, he has become so outstanding and has distinguished himself, and suspect also because in the profession he has chosen he will have influential rivals. Although you have not met my expectations, still, any time you change your mind, you can call on me at my house on the Escolta and I shall put myself sincerely at your service.'

'Can I have used the wrong approach?' muttered Simoun when he was left alone. 'Is it that he mistrusts me and plans his revenge so secretly that he will not trust himself to reveal it to the very solitude of night? Or have the years of servitude stifled all noble sentiments in his heart leaving only the animal instinct to survive and reproduce? If so, the mould is defective and it will be necessary to recast it... in a hecatomb! Let the unfit perish and the strongest survive!'

He added lugubriously as if he were addressing someone:

'Be patient, you who left me a name and a home, be patient! One after the other I have lost them: country, future, contentment, your very graves, but have patience! And you, noble spirit, great soul, generous heart, who lived for only one ideal and sacrificed your life without expecting gratitude or admiration, be patient, be patient. Perhaps the means I use are not yours but they are the swifter. The day is near, and when it dawns I shall myself give you the good tidings. Patience!'

8 • *Happy Christmas!*

WHEN Julí opened her tear-swollen eyes she saw that the house was still in darkness. Cocks were crowing, but the first thing that came to her mind was that the Virgin had made her miracle, after all, and that the sun would not rise at the summons of the cocks.

She rose, crossed herself, and said her morning prayers with great fervour. Then, trying to make as little noise as possible, she went out to the kitchen porch.

There would be no miracle; the sun was about to rise and it promised to be a magnificent morning; there was a delightfully chilly breeze, the stars were pale in the East, and the cocks were crowing louder and more often. It had been too much to ask; the Virgin would find it easier just to send her the two hundred and fifty pesos! Surely that was not too much trouble for the Mother of God! But under the Virgin's image all she found was her father's letter asking five hundred pesos for his ransom. She had to go. Seeing her grandfather motionless, she believed him still asleep and made him native tea for his breakfast. How odd! She found herself calm, she even wanted to giggle. What had she been so upset about the night before? She was not going so far away; she could come home for a visit every two days; her grandfather could go and see her; and as far as Basilio was concerned he had known for some time that her father's affairs were in a bad way, for he had often told her: 'When I get to be a physician, and we are married, your father will not need his fields.'

'How silly I was to cry so much,' she told herself as she packed her things.

She came across the reliquary and raised it to her lips, kissing it, then wiped her mouth hurriedly, afraid of catching the disease of the leper who had given Basilio this jewel of diamonds and emeralds. If she caught leprosy that would really be the end of any hopes of marriage!

It was beginning to be light. She saw her grandfather in his corner following all her movements with his eyes and, taking up her case, she went up to him with a smile to kiss his hand. The old man blessed her silently and she tried to cheer him up with a joke.

'When father comes back tell him that I have gone to school at last. My mistress speaks Spanish. You could not find a cheaper school.'

The old man's eyes filled with tears and she quickly put her case on her head and hurried down the stairs, her slippers gaily slapping the wooden steps.

But when she looked back to see her house, the house where the last dreams of her childhood had vanished and the first illusions of her youth had taken shape, when she saw it forlorn, solitary, abandoned, with half-open windows empty and dark like a dead man's eyes, when she heard the bamboo clumps wave and whisper in the morning breeze as if to bid her farewell, her vivacious spirits fell, she stopped, the tears welled up in her eyes, and, sitting on a fallen tree-trunk by the wayside, she wept disconsolately.

Julí had been gone for hours and the sun was high in the heavens when Old Selo sat by the window watching the people who, in their best clothes, were going to town for High Mass. Almost all of them were leading by the hand or carrying in arms a boy or a girl dressed up for a holiday.

Christmas in the Philippines is, according to the grown-ups, a holiday for children; the children do not perhaps share this opinion and the thought can even be hazarded that they have an instinctive fear of Christmas. Indeed it is a day when they are woken up early, washed, and loaded with new, expensive and showy clothes, silken booties, huge hats, woollen, silk or satin suits, without forgetting four or five little scapulars bearing the gospel of St John, and thus encumbered taken to High Mass for almost an hour, compelled to suffer the heat and the smells of the tightly packed and sweaty congregation, and, if not forced to recite the Rosary, to be quiet and be bored or go to sleep, punished and scolded for every movement or any prank that might soil their new clothes. So it is that they neither laugh nor are merry at all, and in their round eyes can be seen a nostalgia for their old every-day clothes and a protest against so much embroidery. Afterwards they are taken from house to house to visit relatives and greet them, as is the custom, by kissing hands; there they have to dance, sing, and put on exhibition any graces they may have, whether or not they feel like it, and whether or not they are at ease in all their finery, with the usual scoldings and snappings whenever they try to have their own way. The relatives give them coins but these are taken over by their parents and that is the last they hear of these presents. The only thing clear they get from the holiday are the scoldings and the discomforts, and more often than not a stomach-ache from a surfeit of sweets and biscuits in the house of the more generous relatives. But that is the way of the country, and the Filipino children make their entrance into the great world by means of these trials which, after all, turn out to be the least sorrowful, and the least arduous, in their lives.

The grown-ups who live by themselves have a share of their own in the holiday. They visit their parents and their uncles and aunts, bend a knee, and wish them a Happy Christmas; their presents are a sweet, a fruit, a glass of water or some trinket.

Old Selo watched his friends go by and thought ruefully that this year he had no presents for anyone and that his own granddaughter had gone off without giving him one or even wishing him a Happy Christmas. Had Julí been tactful or merely forgetful?

When Old Selo tried to greet the relatives who came to see him with their children he found to his great surprise that he could not say a word. He tried in vain, he could not utter a sound. He rubbed his throat, shook his head: all useless. He tried to laugh and his mouth worked convulsively but all he could produce was a dull sound like the puffing of a bellows. The women looked at one another in dismay.

'He has been struck dumb, struck dumb!' they screamed distraughtly. It made a great sensation.

9 • *Pilates*

NEWS of this misfortune soon spread in the town. Some were sorry; others shrugged their shoulders. Nobody was to blame for it, nobody had it on his conscience.

The garrison commander was completely unmoved. After all he had been given orders to seize all arms and he had only done his duty. He went after the outlaws on every possible occasion and, when Cabesang Tales had been kidnapped, he had organized a pursuit at once and had brought back to town five or six suspicious peasants, tied up elbow to elbow. If Cabesang Tales did not turn up it was because he was not to be found in their pockets or under their skin for they had certainly been searched and shaken thoroughly.

The friar-administrator shrugged his shoulders. It was nothing to do with him: a matter of outlaws! He only did his duty. Of course, if he had not filed a complaint, perhaps the arms would not have been seized and the poor headman would not have been kidnapped; but he, Father Clemente, had to look to his own security and that Tales had a way of looking at one as if he were fixing a target on one's body. It was only natural to defend oneself If there were outlaws that was not his fault, nor was it his duty to go after them; that was the work of the Constabulary. If Cabesang Tales, instead of roaming about his fields, had only stayed home he would not have been kidnapped. In brief it was a judgment sent from Heaven upon those who resisted the demands of his Order.

Sister Penchang, the devout old woman in whose service Julí had entered, let loose two or three pious ejaculations when she heard about it, crossed herself, and added:

'God often sends us these trials because we are sinners or because we have sinful relatives whom we should have reformed and have not.'

She meant Julí who, in her eyes, was a great sinner.

Fancy, a marriageable young lady who still doesn't know how to pray! Lord, what a scandal! The wench says the Hail Mary without pausing after 'the Lord is with thee', as all good God-fearing Christians should, and the Holy Mary without pausing after 'pray for us sinners'! Jesus, Mary, Joseph! She does not know the most common prayers and pronounces Latin with a Tagalog accent!'

She crossed herself in very outrage and gave thanks to God for allowing Cabesang Tales to be kidnapped so that his daughter might be redeemed from sin and taught the virtues which, according to the priests, should be the adornments of every Christian woman. To this end she kept Julí in the house and would not allow her to return and look after her grandfather. Julí had to learn how to pray properly, read the booklets distributed by the friars, and work off the two hundred and fifty pesos.

When she learned that Basilio had gone to Manila for his savings in order to redeem Julí from servitude, the good woman thought that Julí was as good as damned and that the Devil would present himself to her in the student's guise. Boring as it was, that booklet the parish priest had given her was so right! The young who went to Manila to study lost their souls and led others to perdition; and, believing that it was the way to save Julí, she made the young girl read and re-read the booklet by *Tough Old Basio,* a popular religious work of the time, urging her to see the friar in the parish house as often as possible, as did the heroine of the booklet who was so highly praised by its friar author.

In the meantime the friars had reason to celebrate their good fortune; they had definitely won the lawsuit and they took advantage of Cabesang Tales's captivity to hand over his fields to their favoured applicant without the least twinge of shame or delicacy. When the former owner returned at last and learned what had happened, when he saw in the hands of another those fields, his fields which had cost the lives of his wife and daughter and found his own father struck dumb and his remaining daughter in servitude, and what was more when he was given a court order to vacate his house in three days, Cabesang Tales said not a word but seated himself beside his father and scarcely spoke the whole day.

10 • *Wealth and Want*

THE following day, to the great surprise of the neighbourhood, Simoun the jeweller sought lodging in the house of Cabesang Tales. He was accompanied by two servants who carried canvas-covered chests. Even in the depths of his misfortune Tales could not forget the native customs and was embarrassed because he had nothing to offer his foreign guest. But Simoun brought his own food and servants with him, he only required lodging for the day and night, apparently because the house of Tales was the most comfortable in the locality, midway between the towns of San Diego and Tiani whence many of his customers were expected.

Simoun inquired about the state of the roads and asked Cabesang Tales if the revolver he carried with him would be enough to defend him against any outlaws.

'They have long-range guns,' commented Tales absently.

'This revolver does not have a shorter range,' answered Simoun, firing at a *bonga* palm tree two hundred paces away.

Cabesang Tales saw a number of nuts fall but said nothing and remained sunk in thought.

One after the other various families arrived, attracted by the famous jeweller's wares. They wished one another a Happy Christmas and chattered away about Masses, saints and the bad harvest. For all that, they were ready to spend their savings on gems and trifles from Europe. The jeweller was known to be a friend of the Governor-General and there was nothing to lose in being on good terms with him just in case...

Capitán Basilio had come with his wife his daughter Sinang and his son-in-law, ready to spend at least three thousand pesos.

Sister Penchang was there to buy a diamond ring which she had promised the Virgin of Antipolo; she had left Julí behind to learn by heart a booklet which the parish priest had sold her for two centavos; the Archbishop had granted forty days' indulgence to all who read it or heard it read to them.

'Lord,' said the good woman to Capitana Tiká, 'that poor girl grew up here like a mushroom planted by goblins! I have made her read that booklet aloud at least fifty times but nothing stays in her head; it is like a basket, full only as long as it stays in water. Listening to her, all of us, even the dogs and the cats, must have gained at least twenty years' indulgence by now.'

Simoun arranged the two cases he had brought on a table before him; one was rather larger than the other.

'I am sure you do not want mere gold-plate or silver-plate or imitation stones. The lady,' he added, turning to Sinang, 'will want diamonds?'

'That's it, sir, diamonds, old diamonds, antique gems, do you know what I mean? Papa will pay, and he likes antiques, old gems.'

Sinang liked to joke about how much Latin her father knew as well as how little her husband did and how badly he spoke it.

'It just so happens that I have here some jewels of the greatest antiquity,' said Simoun, removing the canvas cover of the smaller case.

It was a box of polished steel with many bronze decorations and heavy complicated locks.

'I have here necklaces that once belonged to Cleopatra, legitimate and genuine, found indeed in the Pyramids, also rings that once were worn by Roman senators and knights, found in the ruins of Carthage...'

'Probably those which Hannibal sent home after the battle of Cannae,' ventured Capitán Basilio in all seriousness and shivering with excitement.

The good man, although he had read much about the ancients, had never seen anything of those times because of the lack of museums in the Philippines.

'I bring also very valuable earrings belonging to Roman ladies, found in the villa of Annius Mucius Papilinus in Pompeii...'

Capitán Basilio nodded, suggesting that he knew about these things and was in a hurry to see such precious relics. The ladies said they would also like to see things from Rome, but they were interested in rosaries blessed by the Pope, relics that secured the forgiveness of sins without Confession, and similar objects of devotion.

The jewel-box was opened and the first tray uncovered of its protective layer of cotton-wool. It displayed rings, reliquaries, lockets, crucifixes, brooches. Diamonds, set together with precious stones of different colours, sparkled amidst golden flowers of various shades striped with enamel and in fanciful designs and rare arabesques.

Simoun lifted the tray and displayed another one crammed with fantastic jewels capable of satiating the desires of seven young ladies on the eve of seven balls in their honour. Here were fantastical designs, pearls and precious stones combined to imitate insects with blue backs and transparent wings; sapphires, emeralds, rubies, turquoises, diamonds, set in the shape of dragonflies, bees, butterflies, wasps, scarabs, serpents, lizards, fish, flowers, clusters of grapes; and there were tiaras, necklaces and chokers of pearls and diamonds so beautiful that a number of young ladies could not suppress exclamations of awe and Sinang was unable to resist clucking her tongue loudly, a betrayal of emotion that her mother, Capitana Tiká, promptly punished, fearful that it would raise the prices. Capitana Tiká still disciplined her daughter by pinching her arms even though she was married now.

'There is your antique jewellery,' observed Simoun. 'This ring belonged to the Princesse de Lamballe, and these earrings to a lady-in-waiting of Marie Antoinette.'

They were lovely diamond solitaires as large as grains of maize, of a bluish tinge, and gleaming with a severe elegance as if remembering with a shudder the days of the Terror in the French Revolution.

'Those earrings!' cried Sinang, her eyes on her father but her hand instinctively protecting the arm nearest her mother.

'Something older still, the Roman ones!' demurred Capitán Basilio with a wink.

The pious Sister Penchang decided that such earrings would surely move the Virgin of Antipolo to grant her dearest wish; she had been praying so long for a sensational miracle involving herself which would immortalize her name on earth and afterwards in Heaven, like the Capitana Inés of the priests' tales. She asked the price. Simoun wanted three thousand pesos. The good woman crossed herself. Good Lord!

Simoun uncovered the third tray.

This was full of watches, wallets, match-holders, and reliquaries garnished with diamonds and the most exquisite enamelled miniatures.

The fourth tray contained loose stones and when they were exposed a murmur of admiration swept the room; Sinang's tongue went clucking again and her mother again pinched her arm but not without herself yielding to an awestruck 'Jesus Mary!'

Nobody had ever seen such wealth before. In the compartments of that tray, lined with dark blue velvet, the dreams of the *One Thousand and One Nights,* the most Oriental fantasies, became realities: diamonds as large as chickpeas glittering with fascinating sparks that raced through all the colours of the spectrum, emeralds from Peru of every shape and cut, Indian rubies like drops of blood, blue and white sapphires from Ceylon, Persian turquoises, Oriental pearls, some rosy, others grey or black—all giving the effect of a giant rocket exploding against a dark blue sky and scattering thousands of sparks more brilliant than the stars.

Simoun, as if to egg on the admiration of those present, stirred the precious stones with his long brown fingers, taking pleasure in their crystalline tinkle and their slippery brilliance, like so many drops of water coloured by the rainbow. So many flashing facets, and the thought of their cost, fascinated all eyes. Cabesang Tales, who had pressed close out of curiosity, shut his eyes and moved away quickly as if to flee from temptation. So much wealth was an insult to his misfortune; this man had come to make a show of his immense riches on the very eve of the day when he, Tales, for lack of a few pesos, for lack of influential protectors, would have to leave the house he had built with his own hands.

'Here we have two black diamonds, among the biggest there are,' observed the jeweller. 'They are very difficult to cut because they are extremely hard. This pinkish stone is also a diamond, like this green one which many take for an emerald. Quiroga the Chinaman has offered me six thousand pesos for it to give as a present to a most powerful lady. Nor are the green ones the most expensive, but these I bluish ones.'

He put aside three stones, not very large, but heavy and beautifully cut, with a slight bluish tinge.

'They are smaller than the green ones but they cost much more. For instance, this one, the smallest of the three, which does not weigh more than two carats, cost me twenty thousand pesos and I would not part with it for less than thirty. I had to make a special trip to acquire it. This other one was found in the Golconda mines, weighs three and a half carats, and is worth more than seventy thousand. The Viceroy of India, in a letter I received day before yesterday, offers me for it no less than twelve thousand pounds sterling.'

Faced with such a treasure gathered in the hands of one man who spoke so nonchalantly, everyone was overcome with mingled respect and fear. Sinang clucked her tongue again repeatedly and her mother did not bother to pinch her, perhaps because she was too absorbed in her own meditations or because she thought that a jeweller like Simoun would not raise his prices five pesos or so merely because of a more or less indiscreet exclamation. All stared at the precious stones but no one showed the least desire to touch them; they seemed terrified to do so. Curiosity was stupefied by awe. Cabesang Tales was looking out to his fields: with only one of those diamonds, perhaps the smallest one, he could redeem his daughter, save his house, and perhaps clear another farm. God, that one such stone should be worth more than a man's home, a young girl's security, and the peace of an old man's last days!

As if he had read his thoughts Simoun remarked to the families round him:

'And look here, with one of these little blue stones, which seem so innocent and harmless, as pure as stardust, with one of these, given as a present to the right people at the right time, a man has been able to secure the exile of his enemy, the father of a family, as a disturber of the public peace... and with another little stone like this one, red as heart's blood and the thirst for revenge, as bright as orphans' tears, freedom was recovered, the man was returned to his home, the father to his children, the husband to the wife, and a whole family saved from a miserable future.'

He tapped the coffer and added loudly in bad Tagalog:

'Here, as in the chests of physicians, I have life and death, poison and antidote; with a handful I can plunge all the people of the Philippines into tragedy.'

All stared at him in fear for they knew that he was right. There was a strange timbre in Simoun's voice and a sinister gleam behind his dark glasses.

As if to break the spell which the precious stones had cast on such simple people Simoun once again raised the tray and revealed the bottom of the casket where he kept his choicest wares. Cases of Russian leather, separated by cotton-wool, filled the bottom which was lined with grey velvet. All expected new marvels. Sinang's husband was sure he would see carbuncles flashing fire and shining in the darkness. Capitán Basilio fancied himself on the threshold of eternity; he was going to see something positive, something real, the very shape of what he had so often dreamed.

'This is the necklace of Cleopatra,' announced Simoun, displaying with great care a plain box shaped like a half-moon. 'It is a jewel whose value cannot be assessed; it is a museum piece, only rich governments can afford it.'

The necklace was composed of an interlaced series of little golden idols, green and blue scarabs, joined in the centre by a vulture's head with two wings outstretched carved from rare jasper, the symbol and ornament of the Egyptian queens.

Sinang wrinkled her nose when she saw it and pouted childishly and Capitán Basilio himself, for all his love of antiquities, could not repress an exclamation of disillusionment.

'A magnificent jewel, very well preserved. It is almost two thousand years old.'

Sinang made her scorn audible to keep her father from falling into temptation.

'Idiot!' cried her father, who had overcome his first feeling of disappointment. 'For all you know, this necklace is responsible for the present state of the whole world! With it Cleopatra may have captivated Caesar, Mark Antony; it may have heard the love-making of the two greatest warriors of their time, and in the purest and most elegant Latin at that. You would be lucky enough to have had it on!'

'Me? I wouldn't give three pesos for it.'

'Silly!' put in Capitana Tiká with a knowing air. 'You could give twenty. The gold is good and it could be melted down to make other pieces.'

'This is a ring that may have belonged to Sulla,' continued Simoun imperturbably.

It was a broad ring of heavy gold with a seal.

'With it he probably decreed the proscriptions during his dictatorship,' breathed Capitán Basilio, pale with emotion.

He examined the seal and tried to decipher it but, knowing nothing of palaeology, he could make nothing out, turn it round and round as he would.

'What a finger this Sulla had,' he remarked at last. 'Two of mine can fit into this ring. Ah, well, as I have always said, we are on the decline.'

'I have many other jewels...'

'If they are all that kind, no, thank you,' protested Sinang. 'I prefer more modern pieces.'

They made their choices: a stone, a ring, a watch, a locket. Capitana Tiká bought a reliquary containing a chip of the rock on which Our Lord rested after His third fall on the Way of the Cross; Sinang, a pair of earrings; Capitán Basilio, the watch-chain for the lieutenant, the lady's earrings for the parish priest, and other presents. The families from Tiani, to keep up with those from San Diego, also emptied their pockets.

Simoun was also buying old jewellery and was ready to barter, so the frugal housewives had taken with them those pieces they no longer fancied.

'And you, sir, have you nothing to sell?' Simoun asked Cabesang Tales, seeing the latter watch all these sales and barters with covetous eyes.

Cabesang Tales replied that his daughter's jewels had all been sold and there was nothing worthwhile left.

'What about María Clara's reliquary?' asked Sinang.

'That's right!' Tales exclaimed and his eyes flashed.

'The reliquary has diamonds and emeralds,' Sinang informed the jeweller. 'My friend used to wear it before she went into the nunnery.'

Simoun did not answer. He was watching Cabesang Tales anxiously.

After rummaging through a number of drawers Tales found the jewel. Simoun studied it, opening and closing it a number of times. It was the same reliquary that María Clara had worn during the town fiesta of San Diego and that she had given to a leper on a generous impulse.

'I like the design,' said Simoun. 'How much do you want for it?'

Cabesang Tales scratched his head, then his ear, in perplexity and cast a look at the women.

'It has caught my fancy,' continued Simoun. 'Would you sell it for a hundred—five hundred pesos? Do you want to trade it for another jewel? Take your pick.'

Cabesang Tales remained wordless, staring stupidly at Simoun as if he doubted what he heard.

'Five hundred pesos?' he muttered.

'Five hundred,' the jeweller replied in a strange voice.

Cabesang Tales took the reliquary and turned it over and over. His temples were pulsing violently; his hands were trembling. Suppose he asked for more? That reliquary could rescue them all; it was a wonderful chance which would never come again.

All the women signalled him with winks to sell, except for the woman to whom Julí had mortgaged her services and who, fearing that the girl would thus be ransomed, observed piously:

'I would keep it for a relic. Those who have seen María Clara in the convent found her so thin, so wasted away that they said she could scarcely say a word; they believe she will die a saint. Father Salví speaks very highly of her, and he is her confessor, you know. Perhaps that is why Julí did not want to lose the reliquary and rather went into service than do it.'

Her comment was effective.

The memory of his daughter gave Cabesang Tales pause. 'If you will allow me,' he said, 'I'll go to town and ask my daughter what she thinks. I'll be back before nightfall.'

They agreed on that and Cabesang Tales left immediately.

But when he had left the barrio behind he caught a glimpse along a trail which led to the woods, of the friar-administrator and the man whom he recognized as the one who had taken over his lands. A husband surprising his wife in a secret rendezvous with another man could not have felt more anger and jealousy than Cabesang Tales did when he saw those two on the way to his fields, the fields he had worked with his own hands and which he had hoped to hand down to his sons. He imagined them laughing at him, mocking his impotence; and he remembered that he had sworn that he would never yield his lands except to one who had watered them with his own blood and buried in them his wife and daughter.

He stopped, drew his hand across his brow, and shut his eyes. When he opened them again he saw the new tenant doubled up with laughter; the friar-administrator had his hands on his belly as if to keep it from bursting with merriment; both gestured towards his house and broke out again into laughter.

His ears hummed; he felt a whiplash on the temple; again he saw red, and through the red cloud the corpses of his wife and daughter, and beside them the friar and the new tenant holding their sides with laughter.

He forgot everything, turned round, and followed the trail on which he had seen the pair—it was the trail to his lands.

Simoun waited in vain for Cabesang Tales that night.

The next day when he awoke he saw that the leather holster of his revolver was empty. He opened it and found inside a sheet of paper wrapped round the golden reliquary with its emeralds and diamonds. On it were written a few lines in Tagalog.

Sir,

Forgive me; I have taken what is yours although you are my guest. But I had to do it, and in exchange for your revolver I have left you the reliquary you wanted so much. I need weapons. I leave to join the outlaws. I advise you not to go on; if you fall into our hands you will no longer be my guest and we shall demand a heavy ransom.

Telesforo Juan de Dios

'At last I have my man,' sighed Simoun. 'Rather scrupulous perhaps, but so much the better. He will keep his word.'

He ordered his servant to go on with the larger chest to Los Baños by way of the lake and await him there; he himself would go overland with the case containing his famous jewellery.

The arrival of four Constabulary soldiers definitely put him in the best of tempers. They had come to arrest Cabesang Tales; not finding him, they took away Old Selo, his father.

Three murders had been committed the night before. The friar administrator and the new tenant had been found dead on the boundaries of the lands of Cabesang Tales; both of their heads had been bashed in, and their mouths filled with earth. The wife of the new tenant had also been found dead at dawn, her mouth likewise stuffed with earth and her throat cut.

Beside her was a sheet of paper on which a finger had written with blood the name Tales.

Do not be alarmed, peaceful citizens of Kalamba! None of you is called Tales, none of you committed the crime! You are called Luis Habaña, Matias Belarmino, Nicasio Eigasani, Cayetano de Jesús, Matéo Elejorde, Leandro López, Antonino López, Silvestre

Ubaldo, Manuel Hidalgo, Paciano Mercado — you are the whole town of Kalamba!
You cleared your fields, you spent on them the labours of a lifetime, savings, sleepless
nights, privations, and you have been stripped of all, driven out of your homes, deprived
by order even of the hospitality of others. They were not content with doing violence to
justice; they broke the most sacred traditions of our country. You served Spain and the
King, and when you asked for justice m their names you were exiled without trial and
torn from the arms of your wives and the kisses of your children. Any one of you has
suffered more than Cabesang Tales, and yet none of you, not one, has taken the law in
his own hands. There was neither pity nor human feeling for you, and like Mariano
Herbosa you have been persecuted even beyond the grave. Weep or laugh in the solitary
islands where you wander, idle and uncertain of the future. Spain, generous Spain,
watches over you, and sooner or later you shall have justice!

11 • Los Baños

HIS EXCELLENCY the Commander-in-Chief and Governor-General of
the Philippine Islands had gone shooting in Bosoboso. But since such an
exalted personage could not be less than the wooden images carried in
processions and must therefore be escorted by a brass band, and since an
appreciation of the divine art of St Caecilia had not yet become widespread
among the deer and wild boar of Bosoboso, His Excellency, with his brass
band and his cortege of friars, officers and bureaucrats had, alas, shot not a
single mouse, not one sparrow.

The provincial authorities foresaw dismissals and transfers; the poor mayors
and local headmen were so worried they could not sleep, fearful that it might
occur to the godlike hunter to make them take the place of the recalcitrant
denizens of the forest, just as some years before a provincial governor had
gone travelling on the shoulders of some road-workers just because no horses
could be found quiet enough to be trusted with his person. Nor was there
lacking a malicious rumour that His Excellency was set on taking drastic
measures because he saw in the situation the first symptoms of rebellion
which it was needful to suppress at birth—a hunt that bagged nothing injured
the prestige of the Spanish name! The authorities were looking speculatively
at one unfortunate and thinking of disguising him as a stag when His
Excellency, in an act of clemency that Ben Zayb could find no phrases to
praise, dispelled all anxieties saying that he found it disagreeable to sacrifice
the beasts of the forest to his pleasure.

The truth was that His Excellency was inwardly pleased and happy: what would have happened if he had missed, say, one of those stags that had no idea of political expediencies? Where would the prestige of sovereignty have fallen then? What, a veritable Commander-in-Chief of the Philippines missing his target like some novice? What might not have been said among the natives, among whom there were excellent shots? Then indeed the integrity of the nation would have been in dire peril!

So it was that His Excellency, with a high-pitched giggle and the air of a disappointed sportsman, ordered an immediate return to Los Baños, although not without descanting during the ride on his hunting feats in this or that forest of the Peninsula and suggesting, somewhat deprecatingly, and rather conveniently, that he did not much care for hunting in the Philippines, pshaw! The baths at Dampalit, the sun-bathing on the shores of the lake, a game of ombre in the summer-house, with little side-trips to the neighbouring falls or the crocodile lake, were more attractive and less risky for the integrity of the nation.

In the last days of December, therefore, His Excellency found himself at cards in his living room, waiting for the luncheon hour. He had come from the baths and, sipping the traditional glass of coconut water and nibbling the tender coconut meat that floated in it, was in the best of tempers to grant favours and privileges. His good humour increased apace with his winnings, for Father Irene and Father Sibyla, who were gaming with him, were each using all their wits to lose unobtrusively to the mounting annoyance of Father Camorra, who had only arrived that morning and was not aware of what was afoot. The friar-gunner was playing in good faith and with the utmost concentration; he flushed and bit his lips every time Father Sibyla was distracted or played the wrong card but dared not say a word out of respect for the Dominican. He took it out instead on Father Irene whom he considered a low-born flatterer and whom, for all his own coarseness, he despised. Father Sibyla did not even deign to look at Father Camorra and let him snort unregarded; Father Irene, more modest, made his excuses while fondling the tip of his large nose. His Excellency was enjoying himself and took advantage of his opponents' mistakes like, the canon suggested smoothly, the excellent tactician that he was. Father Camorra was unaware that the intellectual development of the Filipinos through the teaching of Spanish was at stake on the gaming table; if he had known it, he would have joined, happily enough perhaps, in the intrigue.

A fresh invigorating breeze blew in through an open balcony which overlooked the lake, its sweetly murmuring waters lapping the foot of the house in homage. Far off to the right could be glimpsed the isle of Talim, a pure blue; in the middle of the lake, almost directly opposite, the deserted isle of Kalamba, green and shaped like a half-moon; and to the left the lovely shoreline embroidered with bamboo, a hill overhanging the lake, beyond it great cultivated fields, then red roofs glimpsed among the dark green of trees—the town of Kalamba; finally the coast lost itself in the distance, with the sky bringing down the horizon on the waters, giving the lake the appearance of a sea and justifying the name which the natives gave it: 'the sweet-water sea'.

At one end of the living room, seated at a small table with papers, was a secretary. His Excellency was very hard-working and did not want to waste time so that he attended to official business when he was dummy or when the cards were being shuffled and dealt.

In between such times the poor secretary yawned in desperation. That morning they had taken up everyday matters like transfers, suspensions, deportations, concessions, but they had not yet come round to the great issue which had aroused so much interest, the student petition for a permit to open an academy for the teaching of Spanish.

Three men—Don Custodio, a high official, and a friar called Father Fernández, whose downcast head suggested that he was either thoughtful or depressed—walked up and down the room. From an adjoining chamber came the sound of ivory balls in collision, laughter, guffaws, and the dry cutting voice of Simoun: the jeweller was playing billiards with Ben Zayb.

Suddenly Father Camorra sprang to his feet and flung the two cards in his hand at Father Irene's head.

'By golly, Jesus Christ Himself wouldn't take my place! By golly, I had that trick won, if not the game, and I am robbed! By golly, Jesus Christ Himself couldn't stand it!'

He was in a perfect rage and called on everyone in the room, particularly the three bystanders, to sit in judgment: the General had been leading against him, Father Irene had the trick under control, for his part he had played a spade, and by golly, that nincompoop Father Irene had trumped him! Jesus Christ! This mother's son had not come to break his head against a stone wall and throw away his money!

'The dear old boy,' he added, red with fury, 'seems to think I pick my money from the trees! And to think that my natives are even beginning to jew me down!'

Father Irene tried to explain himself, rubbing his nose to conceal a subtle smile, but Father Camorra stamped off grumbling to the billiard-room.

'Would you like to join us, Father Fernández?' asked Father Sibyla.

'I am a very bad player,' replied his fellow Dominican, making a face.

'Then we must have Simoun,' said the General. 'Hello, there, Simoun, hey mister! Do you want to have a hand?'

'What is the decision on small firearms?' asked the secretary taking advantage of the lull.

Simoun peered out of the billiard-room.

'Do you want to take Father Camorra's place, Mr Sinbad the Sailor?' asked Father Irene. 'You can use your diamonds for chips.'

'No objection,' replied Simoun approaching the table and blowing the chalk-dust from his fingertips. 'And what will you bet?'

'What will we use for chips?' echoed Father Sibyla. 'Well, the General can do what he likes, but we religious, we priests...'

'Bah,' Simoun interrupted sardonically, 'you and Father Irene can pay with acts of charity, prayers, virtues, is that it?'

'You should know,' countered Father Sibyla gravely, 'that any virtues one may possess are not like diamonds that can be passed from hand to hand, or sold and re-sold. They reside in the person himself, properties inherent in the subject..'

'Then I shall be satisfied with mere words,' Simoun replied cheerfully. 'You, Father Sibyla, instead of giving me five chips, will say, for example, "I renounce poverty, humility and obedience for five days", and you, Father Irene, "I renounce chastity, generosity, etc." You see, it's very little, and I stake my diamonds.'

'What a singular character this Simoun is, really,' laughed Father Irene. 'What wit!'

'And this one,' Simoun continued, giving His Excellency an intimate tap on the shoulder, 'he is going to pay me for five chips, a blank order of detention for five days in gaol; fifty chips, five months; two hundred chips, a deportation order in blank; and five hundred chips, well, say, a summary execution by the Constabulary while my man is being taken from one town to the next.'

The challenge was unique. The three bystanders came closer.

'But, Mr Simoun,' objected the high official, 'what do you gain from promises of virtue, prison sentences, deportations and summary executions?'

'Why, quite a lot! I am tired of hearing about virtues and I should like to have them all, all there are in the world, to put them in a sack and throw them into the sea, even if I have to use all my diamonds for ballast.'

'What a whim,' chuckled Father Irene. 'And the deportations and summary executions?'

'Why, to clean up the country and destroy all the seeds of evil.'

'Come now, you are still furious at the outlaws and, look here, they might well have demanded a bigger ransom or kept all your jewels. Don't be ungrateful, man!'

Simoun had told them that he had been held up by a band of outlaws who, after entertaining him for a day, had let him go on his way, asking no more ransom than his two magnificent Smith revolvers and two boxes of cartridges which he had with him. He had added that the outlaws had sent their best regards to His Excellency the Commander-in-Chief.

In view of this incident, and because Simoun had said that the outlaws were very well equipped with shotguns, rifles and revolvers and that against such people one man alone, no matter how well armed, could not possibly defend himself, His Excellency was about to issue a new decree regarding sidearms to prevent the outlaws from acquiring any more weapons in the future.

'On the contrary,' Simoun protested. 'Why, in my view the outlaws are the most honest men in the whole country! They are the only ones who really earn their daily rice. Do you think that if I had fallen into the hands of, well, for example, you, Father Irene, you would have let me go without taking at least half of my jewels?'

Don Custodio was on the point of raising a scandalized outcry: this Simoun was undoubtedly a coarse American mulatto who was abusing his friendship with the Governor-General to insult Father Irene (although it was also true that Father Irene would really not have let Simoun go for so little).

'The trouble is not that there are bandits in the mountains and in uninhabited places,' Simoun continued. 'The trouble lies with the bandits in the towns and cities...'

'Like you,' the canon suggested with a laugh.

'Yes, like me, like us; let us be frank,' the jeweller went on, 'there is no native around to overhear us. The trouble is that we are not openly professed bandits; when we become that and go to live in the forests, that day the country will have been saved, that very day a new society will have been born capable of running its own affairs, and Your Excellency will then be able to play cards at your ease without being bothered by your secretary.'

At that point the secretary was in full yawn, raising his arms above his head and stretching his crossed legs as far as possible under the table.

They all burst into laughter when they caught sight of him. His Excellency did not like the turn the conversation had taken and, dropping the cards which he had been shuffling, said half serious and half jolly:

'Come, come, enough of jokes and games. To work, let's get down to some serious work, there is still half an hour before luncheon. Is there a lot of business?'

All became attentive. That day battle would be joined on the issue of the teaching of Spanish, and to debate it Father Sibyla and Father Irene had been waiting there for days. It was known that the first, as Vice-Rector of the University, was opposed to the project, and that the second, with the support of the Countess, the General's wife, was in favour.

'What is there to decide?' asked His Excellency impatiently.

'The matter of small-calibre firearms,' said the secretary between yawns.

'Let them be forbidden.'

'I beg your pardon, General,' said the high official earnestly. 'Your Excellency will permit me to observe that the possession of sidearms is allowed in every country in the world.'

The General gave a shrug.

'We do not imitate any country in the world,' he said drily.

His Excellency and the high official were in perpetual disagreement, and it was enough for the latter to make the least comment for the former to remain obdurate.

The high official felt his way along another approach.

'These small-calibre firearms can only harm rats and chickens,' he began. 'It might be said...'

'That we are chicken-hearted?' the General asked with another shrug. 'What do I care? I have proved that I am not.'

'But there is another point,' put in the secretary. 'Four months ago. when the possession of firearms was prohibited, the foreign importers were given the assurance that sidearms would be allowed.'

His Excellency frowned.

'There is a way out,' said Simoun.

'What?'

'Very simple. Almost all sidearms have a calibre of six millimetres, at least those now in the market. Let the sale be authorized only for those firearms that are not of six-millimetre calibre.'

Simoun's sally was well received by all except the high official who told

Father Fernández in a whisper that this way of doing things was not serious, it could not be called governing.

'The schoolmaster of Tiani,' continued the secretary, leafing through his papers, 'requests that better quarters be provided for his school.'

'Better quarters!' interrupted Father Camorra who had joined the group, forgetting his grievances. 'But he has a barn all to himself!'

'He says it has lost its roof,' observed the secretary, 'and that having bought maps and pictures out of his own pocket he cannot leave them exposed to the weather.'

'But I have nothing to do with that,' muttered His Excellency. 'He should address himself to the Administrative Director, the Provincial Governor, the Nuncio...'

'What I want to tell you is,' Father Camorra blurted out, 'that this so-called schoolmaster is a discontented small-time agitator. Fancy, this heretic is spreading the word around that dead men who are buried with solemn rites rot just as quickly as those who are not! Some day I am going to smash his face in!'

And Father Camorra clenched his fists.

'To tell the truth,' Father Sibyla remarked, addressing Father Irene, 'who really wishes to teach, teaches everywhere, in the open air: Socrates in the public squares, Plato in the groves of Academe, Christ in the mountains and lakes.'

'I have received several complaints against that schoolmaster,' said His Excellency, exchanging glances with Simoun. 'I think it would be best to suspend him.'

'Suspended,' repeated the secretary.

The high official felt a pang at the fate of this poor man who had asked for help and had lost his job instead, and wished to do something for him.

'There can be no doubt,' he suggested with a certain hesitation, 'that proper attention has not been given to educational facilities.'

'I have already released great sums for the purchase of school materials,' said His Excellency haughtily, as if to say that he had already done more than enough.

'But suitable quarters are lacking, and any materials that may be bought will be spoiled.'

'We cannot do everything at once,' His Excellency curtly interrupted, 'the local schoolmasters do wrong in asking for schoolhouses when their colleagues in the Peninsula do not even have enough to eat. It is a bit much to want to be in a better position than in the Mother Country itself'

'Subversion...'

'The Motherland above all, above all we are Spaniards,' added Ben Zayb, his eyes gleaming with patriotism, but he blushed when he found himself unsupported.

'From now on,' the General said, putting an end to the argument, 'anyone who complains shall be suspended.'

'If my project were approved...' Don Custodio ventured to murmur, as if talking to himself.

'Regarding schoolhouses?'

'It is simple, practical and economical like all my projects, the fruit of long experience and knowledge of the country. The towns would then have schoolhouses without the government spending a centavo.'

'Meaning,' said the secretary sardonically, 'that the towns would be obliged to construct schoolhouses at their own expense.'

There was general laughter.

'No, sir,' cried Don Custodio flushing with annoyance, 'the buildings I refer to are already built and ready for use. They are hygienic, spacious, with every advantage...'

The friars looked at one another uneasily. Was Don Custodio proposing to turn the churches and the parish houses into schools?

'Explain yourself,' said the General with a frown.

'Well, General, it is very simple,' replied Don Custodio, drawing himself up and using a grave official tone of voice. 'Schools are only open on workdays, and cockpits on holidays. Well, then, let the cockpits be used as schoolhouses, at least on weekdays.'

'Good heavens, man!'

'Here we go again!'

'But, Don Custodio, where do you get these ideas!'

'Never heard a funnier proposition!'

'This beats them all!'

'But, gentlemen,' argued Don Custodio almost in a scream, hearing so many objections, 'let us be practical. What buildings are more suitable than the cockpits? They are large, they are well built, and they are utterly useless on weekdays. Even from a moral point of view my project is most commendable: it would serve as some sort of expiation, a week-long purification, so to speak, of a temple of vice.'

'But the point is that sometimes there are cockfights on weekdays,' remarked Father Camorra, 'and it is not fair that the cockpit contractors, having paid their fees to the government...'

'Well, then, close the schools on those days.'

'Good heavens, man,' exclaimed the scandalized Commander-in-Chief, 'such a shocking thing will never happen while I am Governor-General! To close the schools for cockfights! Good Lord, man, I would resign first!'

His Excellency was truly distressed.

'But, General, it is preferable that they should be closed for a few days than for months on end.'

'It would be immoral,' cried Father Irene who was even more indignant than His Excellency.

'It is even more immoral that the vices should be well housed, and the letters not at all. Let us be practical, gentlemen, and let us not be carried away by sentimentalism. To take one other example: out of deference to public opinion we do not allow the cultivation of the poppy in our colonies yet we tolerate the smoking of opium, with the result that, while we do not combat the vice, we at the same time impoverish ourselves.'

'You forget, however, that opium smoking gives the government, without any work at all, a yearly revenue of more than four hundred and fifty thousand pesos,' argued Father Irene, who was turning more and more pro-administration.

'Enough, gentlemen, enough,' His Excellency cut the debate short. 'I have my plans on this matter, and I am giving special attention to public instruction. Anything else?'

The secretary looked at Father Sibyla and Father Irene with some anxiety. The big issue was coming up. Both braced themselves.

'The application of the students for a permit to open a Spanish academy,' said the secretary.

There was a general stir in the chamber, and after exchanging glances all eyes were fixed on the General to guess what he would decide. The application had been pending decision for six months and had become a kind of *casus belli* in certain spheres. His Excellency kept his eyes lowered as if to prevent his thoughts from being read.

Presently the General felt that the silence was turning awkward and asked the high official:

'What is your opinion?'

'What else should I think, General!' he answered with a shrug and a bitter smile. 'What else than that the petition is well founded, very well founded indeed, and that it seems to me strange that six months should have been spent in considering it.'

'Still, there are certain considerations involved,' interjected Father Sibyla coldly, closing his eyes.

The high official gave another shrug as if he did not understand what such considerations could be.

'The petition is not only untimely,' the Dominican continued, 'it not only implies a certain conflict with our prerogatives...'

Father Sibyla did not dare proceed and looked to Simoun.

'The application appears to be rather suspicious,' the latter concluded, exchanging looks with the Dominican.

The latter blinked twice. Father Irene, who saw them, realized that his cause was almost lost; Simoun was against it.

'It is a peaceful rebellion,' added Father Sibyla, 'a revolution under official auspices.'

'Revolution, rebellion?' asked the high official, looking at one and the other as if he did not understand.

'The movement is led by certain young men who are suspected of seeking excessive reforms, of being far too progressive, to say nothing more,' supplied the secretary, his eyes on the Dominican. 'There is among them a certain Isagani, a hothead, the nephew of a secular priest...'

'He is a student of mine,' remarked Father Fernández, 'and I am very well satisfied with him.'

'By golly, you are easily satisfied,' exclaimed Father Camorra. 'We almost came to blows aboard ship; he thinks a lot of himself; I gave him a push and he pushed me back!'

'Then there is a certain Macaragui or Macarai...'

'Macarai,' interrupted Father Irene in turn, 'a very pleasant and likeable chap.'

And he whispered in the General's ear:

'He is the one I was telling you about. He is very wealthy. Milady the Countess has recommended him in the highest terms.'

'Ah?'

'A medical student, a certain Basilio...'

'I have nothing to say about this Basilio,' said Father Irene, raising his hands palms outward as if to call upon them the peace of the Lord. 'Still waters there. I have never been able to tell what he wants or what he is thinking about. What a pity Father Salví is not with us to give us some idea

of his background. I think I have heard it said that when he was a boy he was
involved in some incident with the Constabulary; his father, at any rate, was
killed in some riot I do not recall.'

Simoun smiled slowly, silently, showing his white even teeth.

'Aha, aha,' exclaimed His Excellency, nodding, 'so that's how it is, eh?
Take down that name.'

'But, General,' protested the high official, seeing that things were taking
a bad turn, 'to this moment we know nothing for sure about these young
men. Their petition is very well founded and we have no right to deny it on
the basis of mere conjectures. My opinion is that the government should
grant the petition, thus proving its confidence in the people and in the
stability of the regime, without prejudice to withdrawing the permit when
it appears that its generosity has been abused. There will always be reasons
and justifications for withdrawal; we can keep an eye on these young men;
but why disappoint them at the risk of antagonizing them when what they
ask is indeed commanded by royal decrees?'

Father Irene, Don Custodio and Father Fernández nodded in agreement.

'But the natives should not know Spanish, don't you realize that?' shouted
Father Camorra. 'They should not be allowed to know it because afterwards,
when they do, they start arguing with us, and the natives have no business
arguing, all they should do is pay and obey, they have no business interpreting
laws and books, they are such shysters, they see a double meaning everywhere.
As soon as they know Spanish they become enemies of God and Spain. If you
don't believe me, read *Tough Old Basio*—now, there's a book for you! It has
arguments like these!' And he shook his fists.

Father Sibyla drew his hand across his brow in an impatient gesture.

'One word, please,' he said, adopting in spite of his annoyance a conciliatory
tone of voice. 'What is at issue here is not only the teaching of Spanish. This
is an undeclared war between the University of Santo Tomás and its students;
if the students have their way our prestige will be destroyed, they will say
that they have beaten us and they will crow over us, and then, good-bye
moral influence and good-bye everything else! Once the first dam is broken,
what is going to hold these young people back? Our fall will only herald
yours! After us, the Government!'

'By golly, not that!' roared Father Camorra. 'Let's see who can lick whom!'

Now Father Fernández, who had been content to smile during the
discussion, intervened, drawing the general attention because they knew he
had a good head on his shoulders.

'Do not hold it against me, Father Sibyla, if I differ from your way of looking at things in this affair, but it is my peculiar misfortune to be almost always in disagreement with my brethren. I say then that we should not be such pessimists. The teaching of Spanish can be allowed without any danger at all and, so that it may not appear to be a defeat for the University, we Dominicans should make an effort and be the first to rejoice over it: that is the right policy. Why should we always be at odds with the people when, after all, we are the few and they are the many, and when we need them while they do not need us? Now wait a while, Father Camorra, wait a moment. Admitted that for the time being the people are short on knowledge and power; I agree, but they will not be the same tomorrow or the day after. Then they will be the stronger, they will know what is good for them, and we shall not be able to stop them from getting it, any more than children can be prevented, when they have reached a certain age, from knowing a number of things. I say, then, why not take this opportunity, when they are still ignorant, to change our policies completely, to place those policies on a solid and permanent foundation, say, that of justice, instead of ignorance? There is nothing like being fair; I have always told my brethren that, although they do not want to believe me. The natives, like any young people, idolize justice; they even ask to be punished when they are at fault, but by the same token they are exasperated by being punished when they do not deserve it. Is what they want reasonable and fair? Then let us give it to them; let us give them all the schools they want, they will soon tire of them, youth is lazy and only our opposition makes them active. The bonds of prestige, Father Sibyla, are very much worn out; let us make ready other bonds, say, the bonds of gratitude. Let us not be stupid; let us do what the crafty Jesuits do...'

'Oh, no, Father Fernández!'

No, Father Sibyla could endure anything except take the Jesuits for a model. Pale and shaken he broke out into bitter recriminations and exclaimed almost beside himself:

'I would be a Franciscan first, anything but a Jesuit!'

'Oh, now!'

'Oh, yes!'

A discussion flared up in which everyone, ignoring the Governor-General, intervened, speaking at the same time, shouting, contradicting without understanding one another; Ben Zayb and Father Camorra were shaking their fists at each other, one spoke of boobies and the other of hack-writers; Father Sibyla was appealing to the Chapter, Father Fernández to the *Summa* of St Thomas; until the parish priest of Los Baños appeared and announced that luncheon was served.

His Excellency rose to his feet and thus cut the debate short.

'Come, gentlemen,' he said, 'we have worked like niggers even though we are on holiday. Someone has said that serious matters should be discussed over dessert. I agree absolutely.'

'We may suffer an indigestion,' observed the secretary.

'Then we shall leave it for tomorrow.'

All rose.

'General,' said the high official, 'the daughter of Cabesang Tales has come again to ask that her ailing grandfather, who is being held in place of her father, be released.'

His Excellency gave him a look of exasperation and passed his hand over his broad brow.

'Good God, one cannot even have lunch in peace!'

'It is the third day she has come, poor girl.'

'Ah, the devil take it,' exclaimed Father Camorra, 'I knew I had something to tell the General; that is why I came, to support this girl's petition!'

The General scratched himself behind an ear.

'Oh, very well,' he told the secretary, 'send the garrison commander a memorandum to release him. They can't say we are neither merciful nor understanding!'

He looked at Ben Zayb and the newspaper man blinked.

12 • *Placido Penitente*

RELUCTANTLY and almost with tears in his eyes Plácido Penitente was going along the Escolta towards the University of Santo Tomás, which was then in the Walled City on the other side of the river.

It was scarcely a week since he had arrived from his home town but he had already written twice to his mother that he wanted to give up his studies to go home and work. His mother had replied asking him to be patient; he should at least take the degree of bachelor of arts; it would be a pity to abandon his studies after four years of expenses and of sacrifices on their part.

Why was it that Penitente had conceived such a dislike for study when he had been one of the most conscientious students in the famous college of Father Valerio in Tanawan? Penitente had been considered one of the best Latin scholars and most subtle logicians in his native province of Batangas, one who was perfectly capable of disentangling the most complex questions and of ensnarling the simplest; his townmates looked on him as the cleverest of them all; and his parish priest, under the influence of this reputation, already considered him subversive, sure proof that he was neither stupid nor irresolute. His friends were consequently at a loss to understand his desire to go home and give up his studies; he was not one who went after the girls; he was not a gambler and scarcely knew or had tried his hand at the most popular card-games of the day; he did not take the advice of the friars seriously and made fun of *Old Basio;* he had money to spare and smart clothes; and yet he went to his classes reluctantly and looked on his books with distaste.

Now, on the Bridge of Spain—a bridge that took only its name from Spain since even its smallest nail had come from foreign parts—he found himself in a long procession of young people going to their respective schools in the Walled City. Some were dressed in European clothes, walked briskly, carrying a load of books and notebooks, and seemed engrossed in thinking about their lessons and their assignments: these were the students of the Jesuits' Ateneo. Those from the Dominicans' Letran could be distinguished from the others because almost all of them were dressed in the native fashion, were more numerous, but carried fewer books. The University students were dressed more neatly and elegantly and strolled about, carrying not books but a walking-stick. Students in the Philippines of that time were not very boisterous or mischievous; they went about with a worried air and looking at them one would have thought that they saw before them no hopes of a rosy future. The procession was brightened here and there by the girl students of the Municipal School, ribbons round their shoulders, books on their arms, attended by maid-servants, but although they struck a charming and colourful note there was scarcely a laugh to be heard or a joke, not one song or witty compliment; at the most there were pranks and fist fights among the smaller fry. Their elders almost always went their ways gravely and well behaved like German students.

Plácido was going along Magallanes Drive to enter the Walled City through the breach—once a gate—of Santo Domingo when he suddenly felt himself slapped on the back. Not in the best of tempers he turned round.

'Greetings, Penitente, all hail!'

It was Juanito Peláez, a classmate, favourite buffoon of the professors, a cunning rogue like no one else, with the slyest of looks and the gayest of smiles. He was the son of a Spanish half-breed, a rich merchant in one of the suburbs who pinned all his hopes and joys on the young man's talents; indeed, his escapades gave some sort of promise. His practice of playing disagreeable jokes on everyone and then hiding behind the back of whoever was around, had given him a peculiar hunch which became more pronounced every time he got away with one of his pranks and doubled up with laughter.

'Did you have a good time, Penitente?' he asked now, slapping Plácido heavily on the back.

'So, so,' answered Plácido, rather annoyed. 'And you?'

'I had a marvellous time! Fancy, the parish priest of Tiani invited me to spend the holidays in his town, I went, and... boy! Do you know Father Camorra? Well, he is a very liberal priest, a good fellow, frank, very frank, something like Father Paco. And since there were some smashing girls around, we had a time serenading them, he with his guitar and songs, and I with my violin. I tell you, boy, we had a devil of a time, not a house but we were asked up.'

He whispered in Plácidos' ear and burst into laughter. Plácido looked rather doubtful, and Peláez added:

'I swear it! They can't help it! With a simple confidential complaint he can get rid of the father, the husband or the brother, and then Happy Christmas! However, we did meet one booby, the sweetheart, I believe, of Basilio—what a fool that Basilio is, you know, to have a sweetheart who knows not one word of Spanish, has no money at all, and was once a servant-maid! Shy as anything, but pretty. Father Camorra beat up two young men who were serenading her one night; I don't know how they got away with their lives. For all that she was as stand-offish as ever. But she'll have to go through the business like all the others!'

Juanito Peláez roared with laughter as if it was the greatest thing - in the world. Plácido looked at him with disgust.

'Listen,' said Peláez, changing the subject, 'what did the professor lecture on yesterday?'

'There was no lecture yesterday.'

'Great! And day before yesterday?'

'It was a Thursday, man!' At that time Sundays and Thursdays were school holidays.

'That's right! What a blockhead I am! Do you know, Plácido, that I am turning into a blockhead? And Wednesday?'

'Wednesday? Wait a moment... oh yes, it rained on Wednesday.'

'Marvellous! And Tuesday, dear boy?'

'Tuesday was the professor's name-day and we went to greet him with an orchestra, a bouquet of flowers and some gifts.'

'Oh golly,' exclaimed Juanito, 'I forgot all about it. What a blockhead! Listen, did he ask for me?'

Penitente shrugged.

'I don't know, but they gave him the list of those who had subscribed for the presents.'

'Oh golly! Listen, what happened on Monday?'

'Well, since it was the first day of class, he called the roll and assigned the lesson. On mirrors. From here to here, by heart, word for word. Skip this part entirely and recite this one.'

He was pointing out in the textbook the passages assigned when suddenly the book flew through the air, slapped up by Juanito.

Oh, skip the lesson, man, and let us have an in-between holiday.

Manila students called a day between two regular holidays an in-between holiday, declared, so to speak, by the beneficiaries.

'You know, you really are a blockhead!' Plácido replied in a fury, picking up his book and notes.

'Come on, an in-between!'

Plácido was not for it; a class of more than a hundred and fifty was not going to be sent home for an extra holiday just because the two of them were absent. Nor could he forget the exertions and economies of his mother, who was supporting him in Manila by denying herself everything.

They were passing through the Santo Domingo breach in the city wall when Juanito, on seeing the little square in front of the old Customs-house, exclaimed:

'Now I remember! You know, I have been put in charge of collecting the contributions.'

'What contributions?'

'For the monument.'

'What monument?'

'Why, Father Baltazar's! Didn't you know?'

'And who is this Father Baltazar?'

'What else? A Dominican! That is why the Fathers have appealed to the students. Come, give three or four pesos so they will see we can be generous. Let it never be said that to raise a statue the friars have had to put their hands in their own pockets! Come now, Plácido boy, you won't be throwing away your money!'

Peláez gave him a meaningful wink.

Plácido remembered the case of a student who passed his subjects giving presents of canaries, and handed over three pesos.

'Look here, I shall write your name down in big block letters so the professor won't miss it. See, Plácido Penitente, three pesos There! Oh, I say, it will be the feast-day of the professor of Natural History two weeks from now. You know he's very easy to get along with, never marks absences, never asks any questions. Dear boy, one should be grateful.'

'That's true.'

'What do you say if we set the contributions at two pesos per head? Go ahead, Plácido boy, you start it; then you'll be at the head of the list.'

When he saw that Plácido was handing over the two pesos without a moment's thought he added:

'Look, give me four; I'll give you back two later on. I want it as a come-on.'

'But if you're going to give them back to me anyway, why give them to you now? Why not just write down four?'

'That's right! Golly, what a blockhead I am, do you know I'm losing my grip? But give me four anyway so I can show them around.'

Plácido, living up to his name, handed over what he was asked.

They reached the University.

At the entrance and along the pavement the students were waiting for their professors in lively groups: seniors of secondary school, students of the preparatory courses in Law and Medicine, the last easily recognized by their clothes and a certain air that the others lacked; they were mostly from the Ateneo, and among them could be seen the poet Isagani explaining to a classmate the theory of the refraction of light. One circle discussed and debated, citing the lecturer, the textbook, the principles of Scholastic Philosophy; in another, the students brandished their books in the air or illustrated their theories by sketching on the pavement with their walking-sticks; farther on, other students amused themselves by staring at the women entering the neighbouring church and making cheerful commentaries. An old woman was passing by, leaning on a girl's arm and limping with an air of devout self-sacrifice; the girl walked with downcast eyes, shy and embarrassed to run the gauntlet of so many observers. The old woman raised her coffee-coloured skirt, the habit of the Sisters of St Rita, and showed a pair of plump feet and white stockings; she scolded the girl and darted furious looks at the curious bystanders, grumbling:

'Little monkeys! Don't look at them! Lower your eyes!'

Everything attracted the attention of the students and gave rise to jokes and comments.

Now it was a magnificent carriage stopping at the church door with a pious family visiting the Virgin of the Rosary on her special day, and the bystanders sharpened their eyes to catch a glimpse of the size and shape of the young ladies' feet as they alighted; now it was a fellow student emerging from the door with devotion still visible on his face after praying to the Virgin to make the day's lesson intelligible, or another who had been to church merely to see if his sweetheart was there, to exchange a few looks with her, and to go to class with the memory of her loving eyes.

But the arrival of a coach drawn by a well known pair of white horses caused a greater stir than usual, a certain expectation, and Isagani fell silent and lost colour. It was the coach of Paulita Gómez and she had already sprung to the ground, light as a bird, without giving any roguish eye a glimpse of her ankle. With a graceful turn of the body and gesture of the hand she arranged the folds of her skirt, and in one swift and seemingly careless look saw Isagani, nodded and smiled. Doña Victorina alighted in turn, stared through her *pince-nez,* saw Juanito Peláez, smiled and waved affably.

Isagani, flushed with emotion, answered with a shy greeting; Juanito gave a deep bow and swept off his hat with the gesture of a great comedian acknowledging a round of applause.

'Lord, what a girl!' cried one of the students. 'Tell the professor I am seriously ill.'

Tadeo, which was the sick youth's name, hurried to the church to follow Paulita.

Tadeo went every day to the University to inquire whether or not there would be classes, and was more and more amazed that there would be; he had a vague dream of a perpetual holiday that was just beneath the surface of events, and he awaited its arrival from one day to the next. Every morning, after proposing in vain that everyone take a holiday, he would go off on the pretext of important business, previous engagements, illnesses, just at the moment when his fellow students were about to enter their classes. Yet, no one knew by what magic arts, Tadeo always passed his courses, was a favourite of his professors, and had before him a beautiful future.

Now the students began to move: the professor of Physics and Chemistry was on his way. His students, giving exclamations of disappointment as if some legitimate hope had been defrauded, trooped into the building. Plácido Penitente was following the crowd when someone called out to him.

'Penitente, Penitente, sign this!'

'What is it?'

'Never mind, sign it.'

Plácido had a feeling that his ears were being pulled. He remembered a headman of his home town who had signed a document he had not read and had afterwards found himself in gaol for months and subsequently deported; an uncle of his, to engrave the lesson in his memory, had pulled Plácido's ears so sharply that whenever he now heard anyone speak of signatures the sensation of pain was reproduced in the cartilage of his ears.

'Dear boy, forgive me, but I never sign anything without knowing what I am signing.'

'Oh, don't be tiresome! Look, it's signed by two "heavenly guardsmen", so what do you have to worry about?'

The participation of 'heavenly guardsmen 'was certainly enough to inspire confidence. They were members of a pious confraternity organized to help God in the war against the evil spirit and to prevent the introduction of heretical contraband in the market-places of the New Jerusalem.

Plácido was about to sign to get it over with; he was in a hurry, his classmates were already reciting the opening prayer; but he had a feeling that his uncle was pulling his ears and he said:

'After class. I want to read it first.'

'It's very long, see? It is a counter-petition, or rather, a protest, understand? Makaraig and others have submitted a petition to open a school in Spanish which is really nonsense...'

'All right, dear boy, later, the class is starting,' said Plácido trying to get away.

'But your professor never calls the roll!'

'Yes, he does, sometimes. Later, later! Besides... I don't want to go against Makaraig.'

'But it's not going against him at all, but only...'

Plácido was no longer listening; he was beyond earshot and was hurrying to his classroom. He heard a succession of 'present'... 'present'... 'present'! Good Lord, they were calling the roll! He quickened his steps and arrived at the door just when the roll was at the letter Q.

'Blast it!' he muttered, biting his lips.

He hesitated, uncertain whether to enter or not; there was already a mark against his name and it was not going to be erased. One went to class not to learn but to avoid the mark; there was nothing else to the class except to recite the lesson by heart, to read the textbook, and at most to answer one or two questions, abstract, profound, misleading, enigmatic; there was never lacking, it is true, the usual little homily on humility, submission and respect for the religious, but he, Plácido, was already humble, submissive and respectful. He was about to go when he remembered that the examinations were coming closer and his professor had not yet called on him to recite and indeed had not seemed to notice him at all; this was a good opportunity to attract his attention and make himself noticed. To be noticed was to have the year to the good for, if it cost a professor nothing to flunk someone he did not know, one had to have a hard heart indeed not to be moved by the sight of a young man w ho by his very presence would be a daily reproach for the loss of a year in his life.

So it was that Plácido entered the classroom, and not on tiptoe as he usually did but with his heels striking noisily against the floor. He had overdone it! The professor stared at him, frowned, and shook his head as if to say:

'Insolent puppy! You haven't heard the end of this!'

13 • *A Class in Physics*

THE classroom was a spacious rectangle amply lighted and aired by large windows. Three broad stone tiers, encased in wood, ran along the walls like an amphitheatre and were now filled with students arranged in alphabetical order. The professor's platform, with steps on both sides, stood at the end of the room opposite the entrance, under a picture of St Thomas Aquinas. Except for an impressive blackboard framed in mahogany, which had scarcely been used to judge from the undisturbed *Hurrah* scrawled on it the first day of school, there was no equipment to be seen in the classroom, whether useful or useless. The whitewashed walls, wainscotted with tile to protect them from grime, were wholly bare; not one design, drawing or even outline of laboratory equipment; the students were not thought to need any such thing and nobody missed the practical teaching of an eminently experimental science. For years and years Physics had been taught without laboratory experiments and the Philippines had not thereby gone to seed; far from it, the country was as good as ever. Once in a while, as if descended from Heaven, a little machine might be shown to the class from afar, like the Blessed Sacrament to a congregation in obeisance, bidden to gaze but not to touch. From time to time, when the professor was inclined to spoil his class, one day in the school year was set aside for the students to visit the mysterious Laboratory where they might admire at a distance the enigmatic equipment displayed in the cabinets; nobody could have reason for complaint for on such a day there was much brasswork and glass to be seen, many tubes, disks, wheels, bells; the affair did not go farther than that, but neither did the Philippines go to the dogs. In any case the students were convinced that the equipment had not been bought for their benefit; the friars were not such simpletons! The Laboratory had been set up to be shown to foreigners and high officials from the Peninsula, to make them nod approvingly while their guide smirked as if to say:

'Aha! You thought you were going to deal with a pack of backward monks, didn't you? Well, we are abreast of the age; we have a Laboratory!'

And the foreigners and the high officials, having been lavishly entertained, would afterwards write in their travel journals and memoirs: 'The Royal and Pontifical University of Santo Tomás in Manila, under the direction of the erudite Dominican Order, is equipped with a magnificent Physics Laboratory for the instruction of youth. Some two hundred and fifty students take this course every year but, either from apathy, laziness, the native's mental deficiencies, or other causes, ethnological or beyond comprehension, the Philippine-Malay race has yet to produce a Lavoisier, a Secchi, or a Tyndal, even in miniature!'

However, to be fair, some thirty or forty students in the preparatory courses did have their classes in this Laboratory under the charge of a competent professor but, coming as the majority of them did from the Jesuits' Ateneo, where the sciences were taught empirically in the laboratory itself, the Laboratory of the University was not so useful as it would have been if it had also been used by the other two hundred and fifty students who also paid their fees, bought their textbooks, and spent a year of study to learn nothing in the end. For, with the exception of some unusual scholar or attendant who had these establishments under his care for years on end, no student had ever been known to profit from the lessons so painfully learned by heart.

To return to the Physics class:

The professor was a young Dominican who had made a name for himself teaching a number of subjects in the College of San Juan de Letran with a great show of discipline. He had the reputation of being as clever a logician as he was profound a philosopher, and was considered among the most promising in his faction — for there were factions in the Order—; the older Dominicans treated him with respect, the younger ones envied him. This was his third year of teaching and, although it was the first time he had taught Physics and Chemistry, he was already considered an authority on these subjects not only among the students, who were easily impressed, but also among the other professors; indeed Father Millón was not one of the common run of what one might call nomad professors, wandering from subject to subject in search of scientific commonplaces, as much students as those in their classes, although with the advantage of taking only one course at a time, of asking questions instead of having to answer them, of knowing rather more Spanish and of not being subject to an examination at the end of the year. Father Millón, on the other hand, took science seriously; he knew both Aristotle and Father Amat; he read Ramos's textbook conscientiously and now and again took a dip in Ganot's. For all that, he often shook his head with an air of scepticism, smiled wryly, and murmured, 'Well, let it pass.' He was considered to have more than a passing knowledge of Chemistry ever since, on the basis of a saying of St Thomas that water is a compound, he had proved beyond reasonable doubt that the Angelic Doctor had anticipated by far Berselius, Gay Lussac, Bunsen, and other more or less self-important materialists. Nevertheless, and although he had once taught Geography as well, he still had certain doubts that the world was round, and in discussing its revolutions and rotations round the sun was seen to smile slyly and heard to whisper:

The lying of the stars
Is a star-eyed lying.

He smiled even more scornfully at certain theories in Physics and considered the Jesuit Secchi a visionary, if not actually a madman, accusing him of being so carried away by his theories in Astronomy that he had made geometrical sketches on the Host, for which reason, Father Millón claimed, the Jesuit had been forbidden to say Mass. An odd aversion was observed in him against the very subject he was teaching but this weakness was of no importance, it was a prejudice attributable to his particular scholastic discipline and the Order to which he belonged, and was easily explained not only by the fact that the science of Physics is eminently empirical, founded on observation and induction, while his forte lay in Philosophy, which is purely speculative, abstract and deductive, but also by the fact that like a good Dominican, enamoured of the glories of his Order, he could not feel any attachment for a science in which none of his brethren had been outstanding—apparently he was himself the first to disbelieve in the Chemistry of St Thomas! — and in which indeed so much fame had been won by Orders that were the enemies, or rather the rivals, of the Dominicans.

This was the professor who on the morning in question, the roll having been called, now required his students to recite the day's assignment by heart and word for word. The human phonographs went to work, some well, others badly, some stuttering, others helped out by friendly promptings. Whoever accomplished a flawless recitation gained a good mark; whoever made three mistakes, a zero.

A plump youngster, with a sleepy face and hair that stood on his head as stiff and straight as a brush, was stretching himself so heartily he might have been in bed and yawning so hard that he might well have dislocated his jaw, when the professor, catching sight of him, decided to make an example of him.

'Allo, allo, sleepy head, whassamalah, ha? Velly lazy, mebbe you not knowing lesson, ha?'

Father Millón not only treated his students with the familiar *tu*, like a good friar, but also spoke to them in pidgin, a practice he had picked up from the professor of Canon Law; whether the latter thus wanted to degrade his students or the sacred decrees of the Councils was an issue which had still to be resolved despite the lengthy discussions which had already been held on the point.

Father Millón's interjection did not offend the class; on the contrary, the class was amused and many burst out laughing; it was an everyday affair. The sleepy head, however, did not laugh; he leapt to his feet, rubbed his eyes and, as if a needle had been dropped on a phonograph record, began to recite:

'A mirror is any polished surface designed to reflect the images of objects placed before it; it is classified, according to the materials which compose the surface, into metallic mirrors, glass mirrors . . .'

'Whoa, whoa, whoa!' the professor interrupted him. 'My Lord, what a rattle you are! Let us see now: mirrors may be of metal or of glass, hey? Now then, suppose I were to show you a piece of wood, say mahogany, well polished and varnished, or a slab of burnished black marble, or a sheet of jet which would undoubtedly reflect the images of objects placed before it, how would you classify such mirrors?'

The student, either because he did not know the answer or because he did not understand the question, tried to extricate himself by showing that he had learned the lesson and rushed on desperately:

'The first are made of brass or of alloys of different metals, and the second are made with a sheet of glass whose two surfaces are highly polished, one of them being coated with tin amalgam.'

'Tut, tut, tut, that is not the question. I say *God be with you,* and you reply *Rest in peace!*'

The professor repeated his question in pidgin.

The wretched young man was unable to extricate himself: should he classify mahogany among the metals, marble as glass, and leave jet as something neutral? His neighbour Juanito Peláez slyly prompted him:

'The mahogany mirror is classified as a wooden mirror!'

No sooner said than echoed, and half the class burst into laughter.

'And you as a blockhead,' said the professor, laughing in spite of himself 'Let us see now, what would you say a mirror is: its surface, as a surface, in so far as it is a surface, or the body of which it is the surface, that is to say, the material on which the surface depends, the substance itself which is modified by the nonessential surface, because, of course, since the surface is merely an incident of the substance, it cannot exist without the substance. Now, then, what do you say to that?'

Me? Say to that? Not a thing, the miserable young man was about to reply; he no longer knew what it was all about; he was bewildered by so many surfaces and incidents hammering cruelly at his brains; but an instinctive pride prevented him and, running with anguished sweat, he proceeded to recite between clenched teeth:

'A mirror is any polished surface . . .'

'So that, according to you, the mirror is the surface,' interrupted the professor, taking him up on this point. 'Well, then, resolve this difficulty. If the mirror is the surface, then it does not matter, so far as the essence of the mirror is concerned, what lies behind that surface, since what is behind cannot affect the essence of what is in front, that is to say, of the surface; in other words, what is on top, which is called the surface, is whatever can be seen on top. Do you admit that or not?'

The young man's hair stood even more on end as if raised by a magnetic force.

'Do you grant it or not?'

I grant anything, anything you say, Father, he thought, but did not dare say so for fear of being laughed at. He was certainly in straits, and he had never known them so strait. He had a vague feeling that one could never grant the most insignificant thing to friars without their making the most of it, witness their parishes and estates: his better instincts suggested that he should deny everything with all his spirit and all the rebelliousness of his hair, and he was about to let loose a magnificent denial, particularly because he suddenly remembered that a court official had once told him that whoever denies everything commits himself to nothing, when the bad habit of not listening to the voice of his own conscience, of having little faith in lawyers, and of seeking the help of others when one is sufficient to oneself, ruined him. His classmates were signalling him to grant, most of all Juanito Peláez, and allowing himself to be carried away by his evil genius he blurted out instead: 'Granted, Father!' in a voice so faint that he might have been saying 'Into Your hands I commend my spirit!'

'You grant the premise,' smirked the professor. 'Good. Therefore, according to you, I could scrape the silver amalgam from the back of a mirror, cover it with a rice-cake instead, and we would still have a mirror, hey? Now, what would we have then?'

The young man glanced at his prompters and, seeing them amazed and unable to say a word, his face fell with bitter recrimination, his eyes praying: 'Oh God, why hast Thou forsaken me!' while his lips muttered: 'I'll be damned!' In vain he cleared his throat, tugged at his shirt-front, shifted his weight from one foot to the other; he could not find a way out.

'Come, what would we have then?' insisted the professor, relishing his arguments to the full.

'Rice-cake!' Juanito Peláez prompted. 'Rice-cake!'

'Oh, shut up, you ass!' the young man shouted at last, in desperation and also in order to turn his predicament into a quarrel.

'Ah, Juanito, it's you, is it?' the professor turned to Peláez. 'Well, then, let us see if you can resolve our little difficulty.'

Peláez, who was one of his favourites, stood up leisurely, not without nudging Plácido Penitente, who was next to him on the roll. It was an appeal for help.

'I deny the conclusion, Father,' he said resolutely.

'Oho! Well, then, I shall prove the conclusion. According to you, the polished surface constitutes the essence of the mirror...'

'I deny the supposition,' Juanito interrupted, feeling a tug at his jacket from Plácido.

'What's that? According to you...'

'I deny it.'

'Therefore, you are of the opinion that what is behind affects what is in front?'

'I deny that too!' he cried with even greater vigour, feeling another tug at his jacket.

Juanito, or rather Plácido who was prompting him, was unwittingly adopting the strategy of the Chinese: avoid invasion by never admitting even the most innocent-looking foreigner.

'Well, where are we then?' asked the professor rather disconcerted and staring uneasily at this intransigent student. 'Does the substance which is behind the surface affect the latter or not?'

Faced with this precise and categorical question, a kind of ultimatum, Juanito was unable to answer; his jacket was no help; in vain he wiggled his hands at Plácido; Plácido himself was in a quandary. The professors' eyes wandered to one of the students who was easing himself out of his tight boots, and Juanito seized the opportunity to stamp on one of Plácido's feet.

'Come on, say something!'

'I distinguish—ouch! You beast!' Plácido cried out angrily, holding one of his patent-leather shoes.

The professor heard the exclamation and guessed at a glance what was afoot.

'Hey, you, Mr Ghost,' he called out to Plácido. 'I wasn't asking you, but since you think so highly of yourself as the saviour of others, let me see if you can save yourself. You answer the question!'

Juanito sat down happily and by way of appreciation stuck out his tongue at his prompter. In the meantime the latter, flushing with embarrassment, got to his feet mumbling unintelligible excuses.

Father Millón looked him over for a moment as if savouring a new dish. It would be pleasant to humiliate and put to ridicule this young gallant, always so neatly dressed, with his head held high and his self-possessed look. It would be an act of charity, really, so the charitable professor took it upon himself to perform it in all good conscience, repeating his question slowly.

'The book says that metallic mirrors are made of brass or of alloys of different metals. True or false?'

'If the book says so, Father...'

'The book does say so, and so it is. You are not going to claim you know more than the book, are you?' He then recalled that glass mirrors are made with a sheet of glass whose two surfaces are highly polished, one of them being coated with tin amalgam: 'Mark that. True?'

'If the book says so, Father...'

'Is tin a metal?'

'It would seem so, Father, according to the book...'

'Of course it is. And the word amalgam indicates that it is mixed with mercury, which is another metal. Therefore, a glass mirror is a metallic mirror; therefore, the terms on which the classification is based are interchangeable; therefore the classification itself is erroneous; therefore... Well, how do you explain that, Mr Ghost?'

The professor relished every 'therefore', winking as if to say: 'Your goose is cooked!'

'The thing is... That is to say...' Plácido stammered.

'That is to say, you have not understood the lesson, you miserable ghost, who tries to save others when he himself is lost!'

The class did not resent this; on the contrary, many found the rhyme amusing and laughed. Plácido bit his lips.

'What is your name?' asked the professor.

Plácido gave it curtly.

'Aha, Plácido Penitente! Well, you seem more placid than penitent to me but I shall give you something to be penitent about.'

Self-satisfied with this further play on words the professor now called on him to recite the lesson for the day. The young man was by now in such a state of mind that he made three mistakes, at which the professor, nodding his head, slowly opened the class roll and with all deliberation went through it, muttering the names in order.

'Palencia, Palomo, Panganiban, Pedraza, Pelado, Peláez, Penitente—aha, Plácido Penitente! With fifteen absences!'

Plácido snapped to attention.

'Fifteen absences, Father?'

'Fifteen deliberate absences,' the professor emphasized. 'So you need only one more to be sent down.'

'Fifteen absences, fifteen absences!' the bewildered Plácido repeated. 'I have only been absent four times, and with today's, if that is to be counted at all, five.'

'Thassolaih, sah, thassolaih,' the professor answered peering at the young man over his gold-rimmed glasses. 'You admit you have been absent five times, and God only knows how many more times than that. Now, since I call the roll only rarely, every time I catch anyone absent I give him five black marks. Now then, what are five times five? I bet you have forgotten your multiplication table. Five times five?'

'Twenty-five.'

'Thassolaih, thassolaih. So you are even short ten black marks because I have caught you out only three times. If I had caught you every time, ouch! Now, then, three times five?'

'Fifteen.'

'Fifteen, allah same, fish and game.' concluded the professor, closing the roll. 'One more and out you go, goobay! Out op de door! Ah, and now a zero in recitation.'

He opened the roll again, looked for the young man's name, and placed a zero against it.

'Well, well! Well now, such a pretty zero, that's nice, you haven't got one yet.'

'But, Father,' exclaimed Plácido, barely restraining himself, 'if Your Reverence gives me a bad mark in recitation, surely he should erase my bad marks for absence today!'

His Reverence did not reply. Having first put down the zero, he studied it, shaking his head — the zero must be drawn artistically — then closed the roll and asked with heavy irony:

'Oh sah, whassamallah?'

'It is impossible to understand, Father, how one can be absent and yet recite the day's lesson. As Your Reverence would say, to be and not to be...'

'Oh, help! Ouch! a peelosoper already, but maybe not yet! So it is impossible to understand, hey? *Sed patet experientia* and *contra experientiam negantem, fusilibus est arguendum,* savvee? Facts is facts and anybody argue against facts, more better shoot him! And can you not conceive, dear philosopher, that one can be absent from class and not know the lesson too? Does absence necessarily imply knowledge? What do you say, my apprentice philosopher?'

This last gibe broke the camel's back. Plácido, who was reputed to be a logician among his friends, lost his temper, hurled away his text-book, rose and faced the professor.

'That's enough, Father, enough! Your Reverence can give me all the bad marks he wants but he has no right to insult me. Your Reverence can keep his class; I am not taking any more.'

And without further ado he walked out.

The class was aghast: such a display of personal dignity was almost never witnessed. Who would have thought that Plácido Penitente...! The professor, taken by surprise, bit his lips and, with an ominous shake of the head, watched Plácido leave. Then, in a shaking voice, although with more feeling and eloquence than usual, he launched a sermon on the familiar themes of the growing conceit, the innate ingratitude, the presumption, the disrespect for superiors, the very arrogance, that the evil spirit was infusing in the youth of the day, their rudeness, their ungentlemanliness; thence he proceeded to pour gibes and witticisms on those popinjays who now presumed to teach their teachers by opening an academy for the study of Spanish.

'So those who yesterday scarcely knew how to say *Yes, Father, No, Father,*' he sneered, 'now want to know more than those who have grown old teaching! Who wants to learn, learns, with or without academies! No doubt that rascal who has just gone out is one of those behind the proposal! God save the Spanish language from such friends! Where will you find the time to attend this academy when you can hardly fulfil your classroom obligations? Of course we should like all of you to know Spanish, to speak it properly, if only to save our ears from your f's and p's, but duty comes first, and hobbies afterwards; attend to your studies first, and then learn Spanish, write books in it if you feel like it...'

And so on and so on until the bell rang putting an end to the class, and two hundred and thirty-four students, after saying the closing prayer, left the room as ignorant as when they entered it but sighing as if they had been relieved of an immense burden. Each of them had lost one more hour of his life and with it a measure of his dignity and self-respect, an hour which, on the other hand, had added to the discouragement, resentment and aversion to study in his heart. After that, who could ask them for a greater love of science, more dignity, more gratitude! After that, what a sombre judgment upon us all!

For, just like the two hundred and thirty-four, thousands upon thousands of other students before them had wasted their time and, if matters were not set right, so would others still to come, to be brutalized, to have their dignity outraged and their youthful enthusiasms turned to indolence and hatred, like waves on a polluted beach that one after the other accumulate the garbage upon it. Yet He who from eternity sees the consequences of an act unravel like a thread throughout the centuries, He who weighs the worth of a second, and has imposed upon His creatures the primordial law of progress and perfection, would, if He were just, demand a strict accounting of those responsible for millions of minds darkened and blinded, for the outraged human dignity of millions, for the wasted centuries and the fruitless labour.

And if the doctrines of the Gospels have a foundation of truth, those millions also, for their part, would have to answer for the light of their minds and the dignity of their souls which they had not known how to keep, like the steward asked by his Master to account for the talents of which he had cravenly allowed himself to be robbed.

14 • A Students' Hostel

THE house where Makaraig was lodged was well worth a visit.

It was large and spacious, with two stories above the ground floor, all the windows being fashionably grilled. It was like a school early in the morning and like pandemonium from ten o'clock onwards. During the recreation hours of the lodgers, laughter, shouts, and all manner of hustle and bustle filled the house from the courtyard at the entrance to the main floor. Lightly clad youngsters played native football or performed gymnastics on improvised trapezes. Up and down the staircase eight or nine others fought a mock battle with walking-sticks, pikes, hooks and lassoos. But neither besiegers nor besieged suffered much injury; the blows seemed always to rebound on the back of the Chinese pedlar selling a hodge-podge of indigestible pies at the foot of the stairs. Now he was surrounded by a crowd of boys pulling at his pigtail (by now all undone and every which way), snatching away a pie, haggling over the price of another, and playing on him a thousand tricks. The Chinese screamed and swore in every one of the languages he had picked up, and in his own for good measure; he blubbered, giggled and grinned when scowling did not work, and the other way round.

'Ah, thassa no good, you bad conscience, velly bad Chlistian, you devil, balbalian, lascal!'

Two more blows glancing off from the battle on the stairs— no matter, he turned a smiling face, the walking-sticks had only hit him in the back, and he went about his business undismayed, contenting himself with shouting: 'No mo' joking, ha? No joking!' But when the blows fell on his tray with all its pies, then indeed he let loose all imaginable oaths and curses and swore he would never be back. The boys doubled their pranks to try his temper, but when they saw he was running out of maledictions, and when they themselves were stuffed full of sweetmeat pies and salted water-melon seeds, they paid him scrupulously, and the Chinese went off happy after all, laughing and winking, and taking the light blows which the students gave him to speed him off as if they were acts of endearment.

'Oh me, oh my!'

Upstairs concerts of piano and violin, guitar and accordion, alternated with the clash of walking-sticks in fencing lessons. At a long wide table the students from the Ateneo were at their notebooks, composing essays and solving problems, while others wrote to their sweethearts on pink notepaper fretted with lacework and decorated with pretty drawings. One was composing a play in verse, beside him another was practising the scales on the flute—alas, the verses seemed fated to be greeted with whistles. At one end of the hall the older students, university men in silk hose and embroidered slippers, found their amusement in bullying the youngsters, tweaking their ears, already scarlet with so much abuse. Two or three held a shrieking weeping youngster who was defending with kicks the drawstrings of his underpants: the purpose of the exercise was to reduce him to the state in which he was born: squalling and stark naked. In one of the rooms, round a night-table, four young men were playing cards amid great shouts and laughter, to the manifest annoyance of a fifth who was apparently conning his textbook but who was really awaiting his turn at the game. Another now approached the gaming table with a great show of being scandalized.

'How depraved you are! At cards already, so early in the morning! Well, now, what do we have here? Play the three of spades, you ass!'

And he promptly closed his book and joined the game.

Shouts and the sound of blows came from a neighbouring room: a student sensitive about his limp was fighting with a newcomer from the provinces. The provincial in all innocence had merely asked what was meant by a limping verse and the other had felt insulted. Their companions, while ostensibly trying to explain things, had contrived to make confusion worse confounded and the two had come to blows.

In the dining-room a young man who had just received from home a tin of sardines, a bottle of wine, and other provisions was engaged in an heroic effort to get his friends to share his repast against their equally heroic resistance. Others, for their part, were bathing on the open terrace and, playing firemen, were bombarding one another with bucketfuls of water from the household well to the great amusement of onlookers.

But the noise and the shouting gradually died down with the arrival of student leaders called together by Makaraig to hear a report on the progress of the plan for a Spanish academy. Isagani had a great reception, and also

Sandoval, a Spaniard who had come to Manila as a government employee and had stayed to finish his studies, identifying himself whole-heartedly with the aspirations of the Filipino students. Indeed, the barriers which politics put up between the races collapsed in the classroom, burnt down by the fires of science and of youth.

In the absence of academies and scientific, literary and political clubs in Manila, Sandoval took advantage of any meeting that came his way to display his great oratorical talents, giving speeches on any conceivable subject, this time the teaching of Spanish, to wrest the applause of his friends and admirers.

Makaraig had not yet arrived and everyone speculated on what had happened, on the General's decision, on a possible denial of the permit, on whether Father Irene or Father Sibyla had prevailed, all of them questions which only Makaraig could answer.

Among the young men in the gathering some were optimistic like Isagani and Sandoval, who were sure everything had been arranged and were already talking of the congratulations and praises that would be forthcoming from the Government for the patriotism of the students, expectations that made Juanito Peláez claim for himself a major part of the glory of organizing the movement. To all this the pessimistic Pecson, a stout young man with a madcap's loud guffaw, countered with talk of extraneous influences, of Monsignor A. and the Reverend B. and Father Provincial C., who had or had not been consulted, and who had or had not advised that all the members of the students' movement be thrown into prison, which was enough to make an apprehensive Juanito Peláez stammer:

'Good Lord, now don't you get me mixed up in...'

It was enough to make Sandoval, in his capacity as a Spaniard and a liberal, lose his temper.

'But dammit all,' he cried, 'that is to have a very low opinion indeed of His Excellency! I know he is very close to the friars but on a matter like this he will not let himself be ruled by them. Will you tell me, Pecson, what reason you have to believe that the General cannot think for himself?'

'I said nothing of the sort, Sandoval,' answered Pecson grinning so widely he showed his wisdom teeth. 'Of course, the General can think for himself, that is to say, he thinks what whoever happens to catch his ear wants him to think. That's plain enough!'

'Oh, humbug! Give me one example, cite me just one case!' shrilled Sandoval, adding with an elegant gesture: 'Let us eschew empty phrases and generalizations, and go to the facts. Facts, gentlemen, facts! The rest is pure prejudice which I refrain from characterizing as subversive.'

Pecson burst out laughing.

'I was expecting that: subversion, indeed! It seems we cannot discuss anything without resorting to threats!'

Sandoval protested and in a brief harangue repeated his demand for facts.

'Well, then,' replied Pecson, 'not so long ago some laymen had a lawsuit against certain friars, and the Acting Governor-General decided it by submitting the case to the Father Provincial of the friars' Order.'

Chortling with glee as if it were the most innocuous of subjects he gave names, dates, and promised to produce documents which would prove the way justice was being administered.

'But on what basis, tell me, on what possible basis,' insisted Sandoval, 'could they deny a permit for the academy when it is obvious that the teaching of Spanish is highly useful and even necessary?'

Pecson gave a shrug of the shoulders and answered in the manner of a clerk of court reading from a brief:

'It endangers the integrity of the nation...'

'That's a good one! What have the rules of grammar to do with the integrity of the nation!'

'Holy Mother Church has doctors enough for any doctrine. How should I know? Perhaps it is feared that we might then understand the laws and might even obey them. What shall become of the Philippines the day we can understand one another?'

Sandoval did not like the turn the conversation was taking; an exchange of witticisms was not likely to give him an opening for a worthwhile speech.

'Don't take things so lightly,' he exclaimed. 'These are very serious matters.'

'God save me from taking things lightly where friars are concerned!'

'Well, then, what could they possibly put up as an objection?'

'That,' Pecson continued in the same tone of voice, as if repeating what was only too well known, 'the Spanish classes would have to be held at night and that consequently there would be a danger of immorality, as was said about the proposed Spanish school in Malolos.'

'More humbug! Aren't the classes at the Academy of Painting also held under cover of night? And what about the novenas and the processions?'

'That the classes,' the corpulent Pecson continued imperturbably, 'would imperil the dignity of the University.'

'Let it be imperilled; the University must yield to the needs of the students! Anyway, supposing it were true, then what is the University for? Is it an institution of non-learning? Have then a handful of men gathered together in the name of scientific education only in order to prevent others from securing it?'

'The point is that any initiative that comes from below reveals discontent.'

'And that which comes from above?' someone insinuated. 'What about the School of Arts and Trades?'

'Not so fast, gentlemen,' said Sandoval. 'I am not a partisan of the friars. My liberal ideas are well known. But let us give to Caesar what belongs to Caesar. That School of Arts and Trades, of which I am the most enthusiastic defender, and whose establishment I shall hail as the dawn of a new day for these fortunate islands, that School of Arts and Trades has been placed under the direction of the friars—'

'Or, which comes down to the same thing, of dogs in the manger,' added Pecson, interrupting Sandoval's speech once more.

'Dammit all!' cried Sandoval, furious at losing the thread of his periodic sentence. 'So long as we have no proof of malice, let us not be denigrators; let us not unjustly put in question the Government's freedom of decision...'

And he launched into a beautifully phrased defence of the administration and of its good intentions, a theme whose development Pecson did not dare to interrupt.

'The Spanish Government has given you everything, has denied you nothing. We had absolutism in Spain; you had it too. The friars covered our country with their convents; and convents occupy a third of Manila. Condemned men are strangled to death in Spain; and death by strangling is also the extreme penalty here. We are Catholic, and we have made you Catholic. We believe in Scholastic Philosophy, and Scholastic Philosophy rules your classrooms. In brief, gentlemen, we weep when you weep, we suffer what you suffer, we pray at the same altars, are judged at the same tribunals, suffer the same penalties, and it is only just that we should also share with you the same rights and the same pleasures.'

Free from interruptions he went on from one enthusiasm to another until he reached the future of the Philippines.

'As I have said, gentlemen, the dawn of a new day is not far off; Spain is opening a new age for her beloved Philippines; times are changing, and I am sure that more is being done than we imagine. It would be well to encourage with our confidence that Government which, according to you, is vacillating without a will of its own; it would be well to show that we place our hopes in it; let us, by our conduct, remind it (when it forgets, although I do not think that possible) that we have faith in its good intentions, and that it should not allow itself to be guided by any other standards than those of justice and the common good of all the governed. No, gentlemen,' he continued, in a tone that grew increasingly declamatory, 'in this matter we should not even consider the possibility of negotiating with other bodies that are more or less opposed to our project, for the very idea would imply tolerance of their intervention; your conduct so far has been open, loyal, without hesitations, without suspicions; you have addressed yourselves to the Government simply and directly; the reasons you have given cannot be more worthy of consideration; your objective has been to lighten the burden of the professors in the opening years of the course, and to facilitate the studies of the hundreds of students who fill the classrooms and who cannot be attended to by overworked teachers. If no decision has yet been rendered on the application it is only, to my own knowledge, because of the pressure of other pending business; but I prophesy that the battle is already won, that Makaraig has gathered us here to announce our victory, and that tomorrow we shall see our efforts rewarded with the praise and gratitude of the country—and who knows, gentlemen, if the Government is not contemplating proposing you for honours and decorations which you so well deserve of the nation!'

There was loud applause; everyone was now convinced of success, and many even believed in the honours and decorations.

'Let it be on record, gentlemen,' cried Juanito, 'that I was one of the founders!'

The sceptical Pecson did not share this enthusiasm.

'I hope we won't carry the decorations round our ankles,' he said.

Fortunately for Peláez this remark was drowned by the applause. When calm had been partially restored Pecson countered:

'Good, very good, but let us suppose that, in spite of all that has been said, the General continues to ask for comment, advice and opinion, and in the end denies the permit?'

The supposition came like a dash of cold water.

Everyone turned to Sandoval, who found himself at a loss.

'Then...' he stammered.

'Then?'

'Then,' exclaimed Sandoval, still excited by the applause and in a burst of spirit, 'since the regime proclaims in speech and print that it desires your education and yet, when faced with actualities, prevents it, then, gentlemen, your efforts will not have been in vain since you will have accomplished what nobody else has done, you will have compelled it to unmask itself and throw down the gauntlet!'

'Bravo! Bravo!'

'Good for Sandoval! Long live the gauntlet!'

'So it throws down the gauntlet,' Pecson sneered. 'And then?'

Sandoval was caught up short in the midst of his triumph but, with the vivacity of his race and his orator's instinct, he recovered instantly.

'And then?' he asked. 'Then, if none of the Filipinos dares accept the challenge, then I, Sandoval, in the name of Spain, shall pick up the gauntlet because such a policy would give the lie to all the good intentions that Spain has always cherished for her provinces, and because whoever so prostitutes the office entrusted to him and so abuses his all-embracing powers does not deserve the protection of the Spanish nation or the support of any Spanish citizen!'

The audience was delirious with enthusiasm. Isagani embraced Sandoval; others followed suit. There was talk of nation, union, fraternity, loyalty; the Filipinos said that if only all the Spaniards were Sandovals, there would be none but Sandovals in the Philippines. Sandoval's eyes were gleaming, and it was easy to believe that, if at that moment for any cause a gauntlet had been thrown down before him, he would have mounted the nearest horse and let himself be killed for the Philippines. Mr Cold Water, however, remarked:

'Good, that was very good, Sandoval, I could speak like that too if I were a Spaniard. But, not being one, if I said half of what you have said, you yourself would consider me subversive.'

Sandoval was beginning a speech of protest when he was interrupted by a young man who entered the room at that point and, embracing all and sundry, cried out:

'Good news, friends, good news! Victory! Long live the Spanish language!'

The news was greeted with a round of applause; everyone was embracing everyone else, their eyes bright with tears. Only Pecson did not lose his sceptical smile.

The bearer of the good tidings was Makaraig, the young man at the head of the movement.

This student had two richly furnished rooms to himself in the house, and kept a servant and a groom for his gig and horses. He was high-spirited, well-mannered, elegant and very rich. Although he was studying law only for the sake of the academic title, he had nonetheless a reputation for diligence, and as a logician in the scholastic style he had nothing to envy the most dedicated dialecticians of the University faculty. For all that he was not far behind modern ideas and movements; his wealth put at his disposal all the books and publications which found their way past the censors. It was not to be wondered at that with these qualities, his reputation for manliness founded on certain fortunate encounters in his younger years, and his discreet and unobtrusive munificence, he exercised such influence over his contemporaries that he had been chosen to bring to a successful conclusion a project so difficult as the teaching of Spanish to the Filipinos.

Youth, which always looks on the bright side of things, is inclined to exaggerate its enthusiasms but, once the first outbursts were over, the students wanted to know more about how things had gone.

'This morning I saw Father Irene,' said Makaraig enigmatically.

'Long live Father Irene!' cried a sanguine student.

'He put me abreast of all that happened in Los Baños,' Makaraig continued. 'It seems that they discussed the matter for at least a week, with him upholding and defending our cause against everyone else, against Father Sibyla, Father Fernández, Father Salví, the General, the Vice-Governor-General, Simoun the jeweller,...'

'Simoun the jeweller! But what has that Jew got to do with us? Look here, we make him rich buying his...' said one student.

'Quiet!' he was admonished impatiently by another, who was anxious to know how Father Irene had vanquished such formidable foes.

'Even high officials were against our proposal, the Administrative Director, the Civil Governor of Manila, the Chinaman Quiroga,...'

'The Chinaman Quiroga! That pimp!'

'Shut up, man!'

'In the end,' Makaraig continued, 'they had just about decided to pigeonhole the matter and let it lie for months and months, one can imagine, when Father Irene remembered the Supervisory Committee of Primary Education and proposed that, since the proposal concerned the teaching of Spanish, it should be referred to the Committee for a recommendation.'

'But the Committee has not been functioning for some time,' said Pecson.

'That is exactly what they told Father Irene,' Makaraig continued, 'and he replied that this was a good time to re-activate it and, taking advantage of the presence of Don Custodio, who is a member of the Committee, he proposed that it be reconstituted forthwith. Since he is known to be a good worker Don Custodio was designated to study the matter and make a report on it. The records are now in his hands and he has promised to make his report within the month.'

'Long live Don Custodio!'

'And if Don Custodio makes an unfavourable report?' asked the pessimistic Pecson.

They had not thought of this in their relief at the news that the project was not going to be pigeonholed. Everyone looked towards Makaraig for the solution.

'I put the same objection to Father Irene but, with that roguish smile of his, he told me: "We have gained a lot of ground, we have forced the issue towards a decision and the enemy has been compelled to do battle. If we can only influence Don Custodio to follow his liberal tendencies and make a favourable report, then we shall have won; the General has shown himself absolutely neutral."'

Makaraig paused.

'But how do we influence him?' someone asked impatiently.

'Father Irene suggested two ways.'

'Quiroga the Chinaman!' said one.

'Nonsense! Don Custodio wouldn't pay any attention to him.'

'An expensive present!'

'That's even worse. Don Custodio prides himself on being incorruptible.'

'Oh, I know! I have it!' Pecson exclaimed with a laugh. 'Pepay the dancer!'

'That's it, Pepay the dancer!' chorused a number.

Pepay was a showy beauty who had the reputation of being a very good friend of Don Custodio; contractors, bureaucrats and other intriguers had recourse to her when they wanted something from the famous counsellor. Juanito Peláez, who was also a friend of the dancer, offered his services to arrange the matter but Isagani was opposed; it was bad enough, he said, to have had to use Father Irene; it would be too much to solicit the help of Pepay in such a matter.

'Let's hear the other way then!'

'The other way is to approach Mr Pasta, Don Custodio's legal adviser, the oracle before whom he bows his head.'

'I prefer that,' said Isagani. 'Mr Pasta is a Filipino and was a classmate of my uncle. But how shall we get him on our side?'

'That's the nub!' Makaraig replied, looking at Isagani speculatively. 'Mr Pasta has a dancer too, or rather an embroideress...'

Isagani shook his head again.

'Don't be such a Puritan,' Juanito Peláez told him. 'The end justifies the means! I know the embroideress, her name is Matea and she has a lot of girls working for her in her shop.'

'No, gentlemen,' Isagani insisted. 'Let us first have recourse to honourable means. I shall call on Mr Pasta and, if I get nowhere, then you can do what you like with your dancers and your embroideresses.'

They felt obliged to accept the proposal and agreed that Isagani would call on Mr Pasta that very day and would report to them on the results of his interview that afternoon at the University.

15 • *Mr Pasta*

MR PASTA was considered one of the most brilliant minds in Manila; the friars turned to him in their greatest difficulties. When Isagani called at his house, he had to wait a while because there were a great number of people ahead of him who wanted the lawyer's advice. Eventually it was his turn and he entered Mr Pasta's study.

The lawyer greeted him with a slight cough, peering furtively at Isagani's feet. He did not rise or offer Isagani a chair but went on writing at his desk. Isagani took advantage of this opportunity to look him over: he had aged considerably he was bald to the crown of his head, and what hair he had left was heavily streaked with grey. His face was sour and severe.

There was complete silence in the study except for the distant murmur of the clerks and assistants in the adjoining room and the squeaking of their pens.

At length the lawyer finished what he was writing, dropped his pen, raised his head and, his face brightening when he recognized Isagani, gave him his hand affectionately.

'Well, then, good-bye, young man... I beg your pardon, do sit down. I did not realize it was you. And how is your uncle?'

Isagani's spirits rose and he felt that things would go well. He put the matter to the lawyer briefly, studying the effect of his words. Mr Pasta listened impassively at first; he was already aware of the students' agitation but pretended to know nothing of such puerilities. However, when he got an inkling of what was expected of him and heard that it concerned the Vice-

Rector, friars, the Governor-General, projects, plans, his face slowly darkened until finally he exclaimed:

'This is the country of plans and projects! But go on, go on.'

Isagani was not disheartened. He spoke of the way the issue would be settled and ended by expressing the confidence of the youth that he, Mr Pasta, would intercede in their favour should Don Custodio seek his advice, as was to be expected; Isagani did not dare ask directly that the advice be favourable in view of the grimace that the lawyer made.

But Mr Pasta had already made up his mind to have nothing to do with the matter; he would neither advise nor be advised. He was aware of what had happened in Los Baños; he knew that there had been two factions and that, in fact, Father Irene had not been the only champion of the students nor the author of the proposal to refer the matter to the Supervisory Committee on Primary Education. All the contrary; Father Irene, Father Fernández, the Countess, a merchant who was looking forward to the sale of supplies for the new academy, and the high official who had cited one royal decree after another, had been on the verge of success when Father Sibyla, trying to gain time, had remembered the Committee. The great lawyer had all this in mind and, when Isagani had finished, decided to bewilder the student with evasions, confuse the issue, and then face him on other grounds.

'Oh yes,' he said, pouting and scratching his bald spot, 'I yield to no one in my love of country and in my progressive ideas, but... I cannot commit myself. I do not know whether or not you realize my position; it is very delicate... I have many interests... I must act within the limits of strict prudence... It would be most embarrassing...'

The lawyer wanted to confuse the student with a wealth of language and began to speak of statutes, decrees, indeed he spoke at such length that instead of confusing the young man he almost confused himself with a tangle of citations.

'By no manner of means do we wish to embarrass you,' Isagani replied coolly. 'God forbid that we should make things difficult for those who render such great service to other Filipinos! But, little as I know about statutes, royal decrees, and the legal provisions and orders which are in force in our country, I do not think there can be anything wrong in supporting the progressive policies of the Government and in trying to implement them properly; we seek the same objectives and only differ as to means.'

The lawyer smiled; the youngster had allowed himself to be led to his own chosen ground. He would have him there; he had him already.

'That is precisely the nub, as the saying goes; of course it is praiseworthy to help the Government, when it is done in the proper spirit of submission, following its orders, obeying the spirit of the laws in close harmony with the upright interpretation of the enforcers of the laws, never in contradiction with even the most tentative suggestions and general way of thinking of those who have in their keeping the welfare of the individuals who compose society. That is why it is criminal, it is punishable, as offensive to the high principle of authority, to attempt an action in contradiction with the initiatives taken by authority, even supposing such action to be better than that of the Government, since such action might damage the prestige which is the primordial basis of all colonial structures.'

The old lawyer, sure that this tirade had at least set Isagani's brains awhirl, settled down in his armchair, outwardly grave but laughing to himself.

Isagani, however, replied:

'I had thought that governments would seek firmer foundations the more they were threatened. Prestige is the weakest of all foundations for colonial governments because it does not depend on them but on the good will of those who are governed and lasts only so long as they willingly recognize it. It had seemed to me that justice would provide a more lasting foundation.'

The lawyer raised his head. What! This youngster dared reply and discuss with him, with Mr Pasta? Was he not yet bewildered by big words?

'Young man,' he interrupted, 'you must put such thoughts aside; they are dangerous. What I am telling you is that one must let the Government act for itself.'

'Governments have been made for the good of peoples, and to fulfil their purposes properly they must follow the wishes of the citizens who best know what they need.'

'Those who compose the Government are citizens too, and among the best qualified.'

'But, being men, they are liable to make mistakes and should not close their ears to the opinions of others.'

'We must trust in them; they will give all.'

'There is a saying that is very Spanish: If baby doesn't squawk, baby doesn't suck. You get nothing unless you ask for it.'

'On the contrary,' the lawyer snorted. 'With this Government, it is all the opposite...'

He stopped short as if he had said too much and to cover up his imprudence continued:

'The Government has given us things we have not asked for, which we could not have asked for, because to ask... to ask would have assumed that something was lacking and that the Government had neglected its obligations. To suggest measures, to try, not indeed to oppose, but even to guide it, is to assume that it is capable of making mistakes, and I have already told you that such assumptions threaten the very existence of colonial governments. The masses do not understand this, and the young, who act hastily, do not know, do not understand, refuse to understand that to ask for something is to make sure of the opposite. The very idea is subversive.'

'Pardon me,' broke in Isagani, antagonized by the jurist's arguments, 'when a people ask for something from a government through legal means, it is because the people believe the government to be good and to be ready to give them what is good; and the act of asking, instead of angering, should flatter that government; one asks one's mother, never one's stepmother. In my inexpert opinion our Government is not all-knowing; it cannot see and foresee everything; and even if it were and even if it could, it should not be angered by the act of asking. Witness the Church herself, which does nothing but keep asking God, who sees and knows everything; you yourself ask and demand many things from the courts of this same Government; and neither God nor the courts have taken offence to this date. All of us are conscious of the fact that the Government, being, as it is, a human institution, needs the cooperation of the rest; it must be brought to see and feel the reality of things. You yourself cannot be convinced of the validity of your objections; you yourself must know that a government which, to make a show of strength and freedom of action, refuses to yield out of fear and suspicion, is a tyrannical and despotic government, and that only peoples enslaved by tyrants have the duty of never asking for anything. A people that detest their government can ask only one thing: that it give up power.'

The old lawyer showed his disagreement with grimaces, shaking his head and rubbing his bald spot. Then he said with pitying protectiveness:

'Ah, those are bad theories, bad, bad! It is plain to see that you are young and know little of life. See what is happening to our poor inexperienced young men in Madrid who keep asking for so many reforms: they are all branded as subversive, many do not dare come back, yet what are they asking? Good, old, inoffensive commonplaces! But there are things which I cannot explain to you, they are liable to misunderstanding. Well, now, I must confess that there are reasons other than the ones I have given you which move a prudent government to ignore systematically the desires of the people...

no... we might, however, find ourselves with leaders so stupid and absurd that... but there are always other reasons... even though what one asks is only just... governments are of all kinds...'

The old man hesitated, stared at Isagani, and then made up his mind and gestured as if to brush aside a thought.

'I can guess what you want to say,' said Isagani with a bleak smile. 'You mean to say that a colonial government, for the very reason that its foundations are imperfect, and because it rests on a premise...'

'No, no, not that!' the old man interrupted excitedly, pretending to search for something among his papers. 'No, I did not mean to say... but where are my glasses?'

Isagani pointed them out to him.

Mr Pasta put on his glasses, pretended to read some papers, and then, seeing that the student was waiting, stammered:

'I wanted to say something... I wanted to say... but I have forgotten now. You were too excited, you interrupted me... It doesn't matter... Ah, if you only knew the number of things I have on my mind; I have so much to do!'

Isagani understood that he was being dismissed.

'So we...' he said, rising.

'Ah, ah yes! You would do well to leave the matter in the hands of the Government. It will decide as it sees fit. You say that the Vice-Rector is opposed to the teaching of Spanish. Perhaps he is opposed only with regard to the means, not in principle. They say that the incoming Rector is bringing with him plans for the reform of the educational system. Wait a while; give time to Time, study, the examinations are coming, and, what the devil, you already speak Spanish so well, you express yourself so fluently, why look for trouble? What good will it do you to have special classes in Spanish? I am sure Father Florentino will share my views. Give him my best regards.'

'My uncle,' replied Isagani, 'has always advised me to think of my neighbour as much as myself. I did not come for myself; I came in the name of those who do not enjoy my advantages.'

'Oh, the devil take it! Let them do what you have done; let them scorch their eyebrows over the midnight oil; let them grow bald as I have done learning whole paragraphs by heart. For I believe that if you know Spanish it is because you have studied it; you are not from Manila, and your parents are not Spanish. Well, let them study it as you have studied it, and let them do what I have done. I have been a servant of the friars; I have cooked their chocolate and, while I was stirring it with my right hand, I was holding a grammar in my left; I learnt, thank God, without the help of teachers or academies or government permits. Believe me, he who wants to learn, learns and learns well.'

'But how many among those who want to learn become what you have become? One in ten thousand, and even then!'

'Pshaw, and why more?' the old man answered with a shrug. 'There are already too many lawyers, so many that some are happy to be clerks. Physicians? They insult, calumniate and fight one another over a patient. Arms, sir, sturdy arms for agriculture, that is what we need!'

Isagani realized that he was losing his time but wanted to make his point.

'No doubt,' he answered. 'There are already many physicians and lawyers although I would not say there are too many of them for we have towns that have none at all. Perhaps there is more quantity than quality. But since it is impossible to stop the young from studying, and here there are no other careers open to them, why let them waste their time and effort? If the deficiencies of the educational system do not prevent many of them from becoming physicians and lawyers in the end, why not try to make them good lawyers and good physicians? And for all that, even if it is planned to give this country an agricultural economy, to make us a nation of hewers of wood and carriers of water and to condemn all intellectual activity, I see nothing wrong in training these farmers and peasants, in giving them at least the skills that will enable them to improve themselves and to improve their work, that will allow them to understand many things which now they do not.'

'Nonsense, nonsense,' cried the lawyer, waving his hands as if to drive away such thoughts. 'One does not need such rhetoric to get the harvest in! Dreams, illusions, ideologies! Come now, do you want some good advice?'

He rose and placed a hand affectionately on Isagani's shoulder.

'I shall give it to you, and it is very good advice, because I can see you are clever and it will not be wasted. You are studying Medicine? Well, limit yourself to studying how to apply plasters and leeches, and never try to improve or worsen the lot of your fellows. When you get your degree, marry a rich and pious girl, try to give good prescriptions and equally good bills, and pay no attention to anything that has to do with the state of the nation; hear Mass, go to Confession and Communion with the rest; and you shall see how grateful you shall be to me, if I am still alive to see you. Always remember that charity begins at home; man, as Bentham says, should not seek on earth more than the greatest happiness for himself; if you go in for Quixotic enterprises you shall have neither career nor wife; you shall be nothing. They will all leave you in the lurch and your own countrymen will be the first to laugh at your candour. Believe me; you will remember me and say I was right when your hair is as white as mine!'

The old lawyer stroked his grey hair with a melancholy smile.

'When my hair is as white as that, sir,' replied Isagani just as sadly, 'and, looking back at the past, I should see that I have worked for myself alone, without doing what I very well could and should have done for the country which made me all that I am, for my fellow citizens who helped me to make a living, then, sir, each and every one of those white hairs would be a thorn in my head and, far from being proud, I would be ashamed of them!'

Having said this he bowed and left.

The astonished lawyer remained motionless where he stood, listening to the retreating footsteps. Then he seated himself again murmuring:

'Poor boy! I too once thought like that! Don't we all wish we could say that we have done something for the country and have dedicated our lives to the good of others! Laurels steeped in aloes, withered leaves hiding thorns and worms! That is not life; it does not fill one's stomach or win preferments. Laurels make an indifferent sauce, they do not give peace of mind or win lawsuits; on the contrary. Each country has its own morals as it has its own climate and endemic diseases different from those of other countries.'

He added:

'Poor boy! Perhaps if everyone thought and acted like him... But poor chap! Poor Florentino!'

16 • *A Chinaman's Woes*

THAT night Quiroga the Chinaman, who was hoping to open a consulate for his country in Manila, was giving a dinner at his residence which was located on top of his great shop on the Escolta. His party was very well attended and had drawn friars, bureaucrats, officers, merchants, all his customers, partners and patrons; for his shop supplied the parishes and convents with all they needed, allowed all government employees to open accounts, and was staffed by loyal and active attendants who were eager to please. The friars themselves were not above spending hours in his shop, sometimes in full view of the public, and at other times in inner chambers in agreeable company.

The main reception room had an air all its own that night. It was full of friars and bureaucrats, seated on cane-bottomed chairs or marble-topped stools of dark wood from Canton, playing three-handed ombre at small square tables in front of them, or making conversation in the bright light cast by gilt lamps or the more subdued one from Chinese lanterns ornately decorated with long silken tassels. The walls were covered with a lamentable confusion of delicate blue landscapes painted in Canton and Hong Kong, loud chromos of odalisques and half-naked women, and lithographs of effeminate Christs and the deaths of the Just Man and the Sinner produced by Jewish publishing houses in Germany for sale in Catholic countries. Nor were there lacking Chinese prints on red paper depicting a seated man of venerable aspect, smiling serenely, and behind him an ugly attendant, fearsome, diabolical, menacing, armed with a broad-bladed spear: some of the natives knew him as Mahomet, others as St James, for no known reason; nor could the Chinese themselves give any clear explanation of this popular dual personality. The popping of champagne corks, the clink of glasses, laughter, cigar smoke, and a certain smell peculiar to Chinese houses — a mixture of exotic perfume, opium and preserved fruit — completed the ensemble.

Dressed as a mandarin with a blue-tasselled cap Quiroga strolled from one room to another, erect and grave, although not without alert glances here and there as if to make sure that nobody pocketed anything. In spite of this instinctive distrust he exchanged hand-clasps with all and sundry, greeted some with a courteous and deferential smile, others with a protective air, and still others with certain contempt that seemed to say:

'I know, you come not for me but for my dinner.'

And Quiroga had every reason to think so. The stout gentleman who now sang the praises of his host and spoke of the advisability of opening a Chinese consulate in Manila, suggesting at the same me that the post could not be filled by anyone other than Quiroga, was the same Mr González who under the pen-name of Pitilí attacked Chinese immigration in the press. Another, well on in years, who was peering at the furniture, the lamps and the paintings with grimaces and exclamations of scorn, was Don Timoteo Peláez, Juanito's father, a merchant who usually clamoured against the Chinese competition that was ruining his business. Still another, dark slender man with lively eyes and a bleak smile, had gained fame in the affair of the Mexican pesos which had so discomfited a protégé of Quiroga; he was a bureaucrat who had the reputation in Manila of being a deep one. A fourth, frowning over unkempt moustaches, was a government official who was considered to be the worthiest of office because he had the courage to criticize the deals in lottery tickets between Quiroga and a lady in the highest social circles. Indeed one-half, if not two-thirds, of the lottery tickets were finding their way to China and the few that were available in Manila could not be bought without a premium. This worthy bureaucrat was sure that he would some day win the first prize and was infuriated by the thought of being frustrated by such dodges.

The dinner was coming to an end. Snatches of toasts, bellows of laughter, interruptions, guffaws reached the reception room from the dining-room; the name of Quiroga was heard again and again coupled with the words 'consul', 'equality', 'rights'.

The host did not eat European food and had confined himself to drinking a glass or two with his guests, assuring them that he would join at table those who could not be accommodated at the first serving.

Simoun had already had his dinner at home and was conversing in the reception room with a number of merchants who were complaining about the state of business; nothing was going well, trading was at a standstill, European exchange rates were exorbitant; they were asking the jeweller's advice or suggesting ideas to him in the hope that he would pass them on to the Governor-General. But to every remedy they put forward Simoun replied with a sardonic and ruthless smile. 'Nonsense!' Finally one of them lost his temper and asked Simoun for his own opinion.

'My opinion?' he asked. 'Find out why other countries prosper and do the same.'

'And why do they prosper, Mr Simoun?'

Simoun gave a shrug and did not answer.

'The port works!' sighed Don Timoteo Peláez, 'What a burden for business, and yet they're never finished! As my son says, it's a web of Penelope, woven and unwoven. And then the taxes!'

'You are one to complain!' he was reminded. 'The General has decreed the demolition of all houses of light materials, just now when you happen to have a shipment of galvanized iron sheets!'

'Yes,' agreed Don Timoteo, 'but what that decree has cost me! And then again the demolition will not take place for a month, until Lent, and by then other shipments may come in. I would have wanted the houses to be pulled down straight away but... Besides, how can those poor devils buy anything from me? One is poorer than the next.'

'You could always buy the houses for a song.'

'And then get the decree revoked and sell them at twice what you paid for them. Now there's a good business!'

Simoun smiled coldly and, catching sight of Quiroga, left the complaining businessmen to greet the future consul. The latter lost his self-satisfied expression as soon as he saw the jeweller, took on one more like that of the businessmen, and gave a deep bow.

Quiroga held the jeweller in high esteem not only because he was known to be very rich but also because of the confidential connexion he was said to have with the Governor-General. It was said that Simoun supported the aspirations of the Chinese and was in favour of the consulate; a certain anti-Chinese newspaper, in a celebrated controversy with another which favoured the pig-tailed gentry, had made certain references to Simoun under cover of many circumlocutions, indirect allusions and suppressed phrases. Persons of the utmost prudence added with sundry winks and mumbles that the Commander-in-Chief was being advised by his Grey Eminence to make use of the Chinese to humble the stubborn dignity of the natives.

'To keep a people in submission,' he was said to have advised, 'there is nothing like humiliating and debasing them in their own eyes.'

A suitable opportunity had soon presented itself.

The guild of the halfbreeds and the guild of the natives had always kept vigilant eyes on each other, devoting their energy and their fighting spirit to the indulgence of mutual suspicions and distrusts. One day at Mass it occurred to the leader of the natives, an extremely thin man whose pew was on the right side of the nave, to cross his legs, thus assuming a nonchalant posture that enabled him to exaggerate the size of his calf and show off his elegant boots. The leader of the halfbreeds, who was in the pew across from him, had bunions and moreover was too fat and had too great a belly to be able to cross his legs, and so had taken to spreading his legs wide apart and thrusting forward his paunch, which was encased in an unpleated waistcoat and adorned with a beautiful gold chain with diamonds. The two factions caught on and battle was joined. At the next Mass all the halfbreeds, even the thinnest, developed paunches and spread their legs as wide apart as if they had been on horseback. All the natives for their part were determined to cross their legs, even the fattest, and there was one headman who ended up on his ear. The watchful Chinese thereupon adopted their own posture; they seated themselves as in their shops, one leg tucked in under them, and the other dangling free. There were protests, memoranda, investigations; the municipal police stood at arms, ready for a civil war; the parish priests were in the best of spirits; the Spaniards were hugely amused and made money at everyone's expense. Then the Governor-General resolved the conflict by decreeing that all should sit as the Chinese did because the Chinese paid the most money although they were not the most devout Catholics. The halfbreeds and the natives found themselves in difficulties because, having narrower trousers, they could not imitate the Chinese; but to make the purpose of humiliating them even plainer the decree was enforced with all pomp and circumstance, the church being surrounded by a Cavalry squadron while inside the sweating faithful complied. The affair reached Parliament but there it was reiterated that the Chinese, because they paid, could impose their standards on others, even in religious ceremonies, and even if afterwards they should apostatize and make a mockery of Christianity. The natives and the halfbreeds, for their part, accepted the situation and learned not to lose their time in such trivialities.

Quiroga with his most deferential smile was flattering Simoun in pidgin; his voice was oily, his bows successive, but the jeweller cut him short with a brusque question:

'Did she like the bracelets?'

At this question Quiroga's animation vanished like a dream, his voice turned from a caress to a keening and, bowing even lower and joining his hands at the fingertips before his brow in a Chinese gesture, he moaned:

'Ah, Mr Simoun, such losses! I ruined!'

'What's this, Quiroga? Losses? Ruined? With so much champagne and so many guests?'

Quiroga closed his eyes and made a grimace. The events of that afternoon, the affair of the bracelets, had ruined him. Simoun smiled. When a Chinese merchant complains it is because everything is going well for him; when he pretends that nothing could be better it is because he foresees bankruptcy and is about to run out of the country.

'You have no idea, my losses! I ruined, I finished, Mr Simoun!'

The Chinese, to make his situation even clearer, illustrated it with a gesture of complete collapse.

Simoun felt like laughing at these antics but he restrained himself and explained that he knew nothing, absolutely nothing, of what had happened.

Quiroga took him to another room, locked the door carefully, and explained the reason for his woe.

The three diamond bracelets which he had taken on approval from Simoun, presumably to show to his wife, had not really been for her, a native woman of no importance locked up in her room like a Chinese; they had been intended for a beautiful and enchanting lady, the friend of a powerful gentleman whose influence Quiroga needed in a certain business deal from which he hoped to make a net profit of six thousand pesos. Knowing nothing of feminine tastes and wanting to make a grand gesture he had asked the jeweller for his three best bracelets, each of them costing three or four thousand pesos. Then, with an air of candour and with his most wheedling smile, he had asked the lady to choose the one she liked the best; she, even more ingenuous and accommodating, had declared that she liked all three and had kept them all.

Simoun exploded with laughter.

'Ah, gentleman, I lost, I ruined!' the Chinese cried, slapping his face lightly with his slender hands.

The jeweller laughed on.

'Oh, what a naughty lady! Maybe not a lady!' the Chinese continued, shaking his head disconsolately. 'What, no shame? Maybe I am Chinese but I am also people! Ah, maybe not a lady, even a cigar-maker has more shame!'

'You were had,' Simoun chortled, patting Quiroga's belly, 'you were had!'

'And all people borrow money and never pay, what's the matter?' and he counted them off on his long-nailed fingers: 'Government official, army officer, lieutenant, soldier; ah, Mr Simoun, I lost, I ruined!'

'Come now, don't complain so much,' said Simoun. 'I have saved you from many officers who asked you for money. I lent them the money myself so they wouldn't bother you even though I knew they could not pay me back.'

'But, Mr Simoun, you only lend to officers, I lend to girlfriends, wives, I lend to sailors, every peoples...'

'Well, you'll get your money back sooner or later.'

'Money back? Ah, maybe you not know. Money lost gambling, never come back. Better you, you have consul, can collect; I have no consul.'

Simoun was turning something over in his mind.

'Listen, Quiroga,' he said with an air of absent-mindedness, 'I can take care of collecting what these officers and sailors owe you. Let me have their promissory notes.'

Quiroga moaned that they never signed anything.

'Well, then, whenever they come to you for money, send them to me. I want to save you the trouble.'

Quiroga thanked him effusively but soon returned to his lamentations over the bracelets:

'Even cigar-maker, even cigarette-girl has more shame!'

'Good Lord,' exclaimed Simoun, his eyes on the Chinese's face, 'it just so happens that I need the money and I thought you could pay me now. But there is a way out of everything and I don't want you to go bankrupt over such a trifle. Come now, do me a favour and I'll take seven instead of the nine thousand you owe me. You can get anything you want through Customs: lamps, ironware, chinaware by the crate, copper, Mexican pesos—you even supply the convents with arms, don't you?'

The Chinese nodded but added that he had to give a lot of bribes. 'I give everything to the friars.'

'Well, look here,' Simoun continued in a whisper. 'I want you to get through Customs some crates full of guns which have arrived tonight and I want you to keep them in your warehouse; I cannot keep them all in my house.'

Quiroga took alarm.

'Don't worry. You are not running any risks. These guns are to be planted in certain houses from time to time; then there will be searches, many will be thrown in gaol, and you and I can make a lot of money to get them out again. Understand?'

Quiroga hesitated; he was afraid of firearms. He kept an unloaded revolver in his desk which he never touched except with his face turned away and his eyes closed.

'If you can't do it I shall go to someone else, but then I shall be needing my nine thousand pesos to grease palms and keep eyes shut.'

'All right, all right,' Quiroga finally agreed. 'But you get many peoples in gaol, you make searches soon, eh?'

When Quiroga and Simoun returned to the reception room they found those who had finished dinner; they were engaged in lively discussions, the champagne had loosened their tongues and heated their brains, and they were speaking freely.

A group composed of a number of government officials, some ladies and Don Custodio was talking of a commission sent to India to make a study of army boots.

'And who are on the commission?' asked a prominent lady.

'A colonel, two other officers, and His Excellency's nephew.'

'Four?' asked a bureaucrat. 'What a commission! What happens if they disagree? Are they at least competent?'

'That is exactly what I said,' a colleague added. 'I said there should be a civilian on the commission, someone without military prejudices, a shoemaker for example.'

'That's it,' an importer of shoes agreed, 'but it wouldn't have done to send a native or a Chinese, and the only Spanish shoemaker asked for such allowances...'

'But why make a study of boots at all?' asked an elderly lady. 'Surely not for the benefit of the Spanish artillerymen, and as far as the natives are concerned they can go barefoot as they do in their towns.'

'Exactly, and the Treasury would save money,' added a widow who was unhappy about her pension.

'But look here,' replied a friend of the officers on the commission, 'while it is true that many natives go barefoot in their towns, although not all of them, an army march is not the same as walking about when one pleases; one cannot choose the hour or the way to be taken, one cannot rest when one wishes. Consider, ma'am, that under the noonday sun you could bake bread on the ground; try to march on sand, on rocks, with the sun on your head and your feet burning, and bullets to face...'

'A matter of getting used to it.'

'Like the donkey who was trained not to eat! In the present campaign in the south the greater number of our casualties have been due to foot injuries. Remember the donkey, ma'am, the donkey!'

'Dear boy,' countered the widow, 'consider for your part the amount of money that will be spent on these boots. It would be enough to give many widows and orphans the pensions necessary to maintain our prestige. Oh, do not smile, I am not speaking for myself; I have my pension, although it isn't much, very little indeed compared with the services rendered by my poor husband; I speak of others who are living in misery; it is not fair that, after so much pleading for them to come and after coming all this way across the seas, they should end up by starving to death. What you have said about the native soldiers may be true but I have been here more than three years and I still have to see one of them limping.'

'I quite agree,' said the widow's neighbour, 'why give these natives shoes when they were born barefoot?'

'Why give them shirts?'

'Or trousers?'

'Fancy how much we can save with a stark naked army!' the defender of the soldiers concluded.

An even more heated discussion was taking place in another group. Ben Zayb was orating and declaiming, interrupted as usual at every step by Father Camorra. The journalist-friar, for all his awe of the monkish cowl, never hesitated to tangle with Father Camorra whom be considered a simple-minded semi-friar; thus he contrived to give himself an air of intellectual freedom and to refute the gibes of those who called him Father Ybañez. On the other hand Father Camorra liked his adversary who was the only one to take seriously what he called his reasoning.

It was a question of magnetism, spiritualism, magic, and the words flew through the air, thrown and caught like jugglers' knives and balls.

A great deal of attention had been aroused by a mummified human head, inaccurately described as a sphinx, which was being exhibited at that year's fair in the suburb of Kiapo by an American, one Mr Leeds. Huge wall posters, sombre and mysterious, excited general curiosity in this exhibition. Ben Zayb, Father Camorra, Father Irene and Father Salví had not yet seen it; only Juanito Peláez had been to see it one night and now he was telling the group how impressed he had been.

Ben Zayb, in his capacity as a journalist, sought a natural explanation for the phenomenon, Father Camorra spoke of the Devil, Father Irene smiled, Father Salví was grave.

'But, Father, the Devil doesn't bother with us any more. We are more than sufficient to damn ourselves!'

'There can be no other explanation...'

'But science...'

'Science again, for Heaven's sake!'

'But listen, let me prove it to you. It is all an optical illusion. I have not seen the head myself and I don't know how it is shown to the public. The gentleman here,' and he turned to Juanito Peláez, 'tells us that it is not at all like the usual "talking head". All right. But the principle is the same; it is all an optical illusion; now wait a minute; you place a mirror thus, another one behind it, the image is reflected; I say it is purely an experiment in Physics.'

He took down a number of mirrors from the walls, arranged and re-arranged them, tilted them and, though failing to get the desired effect, concluded:

'As I have said, nothing more or less than an optical illusion.'

'What mirrors are you talking about? Juanito tells us that the head is inside a box which is placed on a table. I see in this a spiritualistic trick, these spiritualists always use tables; and I think that Father Salví, in his capacity as ecclesiastical governor, should ban the exhibition.'

Father Salví was silent, neither agreeing nor disagreeing.

'If you really want to know whether it is the work of the Devil or it is all done with mirrors' suggested Simoun, 'the best thing to do is to go and see this famous sphinx.'

The suggestion seemed to be sensible and was adopted although Father Salví and Don Custodio showed a certain reluctance. Go to the fair, mix with the people, and look at sphinxes and talking heads! What would the natives say? They might take Father Salví and Don Custodio to be men like themselves with the same passions and weaknesses. Then Ben Zayb, with his newspaper man's wits, promised to ask Mr Leeds to keep out the public while their party was in his booth; they were doing him enough of an honour by seeing his show for him to refuse, and surely he would not even charge them the admission fee. To justify this Ben Zayb said:

'You can imagine what would happen if I were to expose how it is all done with mirrors before an audience of natives! I would be snatching the bread from the poor American's mouth!'

Ben Zayb was very scrupulous.

About twelve of Quiroga's guests went off, among them Don Custodio, Father Salví, Father Camorra, Father Irene, Ben Zayb and Juanito Peláez. Their carriages left them at the entrance of the Kiapo square.

17 • *The Kiapo Fair*

IT was a beautiful night and the square was full of life. Tempted by a refreshing breeze and a splendid January moon the people crowded into the fair to see, be seen, and amuse themselves, cheered and stimulated by the twinkling lanterns and by the music that came from the peep-shows of scenes from various parts of the world.

Long lines of stalls, glittering with tinsel and coloured decorations, displayed pyramids of balls, false faces strung together through the eyes, tin toys—miniature trains, carts, Mexican horses, carriages, steamships with tiny boilers, table services for Lilliputians, diminutive Christmas cribs, foreign dolls, blonde and beaming, and—like little ladies beside these gigantic children—native dolls, serious and pensive of aspect. The beating of children's drums, the tootling of tin horns, the heaving music of accordions and steam-organs combined in a carnival concert, and through it all the crowds came and went, shoving, stumbling, eyes on the stalls so that the collisions were not only frequent but also uproarious. The coachmen had to hold their horses back, shouting incessantly for the right of way among the government employees, military men, friars, students, Chinese, girls with their mothers and their aunts, all exchanging greetings winks and more or less cheerful comments.

Father Camorra was in seventh Heaven, there were so many pretty girls; he kept stopping, turning round, nudging Ben Zayb, clicking his tongue, swearing and asking: 'What about that one, you pen-pusher? And that one? And look at that one, what do you say?' He was so happy he allowed himself an intimate familiarity with his former antagonist; he drew a number of glances from Father Salví, but little did he care for Father Salví, and he winked at the girls or threw them roguish looks or pretended to stumble to graze against them.

'By golly,' he asked himself, 'when shall I be parish priest of Kiapo?'

Suddenly Ben Zayb let loose an oath, started, and rubbed his arm; Father Camorra had pinched him in a climax of enthusiasm. A dazzlingly beautiful girl was coming towards them, followed by the admiring stares of the whole square, and Father Camorra, bursting with concupiscence, had taken Ben Zayb's arm for hers.

It was that belle of belles, Paulita Gómez, escorted by Isagani and chaperoned by Doña Victorina; the girl was radiantly lovely and at her approach steps faltered, heads turned, tongues were silenced, and eyes lighted up, while Doña Victorina received deferential greetings.

Paulita wore a richly embroidered native dress, different from the one she had had on that morning at the church of Santo Domingo. The airy and delicate cloth of pineapple fibre gave her head an ideal frame and the natives compared it to the moon in the midst of light white clouds. Her pink silk skirt, gathered by her slender hand in rich and graceful folds, lent stateliness to her body, which she held erect and whose proud movements, pivoting round her swan-like neck, suggested vanity triumphant and coquetry indulged. Isagani appeared to be ill at ease; he did not relish so many curious stares; they seemed to him to steal part of his sweetheart's beauty and her answering smiles had for him the flavour of infidelities.

When Juanito saw Paulita he bowed, his hunch even more pronounced than usual; Paulita returned his greeting negligently but Doña Victorina called him to her side. Juanito was her favourite; her niece preferred Isagani.

'What a gal, what a gal!' murmured Father Camorra almost beside himself

'Come, Father, pinch yourself and leave me in peace,' Ben Zayb said ill-humouredly.

'What a gal! And she has that student, that fellow who goes around pushing people, for a sweetheart!'

And he added after turning round once again to stare after her: 'She's lucky she's not in my parish!' He was sorely tempted to leave the party and follow her, and was dissuaded from doing so by Ben Zayb only with difficulty.

Paulita went on her way, her lovely profile turning here and there with an artless coquetry.

The party from Quiroga's house also went on, though not without heavy sighs from the friar-gunner, until they reached a crowded stall where room was quickly made for them.

It displayed locally made wooden figurines for sale, which depicted in all shapes and sizes the races, professions and distinctive types of the Archipelago: natives, Spaniards, Chinese, half-breeds, friars, seculars, government employees, town mayors, students, military men, etc. Whether it was because the sculptors found it easier to carve the folds of monkish habits or because the friars were most on their minds as a result of the part they played in Philippine society, figurines of friars predominated in the display, executed to perfection, and showing them in life's noblest moments, in contrast to the practice in Europe where they were depicted snoring beside wine-casks, playing cards, emptying glasses, caressing a wench's blooming cheek, and in general having a merry time. The friars of the Philippines were shown to be something quite different: neatly, even elegantly dressed, with tonsures smartly trimmed, serene and well-proportioned faces, contemplative looks, saintly expressions, a touch of pink in the cheeks, walking-sticks in hand, patent-leather shoes on the feet—one felt like putting them under glass and falling on one's knees before them. Instead of the symbols of gluttony and lust put in the hands of their brethren in Europe, the Manila friars were given a book, a crucifix, a martyr's palm; instead of being shown bussing the simple peasant girls, they were seen gravely giving their hands to be kissed by children or even by grown-up men, bent low and almost on their knees; instead of the bursting larder and refectory, their theatres of action in Europe, the friars of Manila were shown in the chapel and in the study; and, while in Europe the friar was shown as a mendicant going from door to door on a donkey, stretching out a sack for alms, the Philippine friar was depicted as showering gold on the poor natives.

'Look, there's Father Camorra!' exclaimed Ben Zayb, who was still under the influence of Quiroga's champagne.

He pointed to the figure of an ascetic friar meditating at a desk, his head resting on one hand, apparently composing a sermon under the light of a lantern.

The contrast raised a laugh.

Father Camorra, who had already forgotten Paulita, did not miss the point and asked in turn, bursting into his clown's guffaw:

'And whom does this resemble, Ben Zayb?'

The figurine was that of a one-eyed dishevelled old woman, squatting on the floor like an Indian idol, ironing some clothes. The steam-iron was well imitated in copper with coals made from tinsel and twists of grimy cotton for wisps of smoke.

'Hey, Ben Zayb, don't you think the fellow who thought this up was a clever one?' the chortling Father Camorra insisted.

'But I don't see the point,' said the journalist.

'By golly, don't you see it's labelled *The Philippine Press?* That iron the old woman is using is called a press here.'

Everyone laughed and Ben Zayb joined in good-naturedly.

Two Constabulary soldiers, labelled as such, were shown in another tableau standing behind a man bound with heavy chains and with his face covered with a hat apparently condemned to death: it was entitled *The Land of Abaka.*

Many in the party had faults to find in the stall's display of figurines. They spoke of the rules of artistic proportions; one pointed out that a certain figure did not have seven heads, that its face was short of one nose, having only three, all of which puzzled Father Camorra, who did not know that the classical human figure was supposed to be seven times the length of the head, and the human face four times that of the nose; another critic insisted that the figurines of natives were too well built to be true to life; a third wondered whether it was sculpture or merely carpentry; everyone had something to say and Father Camorra, who did not want to be left behind, ventured the opinion that each figurine should have at least thirty legs. If the others wanted more noses, why should he not ask for more thighs? They were all then and there embarking on a general discussion of whether or not the native had any artistic abilities and whether or not art should be encouraged among them, when Don Custodio cut it short by declaring that the natives certainly had artistic abilities but that they should dedicate themselves exclusively to carving images of saints.

'Anyone would say this Chinaman is Quiroga,' said Ben Zayb, who seemed full of sallies, 'but, looking at it well, I would say it looks more like Father Irene.'

'And what do you say to this British Indian? It looks like Simoun!'

There was fresh laughter. Father Irene rubbed his nose.

'True, quite true, Simoun to the life!'

'But where is Simoun? Simoun must buy it.'

Simoun had vanished; nobody had seen him.

'By golly,' said Father Camorra. 'What a tightwad! He's probably afraid we'll ask him to pay the admission fees at Mr Leeds's show.'

'Nothing of the sort,' replied Ben Zayb. 'He just doesn't want to be embarrassed. He probably knows that we are going to show up his friend Mr Leeds and he wants no part in it.'

So, without buying the smallest figurine, they left the stall and went to see the famous mummy.

Ben Zayb offered to take the whole matter in hand; the American could not afford to offend a newspaper man who might hit back with a derogatory article.

'You'll see,' he said, 'how it's all done with mirrors. See here...'

He launched once more into a long explanation and this time, not having any mirrors at hand to fit into his theories, he involved himself in so many absurdities that he ended up by not understanding himself

'Anyway, you'll see it's all an optical illusion.'

18 • *An Optical Illusion*

MR LEEDS, a genuine Yankee dressed all in black, received them with great deference. He spoke Spanish fluently, having spent many years in South America. He raised no objections to the party's wishes; he said they were free to examine everything, before and after the show, and asked them only to keep calm while it was going on. Ben Zayb smirked, savouring in advance the American's embarrassment.

The chamber where the show would take place was hung with black and illumined by antique lamps fed with a mixture of spirits and water. A barrier draped in black velvet divided it in two almost equal parts: one was packed with chairs for the audience, the other was taken up by a platform carpeted in a geometric design on which was placed a table covered with a rich black cloth decorated with cabbalistic skulls. The setting was lugubrious and impressed the merry visitors whose jests were stilled and who now conversed in hushed tones; some tried to appear at ease but laughter was difficult. They all felt as if they had entered a house of the dead and a smell of incense and burning wax heightened the illusion. Don Custodio and Father Salví discussed in whispers the expediency of prohibiting exhibitions of this nature.

Ben Zayb, to cheer up the more impressionable and to put Mr Leeds in a predicament, said with a touch of insolence:

'Well, mister, since there is nobody else present and we are not natives who can be fooled, would you allow me to show them how the trick is done? We all know it is a mere optical illusion but since Father Camorra is hard to convince . . .'

He made as if to leap over the barrier without using the wicket provided for the purpose while Father Camorra was breaking out into loud protests, fearful that Ben Zayb would be proved right.

'Why not, sir?' answered the American. 'But please do not break anything. Agreed?'

The newspaper man was already on the platform.

'With your permission,' he said but, without awaiting it, afraid that Mr Leeds would not give it, he raised the black cloth and looked for the mirrors that he thought there must be between the legs of the table. Ben Zayb choked down an exclamation, stepped back and then moved his hands about under the table once more: there was nothing there. The table had three iron thin legs sunk into the floor.

The journalist looked round him as if searching for something.

'Where are the mirrors?' asked Father Camorra.

Ben Zayb looked again and again, felt the table over, raised the cloth once more, and from time to time raised his hand to his brow as if trying to remember.

'Have you lost something?' asked Mr Leeds.

'The mirrors, mister, where are the mirrors?'

'I don't know where you keep yours; I keep mine at my hotel. Were you wanting to look at yourself? You do look rather pale and worried.'

The American's nonchalant joking made a number laugh despite the impression made on them by their surroundings and Ben Zayb returned to his seat, much put out and muttering:

'It can't be; you'll see, he won't be able to do it without mirrors; he'll have to change the table later.'

Mr Leeds put back the cloth on the table and asked his distinguished audience:

'Are you satisfied? Can we proceed?'

'Well, he's a cool one,' remarked the widow.

'Ladies and gentlemen, please take your seats and have your questions ready.'

Mr Leeds went out through a door and after a short while returned with a dark wooden box, worm-eaten, and decorated with hieroglyphs of birds, mammals, flowers and human heads.

'Ladies and gentlemen,' said Mr Leeds with a certain solemnity, 'once visiting the great pyramid of Khufu, a pharaoh of the fourth dynasty, I came upon a sarcophagus of red granite left in a forgotten chamber. My joy was great for I thought to find a mummy of the royal family but to my disappointment, when I had opened the sarcophagus after great efforts, I only found this box which you are free to examine.'

He showed the box to those who were in the first row of chairs. Father Camorra drew back in distaste but Father Salví scrutinized the box as if fascinated by the sepulchral. Father Irene gave an intellectual smile; Don Custodio affected an air of gravity and superiority; Ben Zayb was still looking for his mirrors, they had to be there, for it was all done with mirrors.

'How it smells of dead things,' exclaimed a lady, fanning herself vigorously.

'Smells of forty centuries,' someone commented emphatically.

Ben Zayb forgot his mirrors and looked back to see who had turned the phrase; it was an officer who knew his Napoleon. Ben Zayb wished he had said it and, to turn another phrase which would at least annoy Father Camorra, said:

'Smells like a church!'

'This box, ladies and gentlemen,' the American continued, 'contained a handful of ashes and a fragment of papyrus on which some words had been written. You may look at it but I must ask you not to breathe on it heavily because if any part of the ashes is lost the mummy's head will appear mutilated.'

This rigmarole was pronounced with such gravity and conviction that it was slowly accepted, to such an extent that nobody dared to breathe as the box was passed around; Father Camorra, who had laughed to himself at the frightened looks of sinful women as he described from his pulpit in Tiani the tortures and sufferings of Hell, now covered his nose; and Father Salví, the very same Father Salví who, with lights, transparent figurines, spirit lamps and bits of tinsel, had contrived a representation of the souls in Purgatory on the main altar of a suburban church in order to wheedle alms and orders for Masses on All Souls' Day, now held his breath and, gaunt and wordless, stared at the handful of ashes with mingled fear and suspicion.

'Remember, man, that thou art dust!' murmured Father Irene with a smile.

'Oh, damn!' exclaimed Ben Zayb.

The canon had taken the words out of his mouth.

'Not knowing what to do,' Mr Leeds went on after carefully closing the box, 'I examined the papyrus and saw two hieroglyphs whose meaning was unknown to me. I deciphered the symbols and started to speak them out loud but I had scarcely pronounced the first word when I felt the box slipping through my hands as if borne down by an enormous weight and it slid along the floor defying all my efforts to lift it. My surprise turned to horror when upon opening the box I found in it a human head staring into my eyes with an extraordinary intensity. I was terrified, not knowing what to do before such a marvel, and I remained trembling with amazement for a considerable time. Recovering my wits and believing it was all an empty illusion I tried to compose myself by pronouncing the second word on the papyrus. No sooner had I said it than the box closed, the head disappeared, and in its place I found again the handful of ashes. Unwittingly I had discovered the two most powerful words in all Nature, the words of Creation and Annihilation, of Life and Death!'

He paused to measure the effect of his tale. Then, with grave and measured step, he went to the table, placing upon it the mysterious box.

'Mister, the cloth!' said the incorrigible Ben Zayb.

'Why not?' replied Mr Leeds agreeably.

Raising the box with his right hand, he lifted the cloth with his left, uncovering the table completely and showing it on its three legs. Then he placed the box on the centre of the table once again and approached his audience with great solemnity.

'This I have to see,' Ben Zayb was whispering to his neighbour. 'You'll see how he tries to get out of it now on some pretext.'

Everyone's attention was gripped amid the silence; the noise and bustle of the street could be heard distinctly but they were all in such a state of feeling that even a snatch of dialogue overheard from outside did not disturb them.

'Why also we cannot enter yet?' asked a woman's voice in Philippine Spanish

'Because, missis, the friars and the government officials only are seeing the head of the mummy,' explained a man's voice.

'So the friars are also curious!' said the woman's voice. 'And they do not want yet that we know when they are fooled. What, is this sphinx head a girl friend of the friars?'

In the midst of the profound silence and with a shaking voice the American continued:

'Ladies and gentlemen, with one word I shall now bring this handful of ashes to life and you shall speak with a being that knows the past, the present, and much of the future!'

The magician slowly raised a cry, first keening, and then more vigorous, a mixture of sounds, sharp like curses, hoarse like threats, that raised Ben Zayb's hair on end.

'Deremof!' cried the American.

The hangings in the chamber trembled, the lamps began to flicker and the table groaned. A faint moan rose from the box and all turned pale and exchanged uneasy looks; one terror-stricken lady felt a hot liquid run down the inside of her dress and clung to Father Salví.

Then the box opened by itself, displaying to the eyes of the audience a cadaverous head with long thick black hair. The mummy slowly opened its eyes and gazed out upon the audience. The eyes burned with great brightness, emphasized perhaps by the dark circles underneath them, and, as abyss calls to abyss, they fixed themselves on the deep-set eyes of Father Salví, which were now wide open as if they beheld some spectre. Father Salví was trembling.

'Sphinx,' said Mr Leeds, 'tell them who you are!'

In the deep silence a cold wind blew through the chamber, agitating the blue light of the sepulchral lamps; the more credulous could not repress a shiver.

'I am Imuthis,' answered the mummy in accents that were extraordinarily menacing and seemed to come from the depths of a tomb. 'I was born in the time of Amasis and was killed during the domination of the Persians while Cambyses was returning from his disastrous expedition into Inner Libya. I had come to finish my studies after long journeys through Greece, Assyria and Persia, and I was returning to my native land to live there until Thot should summon me before his dread tribunal. But, to my ruin, as I was passing through Babylon I discovered a terrible secret, the secret of the false Smerdis, the usurper, that daring magician Gautama who was governing through an imposture. Fearing that I might expose him to Cambyses, he decided to ruin me first, using as his tools the Egyptian priests who then ruled my country. There they were lords of two-thirds of the land, knowledge was their monopoly; they buried the people in ignorance and slavery, they brutalized it and made it ready to pass without repugnance from one tyranny to another. The invaders made use of these priests and, knowing their usefulness, protected and enriched them, and indeed some not only depended on their counsel but became their tools. The Egyptian priests lent themselves to the wishes of Gautama with all the greater willingness since they too feared that I would reveal them to the people as cheats. For their purposes they availed themselves of the passions of a young priest of Abydos who was reputed to be a saint...'

A painful silence followed these words: the mummy spoke of priestly intrigues and deceptions and, although these had apparently taken place in other times, the references to them annoyed the friars present, perhaps because they saw in the story an analogy with the actual situation in the Philippines. Father Salví seemed convulsed with terror, he moved his lips soundlessly and stared with fascination and with bulging eyes into the mummy's, heavy drops of sweat were forming on his bony forehead, but no one noticed, absorbed as they all were in their own emotions.

'And what did the priests of your country plot against you?' asked Mr Leeds.

The mummy gave a heartbroken groan and the spectators saw its fiery eyes grow dark and brimmed with tears. Many shuddered and felt their hair stand on end; this was no idle tale, no imposture; the mummy had truly suffered and was telling its own story.

'Ah,' it cried, shaking with grief, 'I loved a damosel, the daughter of a priest, pure as light, as the lotus when it first opens! The young priest of Abydos also wanted her for his own and raised tumult in my name, using some letters of mine which he had obtained from my beloved through craft and guile. The tumult broke out at the very moment when Cambyses was returning in a fury from the disasters of his unfortunate campaign. I was accused of rebellion, seized, and, after briefly escaping, killed in the Lake of Moeris... From eternity I saw the imposture triumph, and even now I see the priest of Abydos day and night harrying the virgin who has taken refuge in a temple of Isis on the isle of Philoe; I see him harry her even in the depths of the earth, turning her mad with terror and suffering, like a gigantic bat tormenting a white dove Oh priest, priest of Abydos, I have come back to life to reveal your infamy and after so many years of silence I call you sacrilegious, a calumniator and an assassin!'

A hollow sepulchral laugh followed these words while a strangled voice replied: 'No, mercy...!'

It was Father Salví who in a fit of terror was falling to the ground, his hands outstretched.

'What is the matter with Your Reverence? Are you ill?' asked Father Irene.

'It's the heat,' someone explained.

'It's the smell of death in here.'

'Assassin, calumniator, sacrilegious priest!' the mummy repeated. 'I accuse you, assassin, assassin, assassin!'

And the hollow laugh, cavernous, menacing, sounded once again as if the mummy, absorbed in the contemplation of the wrongs it had suffered, were blind to the bedlam in the chamber. Father Salví had fainted dead away.

'Mercy! He lives!' he had cried out before losing consciousness. He was as pale as a corpse. Some of the ladies present thought it their duty to follow suit and also swooned away.

'Father Salví is delirious!'

'I told him not to take the birds'-nest soup,' said Father Irene. 'It has unsettled him.'

'But he had nothing to eat,' objected Don Custodio with a shudder. 'I think he was hypnotized by the mummy's fixed stare.'

In its confusion the chamber resembled a hospital, a battlefield; Father Salví had all the appearances of a dead man and the ladies who had swooned, seeing that no one came to their rescue, decided to recover consciousness.

In the meantime the mummy had been reduced to dust and Mr Leeds was replacing the black cloth on the table and thanking his audience.

'This spectacle should be banned!' said Don Custodio as he left. 'It is highly immoral and irreligious!'

'And above all,' added Ben Zayb, 'because it is not done with mirrors.'

Before leaving the chamber, however, he made sure once more, leaped over the barrier, went to the table, and lifted the cloth: nothing, nothing as usual.

He was not, for all that, far off the mark. If he had examined them more closely he would have found grooves in the three table-legs, along which the mirrors, hidden under the platform, were raised and lowered. The box, when placed upon the table, pressed upon a spring which raised the mirrors into position; the latter remained invisible, thanks to the geometrical design of the carpet which they reflected. The box had a hollow bottom which fitted an opening on the table.

Ben Zayb remained baffled and the next day published an article on the occult sciences, spiritualism and such matters. An order of the ecclesiastical governor followed immediately, banning the show, but Mr Leeds had already left for Hong Kong with his secret.

19 • A Leave-Taking

PLÁCIDO PENITENTE left the classroom with his heart overflowing with bitterness, his eyes with tears. He was most worthy of his name as long as he was allowed to go his own way but when provoked he was a veritable raging torrent, a wild beast that could be stopped only by killing or being killed. All the insults which day after day had pricked his heart and had lain there afterwards like coiled serpents, now raised up their heads and shook with fury. His classmates' whistles were mixed in his mind's ear with the professor's sardonic phrases, the asides in pidgin, and he seemed to hear the sound of whiplashes in their laughter. A thousand plans for revenge rose in his mind, overtaking one another and then vanishing like figures in a dream. His self-love, unreasoning and unyielding, called on him to do something.

'Plácido Penitente, show them all that you have dignity, that you come from a brave and chivalrous province where insults can only be washed away with blood. You are from Batangas, Plácido Penitente! Vengeance, Plácido Penitente!'

He growled and ground his teeth, lurching against passers-by on the streets, on the Bridge of Spain, as if intent on picking a fight. On the bridge he caught sight of a carriage bearing the Vice-Rector Father Sibyla and Don Custodio, and he felt a sudden impulse to seize the friar and hurl him into the river.

He went along the Escolta and was tempted to trade blows with two Augustinians who, seated at the entrance to Quiroga's shop, were laughing and exchanging witticisms with other friars who, to judge from their gay banter and loud guffaws, seemed to be in a pleasant gathering inside. A little farther on two cadets barred the way along the pavement, chatting with a shop-clerk in shirtsleeves; Plácido Penitente headed towards them to force his way through but the cadets, who perceived his belligerent intentions and were themselves in a good humour, gave way. Plácido was at that time under the influence of what experts on the Malays know as *amok*.

As he walked to his lodgings in the house of a silversmith, he was trying to thresh out his thoughts, shaping a plan for revenge for which the first step would be to go home, there to show the friars, getting back at them some way, that they could not insult and make fun of a young man of spirit with impunity. He would write immediately to his mother, Cabesang Andang, to let her know what had happened and to inform her that his studies were now at an end for, while it was true that he could always take the year's course in the Jesuits' Ateneo, the Dominicans would most probably refuse to authorize the transfer and, even if they did, he would still have to return to their University the next year.

'They say we don't know how to take revenge,' he muttered to himself 'Let's see what they say when the lightning strikes them!'

But Plácido had not counted on what awaited him at the silversmith's house.

Cabesang Andang had just arrived from Batangas to do some shopping in the capital, visit her son, and bring him money, dried venison and silk handkerchiefs.

After the first exchange of greetings the poor lady, who had remarked from the beginning her son's sullen aspect, could refrain no longer from asking questions. At first she thought he could not be serious and was after something else; she smiled and tried to calm him down with talk of their sacrifices and privations. The son of Capitana Simona, she said, was enrolled in the seminary and was already giving himself in town the airs of a bishop; Capitana Simona already considered herself a veritable Mother of God for, of course, her son was going to be another Christ!

If the son gets to be a priest, joked Cabesang Andang, his mother will never pay us what she owes us—who would dare collect from her then?

But when she realized that Plácido was in dead earnest and saw in his eyes the signs of the storm that was raging inside him, she understood that he was telling her the truth. For a moment she was speechless and then she broke into lamentations:

'Alas, alas, and I promised your father to bring you up, to send you to school, to make you a lawyer! I denied myself everything so that you could go to school! Instead of playing cards at half a peso a point I never dared to play for more than a few centavos, and you have no idea in what company, their smells, the filthy cards! See how often my blouses have been mended! Instead of buying new ones I have spent the money on Masses and offerings to St Sebastian although I must say I am not too happy about it, the priest hurries over the Masses and St Sebastian is a new-fangled saint, he doesn't seem to know how to make miracles and is made of inferior wood. But oh, alas, what will your father say when I die and come face to face with him again?'

The poor lady mourned and wept; Plácido, ever more grim, sighed deeply.

'What will I get out of being a lawyer?'

'What will become of you?' his mother went on, clasping her hands. 'They will call you a *sabersib element* and hang you! How often have I told you to be patient, to be humble! I do not mean you to kiss the friars' hands, I know you are like your father who was very fastidious and could never endure eating European cheese — but we must suffer, keep our mouths shut, say yes to everything — what else are we to do? The friars are everything; if they say no, no one can be a lawyer or a physician; be patient, my son, be patient!'

Cabesang Andang strung out her lamentations; she did not ask him to be a partisan of the friars, she was not one herself; she knew well enough that,

for every good one, there were ten who squeezed money out of the poor and
sent the rich to exile; but one had to be silent, to suffer, to endure; and she
recalled how someone she knew, who hated the friars in his heart of hearts,
had nevertheless risen from being their servant to counsel for the Crown
because he had shown himself patient and humble; and another one who had
been only a poor sacristan but was now rich and could commit any outrage
he wanted because he could be sure of protection against the law, only because
he was humble and obedient and had married a pretty girl, to whose child
their parish priest had stood as sponsor...

Cabesang Andang was still going through her roster of 'humble and patient
Filipinos' and would have gone on to recall those who, lacking these qualities,
had been persecuted and exiled, when Plácido excused himself, left the house
and wandered about the streets.

He meandered through the suburbs of Sibakong, Tondo, San Nicholás,
Santo Cristo, absent-mindedly and in the worst of tempers, oblivious of
the sun and time; only when he felt hungry and realized that he had
given away all his money in subscriptions and contributions did he go
home. He did not expect to find his mother for she had the habit,
whenever she was in Manila, of going at-this time to a neighbouring
house where card games were always going on. But Cabesang Andang
was waiting for him to tell him her plans: she would have recourse to the
Augustinian Procurator to restore her son to the good graces of the
Dominicans. Plácido cut her short with a gesture:

'I'd rather throw myself into the sea; I'd rather turn bandit than go back
to the University!'

When his mother resumed her homily on patience and humility Plácido
went out again without having had a bite to eat and turned his steps
towards the quays.

The sight of a ship raising anchor for Hong Kong gave him an idea: he
would run away to Hong Kong, and make a fortune there with which to
fight the friars. He recalled a story he had heard about Hong Kong, which
was little more than gossip but to which his resentment now gave the
appearances of truth and indeed elaborated with other incidents of the same
nature: it was said that the pious congregation of a certain church had donated
for its services an altar-piece and matching candlesticks and candelabra, all
of solid silver; the friars had had an identical set of ornaments made in Hong
Kong out of silver plate and had melted down the real silver to coin Mexican
pesos. If the religious Orders took all their money to Hong Kong it must be

because business was good there and he could make his own fortune: this vague plan and the desire for a life of freedom nagged at him.

'I want to be free, I want to live like a free man!'

Night surprised him wandering about the waterfront district of San Fernando and, not having come across any friendly sailor, he decided to go home. But it was a beautiful night and the moon shone in the sky, turning the gloomy city into a fantastic fairyland, and he first went to the Kiapo fair. There he wandered aimlessly from stall to stall with no eyes for their contents, obsessed with 'living like a free man' and making a fortune in Hong Kong.

He was about to leave the fair when he saw Simoun the jeweller exchanging good-byes with a foreigner in English; at least it seemed to him to be English, for any language spoken in the Philippines by Europeans which was not Spanish had, to his mind, to be English; besides, he caught the word Hong Kong.

If only Simoun could introduce him to that foreigner who was obviously going to Hong Kong!

Plácido paused. He was acquainted with Simoun for the latter had been to his native town selling jewellery; once he had even accompanied the jeweller on a trip and Simoun had been most amiable, entertaining him with stories of university life in free countries: how different it all was there!

Plácido went after the jeweller.

'Mr Simoun, Mr Simoun!'

The jeweller was about to board his carriage but, recognizing Plácido, stopped.

'I should like to ask you a favour—let me have two words with you!'

Simoun made an impatient gesture which went unnoticed by the excited Plácido. The student told him briefly what had occurred and expressed a desire to go to Hong Kong.

'What for?' asked Simoun, looking fixedly at Plácido through his dark glasses.

Plácido did not answer and Simoun, raising his head and giving him his cold mirthless smile, said:

'Very well, come with me.' He directed his driver to take them to Iris Avenue.

Simoun remained wordless during the journey, as if absorbed in thoughts of great importance. Plácido, waiting to be spoken to, was equally silent and amused himself watching the people who had gone for a promenade in the moonlight: the street was full of young people, affianced or courting couples followed by wary mothers or aunts; groups of students in white which the moon turned whiter still; half-drunken soldiers in hackney-coaches, six to a vehicle, on their way to some nipa-thatched house of ill repute; children chasing one another and Chinese pedlars selling sticks of sugar-cane — all endowed by the moonlight with fantastical shapes and dreamy silhouettes. An orchestra was playing waltzes in a house along the way and he glimpsed a few couples dancing under the light of kerosene lamps: how tawdry it seemed in contrast with the spectacle in the street! He asked himself if moonlit nights in Hong Kong would be as poetical, as sweetly melancholy, as those in the Philippines and his heart was filled with sadness.

Simoun ordered his carriage to stop and they both alighted. At that moment Isagani and Paulita Gómez were passing by, whispering sweet nothings to each other, followed by Doña Victorina with Juanito Peláez, who was speaking in a loud voice, gesturing incessantly, and more hunched up than ever. Peláez passed by oblivious of his former classmate.

'There goes a happy man,' Plácido sighed, looking after the group which was now turning into shadowy silhouettes distinguished only by Juanito's arms which were twirling like a windmill.

'That is all he is good for,' Simoun muttered in turn. 'That is what our youth has come to!'

To whom did Plácido and Simoun refer?

The latter motioned to Plácido; they left the highway and entered a maze of alleys and pathways winding along a number of buildings; now they skipped from stone to stone to cross muddy puddles, now they bent down to slide under fences badly made and in even worse repair. Plácido was puzzled to find the rich jeweller so familiar with such places. At last they reached a large yard where there was a lone miserable hut surrounded by banana and palm trees. A number of bamboo scaffoldings and lengths of bamboo tubing made Plácido suspect that they were in the premises of a maker of fireworks.

'Oh, it's you, sir!'

A man came down immediately from the hut.

'Do you have the gunpowder?' asked Simoun.

'In sacks. I am waiting for the cartridges.'

'And the bombs?'

'All ready.'

'Very well, you must leave tonight and speak to the lieutenant and the corporal. Then go on straight away to Lamayan; there you will find a man in a boat; you shall say to him: "Cabesa", and he will answer "Tales". He must be here tomorrow. There is no time to lose!'

He gave the man a number of gold coins.

'What's up, sir?' asked the man in excellent Spanish. 'Is there anything new?'

'Yes. It must be done by next week.'

'Next week!' The unknown man was aghast. 'The suburbs are not ready. They are expecting the General to withdraw the decree. I thought everything would be left to the beginning of Lent!'

Simoun shook his head.

'We shall not need the suburbs. With Cabesang Tales's men, the dismissed guards, and one regiment, we shall have enough. We can't wait any longer; María Clara may be dead by then. Go at once!' The man obeyed.

Plácido had heard everything that had been said in this brief conversation and with a glimmering of understanding stared at Simoun with panic-stricken eyes. Simoun was smiling.

'Do you find it strange that this wretched native should speak Spanish so well? He was a schoolmaster who insisted on teaching his pupils Spanish and did not stop until he lost his job and was exiled as a disturber of public order and as a friend of the unfortunate Ibarra. I rescued him from exile, where he had nothing to do but prune coconut trees, and turned him into an expert technician in gunpowder.'

They returned to the avenue and went on foot to the suburb of Trozo. A Spaniard leaning on a crutch in the moonlight stood in front of a neat and cheerful little wooden house. Simoun approached him and the Spaniard tried to straighten himself up with a stifled groan.

'Be ready.'

'I always am.'

'For next week.'

'Already?'

'At the first cannon shot!'

Simoun moved away followed by Plácido who was beginning to wonder if it was all a dream.

'Are you surprised to see a Spaniard so young and so infirm? Two years ago he was as vigorous as you are but his enemies contrived to get him assigned to Balakbak in a labour battalion. You see him now racked with the rheumatism and the malaria that will bring him to an early grave. He was unfortunate enough to have a very beautiful wife...'

An empty rig passed by, Simoun stopped it, and had himself and Plácido taken to his house on the Escolta. The church clocks were ringing the time: it was half-past ten.

Two hours later a troubled and thoughtful Plácido left the jeweller's house.

He went down the Escolta, now almost deserted although the cafes were still quite lively. Now and again a carriage drove by at a fast pace, clattering along the cobblestones.

In a room in his house facing the Pasig Simoun stood at an open window and stared across the river at the Walled City with its roofs of galvanized iron glittering in the moonlight, and its church towers dismal, graceless and oppressive in the night's serenity. He had taken off his dark glasses; his white hair framed with silver his bronzed forceful face, now lighted faintly by a lamp whose flame flickered for lack of fuel. He did not seem to notice this and the thickening darkness but was lost in thought.

'Within a few days,' he said to himself, 'when this accursed city, the refuge of senseless arrogance and of the impious exploitation of the ignorant and the unfortunate, is burning at its four corners, and when violence rises in the suburbs and drives through terror-stricken streets my vengeful mobs, bred by folly and greed, then I shall breach the walls of your prison and snatch you from the clutches of fanaticism, and, sweet dove, you shall be a phoenix rising again from the burning ashes. A rebellion plotted by men in the shadows tore me from your side; another one will take me to your arms, will bring me back to life, and before that moon is full it will light the Philippines, scoured clean of their loathsome garbage!'

Simoun abruptly cut himself short. The voice of his conscience asked if he himself were not part of that filth, perhaps the most active poison, in the accursed city; and like the dead rising at the sound of the Last Trumpet a thousand bloody apparitions rose in answer to the cryptic question, wailing phantoms of murdered men, raped women, fathers torn from their families, the lowest passions stimulated and encouraged, virtue scorned. Something in Simoun rebelled for the first time in his criminal career; something in him protested for the first time since in Havana he had decided to fashion, through bribery and corruption, a man without faith, without patriotism and without conscience, a Governor-General who would be an instrument for his designs. He closed his eyes and stood motionless for some time; then he drew his hand across his brow, he would not listen to his conscience, he was afraid; he would not analyse himself, he had not the courage to look back on his past. What, to lose courage just when the time to act was so near, to lose conviction, to lose faith in himself! But the unhappy ghosts of those whose fates he had influenced continued to float before his eyes as if, rising from the glittering surface of the river, they had invaded his room, wailing and stretching out their arms to him, filling the air with reproaches and lamentations, threats and cries of vengeance, and he left the window and, perhaps for the first time in his life, trembled with fear.

'I must be ill, upset... Many hate me, many blame me for their misfortunes, but...'

He rose and went to the window again to cool his burning brow with the night breeze. The silver Pasig flowed beneath him, flecked with gleaming foam lazily swirling in the eddies of the current. The city stood on the farther shore and its dark walls, their meanness ennobled by the light of the moon, seemed to offer mysterious omens. Simoun shivered: he thought he saw before him the stern face of his father, dead in gaol, but dead in a good cause, and the face even more austere of the man who had died for Ibarra, believing that he would achieve the redemption of their native land.

'No, I cannot go back,' he exclaimed, wiping the sweat from his brow, 'the work has gone too far and its success will vindicate me. If I had behaved like you did I would have failed. Away with ideals and empty theories! The cancer can be extirpated only with fire and steel, crime must be punished. If the tool is bad, then let it be broken afterwards. I have thought it all out; this is only a passing fever, it is only natural for my will to weaken now. If I have done evil it was to do good, and the end justifies the means. I must not expose myself...'

With his brain awhirl he went to bed and tried to sleep.

The next morning Plácido listened to his mother's homilies humbly and with a smile on his lips. When she spoke of her plan to get the Procurator of the Augustinians to intercede on his behalf, he neither protested nor opposed her; on the contrary, he offered to speak to the Procurator himself to save his mother the trouble and urged her to return to the provinces as soon as possible, even that very day. Cabesang Andang asked him why.

'Because... because if the Father Procurator learns you are here he will do nothing before you send him a gift and commission several Masses.'

20 • *The Arbitrator*

FATHER IRENE was right; the question of the Spanish Academy, pending for so long, was nearing a solution. Don Custodio, the diligent Don Custodio, the most enterprising of all the arbitrators in the world according to Ben Zayb, had it in hand and spent his days going over the record, only to go to bed without having come to any decision; he rose the next day, went over the whole thing again until it was time to be back in bed; and so it went day after day. How the poor man worked, this most enterprising of all the world's arbitrators! He wanted to get out of the difficulty by pleasing everyone: the friars, the high official, the Countess, Father Irene, and his own liberal principles. He had gone to Mr Pasta for advice and Mr Pasta had left him bewildered and well-nigh senseless by advising a million contradictory and impossible courses of action; he had asked Pepay the dancer for her opinion and Pepay, who had no idea what it was all about, asked him for twenty-five pesos for the funeral expenses of an aunt of hers who had died suddenly for the fifth time, or perhaps it was, after further explanation, the fifth of her aunts to die; she had also wheedled him into giving a cousin of hers, who knew how to read, write and play the fiddle, a job in the Department of Public Works—all of which was far from calculated to inspire Don Custodio with the solution.

Two days after the events in the Kiapo fair Don Custodio was working as usual, going over the record without finding the happy way out. As he yawned, cleared his throat, smoked, and let his mind wander over Pepay's legs and pirouettes, those who so impatiently awaited his decision might well have wondered why Father Sibyla had suggested this distinguished personage to arbitrate such a thorny question and why he had been accepted by the other side.

Don Custodio de Salazar y Sanchez de Monteredondo, alias 'Authoritative Source', belonged to that class in Manila society that could not move a finger without being described in the newspapers as 'indefatigable', 'distinguished', 'zealous', 'diligent', 'profound', 'intelligent', 'well-informed', 'wealthy', as if they might be confused with others of the same name who were lazy and stupid. In any case there was no harm in it and the censors were not disturbed. The nickname 'Authoritative Source' had been given to him because of his friendship with Ben Zayb; when the latter, in two boisterous newspaper controversies in which he had been engaged for weeks and months, had discussed whether bowler hats, top hats, or the native helmet should be worn, and whether the plural of 'handwriting' was 'handwritings' or 'handswriting', he had invariably reinforced his arguments by quoting 'authoritative sources'; later it had transpired, for everything gets about in Manila, that this 'authoritative source' was no other than Don Custodio de Salazar y Sanchez de Monteredondo.

He had arrived in Manila at a very early age, with a good job which had

made it possible for him to marry a beautiful half-breed belonging to one of
the richest families in the capital. Since he had natural talent, nerve and self-
possession, he had known how to take advantage of his connexions, and with
his wife's money had gone into business, specializing in contracts with the
national and city governments. The upshot of it all had been his appointment
as a municipal councillor, then mayor, director of the Economic Association
of Friends of the Philippines, counsellor in the Office of Civil Administration,
president of the executive committee of the government pawnshop, director
of the Associated Charities, adviser of the Hispano-Philippine Bank, etc.,
etc. Nor were these etcetera of the usual type which come after a long
enumeration of titles; Don Custodio, for all that he had never laid eyes on a
treatise on hygiene, had served as vice-president of the Manila Board of
Health; although it must be added that of its eight members only one had to
be a physician, and there was no reason why he of all people should have
been that one. He had likewise been a director of the Central Committee on
Vaccination composed of three physicians and seven laymen, among them
the Archbishop and the Provincials of three religious Orders. He had been a
member of confraternities and arch-confraternities and, as has been remarked,
director-arbitrator of the inactive Supervisory Committee of Primary
Education. All of these provided more than sufficient reason for the
newspapers to bandy adjectives about him, whether he went on a trip or
merely sneezed.

Burdened though he was with so many offices Don Custodio was not like
those timid and lazy members of parliament content to snooze through
sessions and vote with the majority. The reverse of many European monarchs
who still carried the title of King of Jerusalem, Don Custodio made full use
of his titles and dignities, went in for ponderous frowns, resonant phrases
and portentous coughs, and often spent a whole session embroidering an
anecdote, sponsoring a project or duelling with some colleague who had
dared to tell him unpleasant truths. Although he was not yet forty he was
always talking of watching one's step, letting things ripen (adding under his
breath, fiddlesticks!), thinking it over, and going slowly: one had to consider
local conditions because the natives in their present state... because Spanish
prestige... because above all they were Spaniards... because Religion... In
Manila they still remembered the speech he had made when it had first been
proposed to light the streets with kerosene instead of coconut oil; far from
foreseeing in this innovation the ruin of the coconut oil industry, Don
Custodio had only espied the material advantages that might accrue to one

of his colleagues (Don Custodio was far-sighted indeed) and he had opposed the project with all the resources of his oratory, declaring the proposal far too premature and prophesying great social upheavals. No less memorable was his opposition to a serenade for old time's sake, which some of his colleagues wanted to give to an outgoing governor on the eve of his departure; Don Custodio, who was rather resentful because of certain disappointments, found a way to insinuate that the incoming governor was his predecessor's mortal enemy, which was enough to frighten off the would-be serenaders.

There came a time when he was advised to return to Spain for treatment of an affliction of the liver, and the newspapers spoke of him as of an Antaeus, the mythological Greek wrestler whose strength was invincible as long as he touched the earth; Don Custodio, it was inferred, likewise had need to touch his native soil in order to recover his vigour. But the Manila Antaeus instead found himself diminished and insignificant indeed in the Court of Madrid; he was nobody there and he missed the journalistic adjectives of which he had grown fond; he could not afford to mingle with the wealthy, he could not cut much of a figure in scientific circles and literary academies because he did not have the schooling for it, and he was such a priest-ridden reactionary that awhirl in social circles he was soon dizzy, distressed, baffled, unable to get anything straight except that this was a game where the cards were marked and the stakes were high. He missed his meek native servants who pandered to all his wishes and thought them preferable to anything in Madrid; winter placed him in the alternative of roasting himself or catching pneumonia, and he sighed for the Manila winters for which one needed only a scarf; in summer he missed his long-armed chair on which he could curl a leg while a servant fanned him; in brief, he was only one of many in Madrid and, for all his diamonds, he had once been taken for a yokel who did not even know how to walk properly, and another time for a 'get-rich-quick' adventurer from South America. His timidities were mocked and, when he refused to let himself be fooled by petty grafters, the latter shamelessly made him a figure of fun. Disappointed by the Conservatives, who did not take his advice seriously, as much as by the Radicals, who were emptying his pockets, he declared himself a Liberal and returned to the Philippines within the year, if not with a healthy liver, at least with new ideas.

But eleven months in the capital spent among cafe politicians, almost all out of office, the speeches he had caught here and there and this or that leading article in Opposition newspapers, the whole atmosphere of politics taken in earnest, ranging from the hairdresser's where the barber expounded his political programme between snips of his scissors to the great public dinners where the various shades of political opinion, the disagreements, dissidences, discontents, were poured forth in sonorous periods and slogans— all these impressions renewed themselves forcefully within him the farther he got from Europe, like seed that had not had a chance to sprout before because it had been sown among weeds, so that when his ship finally docked in Manila he felt a mission to regenerate the city, and indeed was moved by the noblest aims and the purest ideals.

During the first months after his return he could speak of nothing but the metropolis, of his good friends Minister So-and-so and former Minister Such-and-such, Congressman C., and B. the writer. There was no political development, no scandal at Court, whose smallest details he was not acquainted with; no public official, the secrets of whose private life he did not know; nothing happened that he had not foreseen; no reform was promulgated on which he had not been previously consulted. All this was spiced with sincerely indignant attacks on the Conservatives and praises of the Liberals, an anecdote here, a great man's catch-phrase there, together with tales, told with a reluctant air, of offers of office which he had declined so as to owe the Conservatives nothing. Such was his ardour in those first days that a number of those who gathered at the grocer's shop which he visited on and off for political discussions joined the Liberal Party: an infantry sergeant, retired, a harbour pilot who was also a rabid Carlist, a Customs-house officer, a bootmaker and saddler.

But for lack of both support and opposition Don Custodio's enthusiasm gradually petered out. He did not read the newspapers from Spain because they arrived in batches and bundles whose very sight made him yawn; the ideas he had picked up, all at secondhand, needed to be brushed up and their authors were not there to give speeches for, although there was gambling enough in the Manila clubs and as much sponging as in Court circles, speeches to keep alive political ideals were not allowed. Don Custodio, however, was not lazy, and he did more than wish, he acted. He foresaw that he would leave his bones in the Philippines and understood that his proper sphere of action was in this country; so he lavished his care on it and believed he could make it progressive with a series of the most peculiar reforms and projects. It was he who, having heard in Madrid that the streets of Paris had wooden pavements, an improvement not yet adopted in Spain, proposed that it be done in Manila by covering the streets with planks nailed together like the walls of a house. He it was who, deploring the accidents that overtook two-wheeled vehicles, argued that the best way to prevent these mishaps was to require all such vehicles to have at least three wheels. It was also he who, while vice-president of the Manila Board of Health, took it into his head to fumigate everything, even telegrams from places where epidemics were suspected. And it was he who, moved on the one hand by pity for the convicts who were put to hard labour under the sun, and on the other hand by the desire to save government funds spent on their clothing, proposed that they be clad in loin-cloths and put to work, not in the daytime, but at night. He was puzzled and enraged when these proposals were criticized, but he found comfort in the thought that an able man always had enemies, and took his revenge by attacking and rejecting whatever plans, good or bad, were presented by others.

Since he professed to be a Liberal he would, when he was asked what he thought of the natives, answer condescendingly that they were fit for mechanical work and the 'imitative arts' (by which he meant music, painting and sculpture), adding his usual reminder that one really got to know the natives only after many, very many years in the country. When, however, he heard that one of them had gained distinction in something that was not mechanical or 'imitative', say, in chemistry, medicine or philosophy, he would comment: 'Hmmm, he shows promise... He is not dumb at all!' and was sure that there was a great deal of Spanish blood in that particular native's veins. If despite all his good will he failed to find traces of this ancestry, then he sought a Japanese origin for it was then starting to be fashionable to attribute to the Japanese and the Arabs whatever good there might be in the Filipinos. To Don Custodio the native airs—the *kundiman,* the *Balitaw,* the *kumintang*—were Arab just like the alphabet of the ancient Filipinos, and he was sure of it although he did not know Arabic and had not in fact ever seen the old Filipino alphabet.

'Arabic, the most unadulterated Arabic,' he told Ben Zayb in a tone that brooked no contradiction. 'At best, Chinese.'

And he added with a meaningful wink:

'Nothing can be original, nothing should be allowed to be original, as far as the natives are concerned. Do you follow me? I have a great liking for them but one must not praise them for anything; that only encourages and spoils them.'

At other times he would say:

'I have a great passion for the natives, I have made myself their father and defender, but everything must be put in its proper place. Some are born to command, others to serve; of course, one cannot say this sort of thing out loud, although it is true enough, but it can be put into practice without talking too much about it. And look here, it can be done in little ways. When you want to rule a people you must convince them that they are fit only to be ruled; they will laugh the first day, they will protest on the second, on the third they will begin to doubt, and on the fourth they will be convinced. To keep the native docile one must din it into his ears day after day that he is, and convince him that he can do nothing about it. Anyway, what would it profit him to believe otherwise when it would only spoil him? Believe me, it is an act of charity to keep everyone in his place: that is how to keep order and harmony, that is the science of government.'

Don Custodio was no longer satisfied with the word 'art' when it came to his politics. And when he said 'government' he would stretch out his hand and lower it to the height of a man bent before him on his knees.

As far as religious ideas were concerned he prided himself on being a Catholic, very Catholic—ah, Catholic Spain, land of the Most Blessed Virgin! A liberal could and should be Catholic among a backward people who at the very least set themselves up idols and images; even so a mulatto passed for a white man among the blacks. For all that, he ate meat during Lent except on Good Friday; he never went to Confession, he did not believe in miracles or in the infallibility of the Pope, and, when he went to Mass, he went at ten o'clock or to the shortest one, the garrison Mass. In Madrid he had had unkind words for the religious Orders to keep in harmony with the prevailing atmosphere, and had dubbed them anachronisms, cried horror at the Inquisition, and told one or another dirty story revolving around friars' habits or rather friars without their habits, but when the conversation turned to the Philippines he would hem and haw and say that the country was subject to special circumstances. With a shrewd look he would again stretch out his hand and lower it to the peculiar height that has already been remarked.

'The friars are indispensable. They are a necessary evil.'

He was enraged when some native dared to doubt miracles or the infallibility of the Pope. All the torments of the Inquisition were not enough to punish such audacity.

If it was put to him that to rule or to live taking advantage of another's ignorance would be given a rather more unpleasant description and would be punished by the law if done to an individual rather than to a people, he would reply by pointing to other colonies.

'We can hold our heads up high,' he would say with his public voice. 'We are not like the English or the Dutch who have recourse to the lash to keep peoples in subjection. We have other means at our disposal, milder, surer: the healthy influence of the friars is superior to the English lash.'

This phrase of his caught on and for some time Ben Zayb repeated various versions of it, and with him all of Manila; intellectual Manila applauded it. The phrase reached the Court, it was quoted in Parliament and attributed to a 'long-time resident of liberal beliefs, etc., etc.' The friars, who found honour in the contrast and reinforcement for their prestige, sent him sacks of chocolate, gifts which were returned by the incorruptible Don Custodio whose civic virtue was promptly compared by Ben Zayb with that of Epaminondas, the ancient Greek general who was as famous for the purity and uprightness of his character as for the brilliance of his victories. Yet the modern Epaminondas wielded the lash in moments of anger and advised its use!

In those days the convents, fearing that he would make a recommendation in favour of the students, were renewing their gifts and he was in a greater predicament than ever: his reputation as a man of action was at stake. One afternoon, more than two weeks after the records of the petition had been turned over to him, he recalled that that morning the high official, after praising his zeal, had asked him how he was getting along with the case. Don Custodio had replied with a grave air of reticence, trying to give the impression that he had come to a decision; the high official had smiled, and now the memory of that smile haunted and annoyed him.

He yawned and, between yawns, at a moment when he was opening his eyes and closing his mouth, his eyes fell on a long row of red files arrayed in order in a magnificent mahogany bookcase. Each of them was labelled on the spine: *PROJECTS.*

For a while he forgot his worries and Pepay's pirouettes and considered that everything on those shelves had come out of his fertile brain in moments of inspiration. So many original ideas, so many sublime inspirations, so many remedies for the miseries of the Philippines! Ah, he was sure of immortality and the gratitude of the country!

Like an old roué who stumbles upon a musty bundle of old love-letters Don Custodio stood up and went to the bookcase. The first file, thick, swollen, overflowing, was labelled *PROJECTS Projected*

'No,' he murmured, 'this one has some excellent things in it but it would take a year to go over all of them.'

The second file, also quite full, was identified as *PROJECTS Under Study.*

Not this one, either!

Then came PROJECTS *Under Development* . . . PROJECTS *Submitted* . . .
PROJECTS *Rejected* . . . PROJECTS *Approved* . . . PROJECTS *Suspended* . . .
These last files hat little in them but the last had the least of all: PROJECTS
In Execution.

Don Custodio wrinkled his nose. What could there be in it? He had
forgotten what the file might possibly hold. A yellow sheet of paper peeped
out between the covers as if the file were showing him its tongue.

He took it out of the bookcase and opened it: the paper dealt with the
famous project for a School of Arts and Trades.

'What the devil!' he exclaimed. 'But the Augustinians have been put in
charge of this...'

Suddenly he slept his forehead and arched his eyebrows, success shining
all over his face.

'Now I have it,' he cried out with an oath. 'I've got my bloody
recommendation!'

'And snapping his oaths gaily about him he went to his desk and happily
picked up his pen.

21 • *Manila Characters*

THAT night there was to be a gala performance at the Variety Theatre.

The French operetta company of M. Jouy was opening in *Les Cloches de
Corneville* and would reveal to the public eye for the first time the charms
which the press had been proclaiming for days. It was said a number of the
actresses had lovely voices, figures lovelier still, and, if gossip was to be
believed, were even more loving than lovely.

By seven-thirty in the evening there was not a seat to be had, not even for
Father Salví himself who was dying for one; the queue even for the cheapest
seats was interminable; at the box-office brawls and quarrels broke out, there
were charges of subversion and race prejudice: but all this did not yield any
tickets. By a quarter to eight fabulous prices were being offered for the lower
boxes. The facade of the theatre, brilliantly lit and decorated with potted
plants and sprays of flowers at every door, drove late-comers to excited
exclamations and back-slapping. A great crowd bustled about, staring
enviously at the early-comers who were taking no chances of losing their

seats; speculative murmurs and then laughter greeted those who were disappointed and afterwards joined the curiosity seekers, content, since they could not enter, to look at those who could.

One man, however, stood aloof from all this bustle of curiosity. He was tall, thin, and walked slowly, dragging a stiff leg behind him. He wore a ragged coffee-coloured jacket and a grimy pair of check trousers that clung to his thin bony legs; a bowler hat so shattered that it had a rakish air covered his huge head, except for a few strands of hair, of a dirty grey that was almost blonde, long, and curling at the ends like a poet's locks. What was most striking about him was neither his clothes nor his beardless European face, but its deep red colouring which had won him the nickname of The Shrimp, by which he was generally known. He was a curious character: born of a distinguished family, he lived like a tramp, a beggar; Spanish by blood, he mocked the prestige of his race with his rags; he passed for a sort of reporter, and indeed he turned up, his grey eyes rather protruding, cold and thoughtful, wherever anything happened that might be news. How he lived was a mystery to most; nobody knew where he took his meals or had his bed; perhaps, like Diogenes, he lived in a tub.

The Shrimp did not now have his usual hard and indifferent expression, his eyes were illumined with a certain humorous pity. A tiny little old man greeted him gaily.

'Dear friend!' he cried out with a voice as hoarse as a frog's, jingling a fistful of silver pesos.

The Shrimp saw the money and shrugged his shoulders: what did he care?

The old man made a perfect contrast to him: short, almost dwarfish, he covered his head with a top hat that on him looked like a huge hairy caterpillar; he was lost in an enormous frock coat that was much too wide and long for him, but found himself at the end in a pair of trousers so short that they scarcely covered his calves: his torso was thus grandfather to his legs. His shoes were like gunboats; indeed they were a pair of sailor's boots that cried out against the top hat on his head with the stark protest of a nunnery beside a carnival. Where the Shrimp was red-faced, he was dark; the former, a Spaniard, had not a hair on his face; he, a native, had moustaches and a goatee, long, white and sparse. This man with the lively look was known as Uncle Kiko and, like his friend, made his living out of publicity: he made propaganda for the theatres and put up their bills and posters. He was perhaps the only native who could with impunity go on foot in frock coat and top hat, just as his friend was the first Spaniard to make fun of the prestige of his race.

'The Frenchman paid me well,' he grinned, showing gums which resembled a street after a fire. 'I had a bit of luck with my posters!'

The Shrimp gave another shrug.

'Kiko,' he replied in a cavernous voice, 'if they gave you six pesos, can you imagine what they must have paid the friars?'

Uncle Kiko cocked his head with instinctive alertness.

'The friars?'

'You must know,' continued The Shrimp, 'that the convents were responsible for all this rush for seats.'

Indeed, the friars, led by Father Salví, and a number of laymen, headed by Don Custodio, had protested against the performances; even Father Camorra, whose mouth was in fact watering and whose eyes were likely to fall out of their sockets, had nonetheless argued the point with Ben Zayb, who took the other side rather timidly, thinking of the free tickets that the management would be sending him. Don Custodio had talked to him of morals, religion, public decorum.

'But our own vaudeville sketches and farces,' the journalist had stammered, 'have their play on words and double meanings...'

'At least they're in Spanish!' the virtuous councillor had cut him short with a shout, burning with righteous indignation. 'But obscenities in French, good God, man, in French! No, not that, never!'

And he sounded his 'never' with three times the spirit of that Spanish hero Guzmán who had allowed his son to be killed by the Moors rather than surrender the city of Tarifa; in fact he sounded as determined as Guzmán might have been if he had been threatened with the death of a flea and had been required to surrender twenty Tarifas. Father Irene had naturally been on Don Custodio's side; he abominated French operettas, he had been to Paris and had never even stopped on the pavement outside a theatre, God deliver us!

But the French operetta had its partisans in great numbers: Army and Navy officers, among them the General's aides, government officials, and many prominent gentlemen were anxious to savour the delights of the French language spoken by genuine Parisian girls. They were joined by those who had travelled by the French steamship line and had picked up a little French during the trip, by those who had been to Paris, and finally by all who had any pretensions to culture. Manila society was thus divided into two camps: those in favour of the operetta and those against; the latter found themselves backed by elderly ladies, jealous wives thrifty with their husbands' affections, and engaged girls, while those who were free and attractive proclaimed themselves uncompromising partisans of the performances. Volleys of pamphlets were exchanged, there were comings and goings, arguments, meetings, much lobbying and discussion; there was even talk of a native uprising, of indolence, of inferior and superior races, of prestige and such claptrap; but after a great amount of gossip and slander the permit was granted, and Father Salví issued a pastoral letter that was read only by the printer's proof-reader. It was rumoured that the General had quarrelled with the Countess, that she spent all her time in pleasure villas and that His Excellency was bored, that the French consul... that gifts and presents... Many names were mentioned: Quiroga, Simoun, even a number of the actresses.

Thanks to these scandalous preliminaries popular curiosity had been aroused and, ever since the arrival of the troupe the day before, the only topic of conversation had been their first night. The winners of the argument had begun to make ready to enjoy their victory from the very moment the red posters appeared announcing *Les Cloches de Corneville.* In certain offices the personnel no longer spent their time gossiping and reading newspapers; instead they memorized the plot of the operetta, flicked the pages of French novelettes, or scurried out to the water-closets as if stricken by dysentery in order to look up words surreptitiously in pocket dictionaries. This did not help to get official business done, on the contrary, everyone was told to come back the next day; but the public could take no offence for they met with officials who were most courteous, affable in the extreme, who greeted and dismissed them with deep French bows, who dusted off their French and practised it on one another, lightly dropping a *Oui, monsieur* here and a *s'il vous plait* there and a *pardon*! everywhere—it was sheer delight to see and hear them. But the excitement and anxiety reached their highest points in the newspaper offices; Ben Zayb, assigned to translate the plot and review the performance, trembled like some wretched woman accused of witchcraft; he could almost see his enemies catching him out in dreadful blunders and showing up his ignorance of elementary French. During the tour of the Italian Opera Company he had almost been challenged to a duel because he had mistranslated the tenor's name, and an envious critic had immediately published an article calling him an ignoramus, he, the leading intellectual of the Philippines! He had had the very devil of a time defending himself and had been compelled to write at least seventeen articles and to consult fifteen dictionaries. With this salutary experience in mind poor Ben Zayb went as slowly and cautiously as a crab, not to say backwards and sideways as Father Camorra was rude enough to describe it.

'Observe, Kiko,' said The Shrimp. 'Half the audiences come because the friars said they shouldn't; the other half because they told themselves that, if the friars condemned the performance, it must be good. Believe me, Kiko, your posters were all right but better still was the pastoral letter, and remember that nobody even read it!'

'Dear friend,' worried Uncle Kiko, 'do you think Father Salví's competition might drive me out of business?'

'Could be, Kiko, could be,' replied The Shrimp raising his eyes. 'Money is getting tighter...'

Uncle Kiko muttered a string of incoherent words and phrases: if the friars were going into the theatre advertising business, he would have to turn friar himself. With that he said good-bye and went off coughing and jingling his silver pesos.

Indifferent as ever The Shrimp continued to wander here and there, dragging his leg behind him, his eyes half-lidded. His interest was aroused by the appearance of certain strangers who were gathering from various places and signalling one another with a wink or a cough. It was the first time he had seen them on such occasions, and he knew every face in the city. They were men of dark features, bent low, with an air of uneasiness and insecurity, badly disguised, as if they had put on a jacket for the first time. Instead of trying to get to the front row of the crowd to have a better look, they skulked in the shadows, anxious not to be seen.

'Secret police or pickpockets?' The Shrimp asked himself and then gave a quick shrug. 'What is it to me?'

The lantern of an approaching coach cast its light on a group of four or five of them speaking with a man who had the appearance of an Army officer.

'Secret police! Must be a new outfit,' muttered The Shrimp.

He made another gesture of indifference, but then observed that the officer, after consulting two or three more groups, had approached a carriage and was speaking excitedly with its occupant. The Shrimp took a few steps and was not surprised to recognize the jeweller Simoun while his sharp ears caught the following brief exchange.

'The signal will be a shot!'

'Yes, sir.'

'So then . . . be ready!'

The voice died out and shortly afterwards the carriage went off. The Shrimp, impassive though he was, could not help whispering to himself:

'Something's going on... Keep your hands on your pockets!'

But feeling his own empty, he gave still another shrug. What was it to him if the heavens fell?

He went on with his rounds. He passed two men in conversation and heard one of them, who had rosaries and scapulars hung about his neck, say in Tagalog:

'Don't be stupid: the friars are more powerful than the General. He has to go some time, they stay behind. As long as we do it well, we shall be rich. The signal will be a shot!'

'The plot thickens,' muttered The Shrimp, snapping his fingers. 'On one side, the General; on the other, Father Salví... Unhappy country! But what is it to me?'

Shrugging and spitting, the two gestures with which he symbolized his utter indifference, he continued his peregrinations.

In the meantime carriages were coming along at a brisk clatter and halting smartly at the doors of the theatre, bearing the members of high society: the ladies, although there was only the merest breath of night air, carried magnificent shawls, silken cloaks and even spring coats; the gentlemen in full evening dress wore topcoats or carried them on their arms so folded as to show off the rich silk linings.

Among the onlookers were Tadeo, the student who fell ill whenever the professor started his way to the classroom, and a townmate of his, the newcomer whose question on 'limping verses' had had such unfortunate results, and who was still so curious and asked so many questions that Tadeo, taking full advantage of his ingenuousness and inexperience, had the opportunity to weave for him the most stupefying fantasies. Every Spaniard who greeted Tadeo in passing, no matter if he was a minor clerk or shop assistant, was described as a bureau director, a marquess, a count; on the other hand, whoever passed by without a greeting was dismissed as a beginner, an employee in the lowest ranks, a nobody. When there were not enough pedestrians to keep the newcomer at the right pitch of admiration, Tadeo had recourse to the elegant carriages that went past and scattered graceful salutes, waved a friendly greeting, or called out a familiar 'See you soon!'

'Who is it?'

'Oh, the Civil Governor,' Tadeo would answer nonchalantly. Or 'The Vice-Governor-General... Justice So-and-so... Madame ... Friends of mine.'

The newcomer gaped, listened open-mouthed and made sure to keep himself well to Tadeo's left. Tadeo, friend of justices and governors!

Tadeo identified for him all arrivals, and for those he did not know invented surnames, life stories and many curious details.

'See that tall man with dark whiskers, with the cast in his eye, dressed all in black? That is Justice A., the intimate friend of the wife of Colonel B. One time, if it hadn't been for me, they would have come to blows... *See you soon!* Look, here comes the colonel! I do hope they won't start all over again!'

The newcomer held his breath, but the colonel and the justice shook hands heartily; the officer, who was in fact an old bachelor, asked after the justice's family.

'Ah, thank God,' sighed Tadeo. 'I made them friends after all.'

'I wonder,' suggested the newcomer rather diffidently, 'do you think you could ask them to let us into the theatre?'

'Of course not, man! I never ask favours,' replied Tadeo majestically. 'I'm glad to help them but never ask anything in return.'

The newcomer bit his lips, shrank even more and increased the respectful distance between him and his townmate.

Tadeo continued:

'That's H. the musician... And that one, J. the lawyer, who gave as his own a speech you can find printed in any book; you should have heard how his audience congratulated and complimented him!... Doctor K., the chap getting off that hansom cab now, is a specialist in children's diseases; goes by the nickname of Herod... And that's L. the banker, who has only two topics of conversation, his piles of money and his piles... Over there M. the poet who speaks only of stars and the hereafter... And there goes the beautiful Madame N. whom Father Q. just happens to visit when her husband is away... The merchant P., a Jew, who came with a thousand pesos and is now a millionaire... The chap with the beard is Doctor R., who has made more money making people ill than curing them...'

'Making people ill?'

'Yes, man, to get them off military conscription! Look sharp, now! That respectable well-dressed gentleman is not a physician but he is a homoeopathist in his own peculiar way and believes in the attraction of likes; that young captain of cavalry with him is his favourite disciple...This one in the light suit with the tilted hat is S., a government official, who believes in being impolite but who loses his temper if he sees anybody else keeping his hat on. They say he does it to put German hats out of fashion... The one coming with his family is the fabulously wealthy merchant C., who has an income of more than a hundred thousand... What would you say if I told you that he owes me five pesos and twenty-five centavos? Oh well, who would dare ask a man like that to pay up?'

'This gentleman owes you money?'

'Of course! I got him out of a tight fix one day, it was a Friday at seven-thirty in the morning, I remember; I hadn't had lunch yet... That lady followed by the old woman is the famous dancer Pepay. But she doesn't work in the public dance-halls any more, not since a very pious gentleman, a very good friend of mine, insisted she should give it up... There goes Z. Oh, what a hell-raiser! I'm sure he is after Pepay to get her to dance again. He's a good boy, a very good friend of mine; has only one defect, he's a Chinese half-breed but calls himself a Spaniard from Spain. Hey, look there, that's Ben Zayb, the chap who looks like a friar and has a pencil and that great bunch of papers in his hand, that's Ben Zayb the great writer and a very good friend of mine, you wouldn't believe the brains that man has!'

'Tell me, what about that little man with the white whiskers?'

'That chap has put his daughters, those three little girls, on the payroll of the Department of Economic Development... He's a very smart man, very smart indeed! Whenever he makes a mistake, he blames it on... oh, anybody at hand. Whenever he buys a shirt, he charges it to the Treasury. Smart, very smart, very smart indeed!'

Tadeo stopped short.

'And that gentleman with the scowl who looks at everyone over his shoulder?' asked the newcomer pointing to a man who was looking about him with marked arrogance.

But Tadeo did not answer. He was stretching his neck to catch a look at Paulita Gómez, who was arriving in the company of a friend, Doña Victorina and Juanito Peláez. The latter had asked them to his box and was stooping more than ever.

More and more carriages were drawing up; the actresses had arrived at the stage door followed by friends and admirers.

When Paulita had entered Tadeo continued:

'Those are the nieces of the rich Capitán D., the ones in the landau: notice how pretty and healthy they look? Well, in a few years they will be either dead or crazy. Capitán D. won't let them get married, they will soon be as mad as their uncle... That is Miss E., the wealthy heiress courted by the world and the nunnery... Hold on now! I know this one. That's Father Irene in disguise; with false moustaches! I know that nose! And to think that he was so opposed...'

The newcomer stared, properly shocked, and saw a well cut frock coat move away after a group of ladies.

'The Three Fates!' exclaimed Tadeo on catching sight of three spinsters, dried up, bony, haggard, wide-mouthed, and dressed in the worst of taste. 'They are—'

'Atropos?' piped up the newcomer, who wanted to show that he knew something at least about mythology.

'No, man, they are the Balcon sisters, fault-finders, spinsters, poor as rats. They hate everybody: men, women and children. But look, after the disease God sends the cure, although it may come a little late. Those three young men coming after the Fates, the horror of the city, are the pride of their friends, of whom I am honoured to be one. The slender goggle-eyed chap with the stoop, who is waving his hands about because he could not get tickets, is the chemist S., who has written many monographs and scientific reports, some of them prize-winners, all of them worthy of note. The Spaniards say that he is promising, promising… The one who is trying to calm him down with that Voltairean laugh is the poet T., a talented young man, and a very good friend of mine, who is talented enough to know when to put aside his pen. And the third one who is suggesting that they go in by the stage door is the young physician U., who has had such success with his prescriptions. They say that he too is promising… he is not so stooped as Peláez but he is even cleverer. I do believe he can bluff Death itself'

'And the dark man with the bristling moustache?'

'Ah, that is the merchant F., who forgets everything, even his birth certificate. He wants to be a Spanish half-breed at all costs and makes heroic efforts to forget his native tongue.'

'But his daughters are so white…'

'Which is the reason why rice has gone up in price and, mind you, they eat nothing but bread!'

The newcomer did not catch the connexion between the price of rice and the young ladies' white complexions.

'That chap is engaged to one of them, the dark slender one who is walking so slowly behind them and greeting our three friends so condescendingly while they laugh at him. He is a martyr to his ideas, to his consistency.'

The newcomer was overcome with feelings of respect and admiration.

'He looks a fool, but isn't, really,' continued Tadeo. 'He was born in San Pedro Makati. Now he makes many sacrifices: he almost never takes a bath; or eats pork because, so he says, Spaniards never eat it, and for the same reason never tastes rice or the native fish sauce or fish roe even when his mouth is watering for them, no, not even if he starves to death. He has actually eaten a pot of mustard at one sitting to prove he is a European!'

The theatre orchestra was striking up a waltz.

'See that man, that sickly looking chap looking round, fishing for greetings? That is the famous governor of Pangasinan, a good man who loses his appetite whenever a native fails to salute him. He would have languished away if he had not issued his famous order on salutes to which he owes his fame. Poor man, he has lost so much weight since he came here from his province three days ago. But hey, look here, here's the great man himself, take a good look at him!'

'Who? The man with the frown?'

'That's him, that's Don Custodio, Don Custodio the liberal, he's frowning because he has important things on his mind. Ah, if his ideas could only be put into practice! And here comes Makaraig, your housemate!'

It was indeed Makaraig, with Pecson, Sandoval and Isagani. Tadeo stepped forward on seeing them and greeted them.

'Aren't you coming?' asked Makaraig.

'We couldn't get tickets...'

'Well, we have a box,' replied Makaraig. 'Basilio can't come. Do come along with us.'

Tadeo did not wait for the invitation to be repeated. The newcomer, however, was afraid to be in the way and, with the timidity to be expected from a native provincial, excused himself. It was impossible to get him to change his mind.

22 • *The Performance*

THE theatre had the liveliest of airs; it was packed full, and there were many standing in the corridors and galleries, struggling to get their heads clear or at least to find eye-space between somebody else's neck and his neighbour's ear. The open boxes, most of them occupied by ladies, seemed baskets of flowers whose petals were softly stirred by fans amid the humming of a thousand insects. Yet, just as there are flowers whose scent is delicate and others of heavier perfume, flowers that can kill and others that give comfort, so also in the boxes of the theatre the dialogues and conversations

had their share of wounding and poisonous phrases. Only three or four of the
boxes were still unoccupied; it was late, the performance had been set for
half-past eight and it was already a quarter to nine; but the curtain did not
rise because His Excellency had not yet arrived. Those in the cheapest seats
in the gallery, impatient and uncomfortable, were raising an uproar, stamping
and striking the floor with their walking-sticks.

'Raise the curtain!'

The gunners of the Spanish regiment of artillery were not the least of
the trouble-makers. These sons of Mars, as Ben Zayb called them, were
not content with the noise they made. Perhaps believing themselves in a
bull-ring, they greeted the ladies who passed before them with phrases
that are euphemistically called flowery in Madrid but are more often
than not closer to garbage; ignoring the furious glares of the ladies'
husbands, they proclaimed loudly the sentiments and desires aroused in
them by all these beauties.

The ladies were apparently afraid to go down to the stalls, not one was to
be seen there, and amid clouds of smoke and suppressed laughter masculine
voices weighed the merits of the actresses or relayed the latest scandals:
whether or not His Excellency had quarrelled with the friars, whether his
attendance at the performance was to be taken as a provocation or merely
attributed to curiosity. Others had no thought for these matters and were
concerned only with catching the eye of the ladies, striking attitudes that
were more or less interesting, more or less statuesque, making a great play
with their diamond rings, particularly when they thought that they were
under observation through some insistent pair of opera glasses. Still others
openly sent respectful salutes to this or that lady, bowing their heads gravely
while whispering to their neighbour:

'Silly fool! Such a bore!'

The lady in question replied to the salute with the sweetest of her smiles
and an enchanting tilt of her head, and between two lazy waves of her fan
murmured to her sympathetic neighbour:

'What airs he gives himself! My dear, he's obviously head over heels!'

In the meantime the uproar of protest continued; still, there were now
only two empty boxes and, of course, His Excellency's, which was
distinguished by its red velvet hangings. The orchestra struck up another
waltz, the audience protested; fortunately a hero appeared upon the scene at
this point to distract attention and charitably save the impressario. This was
a gentleman who had occupied a stall and now refused to yield it to the

holder of the ticket, Don Primitivo the philosopher. Failing to convince his antagonist with argument Don Primitivo appealed to an usher. 'I don't feel like it,' the hero replied, nonchalantly puffing a cigarette. The usher ran to the theatre manager. 'I don't feel like it,' the hero repeated, ensconcing himself deeper in the stall. The theatre manager was seen to leave while the gunners in the gallery started up a chorus:

'Yes he will! No he won't! Yes he will! No he won't!'

The hero, who had by now attracted everyone's attention, was convinced that to yield now would be to demean himself and clung to the arms of his seat, repeating his answer to the pair of policemen whom the theatre manager had called. The policemen, considering the rebel's rank and status, went off to consult their corporal while the theatre broke into applause, saluting the gentleman's fortitude s he remained seated like a Roman senator.

But now there were whistles and the gentleman who had just displayed his strength of character turned round in annoyance believing they were directed at him; he was wrong, the sound of galloping horses was heard, a hustle and a bustle—a revolution? Or at least a riot? No, the orchestra was cutting short the waltz and striking up the Royal March. His Excellency the Commander-in-Chief and Governor-General had arrived, and all eyes sought him, followed him, lost him, until he appeared at last in his box where, after sweeping the theatre with a look and making a few of the audience happy with a godlike nod, he seated himself like a mere man in the waiting armchair. The gunners had fallen silent and the orchestra began the prelude.

The students were in a box opposite that of Pepay the dancer; the latter's box had in fact been paid for by Makaraig, who had an understanding with her to win Don Custodio to their side. That very afternoon Pepay had sent the famous arbitrator a note, and now she was waiting for the answer in the theatre, where they had agreed to meet. It was for this reason that Don Custodio, despite his strenuous opposition to the French operetta, had gone to the theatre after all, a decision which made him suffer the sneering innuendos of Don Manuel, his customary antagonist at the sessions of the Municipal Council.

'I have come to sit in judgment on the operetta,' he had replied in the accents of a Cato with a clean conscience.

Now Makaraig was exchanging knowing glances with Pepay, who was giving him to understand that she had news for him; she seemed to be in high spirits and everyone forecast that success was theirs. Sandoval, who had just come back from a round of other boxes, was sure that the recommendation had been in their favour and that the Supervisory Committee had taken it up that very afternoon and adopted it. All seemed bright; Pecson himself was losing his pessimism at the sight of Pepay, who was smiling as she waved a letter; Sandoval and Makaraig were congratulating each other; only Isagani remained somewhat cold and scarcely smiled.

What was wrong with him?

Simply that on entering the theatre he had seen Paulita in a box and Juanito Peláez talking to her. He had blanched and believed himself mistaken, but there was no mistake, it was Paulita beyond a doubt, Paulita who greeted him with a charming smile while her lovely eyes seemed to ask his forgiveness and promise an explanation. Indeed they had agreed that Isagani would see the operetta first to find out if there was anything in it that might embarrass a young lady, and now he found her there herself, and in the company of his rival. His feelings were beyond description: anger, jealousy, humiliation, resentment; there was a moment when he wished the theatre would collapse on top of them all; he felt a strong urge to laugh out loud, insult his sweetheart, provoke a quarrel with his rival, and make a scandal, but in the end he contented himself with taking his seat quietly and never looking at her. He could hear the enthusiastic plans that Makaraig and Sandoval were making, but only as distant echoes; the notes of the waltz seemed to him sad and mournful, and all the audience fatuous and idiotic; more than once he had to make an effort not to burst into tears. He was scarcely aware of the gentleman who would not yield his seat or of the Governor-General's arrival. He stared at the drop-curtain which depicted a kind of gallery with luxurious red hangings, looking out into a garden with a fountain at its centre; how desolate the gallery, how melancholy the view! A thousand vague memories slipped through his mind like the distant echoes of music heard in the night, lullaby airs, lonely murmuring forests, dark rivulets, moonlit nights by a sea that stretched endlessly before his eyes... The enamoured youth, who considered himself the most wretched of human beings, took to looking up at the ceiling to keep his tears from falling.

A burst of applause awoke him from his brooding.

The curtain had just been raised, revealing a gay chorus of Corneville peasants, in cotton caps and heavy wooden shoes. The girls, some six or seven, their lips and cheeks heavily rouged, the sparkle of their eyes emphasized by mascara, were displaying white arms, diamond-ringed fingers, and rounded, well shaped legs. As they sang the Norman ditty, *Allez, marchez! Allez, marchez!* they smiled at their respective admirers in the stalls with such brazenness that Don Custodio, after a glance at Pepay's box to make sure she was not doing the same to another admirer, made a mental note of this lewd behaviour and, to make doubly sure, lowered his head to see if the actresses were showing their knees.

'Oh, these Frenchwomen!' he muttered while his imagination ranged on a higher level and made comparisons and plans.

'*Quoi v'la tous les cancans d'la s'maine . . .*' sang Gertrude, a superb wench who was roguishly looking the Commander-in-Chief straight in the eye. 'What is all the gossip of the week?'

But Tadeo, first honours in French in his class, had caught only the word *cancans* and exclaimed: 'We're going to have the cancan! Makaraig, they are going to dance the can-can!'

He was rubbing his hands gleefully.

From the time the curtain had risen Tadeo had had no ears for the music; he was only on the watch for the scandalous, the indecent, the immoral in gesture and dress, and with his smattering of French cocked his ears to catch the obscenities to which his country's stern censors had given such publicity.

Sandoval, who also claimed to know French, had made himself a kind of interpreter for his friends. He knew as little as Tadeo but he depended also on the summaries of the operetta's plot published in the newspapers; his imagination supplied the rest.

'Yes,' he confirmed, 'they are going to dance the can-can and she will lead it.'

Makaraig and Pecson were all eyes and anticipatory smiles. Isagani looked away, embarrassed that Paulita should witness such a show, and wondered if he should challenge Juanito Peláez the next day.

But the young men waited in vain. Serpolette came on, a delicious girl also in a cotton cap, provocative and quarrelsome.

'*Hein! qui parle de Serpolette?*' she asked the gossips with her arms akimbo, ready to fight whoever it was that was 'telling stories' about her.

A gentleman applauded and was followed by everyone in the stalls. Serpolette, without dropping her role of the buxom beauty, cast a glance at the one who had started the applause and repaid him with a smile, showing a row of even teeth that seemed like a pearl necklace in a red velvet case. Tadeo followed her look and saw a gentleman with false moustaches and a remarkably long nose.

'Good Lord! Little Irene himself!'

'Yes,' said Sandoval. 'I saw him backstage chatting with the actresses.'

It was indeed Father Irene, a fanatical music-lover who knew French well, and who had been sent by Father Salví to the theatre as some sort of religious secret police—that, at least, was what he told those who recognized him. Like a good critic who is not satisfied with seeing the exhibits from a distance, he had decided to take a closer look at the cast; he had mingled with the admirers and men of fashion backstage and had sidled into the dressing-rooms where an elementary and compulsory French was being spoken in whispers, a trader's French that served the sellers well enough when the customers seemed ready to pay well.

Serpolette was surrounded by two gallant officers, a sailor and a lawyer when she had seen Father Irene wandering about and poking his long nose everywhere, at every possible opening, plumbing the mysteries of the stage.

Serpolette had cut short her chatter, frowned and raised her eyebrows, opened her mouth, and with the vivacity of a Parisian girl had left her admirers and launched herself like a torpedo on the clerical critic.

'*Tiens, tiens, Toutou, mon lapin!*' she had cried out, catching Father Irene by the arm and shaking him gaily while she made the air ring with her silvery laughter.

'Ssssh, sssh,' Father Irene had scolded, trying to hide himself.

'*Mais, comment! Toi ici, grosse bête! Et moi qui t'croyais...*'

"*Fais pas d'tapage, Lily! Il faut m'respecter! 'Suis ici l'Pape!*"

It was with great difficulty that Father Irene got Lily to be reasonable and quiet: he was regarded as something like a Pope in these parts, he had to be treated with deference and respect. The gay Lily, alias Serpolette, was *enchantée* to find in Manila no other than Toutou her little rabbit, her great beast, her old friend who reminded her of the Grand Opera Theatre backstage. That was why Father Irene, fulfilling the duties of both friendship and theatrical criticism, had started the applause to encourage her: Serpolette deserved it.

In the meantime the students were waiting for the can-can. Pecson was all eyes, but there was everything but the can-can. At one point, if some lawyers had not come along, it seemed that the girls would come to blows and pull one another's hair out, egged on by the mischievous peasants, who hoped, like the students, to see more than just the can-can.

Scit, scit, scit, scit, scit, scit,
Disputez-vous, battez-vous,
Scit, scit, scit, scit, scit, scit,
Nous allons compter les coups.

But the music stopped before the fighting could get started, the men went off without being able to 'count the blows', the girls drifted back one by one and started a conversation that the young men could not understand at all. In fact they were gossiping about one of the absent girls.

'They sound like the waiters in a Chinese restaurant,' commented Pecson in a whisper.

'And the can-can?' inquired Makaraig.

'They are discussing where it would be best to dance it,' Sandoval replied in all seriousness.

'Sound like waiters in a Chinese restaurant,' repeated the disgusted Pecson.

A lady accompanied by her husband now entered the theatre and occupied one of the two empty boxes. She put on a regal air and looked at the audience disdainfully as if to say: 'I have got here later than all of you, you bunch of vulgar provincials!' Indeed some people go to the theatre like donkeys in a race: the last one in wins. Men who should know better would rather go up the scaffold than enter a theatre before the end of the first act. But the lady's self-satisfaction was shortlived. She perceived that another box remained empty, frowned, and started to quarrel with her husband, causing such a disturbance that many in the audience were exasperated.

There were calls for silence.

'Idiots! As if they understood French!' exclaimed the lady, looking round her with supreme contempt and finally fixing her eyes on Juanito's box from where she thought she had heard an imprudent hushing.

Juanito had, in fact, been guilty of it. From the very start of the performance he had pretended to understand everything and had preened himself, smiling, laughing, and applauding at what seemed the proper times as if nothing that was said on the stage could escape him. Yet he was not even guided by the gestures of the cast; he scarcely looked at the stage. The rogue would say meaningfully to Paulita that he did not want to tire his eyes looking so far away when there were much more beautiful women so near at hand. Paulita would blush, hide her face with her fan, and steal a glance at Isagani who seemed to be watching the show silent and absorbed.

Paulita was spiteful and jealous: had Isagani fallen in love with one of those provocative actresses? This thought put her in a bad humour and she scarcely heard the praises which Doña Victorina was heaping on her favourite.

Juanito was playing his role well: at times he would shake his head in disgust, and then throats would be cleared and mutters of disapproval heard in parts of the theatre; at other times he would smile, nod with approval, and seconds later applause would break out. Doña Victorina was enchanted and even conceived vague desires to marry the young man the day Don Tiburcio should die. Juanito knew French, and de Espadaña did not! She lavished sweet nothings on him but Juanito did not notice the change of tactics, he was much too engrossed in keeping an eye on a Catalan merchant next to the Swiss consul; he had heard them converse in French and was basing his reactions on theirs with consummate success.

Scene followed scene, and character after character, comic and ridiculous like the bailiff and Grenicheux, or noble and appealing like the marquess and Germaine. The audience had a good laugh at the slap which Gaspard had intended for the cowardly Grenicheux but which landed on the grave bailiff instead, sending the latter's wig flying through the air amid a noisy tumult on which the curtain fell.

'And the can-can?' asked Tadeo.

But the curtain rose again almost immediately on a scene representing a market where servants would offer their services under three beflagged poles carrying the placards *servantes, cochers* and *domestiques*. Juanito availed himself of the opportunity to tell Doña Victorina loudly enough for Paulita to hear and be convinced of his French:

'*Servantes* means servants, *domestiques*, domestics . . .'

'And what is the difference between *servantes* and *domestiques?*' asked Paulita.

Juanito was not fazed.

'*Domestiques*, those who are domesticated. Have you noticed that some of them have a savage, uncivilized air? Those are the *servantes*.'

'How true also!' added Doña Victorina 'Some are very impolite. I thought everybody in Europe had good manners yet. But maybe because it is happening in France that is the reason.'

'Sssssh! Quiet there!'

But Juanito's time of trial arrived when the market was opened, the barrier lowered, and the servants offering their services ranged themselves by the poles which announced their qualifications. Some ten or twelve rustics, clad in livery and carrying little branches in their hands, were taking their places under the sign for *domestiques*.

'Those are the domestics!' said Juanito.

'Really, they are looking domesticated now only,' commented Doña Victorina. 'Let us see the uncivilized savages also.'

Now a dozen girls, with the gay and vivacious Serpolette at their head, clad in their best dresses and each with a great garland of flowers at the waist, merry and smiling, fresh and luscious, were ranging themselves, to Juanito's despair, at the post marked *servantes*.

'What,' asked Paulita ingenuously, 'are these the ones you call savages?'

'No,' replied the imperturbable Juanito, 'they have made a mistake. They have lost their place. It is those who come behind.'

'The ones with the whips?'

Juanito nodded in an agony of embarrassment.

'So the girls are the *cochers?* '

A violent fit of coughing attacked Juanito to the annoyance of some in the audience.

'Throw him out! Throw out the consumptive!'

A consumptive! Calling him a consumptive in Paulita's hearing! Juanito wanted to find the insolent scoundrel who had said it and make him swallow his own words. When he saw that the ladies were trying to stop him, he gained courage and grew even more belligerent. Fortunately the diagnosis had been made by Don Custodio who, unwilling to attract attention to himself, pretended unconcern and to be taking notes for his review of the performance.

'Oh, if you hadn't been along!' said Juanito, rolling his eyes like the dolls in cuckoo clocks and, to complete the similarity, sticking out his tongue from time to time.

That night Juanito made a name as a brave and honourable man, as far as Doña Victorina was concerned, and she made up her mind to marry him as soon as Don Tiburcio cleared the way.

Paulita was in lower and lower spirits, wondering how girls called *cochers* could possibly hold Isagani's attention; the word reminded her of the schoolgirl term for certain types of affection among them.

The first act ended at last with the marquess taking into his service Serpolette, Germaine, the timid beauty of the troupe, and the stupid Grenicheux as coachman. A burst of applause called them to the curtain, and those who five seconds before had been chasing one another and about to come to blows now appeared hand in hand, bowing to the generous audience, and exchanging knowing looks with a number of spectators.

Amid the momentary disorder of those who were stumbling over one another to go to the dressing-rooms and congratulate the actresses and those who were on their way to present their compliments to the ladies in the boxes, judgments were made on the operetta and the cast.

'Undoubtedly Serpolette is the best,' said one who was giving himself the airs of an intellectual.

'I prefer Germaine. She is the ideal blonde.'

'But she can't sing!'

'I don't want her to sing to me!'

'Well, the tall one has the best shape.'

'Pooh,' said Ben Zayb, 'none of them is worth a damn, not one of them is an artist.'

Ben Zayb was the reviewer for *The Voice of Integrity* and his disdainful pose gave him a great deal of stature among those who did not ask much more than that.

'Serpolette can't sing, Germaine is a bore, and the whole thing is neither musical nor artistic nor anything at all!' he concluded with marked contempt.

There was nothing like being dissatisfied with everything to appear to be a great critic; in any case the management had sent only two complimentary tickets.

In the boxes interest was centred on the owner of the empty box. Whoever it was would have the most *chic* of all for he would be the last to arrive.

Somehow it got around that the box was Simoun's. The rumour was confirmed. No one had seen the jeweller in the stalls, in the dressing-rooms backstage, or for that matter anywhere else in the theatre.

'But I saw him only this afternoon with M. Jouy.'

'And he gave one of the actresses a necklace.'

'Which one?'

'The best of them all, the one who kept her eyes on His Excellency!'

There were knowing looks, winks, exclamations of scepticism, affirmations, broken phrases.

'He's playing Monte Cristo,' commented a lady who prided herself on her literary knowledge.

'Or purveyor by royal appointment!' added her escort, jealous now of Simoun.

In the students' box only Pecson, Sandoval and Isagani had remained. Tadeo had gone to engage Don Custodio in conversation about his favourite projects and so distract his attention while Makaraig saw Pepay.

'Nonsense,' declaimed Sandoval with sweeping gestures, tuning his voice to the neighbouring box where the daughters of Tadeo's wealthy debtor might hear him, 'as I was saying, my dear Isagani, it is all nonsense; French just does not have the rich sonority, the varied and elegant cadences of Spanish. I cannot conceive, I cannot imagine, I just cannot see how the French can be orators, I doubt that there have ever been any, or that it is possible for them to exist in the true sense of the word, in the strict sense of the idea of orators. For let us not confuse an orator with a mere talker or babbler. Talkers and babblers there may be in every country, in every part of the inhabited world, among the cold dry English as well as among the lively and impressionable French...'

Sandoval went on with an impressive description of various peoples, making a display of his most poetic concepts and sonorous adjectives. Isagani nodded in approval while thinking of Paulita, whom he had surprised giving him an eloquent look that meant many things. Isagani wanted to decipher the language of those eyes; they indeed were eloquent and not babblers at all!

'You, a poet, servant of rhyme and metre, son of the Muses,' Sandoval continued with an elegant gesture of the hand as if saluting the Nine Sisters on the far horizon, 'can you conceive, can you imagine that using a language as harsh, as lacking in rhythm, as the French there can be poets of the gigantic stature of our Garcilasos or Herreras or Esproncedas and Calderons?'

'Nevertheless, 'objected Pecson, 'Victor Hugo...'

'Victor Hugo, my dear Pecson, if he is a poet, owes it to Spain... because research has established, established beyond all doubt, and it is admitted even by the French themselves, who are so envious of Spain, that if Victor Hugo is a genius, if he is a poet, it is because he spent his childhood in Madrid; it was there that he formed his first impressions, there that his brain took shape, there that his imagination was fired, his heart touched, and all the most beautiful ideas of his intellect born. Yet after all, who is Victor Hugo? Is he at all comparable with our modern poets?'

But the arrival of Makaraig, downcast and a bitter smile on his lips, cut the orator's peroration short. He had a paper in hand which he passed wordlessly to Sandoval.

Sandoval read:

Darling pigeon:

Your letter came too late; I had already submitted my recommendation and it had been approved. However, as if I had guessed your thoughts, I decided the matter in accordance with the wishes of your protégés.

I am going to the theatre and will wait for you at the exit.

Your tender little dove,

CUSTODINING.

Tadeo was touched. 'What a dear man he is!'

'Well?' asked Sandoval. 'I don't see anything wrong, all the contrary!'

'Oh yes, in accordance with our wishes indeed!' replied Makaraig sourly. 'I have just seen Father Irene.'

'And what does he say?' asked Pecson.

'The same as Don Custodio. The rascal even had the nerve to congratulate me. The Committee, making the arbitrator's recommendation their own, express their approval of the plan and congratulate the students on their patriotism and their thirst for knowledge...'

'And then?'

'Nevertheless, considering our other duties, and in order, says the Committee, that the plan may not end in failure, the Committee understand that its administration and execution should be entrusted to one of the religious Orders in the event that the Dominicans may not wish to incorporate the Academy in the University.'

There were cries of disappointment. Isagani rose to his feet but said nothing.

'And in order to demonstrate that we participate in the administration of the Academy,' Makaraig continued, 'we are placed in charge of the collection of contributions and fees with the obligation of turning them over afterwards to the treasurer who may be designated by the administering Order, and who will issue the corresponding receipts...'

'Tax collectors, no less!' commented Tadeo.

'Sandoval,' said Pecson, 'there's the gauntlet, pick it up!'

'That's no gauntlet, smells like an old sock to me.'

'The funniest part of it is,' Makaraig went on, 'that Father Irene suggests we celebrate the event with a dinner or a torchlight serenade, a mass student demonstration to thank all those who have intervened in the affair!'

'After the beating, songs of thanksgiving! *Super flumina Babylonis sedimus!* By the waters of Babylon we sat down and wept...'

'The condemned man ate a hearty breakfast,' said Tadeo.

'A banquet, with everyone dressed in mourning, and funeral speeches,' suggested Sandoval.

'A serenade with the Marseillaise and funeral marches,' proposed Isagani.

'No, gentlemen,' said Pecson with his clown's guffaw, 'for a celebration there is nothing like a dinner in a Chinese restaurant served by shirtless Chinamen, definitely shirtless!'

The grotesque and sarcastic idea was accepted; Sandoval was the first to applaud it, for some time now he had wanted to enter one of these establishments which looked so gay and lively at night.

It was just as the orchestra was playing the opening bars of the second act that the students walked out of the theatre to the scandal of the audience.

23 • *The Deal*

TRUE enough, Simoun had not gone to the theatre.

He had left his house at seven in the evening, troubled and sombre; twice his servants saw him return, accompanied by different men; at eight o'clock, as the church bells were tolling the hour, Makaraig came across him wandering about Hospital Street, near the nunnery of St Clare; at nine The Shrimp saw him again around the theatre, talking to someone who looked like a student; he had entered and then left to disappear into the shadows.

'What is it to me?' The Shrimp repeated. 'What do I get out of warning the people?'

Basilio, as Makaraig had intimated, had not attended the performance either. The distraught student, ever since returning from San Diego where he had ransomed his sweetheart Julí from domestic service, had turned once again to his books, spending his time in the hospital, keeping Capitán Tiago under observation and trying to halt the onslaughts of his disease with the proper treatment.

His patient had become unbearable; when Basilio tried to moderate his consumption of opium, he would fall into depths of depression and in this evil mood would insult, maltreat and make all sorts of accusations against Basilio; the latter would swallow everything resignedly, in the consciousness that he was doing good to one to whom he owed much, and only yielded to the old man's demands when it was no longer possible to resist; his craving once satisfied and the monstrous vice appeased, Capitán Tiago would, in the best of spirits, turn sentimental, call him a true son, whining and snivelling about his services and how well Basilio administered his estates, and talk of making the student his heir; Basilio would smile ruefully and ponder that in this life the indulgence of vice is better rewarded than the fulfilment of duty. Not seldom he was tempted to give free rein to the disease and lead his benefactor to the tomb along a flowery path of happy dreams; better that than to lengthen his life by privations.

'What a fool I am,' he would often tell himself. 'He may be wrong but he pays the bill...'

But he would shake his head, thinking of Julí and his promising future: he wanted to live with nothing on his conscience. He would follow the prescribed treatment and keep watch.

For all that, the patient seemed to be getting worse day by day, despite sporadic improvements. Basilio, who was determined to cut down Capitán Tiago's dose of opium gradually or at least not to allow him to smoke more than usual, would find his patient, when he returned from the hospital or from some call, sleeping the heavy slumber of the opium addict, slavering and pale as a corpse. The young man could not understand where Capitán Tiago was getting the drugs; only Simoun and Father Irene ever called at the house, and the jeweller only rarely, while the latter never tired of urging him to be stern and inexorable in his treatment and to pay no attention to the patient's outbursts since the main thing was to save his life.

'Do your duty, young man,' Father Irene would say, 'do your duty.'

And he would deliver himself of a homily on this theme with such conviction and enthusiasm that Basilio even began to feel attracted to the preacher. Father Irene also promised to find him a good assignment in a rich province and even hinted at the possibility of getting him named to a professorial chair. Basilio, without allowing himself to be carried away by dreams, pretended he took the friar at his word and went on doing what his conscience told him.

That night, during the performance of *Les Cloches de Corneville*, Basilio had been studying at an old table, by the light of an oil lamp whose opaque glass shade left his melancholy features half in darkness. An old skull, some human bones and a number of carefully arranged books were on the table, together with a basin of water and a sponge. The smell of opium from the adjoining room made the air heavy and the student sleepy, but he fought it off, moistening his temples and his eyes fro m time to time, determined not to sleep until he had finished the book before him. It was Mata's *Legal Medicine and Toxicology,* a book he had borrowed and must return as soon as possible. Basilio's professor insisted on lecturing on the basis of this text and Basilio could not afford to buy his own copy; on the ground that it had been banned by the Manila censors and many officials had to be bribed before it could be brought in, the bookshops sold it at a very high price. So intent was he on his studies that he had ignored certain pamphlets that had been sent to him from abroad, no one knew from where exactly, pamphlets dealing with the Philippines, among which were some that had aroused great interest at that time because of the harsh and insulting way they dealt with the natives. Basilio had not had the time even to open them; or perhaps he had been deterred by the thought that it was not pleasant at all to be insulted and provoked without having means of defence or rebuttal. Indeed the censorship allowed the natives to be insulted but forbade them to reply.

In the silence that filled the house, broken only occasionally by weak snores from the next room, Basilio caught the sound of light footsteps on the stairs, steps that went on across the hall towards the room where he was. He raised his head, saw the door open, and to his great surprise beheld the grim figure of the jeweller Simoun.

Since they had last met in San Diego Simoun had not seen the young man again or, for that matter, Capitán Tiago.

'How is the patient?' asked Simoun throwing a quick look about the room and noticing the unopened pamphlets.

'Heart-beat imperceptible, pulse very weak, appetite gone completely,' whispered Basilio with a sad smile. 'He sweats profusely in the early hours...'

Seeing from Simoun's look that he had noticed the pamphlets and fearing that the jeweller would renew their argument in the wood, he continued:

'The organism is saturated with poison and may die any day as if struck by lightning . . . the least cause, a bit of nothing, a little excitement can bring death.'

'Like the Philippines,' Simoun commented darkly.

Basilio could not refrain from starting but he was determined not to be drawn into the argument again and continued as if he had not heard a word:

'What weakens him most are his nightmares, panic . . .'

'Like the Government,' said Simoun.

'Some nights ago he awoke in the darkness and thought he had gone blind; he made an outcry, bewailing his fate and accusing me of having plucked out his eyes. When I entered with a light he took me for Father Irene and called me his saviour...'

'Exactly like the Government!'

'Last night,' Basilio went on, turning a deaf ear, 'he got up and asked for his fighting cock, a bird dead these last three years; I had to give him a hen, and then he lavished his blessings on me and promised to give me many thousands of pesos.'

Just then a clock struck half-past ten.

Simoun shivered and cut the young man short with a gèsture.

'Basilio,' he whispered, 'listen to me carefully for every moment counts. I see that you have left unopened the pamphlets I sent you. You do not care about your country?'

The young man started to protest.

'Doesn't matter,' said Simoun curtly. 'Within an hour the revolution will start at my signal and tomorrow there will be no more studying, no more University, nothing except fighting and death. I have everything ready and I am sure of success. When we win, all those who could have helped us but did not, will be treated as enemies. Basilio, I have come to offer you death or a future!'

'My death or my future!' Basilio echoed dully.

'With the Government or with us,' replied Simoun. 'With your oppressors or with your country! Make up your mind, there is no time to lose. I have come to save you because of the memories that bind us together.'

'With my oppressors or with my country!'

Basilio's mind was awhirl; he stared at the jeweller with eyes that gleamed with fear; he felt his limbs go numb and a thousand confused thoughts ran through his mind; he could see the streets running blood, could hear the rattle of musketry and, imagining himself among the dead and wounded, could, in the singular passion of his vocation, watch himself in a surgeon's smock amputating legs and extracting bullets.

'I control the Government's power of decision,' Simoun went on. 'I have committed and spent its sparse strength and resources on foolish expeditions, dazzling it with profits which it might pocket; its heads are now in the theatre, at ease and distracted with thoughts of a night of pleasure, but none of them will rest again on a pillow. I have regiments at my command. I have led some to believe that the General wants the revolution, and others that the friars are behind it. I have bought some with promises of office and money; many others, very many, are out for revenge because they are oppressed and realize they must kill or be killed. Cabesang Tales is downstairs, he came here with me. I ask you again: are you with us or do you prefer to expose yourself to the reprisals of my followers?

In these moments of decision to declare yourself neutral is to invite the anger of both contending parties.'

Basilio drew his hand across his brow time and again as if he wanted to awaken from some nightmare; his forehead was icy cold.

'Make up your mind,' Simoun repeated.

'And what... would I have to do?' he asked in a voice that was breathless, broken, weak.

'A very simple thing,' answered Simoun, whose face lighted up with hope. 'Since I must lead the whole movement I cannot concentrate on any single operation. What I want you to do is to lead a detachment and, while the city's attention is drawn to other places, force the gates of the nunnery of St

Clare and take away from there one whom only you, outside of myself and Capitán Tiago, can identify. You will not be running any risks at all.'

'María Clara!' exclaimed Basilio.

'Yes, María Clara,' confirmed Simoun, and for the first time his voice took on a sad and human accent. 'I want to rescue her, I have wanted to live only to rescue her, I have returned... I make a revolution because only a revolution can open for me the gates of the nunneries!'

'Ah,' said Basilio, clasping his hands, 'you are too late!'

'Why?' asked Simoun with a frown.

'María Clara is dead.'

Simoun sprang to his feet and seized Basilio.

'Dead?' he asked in a terrible voice.

'This afternoon, at six. Now she should be...'

'A lie!' roared Simoun, pale and broken. 'It can't be true! María Clara lives, she must! This is a cowardly excuse. She is not dead and tonight I shall set her free or tomorrow you die!'

Basilio shrugged.

'She had been ill for some time and I would go to the convent for news. Look, here is Father Salví's letter, Father Irene brought it. Capitán Tiago wept all night, kissing his daughter's picture and begging her forgiveness. In the end he smoked a huge dose of opium. This afternoon they tolled the bells for her.'

Simoun gave a great cry and, holding his head in his hands, remained motionless.

'Dead,' he whispered as to a shade. 'Dead and I did not see her again, dead without knowing I lived for her, dead in pain...'

Then feeling in himself a terrible storm, a storm of thunder and whirlwinds without a drop of rain, sobs without tears, wordless cries, that threatened to break out like burning lava too long repressed, he fled from the room. Basilio heard him go down the stairs with hurrying, uneven step; he heard a cry, choked down, a cry that seemed to greet Death, deep, overwhelming, agonizing, so that he started out of his chair, pale and trembling; but then he heard the steps fade away and the street door slammed shut.

'Poor man,' he muttered, and his eyes filled with tears.

Forgetting his studies, his eyes looking out vaguely into space, he pondered on the fate of these two human beings, one of them a rich and cultured young man, free, master of his destiny, with a brilliant future before him, and she, beautiful as a dream, pure, full of faith and innocence, cradled in love and smiles, destined for a happy life in her family's affection and the world's esteem; yet, of these two, so full of love, illusion and hope, one had been driven by a fatal destiny to wander through the world carried along relentlessly in a whirlwind of blood and tears, sowing evil instead of doing good, crushing virtue and fomenting vice, while she perished in the mysterious depths of the cloister where she had sought peace and had perhaps found suffering, where she had entered pure and without stain and died a broken flower.

Sleep in peace, unhappy daughter of my unfortunate country! Bury in the grave the delights of your youth, withered in full bloom! When a people cannot offer their virgins a peaceful home under the protection of sacred liberties, when man can only bequeath shame to his widow, tears to his mother, and slavery to his sons, then you did well to condemn yourself to perpetual chastity, drowning in your womb the seed of an accursed generation! Ah, you are blessed indeed for you shall not tremble in the grave hearing the cry of those who die in agony in the dark, those who beat their wings against their chains, those who cannot draw breath for lack of freedom! Go, go with the poet's fancy to the far reaches of infinity, a woman's shade glimpsed in a ray of moonlight, summoned by the supple branches of the bamboo groves… Happy she who dies and is mourned, who leaves in the loving heart an immaculate vision, a holy memory, unstained by the petty passions that sour with the years! Go, we shall remember you! In the clear air of our country, under its blue sky, on the waves of the lake that sapphire mountains and emerald shores enclose, in its crystal brooks shaded by bamboo, banked with flowers and alive with the capricious darting of dragonflies, and fluttering butterflies that seem to mock the air, in the silence of our forests, in the music of our rivers, in the diamond rain of our waterfalls, by the shimmering light of our moon, in the sighing of the night wind, in everything that calls forth the image of the beloved, we shall see you always as in a dream, fair, beautiful, smiling with hope, pure as light, and yet forlorn and sorrowful in the contemplation of our misfortunes!

24 • Dreams
Love, what star art thou?

THE next day, a Thursday, some hours before sundown, Isagani went along the lovely promenade of María Cristina towards the Malecon Drive to keep an appointment which Paulita had made with him that morning. He had no doubt that they would speak about the last night's events and, determined as he was to demand an explanation, yet knowing how proud and overbearing she could be, he foresaw a final quarrel. For this eventuality he had brought along Paulita's only two letters to him, two scraps of paper on which a few lines had been hastily scribbled, with a number of erasures and spelling mistakes, defects which had not prevented the young man from keeping them with even more devotion than if they had been autographed poems of Sappho herself or the very Muse of Sacred Poetry.

His decision to sacrifice love to self-respect and the consciousness of suffering for what he believed to be right did not stop Isagani from feeling melancholy. He thought back on delightful days and nights even more delightful when they had whispered sweet nonsense to each other across the flower-decked grill of a ground-floor window, nonsense that withal had for him such gravity and importance that they seemed the only concepts worth the attention of the most highly developed human intellect. Isagani remembered promenades, moonlit nights, the fair December mornings after early Mass, the holy water he would offer her and she would accept gratefully with a look full of love's poetry, both of them set trembling by the touch of their fingers. His breast bursting with sighs, he called to mind all the verses, all that had ever been written in prose and poetry, on woman's inconstancy. He damned the theatre and French operettas and swore to avenge himself on Peláez at the first opportunity. Everything about him seemed dark and gloomy: the bay seemed lonelier still because there were so few ships at anchor; the sun was setting behind Mariveles but shorn of poetry and enchantment, naked of the richly coloured and fanciful clouds of happier twilights; the monument to Anda struck him as being in bad taste, paltry yet over-ornate, without style, without grandeur, like an ice or at best a pastry; the gentlemen taking the air along the Malecon, despite their happy and self-satisfied air, seemed sour, haughty, vain; and naughty and badly brought up, the children playing on the beach, sending flat stones skipping on top of the waves, or hunting in the sand for the cockles and winkles that they caught for the mere pleasure of catching them, and killed for no visible good. In brief, even the interminable port works, to which in other times he had dedicated no less than three odes, appeared to him absurd, ridiculous, puerile.

The port, ah, the port of Manila, a bastard that from the moment of conception had brought only humiliation and shame to all! If, at least, after so much sacrifice, it were not to turn out a disgusting abortion!

He greeted two Jesuits, who had been his teachers, absentmindedly; he scarcely noticed a tandem driven by an American which was exciting the envy of a number of men of fashion driving their own rigs; near the Anda monument he overheard Ban Zayb saying that Simoun had suddenly fallen ill the night before and now refused to receive any visitors, even the General's aides.

Ah, he thought bitterly, care is lavished on him because he is rich but nobody cares to visit the soldiers who return sick or wounded from the expeditions to the Carolines!

He meditated on these expeditions, on the fate of the poor soldiers, and on the resistance of the islanders to the foreign yoke, thinking that, death for death, that of the soldiers was noble because they were doing their duty but that of the islanders glorious because they were defending their homes.

The strange fate of some peoples! Because a passing traveller came to their shores, they lost their freedom and became the subjects and slaves not only of the traveller or of his heirs but even of his countrymen, and not for one generation alone but for ever more! What a strange idea of justice! A situation like that gave one more than enough right to slaughter every foreigner like the most ferocious monster spewed up by the sea.

He pondered that those islanders with whom his country was at war were, after all, guilty of nothing but weakness. Travellers had landed on the shores of other peoples but, finding them strong, had not advanced such singular claims. Yet, weak though they were, these islanders seemed to him to be making a magnificent demonstration, and the names of these enemies, whom the newspapers so carefully called cowards and traitors, seemed glorious to him for they fell gloriously in the ruins of their primitive fortifications, and with a greater glory still than the heroes of ancient Troy because these islanders had never kidnapped a Philippine Helen. With his poet's fervour he thought of the young men of those islands who could cover themselves with glory in the eyes of their women and, unhappy in love, he envied them because they could find a memorable death.

Ah, he too would like to die, to become nothing, to leave to his country a glorious name, to die for her, defending her against foreign invaders, and let the sun afterwards shine on his dead body, an immovable sentinel on the rocks of the sea!

The conflict with Germany came to his mind and he almost regretted it had been settled; he would have gladly died for the flag of Spain and the Philippines before submitting to the foreign foe.

Because, after all, he thought, we are bound to Spain by firm ties: the past, history, religion, language...

Language, yes, language! He smiled sarcastically; that night they were holding their dinner at a Chinese restaurant to 'celebrate' the death of the

Academy of Spanish.

If the liberals in Spain were like the liberals in the Philippines, the Mother Country would soon count the number of her adherents on two hands!

Night was falling slowly, heightening the young man's melancholy; he had almost lost hope of seeing Paulita. The promenaders were gradually leaving the Malecon for the esplanade of the Luneta from where the fresh evening breezes brought snatches of music. The sailors of a warship anchored in the river were at their sundown tasks, scurrying about the rigging as light as spiders; the other vessels were coming to life and putting on their riding-lights; and the shore, in the words of the poet Alaejos,

> *Where the wind with gentle moan*
> *Sends the billows swiftly on*
> *In the silence and alone...*

released distant tenuous mists that, in the light of the full moon, were gradually transformed into a transparent and mysterious cloud...

Isagani turned his head at the sound of an approaching clatter and his heart pumped faster: a carriage was coming, drawn by white horses, the white horses he could tell from among a hundred thousand. In it were Paulita, Doña Victorina, and Paulita's friend of the night before.

Before the young man could take a step forward Paulita had already alighted, nimble as a sylph, and giving Isagani a smile of reconciliation. Isagani smiled back and it seemed to him that all the dark thoughts that had beclouded his mind now vanished; the sky was alight, there was music in the air, and flowers in the grassy paths. Unfortunately Doña Victorina was also there, Doña Victorina who was drawing the young man to her own side to ask news of Don Tiburcio. Isagani had engaged himself to discover her husband's hiding-place through some of the students of his acquaintance.

'Nobody has been able to tell me anything so far,' he reported, and he was telling the truth because Don Tiburcio was hiding away precisely in the house of Isagani's own uncle, Father Florentino.

'He should know also,' raged Doña Victorina, 'that I am going already to the Constabulary. I want to know where he is, dead or alive. Imagine, otherwise I am waiting ten years before I am having another husband!'

Isagani stared at her; so Doña Victorina was thinking of getting married again! Who could the unfortunate candidate be?

'What is your humble opinion only of Juanito Peláez?' she suddenly asked him.

'Juanito?'

Isagani did not know how to reply: he felt like speaking as badly as he could of Peláez, but his fine scrupulousness triumphed in the end and he spoke well of his rival, precisely because he was a rival. Doña Victorina, all happiness and enthusiasm, broke out into praises of Peláez and she was about to confide her new-found affections to Isagani when Paulita's friend came running to say that the girl's fan had fallen in between some of the rocks that bordered the Malecon. Whether it was a trick or just a lucky chance, the mishap gave Isagani an opportunity to reach an understanding with Paulita while the latter's friend kept Doña Victorina company. For the rest of it Doña Victorina was glad enough to encourage Isagani's suit, now that she wanted to keep Juanito for herself.

Paulita had her own tactics; even while thanking him for rescuing her fan she put on a resentful and offended air and suggested subtly that she was surprised to find him there when everybody was now on the Luneta, even the French actresses...

'You had made an appointment with me—how could I possibly...'

'And yet, last night, you never even noticed I was in the theatre; I was watching you the whole time and not once did you take your eyes off those *cochers*...'

Their positions had been neatly reversed; Isagani, who had come to demand an explanation, had to give one himself and considered himself very lucky when Paulita said she forgave him. As far as her being at the theatre was concerned, he should be grateful to her; her aunt had forced her to go and she had finally consented only in hopes of seeing him during the performance. What did she care for that Juanito Peláez!

'It's my aunt who's in love with him,' she giggled prettily.

They both burst out laughing at that; the marriage of Peláez to Doña Victorina made them crazy with joy, they took it to be as good as done; then Isagani remembered that Don Tiburcio was still alive and confided to his sweetheart the secret of his hiding-place after making her promise to tell no one about it. Paulita promised, with the mental reservation of telling her chum.

This turned their conversation to Isagani's home town, which was surrounded by forests and perched on high rocks at whose feet the ocean roared.

Isagani's eyes shone as he spoke of that obscure little corner: pride brought a flush to his cheeks, his voice trembled, his poetic imagination was enkindled and words came to his tongue burning and full of enthusiasm as if he were speaking of one love to another.

'Ah,' he could not stop himself from exclaiming, 'in my solitary mountains I feel free, free as the air, free as light rushing uncontrolled through space!' He would give a thousand cities, a thousand palaces, for that corner of the Philippines where, far from humankind, he could feel really free. There, face to face with Nature, before the mysteries of the infinite, in the forest and by the sea, he could think, speak and act like a man who has no master.

Paulita was inclined to be resentful and displayed a certain jealousy of this home town so enthusiastically praised; she could not wholly understand it for she was used to hearing the country criticized and would sometimes do so herself.

But Isagani quickly put her at her ease.

He had loved the town more than anything else—before he had known her. He had delighted in wandering in the forests, sleeping under the shade of some tree, or perching on a rock where he could look down upon the blue waves of the Pacific rolling beneath him, bringing him echoes of songs learned on the shores of free America. Before knowing her that sea had been his whole world, his enchantment, love and illusion. When the sea was calm and the sun shone high overhead, he had found pleasure in staring down at the depths fifty metres under him, searching with his eyes for monsters in the undersea forests of coral and madrepore that could be descried through the limpid blue, perhaps some of the huge serpents that, according to the mountain folk, left the jungles to live in the sea and take on horrifying shapes. In the afternoons when, it was said, the sirens appeared, he would seek to espy them between one wave and the next, so earnestly that once he thought he had actually seen them gambolling at their divine games amid the spume and heard their songs of freedom and the sound of their silver harps. He had spent hour after hour watching the transformation of the clouds, or contemplating some solitary tree in the plain or some boulder, without knowing why or being able to explain the indefinable emotions that they aroused in him. His uncle had talked to him at length about this and had even thought of taking him to a doctor, fearful that his nephew might sink into a state of depression. But then he had seen her and fallen in love, and during these last holidays he had found his old haunts somehow wanting, the forest dark, the river running through it dreary, the sea monotonous, the horizon empty. If she were to go there just once, walk along those paths, dip her fingertips in the brook, look upon the sea, sit upon the rocks, fill the air with her voice, then the forest would become a very Eden, the river would sing, the dew would turn into diamonds and the froth of the sea into pearls!

But Paulita had heard that the way to Isagani's home town was over mountains full of leeches and she gave a convulsive shudder at the very thought. She was spoiled and used to every comfort, and declared that she would make the trip only by coach or railway.

Isagani, who had thrown aside all his pessimism and saw thornless roses all about him. was ready with an answer.

'Soon all the islands will be criss-crossed by iron tracks on which, as someone has said,

> *Locomotives will fly*
> *To the far and the nigh!*

Then the most beautiful corners of the Archipelago will be open to all.'

'Then? And when will that be? When I am a doddering old woman.'

'Oh, come now, you don't realize what we can do in a few years,' replied Isagani. 'You have no idea of the country's energy and enthusiasm that have now been roused after so many centuries of lethargy. Spain keeps an eye on us. Our young men in Madrid are working day and night, dedicating to the country all their intelligence, time and effort. We have friends there who are generous enough to join their voices to ours, politicians who understand that there are no stronger bonds than a community of interests and ideals. We are being treated fairly and everywhere are signs of a happy future for all. It is true that we students have just suffered a minor defeat but we are winning all along the line. Everybody knows it! The stab in the back they just gave us is only one of the last convulsions of the dying. Tomorrow we shall be citizens of the Philippines, whose destiny will be brilliant because it will be in the care of loving hands. Oh yes, the future is ours! I see it rosy, I can see life stirring in this land so long lethargic, dead. I see towns springing to life along the railways, everywhere factories and buildings. I can hear the steam whistles, the clatter of trains, the thunder of the machines; I can see their smoky breath; and I can smell the oil which these monsters will sweat in their unceasing labours. We shall see this port, whose development has been so difficult, and this river, where to all appearances trade is dying; well, we shall see them so full of masts that we may have an idea from them of the leafless forests of the European winter. This air, which is so pure, these stones so clean, will be covered with coal-dust, with barrels and packing-cases, the products of human industry; but, never mind, we shall be able to go swiftly in comfortable railway coaches to seek in the interior another atmosphere, other views on other shores, cooler climes on mountainsides. Our Navy's warships will guard our shores; the Spaniard and the Filipino will be rivals in their zeal to repel any foreign invasion, to defend our homes and to let you women laugh and enjoy yourselves in peace, loved and respected. Freed from exploitation, distrust and despair, the people will work because work will have ceased to be shameful and servile as something required of a slave; then the Spaniard will no longer have reason to sour his character with ridiculous pretensions to despotism and, eye to eye, with stout hearts, we shall take each other by the hand. Then commerce, industry, agriculture, science will be free to develop under the protection of wise and equitable laws as in prosperous England.'

Paulita smiled sceptically and shook her head.

'Dreams, nothing but dreams,' she sighed. 'I have heard that you have many enemies. Aunt Torina says that this country will always be enslaved.'

'Because your aunt is a fool! She cannot live without slaves and, when she cannot have them, dreams of getting them in the future and, when even that is impossible, she imagines she will. Of course, we have enemies, of course we shall have to fight, but we are going to win. The old regime may turn the ruins of lost castles into hasty barricades; we shall take them to the tune of the songs of freedom, under the light of your eyes, to the applause of your beloved hands! As for the rest of it, have no fears, the fight will be peaceful; it is enough that you should keep us at our studies, awaken in us high and noble thoughts, and encourage constancy and heroism with the reward of your tenderness!'

Paulita was thoughtful but kept her enigmatic smile; she was looking out on the river, lightly tapping her cheek with her fan.

'And if you achieve nothing?' she asked absent-mindedly.

The question hurt Isagani. He looked into the eyes of his beloved, caught her softly by the hand, and replied:

'Listen, if we achieve nothing...'

He hesitated and stopped.

'Listen, Paulita, you know how much I love you and adore you. You know that I am quite another man when you look at me and I see in your eyes a spark of love. Yet, if we should achieve nothing I would dream of another look in your eyes; I should be happy to die if you would have in your eyes one day a gleam of pride as you told the world, pointing to my body: "My love has died fighting for the rights of his people!" '

'Let us go home already,' Doña Victorina shouted. 'Foolish, maybe a cold is catching you!'

Her voice took them back to reality. It was time to go home and the ladies were kind enough to ask Isagani to join them in their carriage; he did not have to be asked twice. The carriage was Paulita's, and so Doña Victorina and Paulita's chum, as her guests, sat in the back while she and Isagani took the occasional folding seats.

To go in the same carriage, have her beside him, drink in her perfume, brush against her silken dress, see her pensively crossing her arms under the native moon that endows commonplaces with illusion and enchantment — this was a dream that Isagani had never dreamed! How miserable they looked, all those people who were going home on foot, alone, scrambling out of the way of the swift carriage! They were going along the shore, by the promenade of the Sabana, over the Bridge of Spain, but Isagani saw nothing but a tender profile, lustrous tresses, and a supple neck that lost itself in the gauze of her shawl. A diamond winked at him from the lobe of a tiny ear, a star amid silvery clouds. Isagani heard distant voices asking him about Don Tiburcio de Espadaña, the name of Juanito Peláez was mentioned, but they were as bells ringing afar off, confused voices in a dream.

He had to be told that they had reached the square of Santa Cruz.

25 • *Laughter and Tears*

THE dining hall of the Macao 'Good Taste' Restaurant had an extraordinary appearance that night.

Fourteen young men from the principal islands of the Archipelago, ranging from pure native (if there was such a thing) to peninsular Spaniard, had gathered to hold the dinner suggested by Father Irene to mark the decision taken on the teaching of Spanish. They had reserved all the tables, called for more lights, and placed on the wall, among the Chinese landscapes and picture scrolls, these curious verses:

GLORY TO CUSTODIO WHO LIEST AND NOODLES
ON EARTH TO BOYS OF GOODWILL!

This was probably the best way of commemorating the happy thought of the egregious Don Custodio in a country where the grotesque was invariably disguised with an air of gravity, where many rose to the heights propelled by smoke and hot air, and what was truly serious and sincere was apt to be heart-breaking and a threat to public order. The butts of the joke were replying with laughter and they were matching the official pie with a plate of noodles.

Yet, for all the banter and laughter, the gaiety seemed strained, the laughter had a certain nervous pitch, eyes sparkled but in some it was the sparkle of tears. These young men were nonetheless cruel and unfair: it was not the first time that the most inspiring plans had come to such an end or that hopes had been defrauded with big words and little action; Don Custodio had many, very many, predecessors.

There were four round dining-tables in the hall symmetrically arranged to form a square under red lanterns. The seats were equally round wooden stools. As usual in the restaurant there were at the centre of each table four coloured saucers with four little pies in each, four red porcelain Chinese teacups covered with lids, and before each stool a bottle and two gleaming wine-glasses.

The curious Sandoval scrutinized everything, sampled the pies, examined the pictures and read the price-list. The rest discussed the topics of the day: the actresses in the French operetta and the mysterious illness of Simoun who, according to some, had been found wounded in the street and, according to others, had tried to kill himself. Not unexpectedly they were lost in conjecture. Tadeo had his own version on what he called good authority. Simoun had been assaulted by an unknown man in the old square of Vivac; the motive had been revenge, which was proved by the fact that Simoun himself refused to give the least explanation. They went on to talk of mysterious avengers and then, by a natural connexion, to monkish exploits; each of them had a story to tell of the feats of their parish priests.

A quatrain in large black letters could be read on the frieze of the hall:

The management regrets it is not able
To take any responsibility
For whatever it may be
That is left on the chairs or table.

'Now there's a warning for you!' exclaimed Sandoval. 'Sign of confidence in the gang, eh? And what verses: Don Tiburcio turned into a jingle, two feet, one longer than the other, between two crutches! If Isagani sees it, he is capable of sending it to his future aunt!'

'And here comes Isagani!' cried a voice from the staircase.

The happy youth made his entrance bursting with joy. He was followed by two shirtless Chinese bearing huge trays with tureens that spread appetizing odours. They were greeted merrily.

Juanito Peláez had not arrived, but it was already past the time fixed for the dinner and they gaily took their seats at the tables; Juanito was always careless about his appointments.

'If we had invited Basilio instead,' said Tadeo, 'we would have had more fun. We could have got him drunk and got some secrets from him.'

'The prudent Basilio? Secrets?'

'Of course,' replied Tadeo, 'most important secrets. There are certain mysteries to which only he has the key. The boy who disappeared. The nun…'

'Gentlemen,' announced Makaraig, 'noodles *lang-lang* make the soup without compare! As you will see, Sandoval, it is made with mushrooms, prawns or shrimps, beaten egg, rice noodles, chicken, and God knows what else. Let us offer Don Custodio the first fruits: the bones. Let him make a project out of them!'

'If he ever hears of it…'

'He'll come running,' injected Sandoval. 'The soup is excellent. What did you say it was called?'

'Noodles *lang-lang,* that is to say, Chinese noodles, to distinguish them from native noodles.'

'I can't remember that. In honour of Don Custodio I christen it instead *PROJECT Soup!'*

The new name was instantly adopted.

'Gentlemen,' said Makaraig, who had ordered the dinner. 'There are three courses to come. Chinese *lumpia* made with pork…'

'Which is coupled with the name of Father Irene!'

'Hold it,' a young man from Iloilo whispered to his neighbour. 'Father Irene can't eat pork with that nose of his.'

'Then off with his nose!'

'Off with the nose of Father Irene!'

'A little more respect, gentlemen, more respect,' Pecson chided them with mock gravity.

'The third course is a crab omelette…'

'Dedicated to the friars,' proposed the Visayan.

'For the crabs they are,' argued Sandoval.

'Right! And it shall be called friar omelette.'

'Friar omelette!' they chorused.

'I protest on behalf of the crabs,' demurred Tadeo.

'A little more respect, gentlemen, more respect,' repeated Pecson, his mouth full.

'And the fourth course is stewed noodles which is dedicated... to the Government and the country!'

All turned to Makaraig.

'Until recently, gentlemen,' he continued, 'noodles were thought to be of Chinese or Japanese origin, but the fact is that noodles are unknown in China and Japan and would therefore appear to be Filipino. Yet they are cooked by Chinese and it is the Chinese who make money out of them — which is exactly the case of the Government and of the Philippines. At least they look like Chinese but whether they really are or are not is a question we must leave to the doctors of Holy Mother Church. Observe further that everybody eats noodles and likes noodles and yet everybody pretends to be finicky about eating them and makes faces over them. It is the same when it comes to the Philippines and the most disorganized of governments. Let us dedicate the noodles, then, to the country and the Government.'

'Approved!' came the chorus

'I protest!' cried Isagani.

'Respect for the aged, respect for the victims!' appealed Pecson in a hollow voice, waving a chicken bone.

'Let us rather dedicate the noodles to Quiroga the Chinaman, one of the four pillars of the Philippines,' proposed Isagani.

'No, to His Black Eminence!'

'Quiet,' one of them warned cryptically.' We are being watched from the square and the walls have ears.'

Indeed there were groups of onlookers stationed below the windows while the bustle and the merriment in the adjoining restaurants had stopped completely as if everyone there had been listening to what was being said at the students' dinner. It was an unusual silence.

'Tadeo, make a speech,' Makaraig whispered.

It had been previously agreed that Sandoval, the best speaker of them all, would sum up the toasts and speeches of the others.

Tadeo, lazy as ever, had neglected to prepare a speech and now found himself in a predicament. He was casting about for ways to extricate himself until, tucking in a particularly long rice-noodle, he remembered a speech which they had learned in class and decided to plagiarize and adulterate it.

'Dear brethren in project,' he began, gesticulating with his chopsticks.

'Beast! Let go the chopsticks,' said his neighbour. 'You are uncombing my hair!'

'Called by your votes to fill the vacancy left in...'

'Plagiarist!' interrupted Sandoval. 'That is the speech made by the president of our literary club.'

'Called by your votes,' continued Tadeo imperturbably, 'to fill the vacancy left in my... mind (and he pointed to his stomach), a man renowned for his Christian doctrine and for his original ideas and projects, who is worthy of having a better memory—what can he say to you, one like me who is dying of hunger because he hasn't had lunch?'

'Have a neck, boy,' said his neighbour, handing him the neck of a chicken.

'There is a dish, gentlemen, the most treasured possession of a people that is nowadays the talk and laughing-stock of the world, into which the greatest gluttons of the western regions of the globe have greedily stuck their spoons.' He was pointing his chopsticks towards Sandoval who was struggling with a recalcitrant chicken-wing, and the latter promptly added:

'And the eastern too!' He waved his spoon to include all present.

'Interruptions are out of order!'

'I ask for the floor!'

'I ask for fish sauce!' added Isagani.

'Bring on the *lumpia*!'

All called for the *lumpia* and Tadeo resumed his seat, happy enough to be out of his difficulties.

The course dedicated to Father Irene did not seem so appetizing and Sandoval emphasized it cruelly.

'Glistening with grease on the outside, and inside nothing but pig's meat! Bring on the third course, the friar omelette!'

The omelette was not yet ready, the lard could still be heard hissing in the frying-pan, and they took advantage of the interval to drink and call upon Pecson to speak.

Pecson gravely crossed himself and, barely able to repress his clownish guffaw, rose to his feet. In imitation of a certain Augustinian preacher, famous at that time, be began by murmuring the text of a sermon.

'*Si tripa plena laulat Deum, tripa famelica laudabit fratres;* a full belly praiseth God, but an empty belly praiseth the friars. Words spoken by Don Custodio through Ben Zayb, in *The Voice of Integrity,* second article, idiocy number one hundred and fifty seven.

'My dear brethren in Jesus Christ:

'An evil and impure wind blows on the verdant shores of Friarland, commonly known as the Philippine Archipelago. No day passes without an attack, a sarcastic insult, against the reverend, venerable, and preachifying Orders, so defenceless and shorn of all support. Permit me, brethren, to turn myself for a moment into a knight errant sallying forth to the rescue of the unprotected, of the holy Orders that have educated us, thus confirming once again that the maxim "a full belly praiseth God", is truly complemented by that other, "an empty belly praiseth the friars".'

'Hear, hear!'

'Now look here,' said Isagani earnestly, 'I want you to know that there is at least one friar whom I respect.'

Sandoval, who was in his cups by now, started singing:

One friar, two friars, three friars,
A choir of friars full,
Have much the same effect
As a single fighting bull!

'Hearken to me, brethren, and turn back your eyes to the lovely days of your childhood, try to look at the present and to peer into the future. What do you see? Friars, friars, and more friars! A friar baptizes you, confirms you, and watches over you in school with loving zeal; a friar hears your first secrets, first gives you a god to eat, and starts you on the path of life; your first and last teachers are friars; it is a friar who opens the hearts of your sweethearts and makes them susceptible to your sighs, a friar marries you, and sends you off travelling to various islands for a change of climate and amusements; he assists you on your death-beds and, even if you should be sent to the scaffold, the friar will be there to accompany you with his prayers and his tears, and you can be sure that he will not abandon you until he sees you well hung and thoroughly dead. Nor does his charity stop there. When you are dead he will try to bury you with all pomp, he will fight to expose your corpse in church, he will recite over you prayers of intercession, and will rest content only when he can commend you into the hands of the Creator, purified here on earth by temporal punishments, tortures and humiliations. Knowing that the doctrines of Christ close the gates of Heaven to the rich, these new redeemers, true ministers of the Saviour, use every trick to relieve you of your sins, commonly known as dough, and take it far away across the seas to the land of the accursed Chinese and Protestants, thus cleansing the atmosphere, leaving it pure and healthy, so that even if afterwards you should want to do so, it would be impossible for you to find a single peso for your damnation!

'If, then, their existence is essential for our happiness; if, wherever we stick our noses, we come across the friar's fine hand, so eager for kisses that day by day it flattens even more the ill-used appendage we bear on our faces, why not pamper them and fatten them up, why ask for their impolitic expulsion? Consider for a moment the immense vacuum that their absence will leave in our society. The friars are tireless workers, they are constantly improving and multiplying our race; we, for our part, are divided by jealousies and resentments. It is the friars who bind us all in a common fate, in a tight sheaf, so tight indeed that many cannot even move their elbows! Remove the friar, gentlemen, and you shall see the edifice of state tottering for lack of sturdy shoulders and hairy legs to support it; life in the Philippines will grow monotonous without the merry laughter of the playful and carousing friar, without all those uproarious sermons and pious pamphlets, without the witty contrast between great pretensions and scant wits, without the daily lively re-enactment of the tales of Boccaccio and La Fontaine! What shall our women do without religious girdles and scapulars except save the money now spent on them, thus perhaps turning miserly and covetous? Without Masses, novenas and processions, how shall gambling flourish to amuse their idle moments? They will be reduced to doing housework and we shall have to find them nonexistent books to replace the amusing miracle stories they now read. Remove the friar and heroism will vanish for the political virtues will then be within the understanding of the common people; remove the friar and the native will cease to exist for the friar is the Father, the native the Word, the friar the artist, the native the statue; all that we are, all that we think, all that we do, we owe to the friar, to his patience, to his labours, to his constant struggle for three centuries to change the way that Nature made us. The Philippines without friars and without natives: what will happen to the Government left alone with the Chinese?'

'It will eat crab omelette,' replied Isagani, who was bored by Pecson's speech. 'And that's what we should do too! No more speeches!'

However, the Chinese waiter was taking too long to bring in the third course and one of the students got up and went to the back of the restaurant where a balcony overlooked the river. He came back immediately, making cryptic signals.

'They're spying on us, I have just seen Father Sibyla's favourite.'

'Really?' exclaimed Isagani, rising to his feet.

'Too late now, he left when he saw me.'

Going to the window he looked out on the square and motioned to his companions to join him. They saw a young man leave the restaurant, look about him, and then enter, together with a stranger, a coach that was waiting by the kerb. It was Simoun's.

'Ah,' said Makaraig, 'the Vice-Rector's slave is served by the General's master.'

26 • Subversive Posters

BASILIO rose very early the next morning to go to the Hospital. He had his morning planned out: he would visit his patients, go afterwards to the University to make inquiries about his degree, and then see Makaraig about the expenses of his graduation. He had spent a great part of his savings in ransoming Julí and putting up a cottage where she could live with her grandfather, and he did not dare have recourse to Capitán Tiago for fear that the latter would interpret a request for a loan as an advance against the inheritance he was always promising Basilio.

Absorbed in these thoughts he did not notice the groups of students returning from the Walled City too early in the morning for a school day; still less did he remark the worried air of some of them, their whispered conversations, and their cryptic signs to one another. When, therefore, upon his reaching the Hospital his friends asked him about some conspiracy, Basilio was startled, remembering Simoun's plot which had been thwarted by the mysterious accident he had suffered. Deeply disturbed and with a changed voice he asked with pretended ignorance:

'The conspiracy? What conspiracy?'

'The one that has just been discovered,' he was told. Apparently many have been implicated.'

Basilio tried to control himself.

'Many implicated?' he repeated, trying to read the faces of the rest. 'Who?'

Basilio did not think it prudent to ask any more questions fearful of betraying himself, and left the group on the pretext that he had to visit his patients. A professor at the clinic, who was his friend, crossed his path and, putting his hand on Basilio's shoulder enigmatically, asked him in a hushed voice:

'Were you at the dinner last night?'

In his state of mind Basilio thought he heard 'night before last', the night of his meeting with Simoun, and tried to explain.

'Well, this is what happened,' he stammered. 'Capitán Tiago had taken a turn for the worse and I had to finish the Mata...'

'You did well not to go,' said the professor. 'But are you a member of the students' association?'

'I pay my fees.'

'Well, then, some good advice: resign at once and destroy any compromising papers you may have.'

Basilio shrugged, he had no papers except clinical notes, nothing else.

'But is Mr Simoun...'

'Simoun has nothing to do with it, thank God,' said the doctor. 'He was mysteriously wounded at just the right time and is in bed. No, other hands are at work here, no less fearsome.'

Basilio sighed with relief Only Simoun could implicate him. However, there was, he remembered, Cabesang Tales.

'Any bandits...?'

'No, man, only students.'

Basilio had now recovered his serenity so far as to ask:

'What happened, then?'

'Didn't you know? Subversive posters have been found.'

'Where?'

'Dammit all, in the University!'

'Is that all?'

'What the devil more do you want?' asked the professor on the verge of losing his temper. 'The posters are being blamed on the students in the association. Careful now!'

He had seen the professor of Pathology coming, a man who looked more like a sacristan than a physician. He had been appointed by the all-powerful Vice-Rector, who had required no qualifications or degrees other than an unconditional loyalty to the Order; he was considered a spy and an informer by the other members of the Faculty.

The first professor returned his colleague's salute coldly and, with a wink at Basilio, said loudly:

'Yes, I know Capitán Tiago smells of death, the buzzards and the vultures have called on him.'

And he entered the faculty room.

Somewhat more at his ease Basilio took the risk of inquiring after more details. All he could learn was that posters had been found on the doors of the University, and that the Vice-Rector had ordered them to be removed and sent to the Office of Civil Administration. It was said that the posters had been full of threats of massacre and invasion and similar bravado.

It was on this discovery that the students had been making their comments. The news had come from the janitor, who had heard it from a servant, who in turn had heard it from a student working his way through the University as a domestic of the friars. Suspensions, arrests and other reprisals were predicted with, naturally, the members of the students' association as the victims.

Simoun's words came to Basilio's mind: the day they can get rid of you... You will never finish the course...

Had Simoun known what he was talking about? Well, they would see who would win out in the end.

Recovering his self-possession Basilio decided to go to the University to find out where he stood and at the same time to inquire about his degree. He went down Legazpi Street, then followed Beaterio until he reached the corner of Solana, where he perceived that something of importance must indeed have happened.

Instead of the gay and noisy groups of other days, pairs of policemen were on the pavements, keeping the students moving as they left the University, some of them silent, others sullen and annoyed. They were standing about at a distance or taking the way home. Basilio met Sandoval first but called to him in vain; Sandoval seemed to have gone deaf.

'The effects of fear on the gastro-intestinal juices,' thought Basilio.

Then he came across Tadeo who had a face like Christmas. At last it seemed the perpetual holiday was coming true.

'What's new, Tadeo?'

'No classes, for at least a week, boy! It's sublime, magnificent!'

He rubbed his hands with satisfaction.

'But what has happened?'

'They are going to throw us in gaol, all the members of the association!'

'Does that make you happy?'

'No classes, no classes!' and he walked away chortling with glee.

Basilio saw Juanito Peláez coming, pale and suspicious, in such a hurry to get away that his stoop was at its maximum elevation. He had been one of the most active promoters of the association when things had been going well.

'Hey, Peláez, what has happened?'

'Nothing, I know nothing, I had nothing to do with it,' he answered nervously. 'I kept telling them it was all quixotic. Tell me now, isn't it true I said so?'

Basilio did not know whether Peláez had actually said so but in order to be agreeable answered:

'Yes, man, all right! But what is going on?'

'It's true, isn't it? Now look, you're my witness, I have always been opposed to... Now, you're my witness, don't forget!'

'All right, man, all right. But what is happening?'

'Listen, you're my witness, I have never had anything to do with the members of the association except to advise them... Don't deny it afterwards. Be careful, see?'

'No, I won't deny it! But good Lord, what has happened?'

Juanito was already far away, he had seen a policeman coming and was afraid he would be arrested.

Basilio turned his steps to the University to see if perhaps the secretary's office was open and to get more news. The office was closed but there was an extraordinary amount of activity in the building: friars, officers, private individuals, experienced lawyers and physicians went upstairs and downstairs, perhaps to offer their services to the cause in time of danger.

He saw his friend Isagani from afar, his face drawn and deeply moved yet full of youthful beauty, addressing a handful of classmates in a loud voice, as if he did not care though the whole world heard him.

'It seems incredible, gentlemen, absolutely incredible that such a little thing should put us all to flight and that we should scatter like sparrows before a scarecrow! Is this the first time that young men go to prison for the cause of freedom? Where are the dead, the executed? Why be turncoats now?'

'But who was fool enough to write such posters?' an indignant student demanded.

'What do we care?' replied Isagani. 'It is not our business to investigate that, let them do it! Before we know what was written in the posters, there is no need for us to make protestations of loyalty at moments like these. Where the danger is, there we must go, for that is the place of honour! If what the posters say is in keeping with our self-respect and our own sentiments, then whoever wrote them did well, and we should thank him and hasten to join our names to his. If the posters are unworthy of us, then our conduct and our conscience will speak for themselves and defend us against any charge...'

When he heard such language Basilio, although he had a deep affection for Isagani, turned on his heel and left. He had to go to Makaraig's house to speak to him about the loan.

Nearing the rich student's hostel he observed that the neighbours were whispering and signalling one another but Basilio, not knowing what it was all about, calmly went on his way and entered the house. Two policemen stopped him and asked him what he wanted. Basilio realized he had been imprudent but could no longer withdraw.

'I have come to see my friend Makaraig,' he answered coolly.

The policemen exchanged glances.

'Wait here,' said one of them. 'Wait for the corporal to come down.'

Basilio bit his lips and Simoun's words echoed in his ears once more. Had they come to arrest Makaraig? He did not dare to put the question into words.

He did not have to wait long. Just then Makaraig was coming downstairs chatting amiably with the corporal, following a process-server.

'What! You too, Basilio?' asked Makaraig.

'I came to see you.'

'Nobly done,' laughed Makaraig. 'In peaceful times you avoid us...'

The corporal asked Basilio his name and checked a list.

'A medical student? Residing on Anloague Street?'

Basilio bit his lips.

'You have saved us a trip,' said the corporal, placing his hand on Basilio's shoulder. 'Consider yourself under arrest.'

'What, me too?'

Makaraig laughed.

'Don't worry, friend. We shall go by coach and there I shall tell you about the dinner last night.'

With the gracious gesture of a host he invited the corporal and the process-server to enter the coach waiting at the kerb.

'To the Office of Civil Administration,' he ordered.

Basilio, who had recovered from the shock of his arrest, told Makaraig the reason for his visit. The rich student did not let him finish and grasped his hand.

'Count on me. We shall ask these gentlemen,' he added, nodding to the corporal and the process-server, 'to be our guests at the conferment of degrees.'

27 • *The Friar and the Filipino*
The voice of the people is the voice of God.

ISAGANI was haranguing his friends when a student-domestic approached him with the message that Father Fernández, a professor in the preparatory courses, wanted to speak to him.

Isagani was troubled. he had the greatest respect for Father Fernández, who was the one exception he always made whenever the friars were attacked.

'What does Father Fernández want?'

The domestic gave a shrug and Isagani followed him reluctantly.

Father Fernández, who had been present at the discussions in Los Baños, was waiting for him in his cell, thoughtful and depressed, with a meditative frown. He rose when he saw Isagani enter, greeted him with a handclasp, closed the door and then walked up and down the room. Isagani remained standing, waiting for the friar to speak.

'Mr Isagani,' he said finally in a voice that shook faintly with emotion, 'I heard you making your speech from my window—as a consumptive I have sharp ears—and I wanted to speak to you. I have always liked young men who can make themselves understood and who think and act for themselves; it doesn't matter to me that they may have ideas different from mine. I have heard you gave a dinner last night—don't deny it...'

'But I am not denying it!' Isagani interrupted him.

'All the better. It proved that you accept the consequences of your acts. In any case you would be wrong to deny it. I do not censure you, whatever may have been said last night does not matter to me. Nor do I make any accusations against you since after all you are free to say what you like about the Dominicans; you are not one of our products, we have had the pleasure of teaching you only this year, and probably not after that. Do not think I shall- appeal to your sense of gratitude; I do not propose to waste my time on stupid commonplaces. I had you called because I believe that you are one of the few students who act on conviction and, since I like men of conviction, I told myself that I should like to thresh things out with Mr Isagani.'

Father Fernández paused even while he continued walking up and down the room, his head lowered, his eyes on the floor.

'You may sit down if you wish he said, 'I have the habit of talking on my feet. My thoughts come to me more easily that way.'

Isagani remained standing, head held high, waiting for the professor to face the issue.

'I have been a professor more than eight years,' said Father Fernández, 'and in that time I have known and got to know more than two and a half thousand young men. I have taught them, tried to educate them, inculcated in them the principles of justice and self-respect, and yet, in these times when so much is said against us, I have yet to see one of them bold enough to stand his ground when he has found himself face to face with a friar— not even in a speech before a favourable audience—why, there are young men who slander us behind our backs and, when they are face to face, kiss our hands and beg for a look with contemptible smiles. *Pouf!* What would you have us do with such creatures?'

'The fault is not all theirs, Father,' replied Isagani.

'The fault is in those who taught them to be hypocrites, in those who suppress freedom of thought and freedom of speech. Here every independent thought, every word which is not an echo of the will of the powerful, is called subversion, and you know very well what that means. Only a fool would risk persecution for saying what he thinks out loud!'

'What persecution have you suffered?' asked Father Fernández raising his head. 'Have I not allowed you to speak out freely in my class? You are an exception, of course, but if what you say is true I should have silenced you to make the rule generally applicable and to get rid of a bad example.'

Isagani smiled.

'Thank you, I shall not argue now about whether or not I am an exception. I accept your description and hope you will accept mine. You too are an exception, but since we are not going to speak of exceptions nor praise ourselves, at least as far as I am concerned, I would ask my professor to take the discussion on to other grounds.'

Father Fernández, for all his liberal principles, stared at Isagani. The young man was even more independent than he had thought; although he called him professor, at bottom Isagani treated him as an equal and permitted himself innuendos. But Father Fernández was a good diplomat and he not only accepted the fact but brought it up himself.

'Congratulations,' he said. 'But do not look on me as your professor; I am a friar and you are a Filipino student, nothing more nor less, and now I ask you: what do the Filipino students want us to do?'

It was an unexpected question. Isagani was not prepared for it. In fencing it would have been called a riposte, a sudden thrust after parrying a lunge. Isagani, taken by surprise, could only counter like a novice with a violent blow.

'To do your duty!' he said.

Father Fernández drew himself up; the answer was like a cannon-shot.

'Do our duty? Why, are we not doing so? What duties do you assign us?'

'The same which you freely took upon yourselves in entering your Order and those which, once in it, you have afterwards wanted to assume. But as a Filipino student I do not think it is my business to examine your conduct with regard to the Rule of your Order, Catholicism, the Government, the Filipino people, and humanity in general; these are questions which you shall have to settle with the founders of your Order, the Pope, the Government, the people as a whole, or God. As a Filipino student I shall limit myself to your duties to us. The friars in general, as the local supervisors of education in the provinces, and the Dominicans in particular, in monopolizing the higher studies of Filipino youth, have assumed the obligation, before the country's eight million inhabitants, before Spain, and before that humankind of which we are part, of constantly improving the young morally and physically, of guiding them to happiness, of creating an honest, prosperous, intelligent, virtuous, noble and loyal people. Now I ask in turn, have the friars fulfilled this obligation?'

'We are fulfilling it...'

'Ah, Father Fernández,' Isagani interrupted him, 'you, with your hand on your own heart, can say you are fulfilling it but, with your hand on the heart of your Order, on the hearts of all the Orders, cannot say it without fooling yourself Father Fernández, when I find myself with someone whom I esteem and respect, I prefer to be the accused rather than the accuser, to defend rather than offend. But since we have started this discussion, let us finish it. How are the supervisors of education in the towns performing their duty? By obstructing education! And those who monopolize the higher studies, those who to the exclusion of all others want to mould the minds of the young, how are they fulfilling their obligations? By curtailing the pursuit of knowledge as much as possible, by stifling all fervour and enthusiasm for it, by undermining that self-respect which is the soul's main resource, and by implanting in us outmoded ideas, discredited theories and false principles incompatible with progress! When it is a matter of feeding convicts or providing subsistence for criminals, the Government calls for open tenders in order to determine who offers to provide it in the most acceptable conditions or who is least likely to starve them to death. But when it is a matter of giving a whole people moral sustenance, a matter of nourishing the youth, a people's best part, destined to be the whole, the Government not only does not call for competitive tenders but awards the power precisely to that organization which prides itself in not wanting education or any form of progress. What would we say if a prison caterer, after winning the contract through devious means, should then leave the prisoners to languish through malnutrition, giving them only rank and spoiled provisions, and should excuse himself by saying that healthy prisoners do not suit his convenience because health brings happy thoughts, happiness improves men, and man should not be improved because the more criminals there are, the better for the prison caterer? What would we say if the Government and the caterer were then to conspire together so that the former might pocket half the profits of the latter?'

Father Fernández was biting his lips.

'These are very harsh accusations,' he said. 'You are going beyond the agreed limits of our discussion.'

'No, Father, I am still speaking of the student question. The friars—and I do not include you among the rest—the friars of all the Orders have become our intellectual caterers and yet they say openly, loudly and without shame that our education does not suit them because some day we shall proclaim our independence! This is to desire the malnutrition of the prisoner so that he may not improve and leave prison. Freedom is to man what education is to the mind, and the opposition of the friars to our education is the source of our discontent.'

'Education is given only to those who are worthy of it,' Father Fernández answered drily. 'It would be a prostitution of education to give it to men without character or morality.'

'And why are there men without character and morality?'

The Dominican shrugged his shoulders.

'These are failings that are bred from childhood, that are due to the family environment—how do I know?'

'Oh no, Father Fernández,' the young man cried impetuously, 'you refuse to go deeper into the matter, you do not want to look down into the abyss for fear of finding there the shadow of your brethren. You have made us what we are. An oppressed people is compelled to be hypocritical; whoever is denied the truth, is given falsehood; the tyrant begets slaves. No morality, you say. Very well, although you might be belied by the statistics because crimes that are committed by many peoples blinded by their boasts of morality, are not committed here. But I do not want to analyse now what constitutes character or to what extent morality is affected by education, and I agree with you that we have our failings. Who is to blame for them? You, who have had our education in your hands for three and a half centuries, or we, who have submitted to everything? If after three and a half centuries the sculptor has produced nothing but a caricature, he must be stupid indeed.'

'Or the material he worked on, poor indeed.'

'The more stupid then because, knowing that the material is poor, he does not give it up and continues to waste his time. And not only stupid but dishonest because, knowing the futility of his work, he continues it in order to collect his fees. And not only stupid and dishonest but infamous because he is against anybody else trying his hand at it to see if he can produce something worthwhile. Such are the fatal jealousies of stupidity!'

The reply was energetic and Father Fernández felt trapped. He stared at Isagani, who now appeared to him gigantic, invincible, paramount, and for the first time in his life he believed himself defeated by a Filipino student. He was sorry he had provoked the discussion but it was too late. In his straits before such a formidable adversary he searched for a good defence and put up the Government.

'You blame us for everything that is wrong because you only see us who are close to you,' he said with less arrogance. 'That is only natural. I understand. The people hate the soldier or the process-server who makes the arrest but not the judge who issued the order of imprisonment. Both you and we are all dancing to the same tune; if you move your feet at the same time that we do, do not blame us for it. Our movements are dictated by the music. Do you believe that we friars do not have consciences and do not desire what is good? Do you believe that we do not think of you, that we are not conscious of our duties and that we only eat to live and live to rule? I wish it were so. But, like you yourselves, we must follow the tune. We are between the Devil and the deep blue sea. Either you throw us out or the Government does. The Government has the power of command and whoever is in command, commands, and ours but to do and die.'

'The conclusion that can be drawn from that,' observed Isagani bitterly, 'is that the Government desires our demoralization.'

'Oh no, I did not mean to say that! What I wanted to say was that there are beliefs, theories, laws which with the best of intentions have the most deplorable consequences. I shall make myself better understood by giving you an example. Thus, to remedy a minor evil numerous laws are promulgated which cause even greater evils. *Corruptissima in republica plurimae leges,* said Tacitus. The state is most corrupt when there are too many laws. In order to prevent one case of official corruption, a million and a half rules and regulations are promulgated, cautionary but insulting, which have the immediate effect of challenging the people to evade and circumvent these precautions. You have only to doubt their honesty in order to turn people to crime. As soon as a law is promulgated, not necessarily here but even in Spain, the search is on for loopholes in it. The trouble is that our legislators have forgotten the fact that the more something is hidden, the more one wants to see it. Why are knavery and cleverness so highly regarded among the Spanish people when there are none so noble, so proud, so chivalrous? Because our legislators with the best of intentions have doubted their nobility, wounded their pride and challenged their chivalry. Do you want to open a road through the rockiest terrain in Spain? Then put up a sign absolutely prohibiting passage, and the people, in protest against such an imposition, will leave the highway to climb over the boulders. If some legislator were to prohibit virtue in Spain and command vice, the next day everyone would be virtuous.'

The Dominican paused.

'But,' he continued, 'you will say that we are straying from the issue. I return to it and say, in the hope of convincing you, that you should not blame us or the Government for your defects; they come from the imperfect organization of our society, which is trying to do too much and as a consequence achieves nothing, ruining itself with excessive prudence, short on necessities and long on the superfluous.'

'If you admit these defects in your society,' countered Isagani, 'why meddle in other societies and try to put them right instead of attending to your own?'

'We are going farther and farther away from the issue, young man. A *fait accompli*, an accomplished fact like the Spanish regime in the Philippines must be accepted.'

'Very well, I accept it because it is a fact but I must go on to ask why you do not change your social organization if it is defective, or at least listen to those who are prejudiced by it.'

'We are still far from the issue. We were speaking of what the students want the friars to do.'

'When the friars hide behind the Government, it is to the Government that the students must have recourse.'

It was a fair reply; there was no way out there.

'I am not the Government and I am not responsible for its actions. What do the students want us to do for them within the limits in which we are confined?'

'Not to oppose the freedom of education but instead to favour it.' The Dominican shook his head.

'Without expressing a personal opinion, I would say that that is to ask us to commit suicide.'

'On the contrary, it is only asking you to give us the right of way that you may not be run over and crushed.'

'Hm.' Father Fernández stood still, deep in thought. 'Begin by asking us something that is not too difficult for us to grant, something that each and every one of us might concede without loss of dignity and privilege. If we could understand one another and live peacefully together, there would be no point in hatred and mistrust.'

'Then let us go to details.'

'Yes. If we go to the foundations we shall bring down the whole structure.'

'To details then,' answered Isagani with a smile. 'Let us leave the ground of principle. Without expressing a personal opinion,' and he emphasized the phrase, 'the students would change their attitude and certain animosities would be allayed if the professors were to give them better treatment than they have had so far. That is entirely up to you.'

'What!' cried the Dominican. 'Have the students any complaints about my conduct?'

'Father, we agreed from the start that we were not speaking about you or me. We are speaking in general. The students not only derive little profit from the years spent in the classroom but many of them usually leave there shreds of their self-respect, if not the whole of it.'

Father Fernández made a grimace.

'No one compels them to study,' he remarked curtly. 'There is work to be done in the fields.'

'Oh, but something does compel them to study,' Isagani replied in the same tone, looking the Dominican in the eye. 'It is every man's duty to improve himself but, apart from that, there is an inborn desire in every man to seek knowledge, a desire that is all the more powerful here when it is most repressed. One who places his wealth and his life in the hands of the State has the right to demand that it give him the knowledge to make his money more easily and to live a better life. Yes, Father, something does compel them and that something is the Government itself; it is you yourselves, who make merciless fun of the unlettered native and deny him his rights because you say he is ignorant. You strip him and then mock his nakedness!'

Father Fernández did not reply and continued to walk up and down the room, rapidly as if excited.

'You say that there is work to be done in the fields,' continued Isagani in a different tone after a brief pause. 'Let us not go into the reasons why, we would not get very far. But do you, Father Fernández, you, a professor, you, a man of science, want a nation of field-hands, of peasants? Do you consider that to be a peasant is to reach the last stage of perfection in human evolution? Or do you want science for yourself and manual labour for the rest?'

'No, I want science for whoever is worthy of it and can profit from it,' the friar replied. 'When the students have given proof of loving it, when we have young men of conviction who will know how to defend its dignity and win its respect, then we shall have science, then we shall have understanding professors. If there are overbearing professors, it is because there are compliant students.'

'When we have real professors, you shall have real students.'

'Begin by changing yourselves. You are the ones who need the change. We shall follow you.'

'Yes,' said Isagani with a wry smile, 'let us begin with ourselves because the difficulty is with us. But you know well enough what awaits the student who stands up to his professor. You yourself, for all your love of justice, for all your good intentions, have been barely able to control yourself when I was telling you the bitter truth. Even you, Father Fernández! What has it profited anyone among us who wanted to sow other ideas? And what injuries have you yourself not suffered because you wanted to do good and do your duty?'

'Mr Isagani,' said the Dominican putting out his hand, 'it may look as if nothing practical has been gained from our conversation but something has been achieved. I shall speak to my brethren about what you have told me and I hope that something can be done. I only fear that they may not believe you exist.'

'I fear the same thing,' answered Isagani, clasping the Dominican's hand. 'I am afraid that my friends will not believe that you exist as you have shown yourself to be.'

He took the meeting to be at an end and said good-bye.

Father Fernández opened the door for him and followed him with his eyes until he went out of sight at a bend of the corridor. He stood for a long time listening to Isagani's footsteps and then re-entered his cell. He waited for the young man to go out into the street and heard him answer a schoolmate who wanted to know where he was going:

'To the Office of Civil Administration. I want to see the posters and join the others.'

The schoolmate had taken fright, stared at him as if on someone who was committing suicide, and run away.

'Poor boy,' murmured Father Fernández, feeling his eyes moisten. 'I envy the Jesuits who educated you.'

Father Fernandez was absolutely wrong. The Jesuits were disowning Isagani and, when they learned that afternoon that he had been arrested, they said he was compromising them.

'That young man is headed for disaster and will do us harm. We want it clearly understood he did not pick up his ideas here.'

The Jesuits were only speaking the truth. Such ideas come only from God through Nature.

28 • *Panic*

WRITING in his newspaper a few days previously that education would be ruinous, absolutely fatal, for the Philippines, Ben Zayb had been prophetically inspired; in view of the subversive posters and the events of that Friday the journalist crowed in triumph to the embarrassment and confusion of his rival Horatius who had dared to make fun of him in his column *Fireworks* in the following language.

'Our colleague *The Voice* writes:

'"Education is ruinous, absolutely fatal, for the Philippines."

'We catch on.

'For some time now *The Voice* has made believe it stands for the Filipino people. *Ergo. . .* as Fray Ybañez would say if he knew Latin.

'But Fray Ybañez turns Muslim when he writes, and we all know how the Muslims deal with education.

'Witnesseth, as a Court preacher used to say, the library of Alexandria!'

But now he had been proved right, he, Ben Zayb—why, he was the only one who used his head in the Philippines, the only one who could foresee events!

The news that subversive posters had been found on the doors of the University had, in fact, spoiled the appetite of some and the digestion of others; it upset even the phlegmatic Chinese who did not dare sit in their shops as usual, with one leg tucked in under them, for fear that they would not be given time to stretch it out again and start running. The uneasiness had increased by eleven o'clock that morning, even though the sun still shone and His Excellency the Commander-in-Chief had not made an appearance at the head of his victorious cohorts, for the friars who frequented Quiroga's shop had not shown up and this was taken to be a symptom and an omen of terrible disasters. If the sun had risen in the shape of a square, and the images of Christ had been discovered wearing trousers, Quiroga would not have been so alarmed; he would have taken the sun for a Chinese playing-card and the sacred images for gamblers who had lost their shirts; but for the friars not to come when he had just received a shipment of the latest goods!

At the behest of a Father Provincial, who was a friend of his, Quiroga prohibited the admission into his gaming houses of any native who was not an old customer; the future Chinese consul was afraid that the wretches might take back by force the money they had lost. After making suitable arrangements to put up the shutters of his shop as quickly as possible in case of emergency, he had himself escorted by a policeman along the short distance from his house to Simoun's. Quiroga saw that this was the most favourable occasion to use the rifles and bullets stored in his warehouse in the manner indicated by the jeweller. It was to be expected that in the days to come there would be searches made and then, ah, what numbers would be thrown into prison, and in the grip of panic hand over all their savings! It was an old trick of the revenue collectors, who would slip unlicensed cigars and tobacco-leaves under a house, make a mock search and then face the unfortunate owner with a choice of a bribe or a fine. The same technique was now being perfected with the difference that, the state tobacco monopoly having been abolished, recourse was had to prohibited arms.

But Simoun would see no one and sent Quiroga the message to leave things as they were. The latter went to see Don Custodio to ask whether or not he should fortify his shop but Don Custodio was not at home to callers either, he was at the time studying a project of defence in case of siege. Quiroga remembered Ben Zayb and went to him for news but, finding him armed to the teeth and using two loaded revolvers as paperweights, the Chinese excused himself as quickly as possible and locked himself up in his house on the pretext that he was not well.

By four o'clock in the afternoon the talk was no longer of mere posters. There were whispered rumours of an alliance between the students and the bandits in the San Mateo mountains; it was stated for certain that plans to take the city by surprise had been made in a Chinese restaurant; there was talk of German warships waiting outside the bay to support the uprising; and a group of young men who, under cover of making a protest against subversion and proclaiming their pro-Hispanism, had gone to Malacañang to place themselves at the orders of the General, were said to have been arrested when found to be bearing arms. Providence had saved His Excellency and had prevented him from giving audience to the precocious criminals because he had then been in conference with the Provincials of the various Orders, the Vice-Rector and Father Irene, who was representing Father Salví. There was considerable truth in these rumours if Father Irene was to be believed. That afternoon he had called on Capitán Tiago and had said that certain persons had advised His Excellency to avail himself of the occasion to institute a reign of terror and give the pseudo-subversives a good lesson once and for all.

'Shoot a few,' one had said, 'send two dozen of these reformers into exile immediately in the dead of night, and the dreams of these disgruntled elements will vanish for ever.'

'No,' another had objected in the goodness of his heart. 'It should be sufficient to make a show of strength with the troops in the streets, for instance the battalion of cavalry with drawn sabres, or a few cannon; that should be enough The people are very timid and everyone will go home.'

'On the contrary, this is the opportunity of ridding ourselves of our enemies,' suggested a third. 'It is not enough for the natives to stay at home. They should be driven out into the open like poisonous fluids drawn out by plasters. If they hesitate to riot they should be incited to do so by *agents provocateurs*. I am of the opinion that the troops should be quietly kept under arms while making a show of negligence and indifference to embolden the natives; then, at the least disturbance, up and at them with energy!'

'The end justifies the means,' was the contribution of a fourth. 'Our end is to protect our Holy Religion and the integrity of the Nation. Proclaim a state of emergency and, at the least trouble, seize all the rich and educated people... and clean out the country.'

Telling Capitán Tiago about this Father Irene added: 'If I had not arrived in time to counsel moderation I am sure the streets would be running blood by now. But I was thinking of you, Capitán. The party of violence did not get much from the General. They felt the absence of Simoun. Ah, if Simoun had not fallen ill...'

What with Basilio's arrest and the search which was afterwards made among his books and papers, Capitán Tiago had taken a turn for the worse. Father

Irene's hair-raising stories now increased his panic. The wretch was seized by an indescribable terror, which first took the form of a slight shuddering but which swiftly grew so overpowering that he was unable to speak. Eyes staring wide, brow wet with sweat, he clutched Father Irene's arm, tried to raise himself but failed, and then, groaning twice, fell heavily back on his pillow. Capitán Tiago's eyes were open and he was frothing at the mouth. He was dead. The frightened Father Irene fled but, as the corpse had its hand on his arm, he dragged it out of the bed in his flight, leaving it lying in the middle of the room.

Panic was greatest by nightfall. A number of incidents had taken place which had led the timid to believe the *agents provocateurs*.

At a christening, as was the local custom, the sponsors had celebrated the event by throwing a handful of coins for the children to scramble for and naturally there had been a certain commotion at the church door. A gallant officer had chanced to pass by at the time and, being on edge, had taken the hubbub for a subversive riot, launched himself on the children with drawn sabre, rushed into the church, and would not have spared a single head if he had not got entangled in a curtain hanging from the choir-loft. One look at this and within seconds the timid had taken to their heels with the news that the revolution had begun. The few shops that remained open had hurriedly put up their shutters, whole bolts of cloth had been left behind by the Chinese, and not a few women had lost their slippers in the streets. Fortunately only one person was wounded and a few suffered bruises, among them the officer himself who had fallen on his face while wrestling with the curtain, which had seemed to him a very cloak for subversion. This feat brought him fame, a fame so stainless that one might wish all military reputations were won in the same way: mothers would have less to weep for and there would be more people alive.

In one of the suburbs the residents had surprised two individuals burying arms under a wooden house. The whole neighbourhood had been alarmed, the residents had been for chasing the strangers, killing them and handing over their bodies to the authorities, until someone had brought them to their senses by pointing out that it was enough to deposit the weapons in the town hall. In any case they were only shotguns so ancient they would have been sure to injure anyone who tried to fire them.

'Very well,' cried a braggart, 'if they want us to riot, forward!'

But he was struck and pummelled and set upon by the women as if he had been the owner of the shotguns himself.

In the village of Ermita a more serious incident took place but it was hushed up although shots had actually been fired. A certain government employee, who was taking no chances and had armed himself to the teeth perceived a dark shape near his house at nightfall, decided without further ado that it was a student and fired two revolver shots. It turned out to be a policeman. He was buried, and the peace of Christ be with ye all! After that, not a word more.

A number of shots were also heard in Dulumbayan which resulted in the deaths of a deaf old man who did not hear the sentry's 'Who goes there!' and of a pig which heard it but did not know what to answer. The old man was not easily buried for he had not left any money for the exequies. But there were no difficulties about eating the pig.

At a sweetshop in Manila, frequented by students because it was near the University, the following comments on the arrests were being made.

'Has Tadeo been arrested yet?' asked the owner.

'Missis, he has been shot already,' answered a student who lived in the Chinese quarter.

'Shot! My sainted mother! But he hasn't paid me his accounts yet!'

'Not so loud, missis, you might be taken for an accomplice. I've already burnt the book he lent me. They might have searched my house and found it. Look sharp, missis!'

'They say Isagani was also arrested.'

'That Isagani was an idiot,' said the indignant student. 'He wasn't going to be arrested at all but he went and gave himself up! Whatever happens to him he deserves it. Shot maybe.'

The shopowner shrugged her shoulders.

'He didn't owe me anything. But what will Paulita do?'

'She won't lack for sweethearts, missis. Maybe she will cry a little, then marry a Spaniard.'

That night was among the saddest in memory. The Rosary was being said throughout the city and pious women were offering up Our Fathers and prayers for the repose of the souls of relatives and friends. By eight o'clock scarcely anyone was to be seen in the streets; from time to time a horse could be heard galloping, a scabbard heavily slapping its flank, followed by policemen's whistles, or coaches that rattled along at full speed as if pursued by a rebellious mob.

However, panic did not rule everywhere.

In the silversmith's at which Plácido Penitente lodged the day's events were discussed with a degree of frankness.

'I don't believe there were any posters at all!' said a silver-worker, thin and spare by dint of years on the blower. 'I think it's all the work of Father Salví.'

The master smith, a most prudent man who nonetheless did not dare cut the conversation short because he was afraid of being taken for a coward, cleared his throat noisily, winked at his assistant and turned his eyes towards the street as if to warn him that they might be overheard.

'Because of the affair of the operetta,' the worker continued.

'Aha, that's exactly what I was saying,' concurred another with a candid face. 'That's the reason why...'

'It's true about the posters, all right,' replied a clerk pityingly. 'But I'll give you the right explanation, Chichoy.'

And he added in a confidential whisper:

'It's all a trick of Quiroga the Chinaman.'

The master smith had a fit of coughing and shifted his betel-nut cud from one cheek to the other.

'Believe me, Chichoy, it's Quiroga the Chinaman. I heard it in the office.'

'My sainted mother! Then it must be true,' exclaimed the simpleton, swallowing the story even before he had heard it.

'Quiroga has a hundred thousand Mexican silver pesos in the harbour,' the clerk continued. 'How smuggle them in? Simple. He invents the affair of the posters using the student troubles as an excuse and while everybody is in a dither—*poum* he bribes the Customs guards and brings the silver in.'

'That's it,' the credulous worker exclaimed, striking his fist on the table. 'That is why Quiroga—'

But he had to stop short, he did not know what to say about Quiroga.

'And we pay the bill?' asked the indignant Chichoy.

The master smith cleared his throat a third time, hearing footsteps in the street.

The footsteps came nearer and everyone fell silent.

'St Paschal is a great saint,' said the master smith in a loud unctuous voice, winking at the rest. 'St Paschal . . .'

Just then Plácido Penitente looked in, accompanied by the gunpowder expert to whom Simoun had given his orders some nights before. The newcomers were surrounded and asked for the latest news.

'I could not get to speak to the prisoners,' Plácido answered. 'There were about thirty.'

'Be prepared,' added the gunpowder expert, exchanging a knowing look with Plácido. 'They say there will be a massacre tonight.'

'What! Oh, blast it,' cried Chichoy looking round for a weapon and, finding none, seizing his blower.

The master smith felt his legs give under him and sat down abruptly. The credulous worker already saw himself with his throat cut and started to weep for his family.

'Go on!' said the clerk. 'There isn't going to be any massacre. Fortunately the Big Man's adviser is ill.'

'Simoun!'

The master smith could still clear his throat.

Plácido and the gunpowder expert exchanged another look.

'If that one had not fallen ill...'

'They would have simulated a revolution,' the gunpowder expert supplied the words negligently, lighting a cigarette at a lamp funnel. 'What would we have done then?'

'Make it in earnest! If they are going to kill us anyway...'

Another violent fit of coughing overcame the master smith and muffled the rest of the sentence. Chichoy must have said some terrible things because he was making murderous gestures with his blower and had the face of a Japanese tragedian.

'Simoun is probably just pretending to be ill because he's afraid to go out. If I come across him...'

The master smith's convulsive coughing returned and he begged the rest to go home.

'Nevertheless, be prepared, be prepared,' said the gunpowder expert. 'If they want to force us to kill or be killed...'

The master smith's coughing persisted and the workers and employees went home with hammers, saws, and other blunt or cutting instruments, prepared to sell their lives dearly. Plácido and the gunpowder expert also left.

'Be careful,' advised the master smith with tearful voice.

'Please look after my widow and orphans,' begged the credulous worker with an even more tearful voice.

The poor man already saw himself shot and buried.

That night the sentries at the city gates were relieved by Spanish gunners. The next day, at the break of dawn, Ben Zayb ventured to take a walk to look over the state of the defences and found on the parapet of the city walls the abandoned body of a half-naked native girl. Ben Zayb was horrified and, after prodding the body with his walking-stick and casting a look at the gates, went on his way, wondering how he could turn his find into a sentimental little tale. However, the event was not referred to in the newspapers in the days that followed although there was plenty of space for accidents and falls caused by banana peels. Ben Zayb himself seemed to be short of news and had recourse to lengthy comment on a cyclone which had destroyed a number of towns in America and killed more than two thousand people. Among other pretty turns of phrase were the following:

'Feelings of charity, always deeper among Catholic peoples than among any other, and the memory of Him who at their impulse sacrificed Himself for humanity, move us to pity for the sufferings of our fellow human beings and to pray that in this country, so battered by cyclones, we shall not witness the heartbreaking scenes which the inhabitants of the United States must have seen.'

Horatius did not lose the opportunity and, although equally silent on the dead and the poor murdered native girl and the abuses that had been committed, replied to Ben Zayb in his *Fireworks* column:

'After so much charity and so much humanity, all that Fray Ybañez, or rather, Ben Zayb, can offer is a prayer for the Philippines 'We understand.

'Because he is not a Catholic and feelings of charity are always deeper, etc., etc., etc.'

29 • *Last Words about Capitán Tiago*

His end befitted his life.

CAPITAN TIAGO had a good end, that is to say, a funeral that had rarely been equalled. True enough, the priest of the parish had reminded Father Irene that Capitán Tiago had died unshriven but the good canon had rubbed his nose and replied with a mocking smile:

'Come now, you should know better than to bring that up! If we were to deny exequies to all who die without going to Confession we would soon forget the rites for the dead! As you well know, one is strict with the impenitent when he also happens to be insolvent, but Capitán Tiago! Why, you have buried heathen Chinese yourself, and with a Mass for the Dead at that!'

Capitán Tiago had named Father Irene the administrator and executor of his last will and testament, which left his estate partly to the nunnery of St Clare and partly to the Pope, the Archbishop, and the religious Orders, with a legacy of twenty pesos for the tuition fees of needy students. This last clause had been suggested by Father Irene in his capacity as protector of studious youth. Capitán Tiago had revoked a legacy of twenty-five pesos to Basilio in view of the young man's ingratitude during his last days but Father Irene announced that he would in conscience respect it and pay it out of his own pocket.

In the house of the deceased, where old acquaintances and friends had gathered the next day, there was much talk of a miracle. It was said that, at the very moment in which he was breathing his last, the soul of Capitán Tiago had appeared to the nuns surrounded by a blinding radiance. God had saved him, thanks to the numerous Masses which he had commissioned and to the pious legacies in his will. The story was commented on, graphically told, elaborated, and by none placed in doubt. The apparition was described in detail: Capitán Tiago's attire—frock coat, of course, his cheek bulging with the betel-nut cud, without forgetting his opium pipe and his fighting cock. The head sacristan, who was in the group, gravely nodded approval and was persuaded that when he died in his turn he would appear with a cup of ginger tea in his hand; without this refreshing breakfast it was impossible to imagine happiness in Heaven comparable to that on earth. Since they could not speak about the previous day's events and since there were gamblers present, various ingenious comments were made on the after-life and those present wondered if Capitán Tiago would challenge St Peter to a cockfight, if bets would be made, if the heavenly birds were immortal or invulnerable and, if so, who would act as a referee and who would win, a discussion which was much to the liking of those who base scientific theories and systems on a text which they consider infallible, divinely revealed, or dogma. Citations were made of passages from novels and hooks of miracles, the sayings of priests, descriptions of Heaven, and other odds and ends. Don Primitivo the philosopher was in his glory citing theological opinions.

'Nobody can lose,' he declared with great authority. 'To lose makes one unhappy and nobody can be unhappy in Heaven.'

'But somebody has to win,' argued the gambler Aristorenas. 'That's the whole point, to win!'

'Well, then, both win, that's simple.'

Martin Aristorenas, who had spent his life in the cockpit, could not swallow that; he had always seen one cock win, the other lose, or at most fight to a

draw. Don Primitivo spouted his Latin in vain, Aristorenas stubbornly shook
his head, for all that Don Primitivo's Latin was easy to understand since he
referred to the greenus *cockus acuto spuro armatus* and to *beati Petri blackus et
whitus cockus.* In the end he decided to use the argument which is commonly
used to silence and convince others.

'You're heading for damnation, my dear Martin, you are going to fall into
heresy! *Cave ne cadas,* beware lest you fall! I cannot play cards with you any
more. You deny the omnipotence of God—a mortal sin, *peccatum mortale!*
You deny the evidence for the Most Holy Trinity, three in one, and one in
three! Be careful! For indirectly you deny that two natures, two minds, two
wills can have a single memory! Beware! The unbeliever shall be damned;
quicumque non crederit anathema sit!'

Aristorenas shrank back, pale and trembling, and Quiroga the
Chinaman, who had listened very attentively to this reasoning, offered
the philosopher a magnificent cigar with marked deference and asked
him in his wheedling voice:

'Maybe, you think, contract with Jesus Christ possible for cockpit? When
I dead, I win contract, eh?'

In other circles more was said about the dead man, or at least about the
clothes in which he would be buried. Capitán Tinong suggested a Franciscan
habit. It just so happened that he had one, old, threadbare, patched up, a
precious robe which, according to the friar who had given it to him in charity
in exchange for thirty-six pesos, preserved the corpse from the flames of
Hell. Capitán Tinong supported this claim with a number of pious anecdotes
culled from pamphlets distributed by priests. He himself placed great value
on the relic but he was willing to yield it to his intimate friend, whom he
had been unable to visit during his illness. But a tailor was quick to object
that the nuns had seen Capitán Tiago going up to Heaven in a frock-coat,
and in a frock-coat he must be dressed here on earth without any need of
preservatives or fireproofing; one went in formal dress to a ball, to a banquet,
and nothing less than that could be awaiting Capitán Tiago in the upper
regions. Now it so happened that he had a frock-coat ready-made which he
was prepared to give for thirty-two pesos, four less than the cost of the
Franciscan habit, because he did not want to make a profit out of Capitán
Tiago, who had been a good customer all his life and would now be his
patron in Heaven. But Father Irene, administrator and testamentary
executor, rejected both propositions and ordered the body to be dressed in
any of Capitán Tiago's old clothes, saying unctuously that God did not

notice what one wore.

The exequies were first-class. There were responsorial chants in the house and in the street outside, with three friars officiating as if one were not enough for so great a soul; all possible rites and ceremonies were held with, it is said, a few more improvised for the occasion like encores at benefit concerts. It was all a delight: much incense was burned, much holy water was sprinkled—Father Irene paid tribute to his friend by singing 'Day of Wrath' himself in a falsetto voice from the choir-loft—and there was so much tolling of the church bells that the neighbours had aching heads for days.

Doña Patrocinio, Capitán Tiago's old rival in religiosity, really wanted to die herself the very next day but not without ordering even more splendid exequies. The pious old woman could not endure it that her old competitor, whom she had considered defeated for good, should in dying rise again amid such pomp. Yes, she wanted to die and she could almost hear the exclamations of those who would witness her funeral rites:

'Now that is what we call a funeral! That, Doña Patrocinio, is to know how to die!'

30 • *Julí*

NEWS of Capitán Tiago's death and Basilio's imprisonment soon reached their province and it was to the honour of the simple inhabitants of San Diego that they felt the latter more and talked about it almost exclusively. As was to be expected, different versions of the story gradually spread: sad and fearful details were added, explanations were given for what was not properly understood, conjectures filled the gaps in the story, these passed for facts, and the phantom thus engendered ended up by frightening its own makers.

It was said in the town of Tiani that at best, at the very best, the young man would be deported and very probably murdered during the trip. The timid and the pessimistic were not satisfied with this and spoke of gallows and courts-martial: January was an ill-omened month; the Cavite affair had taken place in January and its principal native victims, for all that they were priests, had been strangled on the scaffold. So that a poor man like Basilio, without friends or protectors...

'I told him so,' sighed the Municipal Judge as if he had ever given Basilio any advice.

'It was only to be expected,' Sister Penchang added, 'he would go to church and when he saw the holy water the least bit dirty he would not cross himself with it. He was always talking about little insects and diseases—well, serve him right! It's the judgment of God on him! As if holy water could give one diseases; all the contrary, what do you think?'

She told how she had cured herself of an indigestion by moistening her navel with holy water while simultaneously reciting the prayer 'God Most Holy' in Latin, and recommended this treatment to all present should they suffer from dysentery or flatulence or the pestilence; only, in the latter case, they were to say the prayer in Spanish:

> *God Most Holy,*
> *God Most Excellent,*
> *God of all,*
> *Do not let us*
> *Into pestilent*
> *Sickness fall.*

'It is a cure that never fails,' she said. 'But you must apply holy water to the part of the body that is painful or diseased.'

However, many men did not believe in such things, nor did they attribute Basilio's imprisonment to God's vengeance. Neither did they give much credit to the charge of rebellion and subversive posters, knowing that the student was peace-loving and prudent in the extreme, and they preferred to attribute his imprisonment to the vengeance of the friars for having ransomed Julí, the daughter of a bandit, a mortal enemy of a certain powerful Order. This conjecture was considered the most reasonable and justified because they had a bad opinion of that Order's morality.

'I was so right to throw her out of my house,' said Sister Penchang. 'I want no quarrels with the friars. That is why I kept urging her to raise the money she owed.'

The truth was that she resented Julí's emancipation. Julí prayed and fasted for her and, if she had only stayed a little longer, she would have done penance for Sister Penchang as well. If the priests prayed for the people, and Christ died for men's sins, was not Julí to do the same thing for Sister Penchang?

When the news reached the hut where poor Julí lived with her grandfather, it had to be told her twice. She stared at Sister Balí, who was giving her the news, as if she did not understand and could not gather her thoughts together; there was a humming in her ears and a weight on her heart and she vaguely felt a painful presentiment that this event would prove disastrous for her in the future. However, trying to keep alive a ray of hope, she smiled and told Sister Balí that of course she knew it was all rather a bad joke, but she would forgive Sister Balí if she would only say so. But Sister Balí crossed herself with thumb and index finger and kissed her to prove she was telling the truth. From then on Julí; never smiled again. She turned pale, horribly pale, felt all her strength drain out of her and fainted for the first time in her life.

When she was brought round by slaps and pinches and the application of cold water, crosses, and fronds blessed on Palm Sunday, and realized her situation, the tears welled silently in her eyes and fell drop by drop, without sobs, complaints or laments. She was thinking that Basilio had no protectors other than Capitán Tiago and, with him dead, Basilio was left completely defenceless in prison. For it was well known in the Philippines that one needed patrons and protectors for everything, from christening until death, whether it was to secure a passport or to establish an industry or to obtain justice. And since it was said that Basilio's imprisonment was a reprisal provoked by her and by her father, Julí's sorrow reached the point of despair. Now it was her turn to ransom him, as he had done when he had rescued her from domestic service, and an inner voice suggested and pictured in her imagination a horrible way to do it.

Father Camorra, the parish priest!

Julí fell into a melancholy depression.

When her father had committed his crimes, her grandfather had been imprisoned in the hope of compelling Cabesang Tales to give himself up, and only Father Camorra had been able to secure Old Selo's release. But Father Camorra had shown himself dissatisfied with mere words of gratitude and, with his usual bluntness, had asked her to make certain sacrifices… From that time on Julí had avoided meeting him but when they did the parish priest would make her kiss his hand, would pinch her nose or her cheeks, and would wink and joke and laugh and, laughing all the while, would pinch her again. Julí had been the cause of the beating which the stout friar had given some young men who had been going round the neighbourhood serenading the girls. When she passed by, so staid and modest, the evil-minded would say loudly enough for her to hear:

'If she only wanted to, she could get Cabesang Tales pardoned!'

She would return home despondent, with a troubled look in her eyes.

Now there was an even greater change in her. She lost her high spirits and nobody saw her smile, she scarcely said a word, and it seemed that she was even afraid of looking at herself in the mirror. One day they saw her in town with a great streak of charcoal dust on her brow, and she had always been so neat and tidy. Once she asked Sister Balí if those who killed themselves went to Hell.

'No doubt about it,' Sister Balí snapped, and pictured Hell to Julí as if she had been there personally.

When Basilio was thrown into gaol her unpretentious but affectionate relatives had promised to make all manner of sacrifices to save him but they could scarcely raise one peso among them and Sister Balí, as usual, had the best idea.

'What we should do,' she said, 'is to ask the municipal clerk's advice.'

To these artless folk the clerk was what the oracle of Delphos was to the ancient Greeks.

Give him twenty-five centavos and a cigar,' she added, 'and he'll give you enough law to make your head burst. For one peso he can rescue you from the very foot of the gallows. When my neighbour Simon was thrown into prison and beaten up because he could say nothing about a robbery which had taken place near his house, the clerk, would you believe it, got him out of it for fifty centavos and a bunch of garlic. I saw Simon with my own eyes: he could hardly walk and had to keep to his bed for at least a month. His behind was rotting away because of the beating he took, and the pity of it is that he died after all.'

Sister Balí's suggestion was adopted and she offered to consult the clerk herself. Julí gave her one peso and some dried venison provided by her grandfather, who had taken up hunting again.

But the clerk could do nothing; the prisoner was in Manila and his influence did not reach that far.

'If at least he were in the provincial capital, then perhaps...' he said, making a show of his influence.

The clerk knew very well that in fact his influence did not go beyond the boundaries of Tiani but he wanted to keep both his reputation and the venison.

'But I can give you some sound advice,' he added. 'Go with Julí to the Municipal Judge, but, mind you, Julí must go along.'

The Municipal Judge was a rough man but perhaps he would be less rude in Julí's presence: therein lay the soundness of the advice.

The Judge heard Sister Balí, who was acting as spokesman, with an air of gravity although not without stealing a look time and again at Julí, who had cast down her eyes in shame. People would say she was excessively interested in Basilio, they would not remember the debt of gratitude she owed him and the rumour that she had been the cause of his imprisonment.

After belching three or four times, for the Judge had this unpleasant habit, he said that the only one who could save Basilio was Father Camorra—if he wanted to—and he looked at Julí meaningfully. He advised her to speak to the parish priest personally.

'You know how influential he is. He got your grandfather out of gaol. One report from him is enough to send a newborn child into exile or save a man with the noose already round his neck.'

Julí said nothing but Sister Balí found the advice as good as if she had read it in a prayer-book. She was ready to accompany Julí to the parish house. It just so happened that she was expecting the gift of a scapular in exchange for one peso.

But Julí shook her head and refused to go. Sister Balí, who thought she divined the reason for Julí's reluctance—Father Camorra was otherwise known as Father Stallion and was reputed to be a frisky one—tried to calm her fears.

'You have nothing to worry about,' she said. 'I'll be with you, after all. Haven't you read in that booklet of the parish priest, *Tough Old Basio*, that young girls should visit the parish house, even without the knowledge of their parents, in order to report on what goes on in their homes? Well, what do you think that booklet was printed with the permission of the Archbishop, no less!'

Julí, who was anxious to cut the conversation short, begged the devout Sister to go on to the parish house if she wanted to so much, but the Judge observed with a belch that a fresh young face got better results than an old one and that Heaven dropped its dew more abundantly on fresh flowers than on withered ones. The metaphor was not without a sinister aptness.

Julí did not reply and both women went downstairs. Once in the street, however, Julí stubbornly refused to go to the parish house and they took the way home. Sister Balí, who was offended by the lack of confidence in her as a chaperone, took her revenge with a long homily.

The truth was that Julí could not take such a step without damning herself in her own eyes, in the eyes of men and in the eyes of God. They had let her understand time and again, with reason or without, that if she made that particular sacrifice her father would be pardoned and yet she had always refused to make it, remind her though her conscience might of her filial duty. And would she do it now for Basilio, for her sweetheart? That would be to fall amid the scornful laughter of all. Basilio himself would despise her. She could not do it, she could never do it. She would hang herself first or jump over a precipice. Anyway she was already accursed as a bad daughter.

Poor Julí had to suffer in addition the recriminations of her relatives who, with no idea of what there was between her and Father Camorra, made fun of her fears. Was Father Camorra going to give a peasant girl a second look when there were so many girls in town? The good housewives brought up the names of young girls, rich and pretty, who were reputed to have fallen, more or less. And what if in the meantime Basilio was shot?

Julí covered her ears with her hands and looked about her as if searching for a voice that would speak up for her; she looked at her grandfather but he was mute and stared fixedly at his hunting spear.

That night she hardly slept. Dreams and nightmares, mournful or bloody, troubled her sleep and she started awake constantly, drenched in a cold sweat. She dreamed she was hearing shots, in dreams she saw her father, who had done so much for her, fighting in the jungle, hunted like a wild beast because she had hesitated to save him, and then the face of her father changed into that of Basilio, dying with a reproachful look for her. The unfortunate girl would get up, pray, weep, call upon her dead mother, on Death itself, and there was a time when, overwhelmed by panic, she would have, if it had not been night, run straight to the parish house, happen what might.

Dawn came and the grim forebodings, the shadowy fears, vanished in part. The light of the day brought her hope. But in the afternoon there was terrible news; there was talk of executions; and the night was hideous for Julí. In her despair she decided to make the sacrifice as soon as day broke and then to kill herself—anything to avoid enduring such torture.

But dawn again brought fresh hope and Julí would neither leave her hut nor go to church. She was afraid of giving in.

So a number of days passed in prayer and despair, in calling upon God and desiring death. Daytime was a time of truce, Julí still believed in miracles. The news from Manila, although exaggerated, was that some of the prisoners had been released, thanks to their protectors and connexions. But someone would have to be the goat. Who? Julí shuddered and went home biting her nails. Then night came, when fears were redoubled and seemed to become certainties. Julí was afraid of sleep, she was afraid to go to bed, her dreams were an endless nightmare. Reproachful looks pierced her eyelids as soon as she had closed them; plaints and laments were dinned in her ears. She saw her father wandering hungry, unable to rest; she saw Basilio dying by the roadside, with two bullets in him, as she had seen one of her neighbours, who had been taken by the Constabulary. She saw rope cutting into flesh, the blood gushing out of the mouth, and heard Basilio cry: 'Save me, save me, only you can save me!' Someone cackled with laughter and turning her eyes she saw her father who stared at her with eyes that seemed to upbraid her. Julí would awake, rise from the sleeping-mat, brush back her hair from her brow which was wet with cold sweat, the sweat of death, and call upon her mother.

In the meantime those who merrily decided the destinies of whole towns, who ordered legal murder, outraged justice, and perverted the law to dignify power, slept in peace.

In the end a traveller from Manila arrived and said that all the prisoners had been released except for Basilio who had no protector. It was said in Manila, it was added, that he would be exiled to the Carolines and that he had been made to sign beforehand a petition in which he stated that this was being done at his own voluntary request. The traveller had even seen the ship which was to take Basilio away.

The news put an end to Julí's vacillations. Besides, so many sleepless nights and horrible dreams had sapped her resolution. Pale and with a lost look, she sought out Sister Balí and, in a voice that troubled the old woman, told her that she was ready to go. Would Sister Balí accompany her?

Sister Balí was pleased and tried to reassure her but Julí was not listening and seemed only to want to get to the parish house as soon as possible. She had tidied herself up, put on her best clothes and seemed in high spirits; she talked a lot although rather incoherently.

They set out, Julí leading the way, impatient when her companion fell behind. But as they neared the town her nervous energy gradually ebbed, she fell silent, lost her resolution, shortened her sups and herself fell back. Sister Balí had to urge her to go on.

'We are going to be late!'

Julí followed pale, not daring to lift her downcast eyes. She fancied that the whole world was looking at her and pointing her out. A shameful name sounded in her ears but she made herself deaf to it and went on. Nevertheless, when she came actually within sight of the parish house, she stopped and shuddered convulsively.

'Let's go back,' she begged, holding back Sister Balí.

Sister Balí had to take her by the arm and half-drag her on, reassuring her and recalling what was written in monkish booklets. She was not going to abandon Julí, Julí had nothing to fear. Father Camorra had other things on his mind, Julí was only a poor peasant girl...

But when they reached the door of the parish house, Julí stubbornly refused to enter and clung to the wall.

'No, no,' she begged, panic-stricken, 'no, have pity...'

'What a silly fool you are!'

Sister Balí pulled at her gently, Julí resisted, her face bloodless and distorted. She looked as if she were staring at Death itself.

'Oh, very well then, let's go home if you don't want to go on!'

Sister Balí exclaimed at last, in a pet; she did not really believe there was any danger; Father Camorra, for all his reputation, would not dare do anything in her presence.

'All right, let poor Basilio be taken to exile, let them shoot him on the way and say he tried to escape,' she added. 'Once he's dead, then you'll be sorry. For my part, I owe him nothing, he can't complain about me.'

It was a decisive blow. Faced with this reproach Julí closed her eyes as if to shut away the sight of the abyss into which she was about to throw herself and, angrily, despairingly, like a suicide, she resolutely entered the parish house. A sigh that was more like a shudder escaped her lips. Sister Balí followed her giving her advice...

That night there was a great amount of whispered and cryptically worded comment on a number of things that had happened in the afternoon.

A girl had thrown herself out of a window of the parish house, falling upon some stones and killing herself. At almost the same time a woman had run out of the door and into the streets shouting and screaming like one insane. The prudent residents did not dare say the names of the two women aloud and many mothers scolded their daughters for dropping compromising words. Later, much later, at nightfall, an old man had come from an outlying neighbourhood and had knocked at the door of the parish house, which was locked and guarded by the priest's servants. The old man knocked with his fists, with his head, giving hoarse wordless cries like those of a dumb man. He was pushed and beaten and driven away. Then he had gone to the Mayor's house but was told that the Mayor was not at home, he was at the parish house; then to the Judge's house but the Judge was not in either, he had been called to the parish house; to the Vice-Mayor, but he was also in the parish house; to the Constabulary barracks but the commanding officer was in the parish house... Then the old man had gone home weeping like a

child. His howling could be heard in the night and the men of the town bit
their lips, the women clasped their hands, and the frightened dogs went
into the houses with their tails between their legs.

'Oh, God,' prayed a devout woman, gaunt with much fasting. 'You know
neither rich nor poor, neither white nor black. You shall do us justice!'

'Yes,' her husband answered, 'as long as that God they preach about is not
pure invention, a fraud—they are the first not to believe in Him.'

By eight o'clock in the evening seven friars from the neighbouring towns
were said to be meeting at the parish house. The next day Old Selo, carrying
his hunting spear, left the town for ever.

31 • *The High Official*

Spain and her virtue,
Spain and her grandeur,
All are going!
— VICTOR HUGO

THE Manila newspapers were giving so much space to a sensational murder
committed in Europe, to praises and panegyrics of the various preachers of the
capital, and to the ever greater success of the French operetta company, that
they could seldom accommodate an item or two on the crimes committed in
the provinces by a band of outlaws led by a terrible and ferocious chieftain who
called himself *Matanglawin,* that is to say, *Hawk-eyes.* Only when the victim
was a friar or a Spaniard did long articles appear in grisly detail, with demands
for the declaration of a state of emergency and energetic measures. For much
the same reasons the newspapers said nothing about what had happened in the
town of Tiani nor were there any allusions to it, any rumours. There was some
gossip in private circles but it was all so confused, so doubtful, so inconsistent
that not even the name of the victim was known and those who showed the
greatest interest in the story soon forgot it under the impression that some
arrangement had been made with the offended family. The one thing sure was
that Father Camorra had had to leave Tiani on transfer to another town or to
remain for some time in the convent of his Order in Manila.

'Poor Father Camorra,' exclaimed Ben Zayb who wanted to appear generous.
'He was so gay; he had such a good heart.'

It was equally true that the students had been released, thanks to the exertions of their parents who had not spared any expense, donation or sacrifice. The first to be set free was Makaraig, as was only to be expected, and the last, Isagani, because Father Florentino took a week to reach Manila. So many acts of clemency won for the General the reputation of being kind and merciful, and Ben Zayb hastened to add these adjectives to the long list with which he habitually garlanded the name of His Excellency.

The only one who was not set free was poor Basilio, who faced the additional charge of having prohibited books in his possession. It was not clear whether this charge referred to Mata's *Legal Medicine and Toxicology* or to the various pamphlets on Philippine affairs which had been found in his room or to both; in any case he was said to have engaged in the clandestine sale of prohibited works and the full weight of the scales of justice fell upon the unfortunate Basilio.

The story went that His Excellency had been advised:

'It is imperative that *someone* should be punished to maintain the prestige of the authorities; otherwise it might be said that we have made much ado about nothing. Authority above all. There must be at least one left behind to face the music.'

'In fact there *is* only one left, a former servant, according to Father Irene, of Capitán Tiago. Nobody has spoken up for him.'

'A servant and a student!' exclaimed His Excellency. 'Well, then, that's the one, hold him!'

'Begging Your Excellency's pardon,' observed the high official who was present by chance. 'I have been told that this young man is a medical student and that his professors speak highly of him. If he is held in gaol he loses a year in his studies and since this is his last year...'

The high official's intervention in favour of Basilio, instead of helping, harmed him. Between the official and His Excellency there had been for some time a certain tension, certain disagreements worsened by gossip. His Excellency smiled uneasily and answered:

'Really? All the more reason, then, to keep him in prison; one more year of studies will not harm him, on the contrary, it should do him good and benefit everyone who may afterwards fall under his care. More practice never made anyone a bad doctor. All the more reason for holding him! And yet,' he added with a sarcastic laugh, 'our disgruntled reformers will say I do not care for the country!'

The high official realized his mistake and took Basilio's cause to heart.

'But this young man seems to me the most innocent of them all,' he objected cautiously.

'They have seized books on him,' observed the secretary.

'Yes, medical textbooks and pamphlets written by Spaniards, their pages still uncut. What is that supposed to prove? Besides, this young man was not at the dinner in the Chinese restaurant and has meddled in nothing. As I said, he is the most innocent...'

'All the better,' cried His Excellency gaily, 'that way the punishment turns out to be more salutary and exemplary for it will strike more terror. That is the way to govern, my good man; the good of the individual must often be sacrificed to the good of the majority. But I am doing even more: from the good of one man I derive the good of all, maintain the threatened principle of authority, and preserve and enhance the prestige of the regime. With this act of mine I correct the errors of our own officials and of others.'

The high official made an effort to control himself and, ignoring the allusion, took another tack.

'But is not Your Excellency afraid of being... blamed?'

'What have I got to fear?' the General interrupted impatiently. 'Have I not got discretionary powers? Can I not do anything I please for the better government of these islands? What have I got to be afraid of? Can a mere servant take me to court and demand an accounting? Of course not. And even if he had the means to do so he would first have to go through the Colonial Office, and the Minister...'

He made a gesture and burst out laughing.

'The devil knows where the Minister who appointed me is now; he will be honoured enough to salute me when I get back! I don't give a damn for the present Minister, he can go to the devil too. And his successor will have his hands full with his new job and will have no time for trifles. My conscience, my good man, is my only guide, I act according to my conscience, my conscience is satisfied, and I don't give a damn what anybody else thinks. My conscience, sir, my conscience!'

'Yes, General, but the country...'

'Oh, tush! What do I have to do with the country? Have I any obligations to the country? Do I owe my job to the country? Did the country elect me to this post?'

There was a momentary pause. The high official stood with head downcast. Then, as if taking a decision, he raised his head, looked the General in the eye and, pale and rather shaken, said with controlled energy:

'That is not important, General, not too important. For Your Excellency was not elected by the Filipino people but by Spain, which is all the more reason why Your Excellency should treat the Filipinos well so that they may have no cause to blame Spain. All the more reason, General! Your Excellency promised, on his arrival here, to govern justly, to seek the good...'

'Am I doing anything else?' cried His Excellency in exasperation and taking a step forward. 'Haven't I told you that I derive the good of all from the good of one? Are you now proposing to teach me my job? If you do not understand what I am doing, am I to blame? Do I perhaps compel you to share my responsibilities?'

'Of course not,' replied the high official stiffly. 'Your Excellency does not compel me, and cannot compel me, to share his responsibilities. But I have a different understanding of my own responsibilities and I shall say what they are, I have kept silent too long. Your Excellency need not make these gestures; just because I have come here in this or that official position does not mean that I have lost all my rights and have become a slave without any self-respect or a right to speak my mind. I do not want Spain to lose this beautiful possession, these eight millions of submissive and patient subjects who live on hope and disappointment; but neither do I want to stain my hands with their inhuman exploitation; I never want it said that, although the slave trade has been abolished, Spain has continued it on a grand scale, shielding it with her flag and even elaborating it with a wealth of impressive institutions. No, Spain need not be tyrannical to be great; Spain is sufficient unto herself; Spain was greater when she had only her own lands, wrested from the Moor! I too am a Spaniard, but before being a Spaniard I am a man, and before Spain and above Spain come her honour, the high principles of morality, the eternal and immutable principles of justice! You are surprised that I think that way because you have no idea of the greatness of the Spanish name, no idea at all; you identify it with individuals, with private interests; as far as you are concerned the Spaniard can be a pirate, an assassin, a hypocrite, a deceiver, anything, so long as he can keep what he has; but for me the Spaniard should be ready to lose everything, empire, power, riches, everything rather than honour! Sir, we are shocked when we are told that might makes right but in actual practice we applaud when might hypocritically perverts right and uses it to get its own way... It is because I love Spain that I am speaking now and I do not care how much it displeases you. I do not want her to be accused in time to come of having been a stepmother of nations, a bloodsucker of peoples, a despot over a handful of islands, because that would be a horrible mockery of the noble purposes of our ancient kings. How do we fulfil their sacred will and testament? They promised these islands protection and justice, and we make game of the lives and liberties of their inhabitants; they promised civilization, and we begrudge it, fearing that the natives may aspire to a fuller life; they promised light, and we blindfold the natives so they may not witness our excesses; they promised to teach virtue, and we foment vice; and, instead of peace, prosperity and justice, there is distress, commerce withers away and the masses lose their faith. Let us put ourselves in the place of the Filipinos and ask ourselves what we would do. Ah, in your silence I read their right to rebel and, if things do not get better, some day they will rebel, and in truth justice will be on their side as well as the sympathies of all honest men, of all the patriots of the world. When a people are denied inviolable homes, education, liberty, justice, goods without which life is impossible and which are thereby the patrimony of all men, that people have a right to treat whoever so despoils them like a bandit who assaults them on the highway. There are no possible distinctions or exceptions; there is only the fact of a violation of rights, and any honest man who does not take the side of the victim makes himself an accomplice in the crime and stains his conscience. I am not a soldier and age is quenching what little fire there was in my blood but, just as I would let myself be torn to pieces to defend the integrity of Spain against foreign invasion or against the unjustified caprices of her provinces, so also, I can assure you, I would take the side of the Filipinos when they are oppressed because I prefer to fall for the downtrodden rights of humanity than to conquer with the selfish interests of one nation, even though that nation were, as it is, called Spain.'

'Do you know when the next mail-boat leaves?' His Excellency asked coldly when the high official had finished speaking.

The high official looked him in the eyes and then lowered his head and left the palace without another word.

He found his coach waiting for him in the garden.

'When you declare yourselves independent some day,' he said, with an abstracted air, to the native lackey who opened the door for him, 'remember that there were not lacking hearts in Spain that beat for you and fought for your rights.'

'Where to did you say, sir?' asked the lackey, who had not understood a word.

Two hours later, the high official submitted his resignation and announced his return to Spain on the next mail-boat.

32 • *Consequences of the Posters*

AS A RESULT of the affair of the posters many mothers called their sons home to abandon their studies and either work on the land or merely idle their time away.

When the examinations were given at the University there were numerous failures and uncommon indeed was the member of the notorious students' association who passed. The association itself never concerned anyone again. Pecson, Tadeo, and Juanito Peláez all failed to pass; the first received the news with his silly giggle and announced that he would seek an official position in some law-court or other; Tadeo, with his perpetual holiday at last on hand, celebrated with a bonfire of his books; while the other members of the association, who had not fared too well, eventually had to give up their studies to the great rejoicing of their mothers who had always imagined their sons on the gallows should they ever understand what their books said. Only Juanito Peláez took his failure badly; he had to exchange the classroom from then on for his father's shop, where he had been taken into the business, and the rogue found the shop less amusing. Still, after some time, his friends saw him with his stoop as pronounced as ever, which was a symptom of renewed high spirits. Faced with the disaster the wealthy Makaraig was careful not to expose himself again and, having secured a passport by means of bribes, hastily sailed for Europe; it was said that His Excellency the Governor-General, in his desire to do good for its own sake and in his solicitude for the comfort of the Filipinos, made travel difficult for anyone who failed to give tangible evidence beforehand of his ability to spend enough money for a life of ease in the cities of Europe. The ones who fared best were Isagani and Sandoval: the first passed the course under Father Fernández although he failed in the others; the second succeeded in turning the heads of the examiners with his speeches. Basilio alone neither passed nor failed nor went off to Europe: he remained in Bilibid Prison, subjected to interrogations every three days, with almost the same questions being asked again and again by different investigators, as if their predecessors had succumbed or fled in horror before the enormity of Basilio's guilt.

While the reports lay forgotten in their pigeonholes and the files passed slowly from desk to desk, with official papers ever increasing like a quack doctor's plasters on the body of a hypochondriac, Basilio learned what had

happened in Tiani in all its details—the death of Julí, the disappearance of
Old Selo. Sinong, the rig-driver who was beaten up while taking Basilio
to San Diego, was then in Manila and visited the prisoner regularly, keeping
him abreast of everything.

In the meantime Simoun had recovered his health, at least according to
the newspapers. Ben Zayb gave thanks to the Almighty 'who watches over
this precious life' and expressed the hope that the All-Highest would some
day permit the discovery of the criminal whose assault remained unpunished
thanks to the generosity of his victim, who applied too literally the words of
the Great Martyr: 'Father, forgive them for they know not what they do.'
Ben Zayb said these and other things in print; in private he was asking if it
was true that the wealthy jeweller was planning a great party, a banquet
whose equal had never been seen, partly to celebrate his recovery and partly
to say good-bye to a country where he had so markedly increased his fortune.
Indeed it was gossiped that Simoun, who would have to leave with the
Governor-General when the latter's term expired in May, was exerting all
his efforts to secure an extension from Madrid and was advising His Excellency
to launch a military campaign which would give him an excuse to prolong
his stay. But it was also said that His Excellency was turning a deaf ear for
once to the advice of his favourite, making it a point of honour not to retain
even for a single day in excess of his term the power which had been entrusted
to him. This rumour led people to believe that the expected party would
soon take place. For the rest of it, Simoun remained unfathomable; he had
turned even more taciturn, made few appearances in public and smiled
enigmatically when he was asked about the expected banquet.

'Come now, Mr Sinbad,' Ben Zayb had once urged him, 'dazzle us with
something Yankee! Dammit, you owe it to the country!'

'No doubt,' Simoun had replied with his mirthless smile.

'Throw the house out of the window, eh?'

'That's possible, except that I haven't got a house.'

'You should have bought Capitán Tiago's. Mr Peláez got it for next
to nothing.'

Simoun had not continued the conversation. But he was often seen
afterwards in the shop of Don Timoteo Peláez, with whom he was said to
have entered into a partnership. Weeks later, towards the month of April,
the news spread that Juanito Peláez, Don Timoteo's son, would marry Paulita
Gómez, the young heiress pursued by locals and strangers.

'Some men are born lucky,' complained the elder Peláez's envious competitors. 'To buy a house for next to nothing, sell his shipment of zinc roofing at excellent prices, have Simoun for a partner, and marry off his son to a rich heiress—these are plums, you must admit, that do not come the way of all honest men!'

'If you only knew how Mr Peláez got those plums,' Ben Zayb said, his tone suggesting it was through himself; he added with an air of mystery:

'And I can also assure you that there will be a party, and on a grand scale!'

It was true indeed that Paulita was marrying Juanito Peláez. Her first love for Isagani had vanished, like all first loves born of poetry and sentiment. The affair of the posters and prison had stripped Isagani of all his attractions. What a fool to seek out danger, wish to share the misfortunes of his comrades and give himself up when the rest of the world had gone into hiding and denied any connexion with the affair! It was quixotism, madness, and no sensible person in Manila was going to forgive Isagani for it; Juanito was perfectly justified in making fun of him with an imitation of Isagani's postures when he had turned himself in at the Office of Civil Administration. Naturally the brilliant Paulita could no longer have any affection for a young man who had so mistaken a notion of society, and he was condemned by all. She began to consider that Juanito was clever, active, gay, shrewd, the son of a rich Manila merchant and half-Spanish for good measure, or, if Don Timoteo was to be believed, even all-Spanish. On the other hand Isagani was a native provincial, a dreamer in forests full of leeches, with a doubtful parentage and an uncle who was a secular priest and perhaps an enemy of luxury and balls, of which she was very fond. It was not strange, therefore, that one fine morning Paulita realized that she had been an absolute idiot in preferring Isagani to his rival, and since then a marked increase was noticed in Peláez's hunch. Paulita was unconsciously but strictly fulfilling Darwin's theory; the female of the species was giving herself to the fitter male, the one who had known how to adapt himself to his environment, for nobody knew his way round Manila like Peláez, who had known from childhood the most devious means of getting his own way.

Lent ended with the Holy Week and its series of processions and ceremonies. Nothing unusual happened except for an inexplicable mutiny in the artillery regiment, whose cause was never revealed. The houses of light materials were razed to the ground as planned, with the help of a detachment of cavalry ready to charge on the owners in case they should riot. There was much weeping and lamentation but it did not go further than that. The curious, among them Simoun, took a promenade in the site and cast an indifferent eye on the homeless, saying to themselves that they could now sleep untroubled.

Towards the end of April, with all fears forgotten, Manila could think of only one affair. It was the reception that Don Timoteo Peláez was giving on the wedding of his son, for whom the General, gracious and condescending, had agreed to stand as sponsor. It was said that Simoun had arranged it. The marriage was taking place two days before the departure of His Excellency, who would honour the house of Peláez with his presence and give the bridegroom a present. The gossip was that the jeweller would also be giving away handfuls of diamonds and pearls to his partner's son and that, unable to give a party of his own because he lacked a house and a wife to act as the hostess, he would take advantage of Peláez's reception to surprise the Filipino people with a heartfelt farewell. The whole of Manila prepared to be invited; never did anxiety grip hearts so tightly at the thought that they might not be asked. All competed to be in Simoun's good graces, and many a husband was compelled by his wife to buy iron bars and zinc sheets to make the acquaintance of Don Timoteo Peláez.

33 • The Final Argument

AT last the day came.

Simoun had not left his lodgings all morning; he was busy packing his weapons and his jewellery. The fabulous treasure was locked up in the great steel case with the canvas cover. A few caskets remained outside, containing bracelets and brooches which he apparently wished to give away as presents. The Governor-General was leaving at last; afraid of what people might say, he had absolutely refused to prolong his term in office. The cynical suggested that Simoun was not taking the risk of being left behind alone and without his protector; he did not want to expose himself to the vengeance of the many unfortunates whom he had exploited, especially because the General's successor had the reputation of being a model of rectitude and might make Simoun give back all his profits. The superstitious natives, for their part, believed that Simoun was the Devil and would not let his quarry go. The pessimistic winked maliciously and said:

'The field has been eaten bare, and the locust moves on.'

Only a few, a very few, smiled and kept their counsel.

In the afternoon Simoun gave his servant instructions that a young man named Basilio was to be admitted immediately he called. Then he locked himself up in his room, apparently buried in deep thought. Since his illness the jeweller's face had turned harder and more lowering still, the cleft between his brows had become much more marked, he had acquired a stoop and no longer held his head high He was so engrossed in his reflections that he did not hear a knock on the door. When it was repeated he started and called out:

'Come in!'

It was Basilio, but much altered. If the change in Simoun over the past two months hat been great, that in the young student was appalling. His cheeks were sunken, his clothes in disarray, his hair uncombed; the attractive melancholy in his eyes had given way to a dark glitter. He looked as if he had risen from the dead, horrified by what he had seen on the other side of eternity. If not crime, at least its shadow suffused his whole person. Simoun himself was shocked and felt pity for the unfortunate young man.

Basilio entered without a word of greeting and said in a voice that startled even the jeweller:

'Mr Simoun, I have been a bad son and a bad brother. I forgot my brother's murder and the tortures my mother suffered, and God has punished me. Now all I have left is the determination to return evil for evil, crime for crime, violence for violence!'

Simoun listened silently.

'Four months ago,' Basilio continued, 'you were telling me about your plans; I refused to take part and I was wrong, you were right. Three and a half months ago the revolution was about to break out; again I refused to join. When the movement failed, the reward for my conduct was imprisonment and I owe my freedom only to your intercession. You have been right and now I come to ask you to give me arms. Let the revolution come and I shall be ready to serve together with all the unfortunate.'

Simoun's brow suddenly cleared, there was a flash of triumph in his eyes and, as if he had found what he had been looking for, he exclaimed:

'I am right; of course I am right. Truth and justice are on my side because my cause is the cause of the unfortunate. Thank you, young man, thank you. You have come to dispel my doubts and overcome my hesitations.'

Simoun had risen to his feet and his face was shining; the fervour that had possessed him when he had told Basilio of his plans in his ancestral forest four months ago brightened his face again like a red sunset after a murky day.

'The movement failed,' he continued, 'and many deserted me because they saw me lose heart and hesitate at the decisive moment; there was something left in my heart, I was not master of all my emotions and I still loved... Now all is dead in me and there is no sacred dead whose sleep I must respect. There will be no more hesitations. You yourself, the young man of ideals, the dove without malice, understand what is required and come and call me to action. You have opened your eyes rather late in the day. You and I together could have put into execution such admirable plans: with me in the upper circle of society, spreading the death-wish amid all the elegance and wealth, brutalizing the corrupt and corrupting or paralyzing the handful of good men, and you below, among the people, among the young, calling forth a new life in blood and tears! Our work, instead of being bloody and savage, would have been holy, artistically perfect, and success would have surely crowned our labours. But no intellectual would give me his support. I found only womanish fears among the educated, selfishness among the rich, naïveté among the youth, and I found my men only in the mountains, among the exiled, among the wretchedly poor. But it does not matter now; if we cannot carve a perfect statue, polished clean of all imperfections, out of the rough material on which we shall work, those who come after us will do it.'

Basilio heard without fully understanding; now Simoun took him by the arm to his chemical laboratory.

There on a table lay a great box of dark tooled leather similar to the containers of the silver dinner services that kings and millionaires give one another. Simoun opened it, revealing against the red satin lining a most curiously shaped lamp. The vessel itself was in the form of a pomegranate as large as a man's head, partly cut open to show the pulp-coated seeds inside which were made of huge cornelians. The fruit's rind was made out of gold plate and was perfectly imitated, down to the rough surface of the original.

Simoun carefully lifted the lamp out of the box, and withdrawing the lamp-burner, revealed in the interior of the vessel a container with walls of steel about two centimetres thick and with a capacity of rather more than a litre. Basilio looked at Simoun inquiringly, he understood nothing.

Without going into any explanations Simoun removed a flask from a cupboard with great care and showed Basilio the formula written on its label.

''Nitroglycerine!' muttered Basilio, drawing back instinctively. 'Nitroglycerine, dynamite!'

He thought he understood Simoun's horrifying plan.

'Quite right, nitroglycerine,' Simoun repeated slowly, with his bleak smile, gazing at the flask with satisfaction, 'and yet something rather more than nitroglycerine: the essence of tears, the compound of hatred, injustice and wrongs, the final argument of the weak, force against force, violence to match violence. A while ago I hesitated to use it but you came and convinced me. Tonight it will blow to pieces the most dangerous of tyrants, the irresponsible tyrants who hide themselves behind God and the State, whose abuses remain unpunished because there is no one to call them to account! Tonight the Philippines will hear the explosion that will finally destroy the rotten structure whose corruption I have tried to hasten.'

Basilio was aghast, his lips moved soundlessly, he felt incapable of speech, his mouth was dry. It was the first time he had seen this potent liquid of which he had often heard as being distilled in darkness by sinister men at open war against society. Now he had it before his eyes, transparent, rather yellowish, being poured with infinite care into the lovely pomegranate lamp. In his eyes Simoun took the shape of the genie of the *Thousand and One Nights* tale who rose from the bosom of the sea, growing gigantically until he touched the sky with his head, bursting out of the house and making the whole city shake with a shrug of his shoulders; while the pomegranate lamp assumed the proportions of an enormous globe, and the cut in its rind became a hellish grin spouting flames and embers. Basilio was panic-stricken and lost his composure utterly for the first time in his life.

In the meantime Simoun was screwing in a strange and complicated mechanism, replacing the glass funnel and crowning the whole with a lampshade of the greatest elegance. Then he backed away to judge the effect, tilting his head to one side or the other in order to have a better idea of the lamp's magnificent appearance.

Basilio was staring at him with inquisitive and suspicious eyes and Simoun explained:

'There will be a reception tonight and this lamp will be placed in the centre of a small dining pavilion that has been constructed at my instructions for the purpose. The lamp will shine so brightly that no other lights will be needed but after twenty minutes its light will grow dim; when the wick is raised a percussion-cap will detonate a firing charge of mercury fulminate, the bomb will explode and with it the dining pavilion, in whose ceiling and floor I have concealed sacks of gunpowder so that none may escape.'

There was a moment of silence while Simoun contemplated his hidden bomb and Basilio scarcely breathed.

'So my help is not needed.' he remarked.

'No,' replied Simoun thoughtfully. 'You have another mission to accomplish. The bomb will have exploded by nine o'clock and the explosion will have been heard in the neighbouring suburbs, in the mountains and in the caves. The rising which I planned with the gunners failed because of lack of leadership and co-ordination. This time it will be different. At the sound of the explosion the unfortunate and the oppressed and those hunted by the law will take up arms and rendezvous with Cabesang Tales in the suburb of Santa Mesa to fall upon the city. On the other hand, the government forces, whom I have led to believe that the General is simulating a rising in order to have a pretext for remaining at his post, will leave their barracks ready to fire on anyone I should point out. In the meantime the people, thoroughly alarmed and believing that their massacre has been ordered, will rise ready to face death. Since they will be unarmed and disorganized, you and a number of others will put yourselves at their head and take them to the warehouses of Quiroga the Chinaman where I have stored my guns. Cabesang Tales and I will rendezvous in the city and take it while you seize the bridges to the suburbs, entrench yourselves and stand ready to come to our aid, executing not only those actively engaged in counter-action, but all males who refuse to take up arms for us.'

'All?' asked Basilio hoarsely.

'All,' Simoun repeated ruthlessly, 'all, natives, halfbreeds, Chinese, Spaniards, all those who show themselves to be without courage, without resolution. The race must be regenerated! Cowards can only breed slaves, and there is no point in destroying only to rebuild with rotten materials. What, you shudder? You tremble and fear to kill? What is death? What does the massacre of twenty thousand wretches signify? Twenty thousand miseries less, and millions more saved at the source from miserable lives. The most timid of rulers, to satisfy a whim, a fancy, his vanity, does not hesitate to proclaim a law which will lead to the ruin and the slow agony of thousands upon thousands of his subjects, prosperous till then, hard-working, happy perchance. And do you shudder because in one night the moral sufferings of so many slaves will end for ever, because a corrupt and paralytic people will die to make way for a new one, young, active, full of energy? What is death? Nothingness or a dream. Will its nightmares be comparable to the reality of the tortures inflicted on one whole miserable generation? It is important to destroy what is evil, to kill the dragon and bathe the new people in its blood to make them strong and invulnerable. What else is the inexorable law of Nature, the law of struggle in which the unfit must perish so that the defective species may not survive and the process of creation go into reverse? Forget these girlish compunctions. Let the eternal laws be fulfilled, and let us assist in the process; since the earth is all the more fruitful when it is fertilized with blood, and governments all the more secure the deeper they have their foundations in crime and death, let us have no more hesitations, no more doubts! What is the pain of death? A moment's sensation, hazy perhaps, perhaps even agreeable like passing from watchfulness into sleep. What is destroyed? Evil, suffering, miserable weeds that will be replaced by healthy grain. Do you call that destruction? I would call it creation, production, giving sustenance, giving life...'

These ruthless sophisms, stated with cold conviction, stunned Basilio, whose intellect, weakened by more than three months in prison and blinded by the thirst for vengeance, was not prepared to analyse their moral foundations. He should have replied that the most evil or cowardly of men is still something more than a vegetable because he has a soul and a mind that, no matter how corrupt or brutalized, can be redeemed; that no man has a right to decide to cut short the life of anyone else no matter for whose benefit, and that the right to life is inherent in every man like the right to liberty and enlightenment; that, if it is wrong for governments to punish the faults or crimes to which they have driven the criminal by their neglect or stupidity, it is much more wrong for one man, no matter how great or unfortunate, to punish a whole pitiful people for the defects of their governments and their ancestors; that only God can try such methods, that God can destroy because He can also create, that God has eternity in His hands as a recompense to justify His acts, and man has not. But instead of these arguments Basilio could only counter with a commonplace:

'What will the world say to such slaughter?'

'The world will applaud, as always, and acknowledge the right of the strongest, the most ruthless,' answered Simoun with his mocking smile. 'Europe applauded when the western peoples butchered millions of Indians in America, and certainly not in order to found nations that would be much more moral or peace-loving, for look at North America with its selfish freedom, its lynch law, its political frauds, and at South America with its restless republics, savage insurrections, civil wars and military dictatorships, just like in their mother Spain. Europe applauded when Portugal looted the Moluccas; Europe applauds when mighty England destroys the primitive races in the Pacific to make room for her settlers; and Europe will applaud us in the same way that one applauds at the end of a play, even of a tragedy. The common people seldom look to the bottom of things, they only have eyes for appearances. If the crime is done with style, it will be admired and will have more defenders than the most virtuous acts performed with modesty and indecision.'

'Agreed,' said Basilio. 'What does it matter to me in the end that the world should applaud or condemn when that world cares nothing for the oppressed, the poor or the weak? Why should I care for society when it has not cared for me?'

'That's the way to talk,' said Simoun triumphantly.

He took a revolver from a drawer and handed it to Basilio, saying:

'Wait for me at ten o'clock in front of the Church of San Sebastian for my last instructions. Ah, and at nine o'clock you should be far, very far from Anloague Street!'Basilio examined the gun, loaded it and placed it inside his jacket. He took his leave with a curt: 'I'll see you later.'

34 • *The Wedding*

ONCE out in the streets Basilio wondered what he could do until the decisive hour. It was only seven o'clock. All the students had gone home for the holidays; only Isagani had refused to go back to his town, but he was nowhere to be found that morning, no one knew where he was. That was what Basilio had been told when on his release from prison he had gone to visit his friend and ask to be put up. Basilio did not know where to go, he had no money or anything else except the revolver. The memory of the lamp filled his imagination: within two hours the great catastrophe would take place and, thinking of it, he fancied the passers-by without their heads. He had a feeling of fierce joy. Starving and all, that night he would be a figure of terror, so transformed from a penniless student and servant that the morning sun would perhaps find him awe-inspiring, sinister, standing on a mound of corpses and giving orders to all those who now passed by in their magnificent carriages. He felt an irresistible desire to laugh and felt for the butt of his revolver. The cartridge boxes were in his pockets.

He wondered where the play would begin. He had been too excited to ask Simoun but Simoun had warned him to stay away from Anloague Street.

This gave him an inkling of the truth. That afternoon, on leaving gaol, he had gone to the former house of Capitán Tiago to pick up his few possessions and had found it completely changed and decorated for a party, the wedding-feast of Juanito Peláez. And Simoun had spoken of a party!

A long line of carriages was passing by, full of ladies and gentlemen engaged in lively conversation. He fancied he caught glimpses also of great bouquets of flowers but did not give it any thought. The carriages were heading towards Del Rosario Street but had to go slowly, with frequent halts, because of the traffic from the Bridge of Spain. In one of them he saw Juanito Peláez beside a girl dressed in white and a transparent veil whom he recognized as Paulita Gómez.

It was she indeed, in bridal dress, as if she had come from church, and with Juanito Peláez!

He thought of poor Isagani, his friend, so noble and generous, and what had become of him.

He considered briefly whether or not to seek him out and tell him Simoun's plans but Isagani would never want to take part in such slaughter. Isagani had not suffered what he had suffered.

If he had not been imprisoned, he brooded, he too would now be bridegroom or husband, a physician living a life of service to the sick in his corner of the provinces. The image of Julí, broken in her fall, crossed his mind; his eyes gleamed darkly with hatred and once again he stroked the butt of his gun, impatient for the hour of terror. Then he saw Simoun leave his lodgings with the neatly wrapped box that held the lamp, board his carriage and take his place in the wedding cortege. Basilio did not want to lose sight of Simoun's carriage and turned his eyes to the driver; to his surprise he recognized in him the luckless Sinong who had taken him to San Diego and been beaten up by the Constabulary, and who had afterwards visited him in prison to keep him abreast of events in Tiani.

Guessing that Anloague Street would be the scene of coming events Basilio hurried there, leaving the slower carriages behind. He was right, they were all headed for the former house of Capitán Tiago, gathering there for a ball only to end dancing in the air! Basilio laughed inwardly at the policemen on duty, their number was an indication of the importance of the party and the guests. The house itself overflowed with people. Brilliant light poured from its windows, the inner courtyard was carpeted and full of flowers, and on the upper floors, perhaps in his old isolated room, an orchestra was playing gay tunes that could not wholly drown out the confused tumult of laughter and conversation.

Don Timoteo Peláez was almost at the pinnacle of fortune and the reality surpassed his dreams. He was marrying his son off at last to the extremely wealthy Gómez heiress and, thanks to a loan from Simoun, he had decorated the house, which he had bought for half its value, so that it was now fit for a king; he was giving in it a magnificent reception and the highest gods of the Manila Olympus were to be his guests, shedding on him the golden radiance of their prestige. Ever since that morning parodies of hazily remembered phrases from the Communion service had run through his mind with the persistence of a popular song: *The hour of bliss has come, the moment of happiness approaches, soon the admirable words of Simoun shall be fulfilled in thee: I live but not I but the Commander-in-Chief who livest in me*... The Commander-in-Chief standing as sponsor to his son! True, he had not found it possible to attend the wedding and had been represented by Don Custodio but he would come to dinner and bring a wedding present, a lamp unequalled even by Aladdin's... Confidentially, Simoun was contributing it—Timoteo, what more do you want?

Capitán Tiago's house had undergone a remarkable transformation. The walls had been richly re-papered, and the smoke and smell of opium had been completely eliminated. The great reception room, made to seem still more spacious by the huge mirrors that multiplied the brilliance of the chandeliers, was carpeted from wall to wall; the salons of Europe were carpeted and, although the floor of Capitán Tiago's house was made of wide and highly polished wooden beams, Don Timoteo's salon must also be carpeted. Capitán Tiago's ornate furniture had been replaced by another set in Louis XV style. Heavy red velvet curtains, with the initials of the newlyweds embroidered on them in gold, and gathered together in folds with garlands of artificial orange blossoms, hung at the doorways, sweeping the floor with their broad golden fringes. In the corners were displayed huge vases from Japan alternating with others from Sevres of the purest dark blue, placed on square pedestals of carved wood. The only wrong note was struck by the loud chromos with which Don Timoteo, despite Simoun's attempts to dissuade him, had replaced Capitán Tiago's old engravings and lithographs of saints; the merchant would not hear of oil paintings which might be attributed to native artists; what, contribute to the support of Filipino painters, never! His tranquillity, perhaps even his life, would be at stake; he knew how to get along in the Philippines! Of course, he had heard of foreign painters like Raphael, Murillo, Velázquez, but he did not know their addresses, and then again they might turn out to be progressives... But there was no risk in chromos, the Filipinos did not make them, they were cheaper, and to Don Timoteo's eyes the effect was the same if not actually better, the colours more vivid, the execution more precise.

No doubt about it, Don Timoteo knew his way about in the Philippines. The spacious entrance hall, profusely decorated with flowers, had again been turned into a dining-room; there was a large table for thirty in the centre and smaller ones for two and three ranged along the walls, all adorned with flower arrangements, heaps of fruit, ribbons and lights. The bridegroom's place was marked with a cluster of roses, and that of the bride with one of orange blossom and lilies. One might be justified in expecting, amid such elegance and so many flowers, that lightly clad nymphs and Cupids with iridescent wings would serve celestial guests with nectar and ambrosia to the music of lyres and Aeolian harps!

However, the table for the higher divinities was not to be found there but in the middle of the broad terrace, in a pavilion of extreme elegance built expressly for the purpose. Lattice-work of gilded wood, bearing sweet-smelling creepers, hid the interior from the eyes of the lower breeds without preventing the free flow of air necessary to refresh the guests during that time of year. A high platform raised this table above the level of the others where mere mortals would be served, and a cupola decorated by the best artists would shield the august from the envious stars.

The table was set for only seven, the service was of solid silver, the cloth and the napkins of the finest linen, the wines among the most exquisite and expensive. Don Timoteo had sought out the dearest and the scarcest delicacies and would not have hesitated to commit a crime if he had been told that the Governor-General had a taste for human flesh.

35 • The Wedding Feast

Dancing on a Volcano

THE guests began to arrive at seven o'clock: first, the minor divinities: low-ranking officials, division chiefs, businessmen and the like, who began by greeting one another studiously and with reserve as if they had only just learned how to bow—so much light, so many draperies, so much glass, somewhat overawed them—but afterwards, more at their ease, exchanged mock blows, taps on the stomach or even intimate pinches. True, some put on a disdainful air to show that they were accustomed to better things: one lesser goddess yawned openly, finding her surroundings vulgar, and said that she was famished, while another one quarrelled with her husband and started to give him the back of her hand. Don Timoteo bowed here, bowed there, sent a little smile in one direction, and bent his waist in another, took a step backward, made a half-turn, then a full turn, and pirouetted about so much that a third goddess felt compelled to tell her neighbour behind her fan:

'My dear, you would think we were all his brothers and sisters He looks like a puppet in a show!'

The bride and groom arrived with Doña Victorina and the wedding cortège. There were congratulations, handclasps, protective pats on the back for the groom, and for the bride lascivious, anatomically searching stares from the men, and from the women appraisals of her gown, her jewellery, her energy, her health.

'Cupid and Psyche entering Olympus,' thought Ben Zayb. He made a mental note, for use on a better occasion, of this comparison with the maiden who had lost her lover because, having been forbidden to look upon his face, she had lit a lamp one night and, a drop of hot oil falling on his shoulder, he had awakened and fled.

The bridegroom indeed resembled the roguish god of love and, with a modicum of goodwill, his hunch, which was more marked than ever under his trim frock-coat, could be taken for a quiver.

Don Timoteo's waist was beginning to ache, the corns on his feet were growing sorer by the minute, his neck was tired, and the Governor-General had not yet arrived! The major divinities, among them Father Irene and Father Salví, were already on the scene, it was true, but the Thunderer, Jove himself, had not yet made an appearance. Don Timoteo was uneasy, his nerves were in a state, his heart beat violently, he felt like relieving a personal necessity, but smiles and greetings came first, and when he did get away he could do nothing; he sat down, stood up, never heard a word addressed to him or said a word about his anxieties. In the meantime a divinity, who was also by way of being a dilettante of the arts, criticized the chromos and declared that they spoiled the walls.

'Spoil the walls,' Don Timoteo echoed smiling but hardly able to keep his hands off the critic's face. 'But they were made in Europe and they are the most expensive I could find in Manila!' Spoil the walls indeed!

He swore inwardly to collect the very next day all the critics' accounts in his shop.

'The Governor-General! The Commander-in-Chief!'

Pale with emotion Don Timoteo struggled to his feet concealing the pain in his corns and, accompanied by his son and some of the major divinities, went down to receive Great Jove. The aches in his waist vanished before the doubts that suddenly assailed him: should he smile or be serious, put out his hand or wait for the General to offer his? Good Lord, how could he have forgotten to take up these details with his great and good friend Simoun? To conceal his feelings he asked his son in a broken whisper:

'Have you prepared a speech?'

'Speeches are out of fashion, papa, and most of all with this one.'

Jupiter arrived with Juno, who was transformed into a display of fireworks: diamonds in her hair, diamonds on her neck, her arms her shoulders, everywhere! She wore a magnificent silken gown with a long train embroidered with flowers.

His Excellency took Don Timoteo's stammering offer of his house literally and really took possession of it. The orchestra struck up the Royal March and the godlike couple majestically went up the carpeted stairs.

His Excellency's gravity was genuine; perhaps for the first time since his arrival in the Philippines, he was sad and there was a tinge of melancholy in his thoughts. This was to be the last triumph in his three years of supreme power; in two days he would descend from the heights for ever. What was he leaving behind him? His Excellency would not look back and preferred to face the future. He was taking a fortune with him, heavy sums deposited in European banks awaited him, he owned houses and hotels, but he had injured a great number of people, he had many enemies at Court and the high official was waiting for him there. Other generals had enriched themselves as quickly as he had done and now they were bankrupt. Why not stay longer, as Simoun advised him? No, propriety above all! Besides, the bows he received were no longer so deep as before, he noted certain stares and even hostile looks, and he found himself replying ingratiatingly and even essaying a conciliatory smile or two.

'You can tell the sun is setting,' observed Father Irene in Ben Zayb's ear. 'There are many who now look him in the eye.'

The devil take the friar, thought the journalist, he had taken the words right out of his mouth.

'My dear,' commented the lady who had called Don Timoteo a puppet, 'have you ever seen such a skirt!'

'Oh dear, the Palace curtains!'

'Why, I do believe you're right. They are taking everything with them. Just you wait, she'll make a coat out of the carpets yet!'

'That proves nothing except that she has a head on her shoulders and good taste,' her husband remarked reprovingly. 'Women should be thrifty.'

The poor man still had not got over the bill from the dress-shop.

'My dear boy,' replied the annoyed goddess, 'give me curtains at twelve pesos a yard and you won't see me in these rags. My Lord, you'll sing another tune if I follow her example!'

In the meantime Basilio, mixed with the crowd of onlookers before the house, watched the guests as they alighted from their carriages; when he saw so many gay and carefree people, among them the bride and groom followed by the innocent and guileless bridesmaids, and realized that they would find there a horrible death, he felt a wave of pity for them that damped his hatred.

He wanted to save so many innocent lives and thought of notifying the police with an anonymous note, but a carriage arrived and Father Salví and Father Irene alighted, both looking very satisfied with themselves, and his good intentions vanished like a passing cloud

What did he care, let the just pay with the sinners! He was not an informer and he had no right to betray the trust placed in him.

He owed Simoun a great deal more than to the people in the house; Simoun had dug his mother's grave, they had killed her, what were they to him? He had done everything possible to be good and useful, had tried to forgive and forget, had endured every imposition and had asked only to be left in peace. He had kept out of the way and what had they done to him? Let them be blown up, everyone had suffered enough.

Then he saw Simoun arrive, carrying the terrible lamp, and cross the courtyard slowly, with head downcast in thought. Basilio felt his heart miss several beats and his hands and feet turn cold; in his eyes the jeweller's silhouette took sinister shapes surrounded by flames. Simoun hesitated at the foot of the staircase; Basilio held his breath. It was a short-lived pause; Simoun raised his head, went resolutely up the steps and disappeared from view.

The student felt that the house would go up at any moment in one infernal explosion that would send walls, roof, windows, lamps, guests and musicians flying through the air, and looking round him he fancied he already saw the mutilated corpses of the curiosity seekers under a flaming sky, but he recovered his serenity after this passing hallucination which had been abetted by hunger and said to himself that there was no danger while Simoun was in the house and before the Governor-General had arrived.

He tried to appear calm, controlling the convulsive trembling of his legs, and to think of other things, mocked by an inner voice which made him wonder how he would comport himself when he saw blood run and houses burning and when he heard bullets whistle about him, if now, even before the moment of decision, he trembled so.

His Excellency arrived but the young man scarcely had eyes for him, his gaze was fixed on the face of Simoun, who was one of those who had gone down to greet the Governor-General. Basilio read in the implacable features a judgment of death on all those men and then panic seized him anew. He felt cold and leaned against the wall of the house; his eyes on the windows and his ears straining for every sound, he tried to guess what was happening inside. He saw the guests in the main reception room crowd round Simoun and admire the lamp; he heard congratulations, exclamations of praise and repeatedly the words 'dining pavilion 'and 'debut'; he saw the General smile and guessed that the lamp would make its first public appearance that very night, as the jeweller had expected, and of course at the table where His Excellency would dine. Simoun disappeared from view followed by a crowd of admirers.

At this terrible moment Basilio's good heart prevailed, he forgot his hatred, he forgot Julí, and thought only of saving the lives of the innocent. Having taken this resolution, happen what might, he crossed the street and attempted to enter the house. But he had forgotten how miserably he was clothed; the porter stopped him, questioned him roughly and, when he insisted on entering, threatened to call the police.

Just then Simoun, a slight pallor on his face, was going down the staircase and the porter left Basilio to show the jeweller out with all the devotion due to a saint. Basilio understood from Simoun's expression that he was leaving the doomed house for good and that the lamp had been lit. The die was cast and, gripped by the instinct of self-preservation, Basilio thought only of saving himself. Anyone in there might, out of sheer curiosity, raise the wick and set off the percussion cap, and then the lamp would blow up and everything be buried in ruins. He could hear Simoun order his coachman:

'To the Escolta, quickly!'

Terrified, expecting to hear the terrible explosion at any moment, Basilio hurried away from the doomed house; his legs seemed to lack the necessary agility, his feet dragged and slid along the pavement, everyone was in his way, and twenty steps seemed to have taken him five minutes. Some distance away he stumbled upon a young man who stood with his head raised, staring fixedly at the house. Basilio recognized Isagani.

'What are you doing here? Come with me!'

Isagani gave him a vague look, smiled sadly and turned his eyes again towards the open windows where the airy silhouette of the bride could be glimpsed, moving away on the arm of her groom.

'Come along, Isagani, let us get away from this house, come' said Basilio hoarsely, seizing him by the arm.

Isagani quietly freed himself and continued to stare with the same melancholy smile on his lips.

'For God's sake, let's get away!'

'Why should I? Tomorrow she will be a different woman.'

His voice was so pathetic that Basilio momentarily forgot his panic.

'Do you want to die?'

Isagani shrugged.

Basilio tried once more to drag him away.

'Isagani, Isagani, listen to me, there is no time to lose. That house is mined, it may blow up at any moment, out of mere thoughtlessness, mere curiosity. Isagani, everything will be buried in its ruins.'

'In its ruins?' repeated Isagani, trying to understand without taking his eyes off the window.

'In its ruins, yes, Isagani, for God's sake, come along, I'll explain later, but come! Someone, more unfortunate than either you or I, has condemned them all to death. Do you see that white clear light, like an electric lamp, coming from the terrace? It is a lamp loaded with dynamite in a pavilion mined with gunpowder; when it blows up not a single rat will escape alive. Come!'

'No,' replied Isagani with a sorrowful shake of the head. 'I want to stay here, I want to see her for the last time, tomorrow it will be different.'

'What must be, will be,' cried Basilio, hurrying away as fast as he could.

Isagani watched his friend move away with a haste that betrayed a genuine terror but then turned his eyes again to the fascinating window like that German knight, of whom Schiller tells us, who waited for his lady fair to show herself. The reception room was empty, everyone had gone in to dinner. Isagani began to realize that Basilio's panic might have been justified. He remembered Basilio's terror-stricken face; Basilio was always so imperturbable; he began to wonder. One idea was clear in his mind: the house would blow up and Paulita was in it. Paulita would die a horrible death...

This thought banished everything else from his mind; jealousy, pain, moral suffering; his generous heart remembered only his love for her. Without a thought for his own safety, without hesitation, he went to the house and, thanks to his elegant clothes and his air of resolution, easily gained admission.

While these brief exchanges were taking place in the street a scrap of parchment was being handed round in the dining pavilion of the greater divinities, who read on it written in red:

Mane Thecel Phares
Juan Crisóstomo Ibarra

'Juan Crisóstomo Ibarra? Who is he?' asked His Excellency handing the paper on.

'A joke in the worst possible taste,' replied Don Custodio. 'The paper is signed with the name of a would-be subversive dead more than ten years now.'

'A subversive!'

'It's a seditious joke!'

'There being ladies present...'

Father Irene was looking round for the author of the squib when he noticed Father Salví, who was seated to the right of the Countess, turn as white as his napkin while he stared at the mysterious message, the episode of the disembodied head refreshed in his memory.

'What's wrong, Father Salví?' he asked. 'Don't tell me you recognize your friend's signature.'

Father Salví did not answer, he was moving his lips soundlessly and, apparently unaware of what he was doing, wiped his brow with his napkin.

'What's the matter with Your Reverence?'

'It's his handwriting,' he whispered almost unintelligibly. 'Ibarra's own handwriting.'

Falling back in his chair, he let his arms fall to his sides as if he had suddenly lost all his strength.

Uneasiness turned to apprehension and they looked at one another in silence. His Excellency wanted to get on his feet but, fearing it would be attributed to cowardice, mastered himself and looked about him. There were no soldiers to be seen and the servants who waited on them were unknown to him.

'Let us proceed, gentlemen,' he said, 'and give no importance to this joke.'

But his voice did not calm them down and only increased their anxiety for the voice had trembled.

'I suppose this *Mane Thecel Phares* does not mean we are going to be murdered tonight,' said Don Custodio.

They were struck motionless.

'Of course they could poison all of us...'

They dropped their knives and forks.

In the meantime the light was beginning to grow dim.

'The lamp is going out,' said the General apprehensively. 'Would you please raise the wick, Father Irene?'

Just then a man dashed into the pavilion, swift as lightning, knocking over a chair and a servant and, to the general amazement, seized the lamp, hurried to the edge of the terrace and threw it into the river. It had all happened in an instant; the pavilion was in utter darkness.

The lamp had already disappeared in the river when the servants managed to cry out the alarm. 'Thief, thief!' They ran out to the terrace.

'A gun!' one shouted. 'A gun, quick! After him!'

But the stranger, moving even faster, had already raised himself to the brick balustrade and before a light could be brought he dived into the river, leaving behind him only the sound of a splash.

36 • Ben Zayb's Predicament

As soon as lights were brought and Ben Zayb learned what had happened, observing the rather unorthodox postures of the surprised divinities, he was filled with indignation and, having made sure of the approval of the censors, hurried to the ground-floor lodgings which he shared. He would write the most inspiring article that had ever been read in the Philippines. The Governor-General would be broken-hearted if he were to depart before reading the vehement outbursts of praise that Ben Zayb was composing in his mind; he could not allow that in the goodness of his heart. He therefore sacrificed both dinner and dance and did not sleep all night.

Loud exclamations of horror and indignation, to begin with; then a picture of a world turned upside down with the stars, the eternal stars, in collision; next a cryptic introduction, bristling with allusions yet keeping up the suspense; to follow, a narration of events; and then the final paragraphs. He multiplied circumlocutions and exhausted all euphemisms to describe how His Excellency fell on his back and received a belated christening with sauce; he praised the agility with which His Excellency had recovered a vertical position, raising his head to the level where his feet had been and vice-versa; he intoned a hymn to Providence for having watched solicitously over such sacrosanct flesh, and the paragraph turned out so well that His Excellency took on the proportions of a veritable hero and fell from higher up, in the language of Victor Hugo. Ben Zayb went on writing, deleting, elaborating, polishing so that without actually lying—and this was his special merit as a newspaper man—the whole thing should read like an epic, revealing the newspaper man—the whole thing should read like an epic, revealing the greatness of the seven divinities and, on the other hand, the cowardice and degradation of the unknown thief 'who had passed judgment on himself, horrified and convinced, at the very moment of committing it, of the enormity of his crime.' Ben Zayb interpreted Father Irene's dash under the dining table as 'an impetuous act of inborn courage which the vestments of a God of peace and meekness, worn throughout his life, had failed to quench.' Father Irene, it turned out, wanted to hurl himself on the criminal and had taken the most direct route under the table. In passing Ben Zayb made reference to submarine tunnels, mentioned one of Don Custodio's projects on the subject, and recalled the culture and extensive travels of the friar. Father Salví's swooning away was the result of the excessive sorrow which had overcome the virtuous Franciscan when he realized what little profit the natives had derived from his pious exhortations. The frozen immobility of the other guests, among them the Countess who had 'protected' (read, grabbed) Father Salví, proved their serenity and heroic imperturbability, inured to peril in the fulfilment of their duties; beside them the Roman senators surprised by the invading Gauls had been skittish girls frightened by cartoons of cockroaches. Then, to draw a contrast, Ben Zayb pictured the thief: craven, mad, bewildered, scowling, his face twisted and yet—what the moral superiority of race could do!—overcome by superstitious awe upon beholding the august assemblage. All this let logically to a long adjuration, a harangue, an outburst against the perversion of good customs which justified the establishment of a permanent court-martial, 'the proclamation of a state of emergency within the state of emergency already proclaimed, special legislation that will be firmly repressive because it is absolutely necessary and urgently imperative to show the depraved and the criminal that, if the heart can be generous and paternal towards those who are submissive and law-abiding, the hand is strong, steady, inexorable, severe, and hard against those who, against all reason, commit any act against the country and insult its most sacred institutions. This is called for not only by the good of these islands, not only by the good of mankind in general, but also in the name of Spain, the honour of the Spanish name, the prestige of the Iberian nation, because above all things we are Spaniards and the flag of Spain, etc., etc.'

Ben Zayb ended his article with a farewell to the General:

'The indomitable warrior who has guided the destinies of this country with expert hand in such calamitous times can depart with easy mind, and untroubled refresh himself with the sweet breezes of the Manzanares, for we remain behind like faithful sentinels to venerate his memory, admire his wise decrees, and avenge the vile outrage perpetrated on his magnificent gift which we shall soon recover even if we have to dry up the seas, for such a precious relic will be for this country an imperishable monument of his generosity, serenity and courage!'

It was on this somewhat confusing note that the article ended. It was not yet dawn when Ben Zayb sent it, with the previous permission of the censor, to his newspaper and then went to sleep like Napoleon after drawing up his plans for the Battle of Jena.

They awoke him at sunrise; the article was being returned with a note from the editor to the effect that His Excellency had absolutely forbidden any news of the affair and had given instructions to deny any comments or stories that might circulate, classifying them as mere gossip, exaggerated rumours and fairy tales.

For Ben Zayb it was like killing a handsome and gallant son, born and reared in pain and travail. On what other occasion could he make use of his superb Catilinarian, the splendid calls to do battle for justice's sake? To think that in a month or two he would be leaving the Philippines himself and that he could not hope to place the article in Spain, for how was he to say the same things against the criminals in Madrid when other ideas of justice were current there, mitigating circumstances were sought for crimes, evidence was duly weighed, verdicts had to be rendered by juries, and all that? Articles of the type he wrote were like some poisonous spirits made in Europe, good only for sale to Negroes, with the difference that the Negroes were not harmed if they did not drink the liquor while Ben Zayb's articles produced their effects whether or not the Filipinos read them.

If only, he thought to himself, some other crime were to be committed tomorrow or the day after!

Ben Zayb dressed to see his editor, his eyes moistening at the thought of the dead child that would never appear in print, a bud nipped by the frost. The editor shrugged his shoulders: His Excellency had issued the prohibition because if it ever became known that seven major divinities had allowed themselves to be surprised and robbed by a common felon while they had knives and forks in their hands, national unity would be imperilled. He had given orders that neither lamp nor thief should be sought, and planned to advise his successors never to run the risk of dining out without being surrounded by halbardiers and bodyguards. Since those who knew anything about the events in Don Timoteo's house were for the most part government officials and military men, it was not difficult to issue public denials, it was a question of national unity. In the face of this appeal Ben Zayb lowered his head heroically, thinking of Abraham, who had been ready to sacrifice his son, and Guzmán the Good who had actually allowed the Moors to kill his, or at the very least of Brutes and other classic heroes of history.

Such sacrifice could not be allowed to go unrewarded; the god of newspaper men was well pleased with Abraham Ben Zayb.

Almost immediately the rescuing angel appeared in the shape of a provincial correspondent, bearing the sacrificial lamb in the form of an attack made on a pleasure villa on the banks of the Pasig where certain friars were spending the hot season. That was exactly what he needed and Abraham Ben Zayb gave praise to his god.

'The outlaws took more than two thousand pesos and left one friar and two servants badly wounded. The priest defended himself as best he could with a chair until it was smashed to pieces.'

'Hold on, just a moment,' cried Ben Zayb, taking it all down. 'Forty or fifty highwaymen treacherously... revolvers, knives, shotguns, pistols... a veritable lion wielding a chair... smithereens... savagely wounded... ten thousand pesos...'

Beside himself, and not satisfied with these details, he decided to visit the scene of the crime personally and on his way composed a Homeric description of the battle. A harangue by the bandit chieftain perhaps? A disdainful phrase from the friar's lips? All the metaphors and comparisons applied to His Excellency, Father Irene and Father Salví would fit the wounded friar perfectly, and the description of the unknown burglar, each and every one of the highwaymen. In fact the adjuration could be expanded, he might speak of religion, of the Faith, of charity, of the pealing of church bells, of what the natives owed the friars; he could put in a touch of tenderness and lyrical phrases in the style of the great Spanish contemporary orator Castelar. The young ladies of the capital would read his article and exclaim:

'Ben Zayb, brave as a lion, tender as a lamb!'

When he arrived at the scene of the attack he discovered to his great surprise that the wounded friar was no other than Father Camorra, who had been condemned by the Provincial of his Order to expiate his frolics in Tiani in the pleasure villa. He had a small wound in one hand and a bruise on his head which he had acquired in falling on his back. There had been three robbers armed with knives and they had got away with fifty pesos.

'That's impossible,' Ben Zayb protested. 'Shut up, man, you don't know what you're talking about!'

'What do you mean, I don't know-what I'm talking about, dammit all!'

'Don't be silly. There must have been more robbers.'

'Lord, what a hack!'

They had a rousing quarrel. The important thing for Ben Zayb was not to let go his article, to build up events enough to justify his closing paragraphs.

A whisper cut their argument short. The robbers had been caught and they had made important statements. One of the outlaws in the band of Cabesang Tales, who was better known as *Matanglawin,* had arranged a rendezvous with them in the outlying suburb of Santa Mesa. The band would have sacked the convents and the houses of the rich. They would be guided by a tall dark Spaniard with white hair who said he was acting for his very good friend the General. They had also been assured of support from the artillery and other regiments, and so would have nothing to fear. The outlaws would afterwards be given free pardons and could keep a third part of the booty. The signal was to have been a cannon shot but they had waited for it in vain, and the outlaws, believing they had been fooled, had gone home or else had returned to the mountains swearing to avenge themselves on the Spaniard who had broken his word for the second time. The robbers who had been caught, for their part, had decided to make an attempt of their own and had attacked the nearest villa, but they were ready to give the white-haired Spaniard his two-thirds' share if he should ask for it.

The description fitted Simoun and the statements were considered absurd. The robbers were subjected to all types of torture, including even electric shocks, for making such a brazen accusation. But when news came of the jeweller's disappearance, to the sensation of the whole business district, and when sacks of gunpowder and a great quantity of bullets were discovered in his house, the robbers' statements began to sound credible and the whole affair was slowly covered in mystery: vague references, whispers, dry little coughs, suspicious looks, sentences that trailed off, and the many ambiguous phrases useful at such times. Those who were given the facts could hardly recover from their amazement; their faces were pale and mournful, and some almost went out of their minds when certain things were discovered which had passed unnoticed.

'We escaped by the skin of our teeth! Who would have said...

In the afternoon Ben Zayb, his pockets full of revolvers and bullets, called on Don Custodio, whom he found working hard on a project against American jewellers. Between the palms of his hands and in the slightest of whispers he murmured a few mysterious words in the ear of the journalist.

'Really!' exclaimed Ben Zayb, visibly shaken, his hands flying to his pockets. 'And wherever they find him...'

Don Custodio finished his phrase with an expressive mime: he raised both arms to the height of his face, the right at a sharper angle than the left, palms downwards, and, with a wink, stabbed his hands forward twice.

'Pssst, pssst,' he hissed.

'And the diamonds?' asked Ben Zayb.

'If they are found on him...'

He went into another mime with the fingers of his right hand, turning them inwards like a closing fan as if gathering in, like the sweep of a windmill, like a clever prestidigitator. Ben Zayb replied with another gesture, opening his eyes wide, raising his eyebrows and avidly sucking in air, as if it had suddenly been endowed with nutritive elements.

37 • *Mystery*

All is known

IN spite of all precautions the rumours reached the general public, although considerably changed and distorted. They were the topic of conversation the following night in the house of the wealthy Orenda family, traders in jewellery in the busy suburb of Santa Cruz. Their numerous callers had no time for anything else. The usual card-game was abandoned the piano was silent, the little Tinay, the youngest of the daughters of the family, was utterly bored playing the native shell game by herself, unable to understand why everyone was so interested in robberies, conspiracies and sacks of gunpowder when there were so many pretty shells winking and pouting with their little mouths. Isagani, who played with her and let himself be beaten very satisfactorily whenever he called, had no ears for her now and listened instead, sombre and silent, to the stories of Chichoy the silver-worker. Momoy, who was affianced to Sensia, the eldest of the Orendas, a pretty and lively girl who was apt to be a tease, had left the window where they usually spent the evenings flirting. This considerably annoyed the parrot whose cage hung at the window, a parrot that was usually the family's centre of attraction because it would greet the world in the mornings with the eloquent love-talk it had heard the night before. Capitana Loleng, usually so industrious and alert, could neither read nor write in the book of accounts that lay open before her, had no eyes for the trays of unset pearls and diamonds and, forgetting it all, was intent only on listening to what was being said. Her husband, the great Capitán Toringoy (born Domingo), the happiest man in the district, who had nothing to do but dress well, eat, go for a walk and chat with friends while his family busied themselves with their tasks, had stayed home to listen, half-way between frightened and touched by the hair-raising stories of the spindly Chichoy.

He had reason to feel that way. Chichoy had gone that morning to Don Timoteo Peláez's house to deliver a pair of earrings for the new bride, just when the dining pavilion, which the highest authorities had used the night before, was being taken down. At this point of the story Chichoy blanched and his hair stood on end.

'My sainted mother! Sacks of gunpowder under the floor, in the ceiling, under the table, inside the chairs, everywhere! Lucky none of the labourers was smoking!'

'And who put them there?' asked Capitana Loleng, who had a stouter heart than the pale-faced swain, Momoy.

Momoy had been a guest at the wedding-feast and his belated emotions were understandable, he had been seated near the pavilion.

'That is what nobody can explain,' Chichoy relied. 'Who would want to spoil the wedding feast? The famous lawyer Mr Pasta, who was in the house at the time, said it could be only an enemy of Don Timoteo or a rival of Juanito...'

The Orenda girls turned their eyes instinctively to Isagani. Isagani smiled wordlessly.

'You must go into hiding,' Capitana Loleng urged him. 'They might make all sorts of charges against you. Hide yourself!'

Isagani smiled again and said nothing.

'Don Timoteo did not know whom to blame,' continued Chichoy. 'He supervised the construction himself, he and his friend Simoun, nobody else. Everyone was very excited, a police lieutenant was called, we were all sworn to silence, and then I was sent away. But...'

'But... but...' stammered the shaken Momoy.

'My sainted mother,' exclaimed Sensia, her eyes on her sweetheart and trembling in turn when she realized that he had been a guest at the wedding, 'this young man of mine... if it had all blown up...'

She gave her sweetheart a look of mingled anger and admiration.

'If it had all blown up...'

'Nobody would have been left alive on Anloague Street,' concluded Capitán Toringoy, with a show of fortitude and nonchalance for the benefit of his family.

'I went home shaken,' continued Chichoy, 'thinking that one spark, one lighted cigarette, an overturned lamp on all that gunpowder, and now we would have no General, no Archbishop, nothing, not even government officials! Everyone at the wedding feast last night, blown to pieces!'

'Most Holy Virgin! And this young man of mine...'

'Jesus, Mary, Joseph!' exclaimed Capitana Loleng. 'Everyone who owes us money was there! Jesus, Mary, Joseph, we have a house near by! Who could it have been?'

'I'll tell you,' Chichoy went on in a hushed tone of voice, 'but you must keep it a secret. This afternoon I met a friend of mine who is a clerk in a government office and, speaking of this business, he gave me a clue, he had it from some government employees. Who do you think put the sacks of gunpowder there?'

There were shrugs all round. Capitán Toringoy gave Isagani a sideways look.

'The friars?'

'Quiroga the Chinaman?'

'Some students?'

'Makaraig?'

Capitán Toringoy coughed and kept his eyes on Isagani.

Chichoy shook his head, grinning.

'Simoun the jeweller!'

'Simoun!'

An astonished silence followed. Simoun, the Governor-General's evil counsellor, the fabulously wealthy trader from whom they bought loose stones, Simoun who received the young Orenda ladies with such courtesy and polished compliments! The story was believed precisely because it sounded so unlikely. I believe because it is absurd, St Augustine had said.

'But wasn't Simoun at the party?' asked Sensia.

'Yes,' answered Momoy. 'But now I remember, he left the house when we were sitting down to dinner, he said he was going to fetch his own wedding gift.'

'But wasn't he the General's friend, Don Timoteo's partner?'

'Yes, but he became their friend and partner only so he could strike all the better and kill all the Spaniards.'

'Ah,' said Sensia, 'now I understand.'

'What?'

'You never wanted to believe Aunt Tentay. But she always said Simoun is the Devil who has bought the souls of all the Spaniards!'

Capitana Loleng crossed herself and cast an anxious look on the unset stones, afraid of seeing them transformed into embers. Capitán Toringoy took off a ring which had come from Simoun.

'Simoun has disappeared without a trace,' Chichoy added. 'The Constabulary are looking for him.'

'A fine time,' said Sensia. 'Might as well look for the Devil.'

She crossed herself Many things were now quite clear: the sources of Simoun's fabulous wealth, the peculiar smell in his house, the smell of sulphur! Binday, another of the Orenda girls, ingenuous and charming, recalled having seen blue flames in the jeweller's house one afternoon when she had gone there with her mother to buy precious stones.

Isagani listened attentively but in silence.

'That is why last night...' stammered Momoy.

'Last night?' echoed Sensia, half curious and half jealous.

Momoy could not make up his mind to tell but the look Sensia gave him dissipated his fears.

'Last night, when we were at dinner, there was a commotion, the lights went out in the General's dining pavilion, they said an unknown man had stolen the lamp given by Simoun.'

'A robber? The Black Hand?'

Isagani stood up and paced up and down the room.

'Didn't they catch him?'

'He dived into the river. Nobody really had a good look at him. Some say he was a Spaniard, others that he was Chinese, or a native...'

'It is believed that this lamp,' continued Chichoy, 'would have been used to burn down the house and set off the gunpowder.'

Momoy gave a shudder but, realizing that Sensia had noticed, tried to remedy the impression he had given.

'Pity,' he said, making an effort, 'the robber did wrong, they should all have died.'

Sensia stared at him, the ladies crossed themselves, and Capitán Toringoy, who was afraid of politics, started to move away. Momoy appealed to Isagani.

'It is always wrong to take what belongs to another,' replied Isagani with an enigmatic smile. 'If the robber had known what it was about and had had time to think, he never would have done it.'

He added after a brief pause:

'I should not like to be in his place for anything in the world.'

And in this fashion comment followed upon conjecture.

An hour later Isagani took his leave of the family. He was going away to live with his uncle and would not come back again.

38 • *A Trick of Fate*

Matanglawin was the terror of Luzon. His band would strike the province where they were least expected just as often as one where preparations had been made to resist them. One day they would burn down a sugar-mill and its fields in Batangas, on the next murder a municipal judge in Tiani, on another take a town in Cavite by surprise and seize the arms in the town hall. *Matanglawin* plundered the provinces of the Central Valley from Tayabas to Pangasinan, and his sanguinary name echoed as far south as Albay and as far north as Kagayan. The towns, disarmed by the distrust of a weak Government, fell easy prey to him; at his coming the farmers fled, herds were scattered and slaughtered, and he left behind him a trail of blood and fire. *Matanglawin* flouted all the harsh measures decreed against bandits; only the inhabitants of isolated neighbourhoods suffered in fact from these decrees for, either they were taken captive and punished by *Matanglawin* when they resisted him, or, if they came to an arrangement with him, they were flogged and exiled by the Government forces, exiled, that is, if they did not meet with a fatal accident on the way. This agonizing dilemma had induced many of the peasants to take to the hills themselves under *Matanglawin*.

Under this reign of terror trade in the towns, already on the decline, was coming to a complete standstill. The rich did not dare to travel and the poor were terrorized by the thought that they might be arrested by the Constabulary who, under orders to hunt down the outlaws, would often seize upon the first persons they found and subject them to unspeakable torture. The impotent Government sought to make a show of force at the expense of those whom it considered suspicious so that the towns, by dint of cruelty, might not suspect its weakness, a fear that in fact was responsible for these measures.

One afternoon a file of these unfortunate suspects, six or seven of them, bound elbow to elbow and one to the other in a kind of chain of human flesh, were marching on a road that skirted a mountain. They were guarded by ten or twelve soldiers armed with rifles. The heat was extraordinary. The bayonets flashed in the sun, the gun barrels were burning hot, and the sage leaves with which the soldiers had lined their helmets hardly absorbed the heat of the deadly May sun.

Deprived of the use of their arms and joined as closely as possible, one to the next, in order to save rope, the prisoners, for their part, marched hatless and shoeless; at best some of them had handkerchiefs tied round their heads. Panting with exhaustion and covered with dust which their sweat turned to mud, they felt their brains melting and saw bright red spots in the air about them. Their faces carried the marks of exhaustion, anger, discouragement if not outright despair; indefinable emotions, akin to those of a man who dies with a curse, who renounces life, himself, and blasphemes against God. Those with the greatest endurance wiped their faces clear of sweat on the filthy back of the man in front; many were limping but, if one of them fell and hindered the march, one of the soldiers came up, swearing and brandishing a branch torn from a wayside tree, and compelled him to get up, hitting out in every direction. Then the file would start a feeble run, dragging along the fallen man who tumbled in the dust and howled for death; if by chance he managed to struggle back to his feet, he would go on marching, sobbing like a child and cursing the hour he was conceived.

The file would stop from time to time while the guards slaked their own thirst and then went on with dry mouths, dark thoughts and hearts full of hatred; thirst was the least of their sufferings.

'Forward, march! March, you sons of bitches,' shouted the soldier with the branch in Tagalog, his strength refreshed.

The branch whistled through the air and struck the nearest back, or perhaps a face, leaving a welt that was white at first, then red, and later only the colour of the dust of the road.

'March, you yellow bastards!' the guard who was called Mautang, would sometimes shout in Spanish in a voice that he tried to make more commanding.

'Yellow bastards!' repeated the mountain echoes.

The 'yellow bastards' marched faster under the hot iron sky, on a road of fire, pursued by the knotty branch that was torn to shreds on their broken skins. Perhaps the Siberian cold is kinder than the May sun in the Philippines.

One of the soldiers, however, watched these pointless cruelties with disgust; he marched silently and with a frown of disapproval. At length, finding that Mautang was not satisfied with beating the prisoners and was kicking those who fell, he could no longer control himself and shouted impatiently:

'Hey, Mautang, leave them alone!'

Mautang turned in surprise.

'And what do you care? You've come back from the Carolines haven't you?'

'It is nothing to do with me,' answered the Carolinian. 'But I don't like it, they're human too.'

'I can see you're new to the job,' countered Mautang with a pitying laugh. 'How did you handle your prisoners during the campaign over there?'

'Not like that, anyway,' said the Carolinian.

Mautang was silenced for a while; then, having found the argument he needed, he replied coolly:

'Ah well, those were our enemies and fought back; these fellows are... just natives like ourselves.'

He added in the Carolinian's ear:

'What a simpleton you are! You treat them like that so they try to fight back or run away, and then... fire!'

The Carolinian did not answer.

One of the prisoners begged to be allowed to stop and relieve himself

'Too dangerous in this place,' answered the corporal in charge with an apprehensive look at the mountain beside them. 'Forward!'

'March!' ordered Mautang.

The cudgel whistled. The prisoner twisted in pain and cried reproachfully:

'You are worse than the Spaniard himself!'

Mautang replied with more blows. At almost the same instant the whistle of a bullet was heard followed by the sound of a shot. Mautang dropped his rifle with an oath and turning round fell with his hands on his chest, The prisoner watched him writhing in the dust and throwing up blood.

'Halt!' shouted the corporal, suddenly pale.

The soldiers halted and looked round them. A slight wisp of smoke could be seen among some bushes on the slope. There was another shot, another bullet, and the corporal, hit in the leg, doubled up swearing. The column was being attacked by men hidden among the boulders above them.

The corporal, sullen with rage, pointed to the prisoners and ordered his soldiers to fire.

The prisoners fell to their knees in consternation; unable to lift up their hands, they asked for mercy by kissing the dust of the road or straining their heads forward; some spoke of children, of mothers, who would be left unprovided; one offered money, another called upon God; but the gun barrels had already been lowered and a terrible volley silenced them.

Then the soldiers turned their fire on the heights which were slowly crowned with smoke. To judge from this manoeuvre of concealment and from the infrequency of their firing, the unseen enemy had not more than three guns. The soldiers advanced firing under cover of the trees or wriggling forward on their bellies. Chips were struck off boulders, branches were torn apart, or little puffs of earth showed where bullets had struck. The first of the soldiers to try rushing the slope rolled back wounded in the shoulder.

The unseen enemy had the advantage of position; the soldiers, who were brave enough and had never fallen back under fire, were slackening, they stopped where they were and would not advance. This fight against the unseen was demoralizing them. They could only see smoke and rocks; there was not one human voice, not even a shadow; they felt they were fighting the mountain itself.

'Come on, you Carolinian, where's that bloody marksmanship of yours!' shouted the corporal.

At that instant a man appeared on top of a boulder making signs with his gun.

'Shoot him down!' ordered the corporal with an oath.

Three soldiers obeyed but the man remained standing; he was shouting but could not be understood.

The Carolinian stared at the sunlit silhouette and thought he recognized it. But the corporal was threatening to run him through if he did not shoot and the Carolinian took aim and fired. The man on the rock turned round on his heels and disappeared with a cry that stunned the Carolinian.

A movement broke out in the thicket that suggested a dispersal of the enemy. The soldiers began to move forward without resistance. Then another man appeared on a boulder waving a spear; the soldiers fired and he fell slowly, clutching at a branch; another shot and he fell on his face on the rock.

The soldiers climbed the slope nimbly with fixed bayonets, ready for a hand-to-hand fight; only the Carolinian moved reluctantly, with a lost brooding look, haunted by the cry of the man whom he had shot down. The first soldier to reach the heights found an old man dying on a rock; he ran him through with the bayonet but the old man did not flinch; he had his eyes on the Carolinian, a cryptic look, and with bony hand was pointing out to him what lay behind the boulders.

The soldiers turned and saw the Carolinian hideously pale, with mouth open and a madman's stare. He was Tano, the son of Cabesang Tales, just back from the campaign in the Carolines, and he recognized in the dying old man his grandfather, Old Selo, who, no longer capable of speech, was telling him their tale of woe through his dying eyes; and would continue, with dead finger, to point out what lay behind the rocks.

39 • The Last Chapter

IN his secluded retreat beside the sea, whose restless surface could be seen through the open windows stretching out in the distance until it merged with the horizon, the lonely Father Florentino solaced himself by playing grave and melancholy airs on a reed organ to the accompaniment of the crashing waves and the sighing of the nearby woods. The old instrument yielded long full notes, prayerful but nonetheless robust; Father Florentino, who was an accomplished musician, was improvising and, since he was alone, gave free rein to the sadness in his heart.

The old man had reason to be sad. His good friend, Don Tiburcio de Espadaña, had just left him, flying from the persecutions of his wife. That morning the priest had received a note from the commanding officer of the local garrison.

My dear Chaplain:
I have just received the following telegram from headquarters: DISABLED SPANIARD HIDDEN HOUSE FATHER FLORENTINO CAPTURE DEAD OR ALIVE. Since the telegram is quite clear, warn our friend not be there when I go to arrest him at eight o'clock tonight.
Yours ever,
Pérez
Burn this letter.

'Oh, th-th-this Victorina!' stammered Don Tiburcio. 'She's quite c-c-capable of having me shot!'

Father Florentino had been unable to stop him from going forthwith; in vain he pointed out that the description of the Spaniard in hiding as 'disabled' might apply not to Don Tiburcio but to the jeweller Simoun who had arrived two days before, wounded and a fugitive, seeking hospitality. Don Tiburcio would not listen; 'disabled' meant his limp, his personal description; it was all the doing of Doña Victorina who wanted him back dead or alive, as

Isagani had written from Manila; and the poor Ulysses hurried out of the priest's house to conceal himself in a woodman's hut.

Father Florentino, however, had no doubt that the wanted Spaniard was the jeweller Simoun. He had arrived in mysterious circumstances, carrying his treasure-chest himself, wounded, morose, and in a state of extreme depression. The priest, with the open and cordial hospitality of the Filipinos, had welcomed him without attempting to make any indiscreet inquiries although, since news of the events in Manila had not yet reached him, he did not have a clear understanding of the situation. The only conjecture he could hazard was that with the departure of the General, the jeweller's friend and protector, Simoun's enemies, those whom he had injured and outraged, had come out in the open to demand satisfaction, and that the Acting Governor-General was after Simoun to make him surrender the riches he had accumulated. That would explain his flight but why was he wounded? Had he tried to kill himself? Had he been the victim of a personal vendetta? Or were his injuries merely accidental, as Simoun had explained? Had he been wounded while evading capture by the forces sent after him?

This last conjecture seemed to be the most reasonable and the telegram received by the garrison commander confirmed it as well as Simoun's stubborn refusal from the very start to send for the government physician in the provincial capital. The jeweller had been ready to receive treatment only at the hands of Don Tiburcio, and even then only with marked suspicion. In these circumstances Father Florentino wondered what attitude to take when the Constabulary came to arrest Simoun. The condition of the wounded man made moving him, and even more a long voyage, dangerous; yet the telegram had said 'dead or alive'.

Father Florentino stopped playing and went to a window to look out upon the sea. The deserted expanse, where not a ship or a sail could be seen, suggested nothing to him. The solitary islet that could be discerned in the distance only suggested its own solitude which sharpened the solitude of his surroundings. The infinite is sometimes maddeningly silent.

The old priest tried to analyse the sad ironic smile with which Simoun had greeted the news that he was going to be arrested. What did it mean? And that other smile, even sadder and more ironic, when he learned that they would not be coming for him until eight o'clock that night? What was the key to this enigma? Why did Simoun refuse to conceal himself?

The famous plea of St John Chrysostom defending the eunuch Eutropius came to mind: 'Never more than now was it proper to say, Vanity of vanities, all is vanity.'

This Simoun, so rich, so powerful, so feared only a week ago, was now more unfortunate than Eutropius himself and sought shelter not by the altars of a church but in the comfortless house of a poor native priest, lost in the forest by a lonely seashore. Vanity of vanities, all is vanity! And in a few hours this man would be arrested, taken from the bed where he lay, without consideration for his condition, without thought for his wounds; he was wanted by his enemies, 'dead or alive'. How to save him? Where find the moving eloquence of the Bishop of Constantinople? What authority could there ring in his poor words, the words of a native secular priest, the humiliation of whose order Simoun himself in his days of glory had seemed to applaud and encourage?

Father Florentino no longer remembered the cold reception that Simoun had given him when two months earlier the priest had sought to interest the jeweller in securing the release of Isagani, imprisoned for his rashness and imprudence; he had no thought for Simoun's eagerness to hasten the wedding of Paulita, a marriage that had plunged Isagani into depths of depression that were causing his uncle great anxiety; Father Florentino forgot everything and remembered only the wounded man's condition, his own duties as a host, and wracked his brains wondering if he should hide Simoun from justice. But if the man himself did not seem to worry and merely smiled . . .

The good priest was pondering on these questions when a servant gave him the message that Simoun wished to speak to him. He went into the next room, a clean and well-aired chamber with a wooden floor made of broad and well-polished boards and simply furnished with great heavy armchairs of an old-fashioned design, unvarnished and undecorated. At one end rose a great wooden bed with four posts to hold the crown of the mosquito-net; beside it was a table littered with bottles, lint and bandages. A praying-desk at the foot of a crucifix and a small library suggested that it was the priest's own room which he had yielded to his guest in obedience to the Filipino custom of giving the stranger the best table, the best room and the best bed in the house. The windows were wide open to the healthy sea air and the sounds of its eternal lament, and no one in the Philippines of that time would therefore have expected to find a sick man there for it was then the custom to close all the windows, even the smallest openings, as soon as anyone caught a cold or suffered from the slightest headache.

Father Florentino looked towards the bed and to his horror saw that Simoun's face had lost its tranquil and ironic expression; instead, a hidden pain contorted his features, there was a look of anxiety in his eyes and his lips were twisted in a grimace.

'Are you in pain, Mr Simoun?' the priest asked solicitously.

'Somewhat,' he answered, shaking his head, 'but soon I shall be out of it.'

Father Florentino clasped his hands in horror as he realized the terrible truth.

'My God, what have you done? What did you take?' He reached out a hand towards the bottles.

'Useless, there is nothing that can be done,' Simoun answered with another grimace of pain. 'What else did you expect me to do? Not later than eight o'clock... dead or alive . . . dead, yes, but not alive.'

'My God, my God, what have you done?'

'Compose yourself,' Simoun cut him short with a gesture. 'What is done, is done. I must not fall alive into anyone's hands, they might wrest my secret from me. Do not fret, do not lose your head, there is nothing you can do. Listen to me, night is falling and there is no time to lose. I must tell you my secret, I must give you my last will. It is essential to me that you see the whole of my life. At this supreme moment I want to unburden myself, I want to resolve a doubt. You have such faith in God—I want you to tell me if there *is* a God!'

'An antidote, Mr Simoun! I have apomorphine, a quick emetic... Ether, chloroform...'

The priest rummaged for the right bottle until Simoun cried impatiently:

'Useless, I said, useless! Don't lose time or I shall go with my secret.'

The bewildered priest knelt at his praying-desk, prayed at the feet of Christ with his head in his hands, and then rose unsmiling and grave as if he had received from God all the energy, all the dignity, all the authority of the Judge of consciences. He placed an armchair at the head of the bed and leant down to listen.

At Simoun's first words, when he revealed his real name, the old priest fell back and stared at him with fear. Simoun smiled bitterly. Father Florentino was so surprised that he had lost control of himself but he quickly recovered his self-mastery and, covering his face with a handkerchief, bent down once again to listen.

Simoun told his sorrowful story. He had returned from Europe thirteen years ago, full of hope and happy illusions. He was to marry the girl he loved. He was ready to do good and forgive all those who had done him wrong so long as they left him in peace. It was not to be. A secret hand had hurled him into the whirlpool of a rising plotted by his enemies. He had lost his reputation, position, love, prospects for the future, freedom, everything, and had escaped death only because of the heroism of a friend. Then he had sworn revenge. With his ancestral wealth, which had been buried in a forest, he had fled abroad and gone into trade. He had taken part in the Cuban wars, helping now one side, now the other, but always to his profit. There he had met the General, at that time only a major, and had won his confidence in the beginning by lending him money. Later they became close friends because of certain crimes whose secrets were known to the jeweller. By dint of bribes Simoun had secured for him the assignment to the Philippines and once in the country Simoun had used the General as his blind tool, impelling him through his insatiable greed to commit all manner of injustice.

The confession was long and wearisome but the priest no longer gave any sign of being shocked during its course and seldom interrupted Simoun. Night had fallen when Father Florentino, drying his face, stood up and fell into meditation. The chamber was in an ambiguous darkness that the moonlight, streaming in through the window, filled with vague and misty gleams.

The voice of the priest, sad, deliberate, but consoling, broke the silence.

'God will forgive you, Mr... Simoun,' he said. 'He knows we are liable to be deceived. He has seen what you have suffered and, in allowing you to be punished for your crimes by suffering death at the hands of the very men you instigated, we can see His infinite mercy. He has frustrated your plans, one after the other, even the best, first with the death of María Clara, then through lack of foresight, and then in some mysterious way... Let us obey His will and give Him thanks.'

'In your opinion,' Simoun replied in a faltering voice, 'it would be His will that these islands...'

'Should continue in their miserable condition?' the priest finished the question when he saw that Simoun hesitated. 'Sir, I do not know, I cannot read the mind of the Inscrutable. But I know that He has not forsaken those peoples that in times of decision have placed themselves in His hands and made Him the Judge of their oppression; I know that His arm has never been wanting when, with justice trampled under foot and all other recourses at an end, the oppressed have taken up the sword and fought for their homes, wives, children, and those inalienable rights that, in the language of the German poet, shine above us unbreakable and untouchable like the eternal stars. No, God is justice and He cannot abandon His own cause, the cause of freedom without which no justice is possible.'

'Why then has He forsaken me?' asked Simoun in a voice overflowing with rancour.

'Because you chose a means of which He could not approve,' replied the priest sternly. 'The glory of saving a country cannot be given to one who has contributed to its ruin. You believed that what crime and iniquity had stained and deformed, more crime and more iniquity could cleanse and redeem. This was error. Hate only creates monsters; crime, criminals; only love can work wonders, only virtue can redeem. If our country is some day to be free, it will not be through vice and crime, it will not be through the corruption of its sons, some deceived, others bribed; redemption presupposes virtue; virtue, sacrifice, and sacrifice, love!'

'Very well, I accept your explanation,' replied Simoun after a pause. 'I was wrong. But because I was wrong, was this God of yours to deny freedom to a whole people and spare others much more evil than I was? What is my error compared with the crimes of those who govern us? Why should this God of yours give more importance to my iniquities than to the cries of the innocent? Why did He not strike me down and then work the people's victory? Why allow so many who are worthy and just to suffer and, without lifting a finger, find satisfaction in their sufferings?'

'The just and the worthy must suffer so that their ideas may be known and spread. The vessel must be shaken or broken to release the perfume, the stone must be struck to raise a spark. There is something providential in the persecutions of tyrants, Mr Simoun!'

'I knew that. That is why I encouraged tyranny...'

'Yes, my friend, but it was filth that spread more than anything else. You fomented social corruption without sowing a single idea. This fermentation of vices could inspire only nausea, and if anything had sprouted overnight it would have been only a toadstool for only toadstools grow spontaneously in garbage. Of course, the vices of a government are fatal to it and kill it, but they also kill the society in which they are bred. An immoral government is matched by a demoralized people; an administration without conscience, by greedy and servile townsmen and outlaws and robbers in the mountains. The slave is the image of his master: the country, of its government.

There was a brief pause.

'Then what is to be done?' asked Simoun.

'Endure and work.'

'Endure, work!' replied Simoun sarcastically, 'It is easy to say so when there is nothing to be endured, when work is rewarded. If this God of yours requires such sacrifices from men who can scarcely be sure of the present and doubt there will be a future for them... Ah, if you had seen what I have: unfortunate wretches suffering unspeakable tortures for crimes they never committed, the murders done to conceal the crimes or blunders of others, pitiful fathers of families torn from their homes to work uselessly on highways that crumbled the next morning and which seemed to be built only to bury their families in misery—endure, work, it is the will of God! Persuade these people that they are murdered for their own salvation, that they work for the prosperity of their homes. Endure, suffer—what kind of a God is that?'

'A most just God, Mr Simoun,' replied the priest, 'a God who punishes our lack of faith, our vices, the little regard we have for dignity and civic virtues. We tolerate vice and thereby become accomplices in it, sometimes we have to go so far as to applaud it; it is only just, then, very just, that we should suffer the consequences that our children should do the same. He is the God of freedom, Mr Simoun, who makes us love it by weighting the yoke upon our shoulders; He is a God of mercy and of justice, who improves us with His punishments and grants happiness only to those who have merited it with their exertions. The school of suffering tempers the spirit, the fighting arena strengthens the soul. I do not mean to say that our freedom must be won at the point of the sword; the sword now counts for very little in the destinies of our times; but I do say that we must win our freedom by deserving it, by improving the mind and enhancing the dignity of the individual, loving what is just, what is good, what is great, to the point of dying for it. When a people reach these heights, God provides the weapon, and the idols and the tyrants fall like a house of cards, and freedom shines in the first dawn. Our misfortunes are our own fault, let us blame nobody else for them. If Spain were to see us less tolerant of tyranny and readier to fight and suffer for our rights, Spain would be the first to give us freedom because, when the fruit of conception reaches the time of birth, woe to the mother that tries to strangle it! But as long as the Filipino people do not have sufficient vigour to proclaim, head held high and chest bared, their right to a life of their own in human society, and to guarantee it with their sacrifices, with their very blood; as long as we see our countrymen feel privately ashamed, hearing the growl of their rebelling and protesting conscience, while in public they keep silent and even join the oppressor in mocking the oppressed; as long as we see them wrapping themselves up in their selfishness and praising with forced smiles the most despicable acts, begging with their eyes for a share of the booty, why give them independence? With or without Spain they would be the same, and perhaps, perhaps worse. What is the use of independence if the slaves of today will be the tyrants of tomorrow? And no doubt they will, because whoever submits to tyranny, loves it! Mr Simoun, as long as our people are not prepared, and enter the struggle deceived or compelled, without a clear idea of what they are to do, the best-planned movements will fail and it is better that they should fail, for why give the bride to the groom if he does not love her enough and is not ready to die for her?'

Father Florentino felt the dying man take his hand and press it. He fell silent and waited for him to speak but only felt his hand pressed twice again and heard a sigh; then a long silence reigned in the room. Only the sea, whose waves had grown boisterous in the night wind as if awakening from the heat of the day, roared hoarsely its eternal cries as it dashed against the sheer rocks. The moon, delivered from rivalry with the sun, enjoyed its quiet victory in the sky. The trees in the forest, bending towards one another, told their immemorial tales in cryptic murmurs that were carried on the wings of the wind.

Since the dying man had nothing more to say, Father Florentino, engrossed in his own thoughts, whispered:

'Where are the youths who will dedicate their innocence, their idealism, their enthusiasm to the good of the country? Where are they who will give generously of their blood to wash away so much shame, crime and abomination? Pure and immaculate must the victim be for the sacrifice to be acceptable. Where are you, young men and young women, who are to embody in yourselves the life-force that has been drained from our veins, the pure ideals that have grown stained in our minds, the fiery enthusiasm that has been quenched in our hearts? We await you, come for we await you!'

He felt his eyes moisten and freed his hand, rising then and going to the window to contemplate the vast expanse of the sea. A discreet knocking at the door brought him out of his meditations. It was the servant who wanted to know if lights were wanted.

When the priest returned to the bedside he saw by the lamplight that Simoun was still, his eyes closed, and the hand which had pressed his own open and limp at the edge of the bed. For an instant he thought that Simoun slept but, observing no signs of breathing, touched him gently and then realized that he was dead and already turning cold.

The priest fell on his knees and prayed.

When he rose and looked upon the dead body, in whose face was a sadness beyond death, the old priest shuddered and murmured:

'God have pity on those who led him astray!'

While the servants, summoned by him, knelt and prayed for the dead, distracted from their repetitive prayers by curious looks at the bed, Father Florentino took from a cabinet the famous steel chest which contained Simoun's fabulous treasure. He hesitated momentarily but quickly came to a decision, went downstairs, and headed for the rock on whose pinnacle Isagani was wont to sit to stare down into the depths of the sea.

Father Florentino looked below him, where the dark waves of the Pacific beat thunderously upon the hollow rocks while the moonlit spume flashed like sparks of fire, like handfuls of diamonds thrown up in the air by some spirit of the deep. He looked about him, he was alone. The deserted shore lost itself in the distance in vague mists that the moon confounded with the horizon. The forest whispered enigmatic messages. Then the old priest, with an effort of his Herculean arms, hurled the chest through the air and into the sea. It turned round upon itself several times and fell quickly in a shallow curve, its polished surface reflecting a few pale gleams. The old priest saw the splash and heard the broken sound as it plunged into the depths which closed upon the treasure. He waited for some time to see if the depths would throw up anything but the waves kept their unbroken array, as secretive as before without one wrinkle added to the rugged surface, as if into the immensity of the sea only a pebble had fallen.

'May Nature guard you in the deepest of the deep, among the corals and the pearls of the eternal seas,' the priest said, solemnly stretching out his hand. 'When men should need you for a purpose holy and sublime, God will know how to raise you from the bottom of the seas. Until then you will do no evil there, you will not thwart justice or incite greed!'

THE END